Under Currents

"Roberts's latest is full of powerful, magnetic characters who have overcome terrible situations. Suspense and sensual romance are expertly combined in this riveting story."
—*Publishers Weekly*

"Readers can always count on Nora Roberts to deliver high-octane thrillers that focus on the bonds of small-town life, dark secrets, and the prospect of new love complicated by evil lurking around sharp corners. . . . A chilling suspense novel."
—*Shelf Awareness for Readers*

"*Under Currents* is brilliantly plotted and unrelentingly propulsive. It is a beautifully written story about the fragility of life and the power of the past and the need to fight back . . . a highly recommended novel for this summer."
—*The Washington Book Review*

UNDER CURRENTS

Nora Roberts

ANTHOLOGIES

Irish Born Trilogy
BORN IN FIRE
BORN IN ICE
BORN IN SHAME

Dream Trilogy
DARING TO DREAM
HOLDING THE DREAM
FINDING THE DREAM

Chesapeake Bay Saga
SEA SWIFT
RISING TIDES
INNER HARBOR
CHESAPEAKE BLUE

Gallaghers of Ardmore Trilogy
JEWELS OF THE SUN
TEARS OF THE MOON
HEART OF THE SEA

Three Sisters Island Trilogy
DANCE UPON THE AIR
HEAVEN AND EARTH
FACE THE FIRE

Key Trilogy
KEY OF LIGHT
KEY OF KNOWLEDGE
KEY OF VALOR

In the Garden Trilogy
BLUE DAHLIA
BLACK ROSE
RED LILY

Circle Trilogy
MORRIGAN'S CROSS
DANCE OF THE GODS
VALLEY OF SILENCE

Sign of Seven Trilogy
BLOOD BROTHERS
THE HOLLOW
THE PAGAN STONE

Bride Quartet
VISION IN WHITE
BED OF ROSES
SAVOR THE MOMENT
HAPPY EVER AFTER

The Inn BoonsBoro Trilogy
THE NEXT ALWAYS
THE LAST BOYFRIEND
THE PERFECT HOPE

The Cousins O'Dwyer Trilogy
DARK WITCH
SHADOW SPELL
BLOOD MAGICK

The Guardians Trilogy
STARS OF FORTUNE
BAY OF SIGHS
ISLAND OF GLASS

Chronicles of The One
YEAR ONE
OF BLOOD AND BONE

Nora Roberts & J. D. Robb

REMEMBER WHEN

J. D. Robb

Anthologies

FROM THE HEART

A LITTLE MAGIC

A LITTLE FATE

MOON SHADOWS
(with Jill Gregory, Ruth Ryan Langan, and Marianne Willman)

The Once Upon Series
(with Jill Gregory, Ruth Ryan Langan, and Marianne Willman)

ONCE UPON A CASTLE	ONCE UPON A ROSE
ONCE UPON A STAR	ONCE UPON A KISS
ONCE UPON A DREAM	ONCE UPON A MIDNIGHT

SILENT NIGHT
(with Susan Plunkett, Dee Holmes, and Claire Cross)

OUT OF THIS WORLD
(with Laurell K. Hamilton, Susan Krinard, and Maggie Shayne)

BUMP IN THE NIGHT
(with Mary Blayney, Ruth Ryan Langan, and Mary Kay McComas)

DEAD OF NIGHT
(with Mary Blayney, Ruth Ryan Langan, and Mary Kay McComas)

THREE IN DEATH

SUITE 606
(with Mary Blayney, Ruth Ryan Langan, and Mary Kay McComas)

IN DEATH

THE LOST
(with Patricia Gaffney, Ruth Ryan Langan, and Mary Kay McComas)

THE OTHER SIDE
(with Mary Blayney, Patricia Gaffney, Ruth Ryan Langan, and Mary Kay McComas)

TIME OF DEATH

THE UNQUIET
(with Mary Blayney, Patricia Gaffney, Ruth Ryan Langan, and Mary Kay McComas)

MIRROR, MIRROR
(with Mary Blayney, Elaine Fox, Mary Kay McComas, and R.C. Ryan)

DOWN THE RABBIT HOLE
(with Mary Blayney, Elaine Fox, Mary Kay McComas, and R.C. Ryan)

Also Available...

THE OFFICIAL NORA ROBERTS COMPANION
(edited by Denise Little and Laura Hayden)

UNDER CURRENTS

NORA ROBERTS

ST. MARTIN'S GRIFFIN NEW YORK

Published in the United States by St. Martin's Griffin,
an imprint of St. Martin's Publishing Group

UNDER CURRENTS. Copyright © 2019 by Nora Roberts. All rights reserved.
Printed in the United States of America. For information, address St. Martin's
Publishing Group, 120 Broadway, New York, NY 10271.

www.stmartins.com

Designed by James Sinclair

The Library of Congress has cataloged the hardcover edition as follows:

Names: Roberts, Nora, author.
Title: Under currents / Nora Roberts.
Description: First edition. | New York: St. Martin's Press, 2019.
Identifiers: LCCN 2018055444| ISBN 9781250207098 (hardcover) |
    ISBN 9781250246776 (international, sold outside the U.S., subject to rights
    availability) | ISBN 9781250213273 (ebook)
Classification: LCC PS3568.O243 U48 2019 | DDC 813/.54—dc23
LC record available at https://lccn.loc.gov/2018055444

ISBN 978-1-250-21326-6 (trade paperback)
ISBN 978-1-250-76587-1 (international, sold outside
the U.S., subject to rights availability)

Our books may be purchased in bulk for promotional, educational,
or business use. Please contact your local bookseller or the
Macmillan Corporate and Premium Sales Department at 1-800-221-7945,
extension 5442, or by email at MacmillanSpecialMarkets@macmillan.com.

First U.S. Edition: July 2019
First St. Martin's Griffin Edition: May 2020

10 9 8 7 6 5 4 3 2 1

To the Greenbrier Girls
JoAnne, workout companion
Kat, my sweet, sweet Baby Mama
Laura, the handler of everything
Mary, shopping pal
Sarah, spirit magnet

PART ONE

THE CRUELTY OF LIES

Cruelty and fear shake hands together.
—HONORÉ DE BALZAC

Child abuse casts a shadow the length of a lifetime.
—HERBERT WARD

CHAPTER ONE

From the outside, the house in Lakeview Terrace looked perfect. The dignified three stories of pale brown brick boasted wide expanses of glass to open it to the view of Reflection Lake and the Blue Ridge Mountains. Two faux turrets capped in copper added a European charm and that quiet whisper of wealth.

Its lawn, a richly green skirt, sloped gently toward a trio of steps and the wide white veranda banked by azaleas that bloomed ruby red in spring.

In the rear a generous covered patio offered outdoor living space with a summer kitchen and those lovely lake views. The carefully maintained rose garden added a sweet, sophisticated scent. In season, a forty-two-foot sailing yacht floated serenely at the private dock.

Climbing roses softened the look of the long, vertical boards of the privacy fence.

The attached garage held a Mercedes SUV and sedan, two mountain bikes, ski equipment, and no clutter.

Inside, the ceilings soared. Both the formal living room and the great room offered fireplaces framed in the same golden brown brick as the exterior. The decor, tasteful—though some might whisper *studied*—reflected the vision of the couple in charge.

Quiet colors, coordinated fabrics, contemporary without edging over into stark.

Dr. Graham Bigelow purchased the lot in the projected development of Lakeview Terrace when his son was five, his daughter three.

He chose the blueprint he felt suited him and his family, made the necessary changes and additions, selected the finishes, the flooring, the tiles, the pavers, hired a decorator.

His wife, Eliza, happily left most of the choices and decisions to her husband. His taste, in her opinion, couldn't be faulted.

If and when she had an idea or suggestion, he would listen. If most often he pointed out why such an idea or suggestion wouldn't suit, he did—occasionally—include her input.

Like Graham, Eliza wanted the newness, the status offered by the small, exclusive community on the lake in North Carolina's High Country. She'd been born and raised in status—but the old sort, the sort she saw as creaky and boring. Like the house she'd grown up in across the lake.

She'd been happy to sell her share of the old house to her sister and use the money to help furnish—all new!—the house in Lakeview Terrace. She'd handed the cashier's check to Graham—he took care of things—without a second thought.

She'd never regretted it.

They'd lived there happily for nearly nine years, raising two bright, attractive children, hosting dinner parties, cocktail parties, garden parties. Eliza's job, as wife of the chief of surgery of Mercy Hospital in nearby Asheville, was to look beautiful and stylish, to raise the children well, keep the house, entertain, and head committees.

As she had a housekeeper/cook three times a week, a weekly groundskeeper, and a sister who was more than happy to take the children if she and Graham needed an evening out or a little getaway, she had plenty of time to focus on her looks and wardrobe.

She never missed a school function, and in fact had served as PTA president for two years. She attended school plays, along with Graham if work didn't keep him away. She embraced fund-raising, both for the school and the hospital. At every ballet recital since Britt turned four, she'd sat front row center.

She sat through most of her son Zane's baseball games as well. And if she missed some, she excused it, as anyone who'd sat through the nightmare of tedium that youth baseball provided would understand.

Though she'd never admit it, Eliza favored her daughter. But Britt was such a beautiful, sweet-natured, obedient young girl. She never had to be prodded to do her homework or tidy her room, was unfailingly polite. In Zane, Eliza saw her sister, Emily. The tendency to argue or sulk, to go off on his own.

Still, he kept his grades up. If the boy wanted to play baseball, he made the honor roll. Obviously, his ambition to play professionally was just a teenage fantasy. He would, of course, study medicine like his father.

But for now, baseball served as the carrot so they all avoided the stick.

If Graham had to pull out that stick and punish the boy from time to time, it was for his own good. It helped build character, teach boundaries, ensure respect.

As Graham liked to say, the child is the father of the man, so the child had to learn to follow the rules.

Two days before Christmas, Eliza drove the plowed streets of Lakeview toward home. She'd had a lovely holiday lunch with friends—maybe just a couple sips more champagne than she should have. She'd burned that off shopping. On Boxing Day, the family would take its annual ski trip. Or Graham and the kids would ski while she made use of the spa. Now she had a pair of gorgeous new boots to pack along with some lingerie that would warm Graham up nicely after his time on the slopes.

She glanced around at the other homes, the holiday decorations. Really lovely, she thought—no tacky inflatable Santas allowed in Lakeview Terrace—by order of the homeowners' association.

But, no point being modest, their home outshined the rest. Graham gave her carte blanche on Christmas decorating, and she used it wisely and well.

The white lights would sparkle when dusk rolled in, she thought. Outlining the perfect lines of the house, twining around the potted firs on the front veranda. Gleaming inside the twin wreaths with their trailing red and silver ribbons on the double doors.

And of course the living room tree—all twelve feet—white lights, silver and red star ornaments. The great room tree, the same color scheme, but with angels. Of course the mantels, the formal dining table, all tasteful and perfect.

And new every year. No need to box and store when you could arrange for the rental company to come sweep it all away afterward.

She'd never understood her parents' and Emily's delight in digging out ancient glass balls or tacky wooden Santas. They could have all that with their visit to the old house and Emily. Eliza would host them all for Christmas dinner, of course. Then, thank God, they'd head back to Savannah and their retirement.

Emily was their favorite, she thought as she hit the remote for the garage door. No question there.

It gave her a jolt to see Graham's car already in the garage, and she checked her watch. Let out a breath of relief. She wasn't late; he was home early.

Delighted, especially since someone else had the car pool, she pulled in beside her husband's car, gathered her shopping bags.

She went through the mudroom, hung her coat, folded her scarf, removed her boots before sliding into the black Prada flats she wore around the house.

When she stepped into the kitchen, Graham, still in his suit and tie, stood at the center island.

"You're home early!" After setting her bags on the wet bar, she moved quickly to him, kissed him lightly.

He smelled, lightly like the kiss, of Eau Sauvage—her favorite.

"Where were you?"

"Oh, I had that holiday lunch with Miranda and Jody, remember?" She gestured vaguely toward the family calendar in the activity nook. "We topped it off with a little shopping."

As she spoke, she walked to the refrigerator for a bottle of Perrier. "I can't believe how many people are still shopping for Christmas. Jody included," she said, adding a scoop of ice from the ice machine, pouring the sparkling water over it. "Honestly, Graham, she just never seems to get organized about—"

"Do you think I give a damn about Jody?"

His voice, calm, smooth, almost pleasant, set off alarm bells.

UNDER CURRENTS ≈ 7

"Of course not, my darling. I'm just babbling." She kept the smile on her face, but her eyes turned wary. "Why don't you sit down and relax? I'll freshen your drink, and we'll—"

He heaved the glass, smashing the crystal at her feet. A shard dug a shallow slice across her ankle with an added sting as scotch splattered over it.

The Baccarat, she thought with a little frisson of heat.

"Freshen that!" No longer calm and smooth, not nearly pleasant, the words slapped out at her. "I spend my day with my hands inside a human being, saving lives, and come home to an empty house?"

"I'm sorry. I—"

"*Sorry*?" He grabbed her arm, twisting as he slammed her back against the counter. "You're *sorry* you couldn't be bothered to be home? *Sorry* you frittered away the day, and my money, having lunch, shopping, gossiping with those idiot bitches while I spend six hours in the OR?"

Her breath began to hitch, her heart to pound. "I didn't know you'd be home early. If you'd called me, I would've come straight home."

"Now I have to report to you?"

She barely heard the rest of the words that hammered at her. *Ungrateful, respect, duty*. But she knew that look, that avenging angel look. The dark blond hair, perfectly groomed, the smooth, handsome face suffused with angry color. The rage in those bright blue eyes so cold, so cold.

The frisson of heat became electric snaps.

"It was on the calendar!" Her voice rose in pitch. "I told you only this morning."

"Do you think I have time to check your ridiculous calendar? You will be home when I walk in the door. Do you understand me?" He slammed her against the counter again, shooting a jolt of pain up her spine. "I'm responsible for everything you have. This home, the clothes on your back, the food you eat. I pay for someone to cook, to clean so you can be available to me when I say! So you damn well will be home when I walk in the door. You'll damn well spread your legs when I want to fuck you."

To prove it, he rammed his erection against her.

She slapped him. Even knowing what was coming—maybe because of what was coming—she slapped him.

And that rage went from cold to hot. His lips peeled back.

He plowed his fist into her midsection.

He never hit her in the face.

At fourteen, Zane Bigelow's heart and soul centered on baseball. He liked girls—he liked looking at naked girls once his pal Micah showed him how to bypass the parental controls on his computer. But baseball still ranked number one.

Numero uno.

Tall for his age, gangly with it, he longed to get through school, be discovered by a scout for the Baltimore Orioles—he'd settle for any American League team, but that was his number one pick.

Totally *numero uno.*

He'd play shortstop—the amazing Cal Ripken would have retired by then. Besides, Iron Man Ripken was back at third.

This comprised Zane's ambitions. And actually seeing a naked girl in the—you know—flesh.

Nobody in the world could have been happier than Zane Bigelow as Mrs. Carter—Micah's mom—drove the car pool gang home in her Lexus SUV. Even if she had Cher singing about life after love playing.

He didn't have a passion for cars—yet—just a young male's innate knowledge. And he preferred rap (not that he could play it in the house).

But even with Cher singing, his sister and the other two girls squealing about Christmas, Micah deep into *Donkey Kong* on his Game Boy (Micah's desperate Christmas wish was the new Game Boy Color), Zane hit the highest note on the happy scale.

No school for ten whole days! Even the prospect of being pushed into skiing—not his favorite sport, especially when his father kept pointing out his little sister skied rings around him—couldn't dampen his mood.

No math, ten days. He hated math like he hated spinach salad, which was a lot.

Mrs. Carter pulled over to let Cecile Marlboro out. There was the usual shuffling, hauling of backpacks, the high-pitched squeal of girls.

They all had to hug, because Christmas vacation.

Sometimes they had to hug because it was, like, Tuesday or whatever. He'd never get it.

Everybody called out Merry Christmas—they'd called out Happy Holidays when dropping Pete Greene off, because he was Jewish.

Almost home, Zane thought, watching the houses go by. He figured to fix himself a snack, then—no homework, no freaking math—close up in his room and settle in with an hour on *Triple Play* on his PlayStation.

He knew Lois—off till like *après ski*—planned to make lasagna before she left for her own family holiday stuff. And Lois's lasagna was awesome.

Mom would actually have to turn on the oven to heat it up, but she could handle that much.

Better yet, Grams and Pop got in from Savannah tomorrow. He wished they could stay at his house instead of with his aunt Emily, but he planned to ride his bike over to the old lake house the next afternoon and hang awhile. He could talk Emily into baking cookies—wouldn't even have to talk hard for that.

And they were coming for Christmas dinner. Mom wouldn't even have to turn on the oven for that one. Catered.

After dinner Britt would play piano—he sucked at piano, which equaled another regular dig from his dad—and they'd do a sing-along.

Corny, totally corny, but he sort of liked it. Plus, he sang pretty good, so he didn't get ragged on.

As the car pulled over at his house, Zane exchanged fist bumps with Micah.

"Dude, Merry."

"Dude," Micah said. "Back atcha."

While Britt and Chloe hugged as if they wouldn't see each other for a year, Zane slid out. "Merry Christmas, Chloe. Merry Christmas, Mrs. Carter, and thanks for the ride."

"Merry Christmas, Zane, and you're always welcome." She shot him a smile, made eye contact. She was really pretty for a mom.

"Thank you, Mrs. Carter, and Merry Christmas." Britt practically sang it. "I'll call you, Chloe!"

Zane slung his backpack over one shoulder as Britt climbed out. "What are you calling her for? What could you have left to talk about? Y'all never shut up all the way home."

"We have plenty to talk about."

Britt, more than a full head shorter, shared his coloring. The dark hair—Britt's nearly to her waist and pinned back with reindeer barrettes—the same sharp green eyes. Her face was still sort of round and babyish while his had gone angular. Because, Em said, he was growing up.

Not that he was ready to shave or anything, though he did check carefully every day.

Because she was his sister, he felt honor bound to give her grief. "But y'all don't actually say anything. It's like: Ooooh, Justin Timberlake." He followed up with loud kissy noises, making her blush.

He knew Timberlake was her not-so-secret crush.

"Just shut up."

"You shut up."

"You shut up."

They back-and-forthed that until they reached the veranda—switched to snarling looks, as both knew if they went inside arguing and their mother heard, an endless lecture would follow.

Zane dug out his key, as his father decreed the house stayed locked whether or not anyone was home. The second the door cracked open, he heard it.

The snarl dropped from Britt's face. Her eyes went huge, filled with fear and tears. She slapped her hands over her ears.

"Go upstairs," Zane told her. "Go straight up to your room. Stay there."

"He's hurting her again. He's hurting her."

Instead of running to her room, Britt ran inside, ran back toward the great room, stood, hands still over her ears. "Stop!" She screamed it. "Stop, stop, stop, stop."

Zane saw blood smeared on the floor where his mother tried to crawl away. Her sweater was torn, one of her shoes missing.

"Go to your rooms!" Graham shouted it as he hauled Eliza up by her hair. "This is none of your business."

Britt just kept screaming, screaming, even when Zane tried to pull her back.

He saw his father's hate-filled eyes track over, latch on to his sister. And a new fear flashed hot inside him, burned something away.

He didn't think, didn't know what he intended to do. He shoved his sister back, stood between her and his father, a skinny kid who'd yet to grow into his feet. And with that flash of heat, he charged.

"Get away from her, you son of a bitch!"

He rammed straight into Graham. Surprise more than the power of the hit knocked Graham back a step. "Get the hell away."

Zane never saw it coming. He was fourteen, and the only fights he'd ever participated in consisted of a little pushy-shovey and insults. He'd felt his father's fist—a blow to the gut, sometimes the kidneys.

Where it didn't show.

This time the fists struck his face, and something behind his eyes exploded, blurred his vision. He felt two more before he dropped, the wild pain of them rising over the fear, the anger. His world went gray, and through the gray, lights sizzled and flashed.

With the taste of blood in his mouth, his sister's screams banging in his head, he passed out.

The next he knew, he realized his father had slung him over his shoulder, carrying him up the stairs. His ears rang, but he could hear Britt crying, hear his mother telling her to stop.

His father didn't lay him down on the bed, but shrugged him off his shoulder so Zane bounced on the mattress. Every inch of his body cried out in fresh pain.

"Disrespect me again, I'll do more than break your nose, blacken your eye. You're nothing, do you understand me? You're nothing until

I say you are. Everything you have, including the breath in your body, is because of me."

He leaned close as he spoke, spoke in that smooth, calm tone. Zane saw two of him, couldn't even manage to nod. The shaking started, the teeth-chattering cold of shock.

"You will not leave this room until I permit it. You will speak to no one. You will tell no one the private business of this family or the punishment you forced me to levy today will seem like a picnic. No one would believe you. You're nothing. I'm everything. I could kill you in your sleep, and no one would notice. Remember that the next time you think about trying to be a big man."

He went out, closed the door.

Zane drifted again. It was easier to drift than to deal with the pain, to deal with the words his father had spoken that had fallen like more fists.

When he surfaced again, the light had changed. Not dark, but getting there.

He couldn't breathe through his nose. It felt clogged like he had a terrible cold. The sort of cold that made his head hammer with pain, had his eyes throbbing.

His gut hurt something terrible.

When he tried to sit up, the room spun, and he feared throwing up.

When he heard the lock click, he started to shake again. He prepared to beg, plead, grovel, anything that kept those fists from pounding on him again.

His mother came in, flipping the light as she did. The light exploded more pain, so he shut his eyes.

"Your father says you're to clean yourself up, then use this ice bag on your face."

Her voice, cool, matter-of-fact, hurt almost as much as his father's.

"Mom—"

"Your father says to keep your head elevated. You may leave your bed only to use your bathroom. As you see, your father has removed your computer, your PlayStation, your television, items he's generously given you. You will see and speak to no one except your father or me. You will not participate in Christmas Eve or Christmas Day."

"But—"

"You have the flu."

He searched her face for some sign of pity, gratitude. Feeling. "I was trying to stop him from hurting you. I thought he might hurt Britt. I thought—"

"I didn't ask for or need your help." Her voice, clipped, cold, made his chest ache. "What's between me and your father is between me and your father. You have the next two days to consider your place in this family, and to earn back any privileges."

She turned toward the door. "Do as you're told."

When she went out, left him alone, he made himself sit up—had to close his eyes against the spinning and just breathe. On shaky legs, he stood, stumbled into the bathroom, vomited, nearly passed out again.

When he managed to gain his feet, he stared at his face in the mirror over the sink.

It didn't look like his face, he thought, oddly detached. The mouth swollen, bottom lip split. God, the nose like a red balloon. Both eyes black, one swollen half-shut. Dried blood everywhere.

He lifted a hand, touched his fingers to his nose, had pain blasting. Because he was afraid to take a shower—still dizzy—he used a washcloth to try to clean off some of the blood. He had to grit his teeth, had to hang on to the sink with one hand to stay upright, but he feared not doing what he'd been told more than the pain.

He cried, and wasn't ashamed. Nobody could see anyway. Nobody would care.

He inched his way back to bed, breathed out when he eased down to take off his shoes, his jeans. Every minute or two he had to stop, catch his breath again, wait for the dizziness to pass.

In his boxers and sweatshirt, he crawled into bed, took the ice bag his mother had left, and laid it as lightly as he could on his nose.

It hurt too much, just too much, so he switched to his eye. And that brought a little relief.

He lay there, full dark now, planning, planning. He'd run away. As soon as he could, he'd stuff his backpack with some clothes. He didn't have much money because his father banked all of it. But he had a little he'd hidden in a pair of socks. His saving-for-video-games money.

He could hitchhike—and that thought brought a thrill. Maybe to New York. He'd get away from this house where everything looked so clean, where ugly, ugly secrets hid like his video game money.

He'd get a job. He could get a job. No more school, he thought as he drifted again. That was something.

He woke again, heard the lock again, and pretended to sleep. But it wasn't his father's steps, or his mother's. He opened his eyes as Britt shined a little pink flashlight in his face.

"Don't."

"Shh," she warned him. "I can't turn the light on in case they wake up and see." She sat on the side of the bed, stroked a hand over his arm. "I brought you a PB&J. I couldn't get lasagna because they'd know if any was missing from the dish. You need to eat."

"Stomach's not so good, Britt."

"Just a little. Try a little."

"You need to go. If they catch you in here—"

"They're asleep. I made sure. I'm staying with you. I'm going to stay with you until you can eat something. I'm so sorry, Zane."

"Don't cry."

"You're crying."

He let the tears roll. He just didn't have the strength to stop them.

Sniffling at her own tears, swiping at them, Britt reached down to stroke his arm. "I brought milk, too. They won't notice if a glass of milk is gone. I cleaned everything up, and when you're done, I'll wash the glass."

They spoke in whispers—they were used to it—but now her voice hitched.

"He hit you so hard, Zane. He hit you and hit you, and when you were on the ground, he kicked you in the stomach. I thought you were dead."

She laid her head on his chest, shoulders shaking. He stroked her hair.

"Did he hurt you?"

"No. He sort of squeezed my arms and shook me, yelled at me to shut up. So I did. I was afraid not to."

"That's good. You did the right thing."

"You did." Her whisper thickened with tears. "You tried to do the right thing. She didn't try to stop him from hurting you. She didn't say anything. And when he stopped, he told her to clean up the blood on the floor. There was glass broken in the kitchen, to clean it up, to clean herself up and have dinner on the table by six."

She sat up, held out half the sandwich she'd neatly cut in two. In that moment he loved her so much it hurt his heart.

He took it, tried a bite, and found it didn't threaten to come up again.

"We have to tell Emily and Grams and Pop you're sick. You got the flu, and you're contagious. You have to rest, and Dad's taking care of you. He won't let them come up to see you. Then we have to tell people at the resort you fell off your bike. He said all this at dinner. I had to eat or he'd get mad again. Then I threw up when I went upstairs."

He took another bite, reached for her hand in the dark. "I know how that feels."

"When we get back, we have to say you had a skiing accident. Fell. Dad took care of you."

"Yeah." The single word rang bitter, bitter. "He took care of me."

"He'll hurt you again if we don't. Maybe worse. I don't want him to hurt you again, Zane. You were trying to stop him from hitting Mom. You were protecting me, too. You thought he was going to hit me. So did I."

He felt her shift, saw in the faint light of the flashlight she'd set on the bed that she'd turned to stare toward the window. "One day I guess he will."

"No, no, he won't." Inside the pain, fury rose. "You won't give him any reason to. And I won't let him."

"He doesn't need a reason. You don't have to be a grown-up to understand that." Though her tone sounded adult, fresh tears leaked. "I think they don't love us. He couldn't love us and hurt us, make us lie. And she couldn't love us and let it keep happening. I think they don't love us."

He knew they didn't—had known for sure when his mother had come in, looked at him with nothing in her eyes. "We've got each other."

While she sat with him, making sure he ate, he understood he couldn't run away, couldn't run and leave Britt. He had to stay. He had to get stronger. He had to get strong enough to fight back.

Not to protect his mother, but his sister.

CHAPTER TWO

On Christmas Eve, Emily Walker still had half a dozen items left on her to-do list. She always made lists, always worked up a schedule. And invariably every item on every list in her history of lists took longer than she'd thought it would.

Every freaking time.

The other thing about lists? Other items tended to pop up onto it, adding yet more time she hadn't anticipated.

Such as today. In addition to giving the house one last going-over, making her daddy's favorite stuffed pork chops and scalloped potatoes for Christmas Eve dinner, giving herself a much-needed home facial, driving out to Asheville to pick her parents up from the airport, she'd added in a quick trip to the market to pick up a stewing chicken.

Poor Zane had the flu, so she'd also added making that stewing chicken in a nice batch of chicken soup. And that added on delivering the soup to her sister's house across the lake.

Which added on the chore of being sweet and nice to Eliza.

To make it worse, she had to be sweet and nice to Eliza after Eliza decreed that Christmas dinner had to be at the old house.

Oh, not to worry, said Eliza, Emily thought while she threw on fresh clothes. She had to skip the facial, needed or not. No, not to worry, because Eliza had already contacted the caterer and switched the venue.

Venue, for God's sake!

And who in holy hell hired on a caterer for a family holiday dinner? Eliza Snootface Walker Bigelow, that's who.

But she'd be sweet, she'd be nice. She damn well wouldn't start something up with Eliza during their parents' visit. She'd take over the soup still simmering on the stove, have a little visit with her sick nephew.

And she'd sneak him the latest Dark Tower novel, since King, along with a good dozen others, didn't make Eliza and Graham's approved authors list.

What they didn't know wouldn't come back and bite her in the ass. Zane was good at keeping secrets. Maybe too good, Emily thought as she slapped some makeup on her face. Maybe she didn't spend as much time with the kids as she should, but sometimes when she did, she got the sense of . . . something. Something just not altogether right.

Probably her imagination, she admitted, pulling on her boots. Or just looking for something to whack her older sister with. They hadn't been close as kids—opposites didn't always attract, and the nine-year gap between them might have added to it.

They'd grown no closer as adults. In fact, while usually polite— usually—on the surface, there were those undercurrents again. An active mutual dislike.

In fact, if it hadn't been for her parents and her niece and nephew, Emily could have gone the rest of her life never seeing or speaking to Eliza again.

"A terrible thing," she murmured as she hurried downstairs. "An awful thing to think, to feel."

Worse, she feared some of that thinking, that feeling was straight-out resentment on her part—which added shameful.

Eliza was prettier, and always had been. Not that Emily wasn't cute enough herself, even without the home facial. But Eliza could claim double scoops of good looks, and bigger boobs, too. And of course, given that nine-year head start, had done everything first.

She'd starred in school plays, made head cheerleader, wore the crown as homecoming queen, as prom queen. And when she'd graduated, hadn't their grandparents given her a slick silver BMW convertible?

Then she'd gone and bagged herself a doctor. A surgeon, and one handsome as a movie star. Had her fancy-dancy country club engagement party, her snooty-assed bridal shower, her extravagant and splashy white wedding.

And she'd looked just magnificent, Emily remembered as she turned off the heat under the soup. Like a queen in her big, beautiful white dress.

She hadn't resented Eliza that day. She'd been happy for her—even when forced to wear the blush-pink attendant's gown with its poufy shoulders.

But after that, resentment had built right back up again.

"Don't think about it now," she ordered herself, put on her coat, her hat, her gloves. "It's Christmas. And poor Zane's sick."

She got her purse—with the Dark Tower novel already stuffed inside—got hot pads to cart the soup out to her truck and to transfer the soup to Eliza's.

She'd had the truck washed, waxed, and detailed—something crossed off yesterday's list—so sticky notes didn't decorate the dash. And she'd completed a personal check on all the rental bungalows, so when her parents asked—and they would—she could tell them Walker Lakeside Bungalows, the family enterprise, was safe and secure.

She liked being in charge of it now that her parents had retired. Maybe she resented—that word again—cutting the check to Eliza for her share of the profits every quarter. Eliza didn't do a damn thing, but blood was blood, family was family, so she got a share of what her parents had built and she maintained.

At least the house was hers, just hers now, she thought, looking back on it after she settled the soup pot on the floor of the passenger's seat.

She loved the house, the wood and stone ramble of it, the wraparound porch, the views of the lake and mountains. It had been home all of her life, and she intended for it to be home until she died. Since she didn't have kids, and the likelihood of making any looked dim at best, she planned to leave it to Zane and Britt when the time came.

Maybe one of them would live there. Maybe they'd rent it out or sell it off. She'd be dead, so she wouldn't know the difference.

"A cheerful Christmas thought."

Laughing at herself, she climbed in the truck, thinking how pretty the house would look come dusk when all the colorful lights came on, the tree sparkling in the window. Just the way it had every Christmas in her memory. The house smelling of pine and cranberry, of cookies warm from the oven.

As she pulled out to take the lake road, she blew her bangs out of her eyes. A trim hadn't made it on her pre-Christmas list and had to wait.

As she drove around Reflection Lake, she turned the radio on, the volume up, and sang along with Springsteen as she passed the rental bungalows, the docks, the other lake houses, and curved around toward town with the snow-topped mountains rising up into the pale blue of winter sky.

The road rose and fell, twisted and turned—she knew every inch. She cut through Main Street just to see the shops all done up for Christmas and the star rising high above the Lakeview Hotel.

She spotted Cyrus Puffer carting a bag, heading toward his parked truck. She'd been married to Cyrus for almost six months—God, nearly ten years ago, she thought. They'd decided, pretty quick, they made better friends with benefits than husband and wife, and so had had, in her opinion, one of the only truly amicable divorces in the wide world of divorces.

She pulled over to say hey.

"Last-minute shopping?"

"No. Yeah. Sort of." He grinned at her, a good-looking guy with bright red hair and a happy disposition. "Marlene wanted ice cream—nothing but mint chocolate chip would do."

"Well, aren't you the good husband."

He'd found the right woman the second time around. Emily had introduced them herself, and ended up being best man at the wedding.

"Doing my best." That grin just wouldn't quit. "I guess I'm lucky she didn't want pickles to go with it."

"Oh my God!" She gripped his face with both hands. "Oh my God, Cy! You're going to be a daddy!"

"We just found out yesterday for certain. She doesn't want to tell anybody yet, except her folks and mine, but she won't mind me telling you."

"It's in the vault, but oh my God, I'm dancing for you." She yanked him farther through the window to give him a hard, loud kiss. "Best Christmas present ever. Oh, Cy, you tell her merry, merrier, merriest from me. And when she wants to talk about it, just give me a call."

"I will. Em, I'm so happy I could split in two. I gotta get the ice cream home to mama."

"You tell her I want to give the baby shower."

"Really?"

"You bet I do. Merry Christmas, Cy. Oh my God!"

She grinned all the way through town, back to the lake, and into Lakeview Terrace.

As she did every time she turned in, she thought: I'd kill myself if I had to live here.

No question the houses were big and mostly beautiful. And not exactly all the same, as there had been several styles and plans to choose from as she recalled. And many add-on options.

But there was, to her eye, an edging-toward-creepy Stepford air in the development. Perfect perfection, down to the tidy sidewalks, the paved or pavered driveways, the small park—residents and their guests only—with its carefully planted trees, carefully placed benches and walkways.

But her sister loved it, and in truth the perfect rows of McMansions with their manicured lawns suited Eliza very well.

Reminding herself to be sweet, Emily pulled into the driveway. She carried the soup to the door, rang the bell. Like a stranger, she thought, not like family. But they kept their personal palace locked tight.

Sweet, she thought again, and put a smile on her face.

She kept it in place when Eliza opened the door looking just damn beautiful in winter-white pants, red cashmere sweater, her hair in soft, dark waves to her shoulders.

And her eyes, the same sharp Walker green as Emily's, showed only mild annoyance. "Emily. We weren't expecting you."

Not Emily! Merry Christmas. Come in.

But Emily kept smiling.

"I got your message about Zane, and dinner tomorrow. I tried to call you back, but—"

"We've been busy."

"Yeah, me, too. But I felt so bad for Zane, so I made Mama's famous cure. Chicken noodle soup. How's he doing?"

"He's sleeping."

"Eliza, it's cold. Aren't you going to let me in?"

"Who is it, sweetheart?" Graham, gilded, handsome—in cashmere, of course, his sweater a silvery gray—stepped up behind Eliza. He smiled, but as Emily noted often, it didn't really reach his eyes.

"Emily! Merry Christmas. This is a surprise."

"I made soup for Zane. I wanted to bring it by, see him, before I pick up Mama and Daddy from the airport."

"Come in, come in. Let me take that."

"It's hot. I'll just take it back to the kitchen if that's okay."

"Of course. That's very sweet of you, the soup. I'm sure Zane will appreciate it."

She carried it back, with Graham beside her, past the magazine perfection of holiday decor. "The house looks amazing." She set the pot on the stove top. "Why don't I take Zane up a bowl, sit with him a few minutes. Bet he could use a little company."

"I told you, he's sleeping."

She glanced at her sister. "Well, maybe he's—"

"And contagious," Graham added, slipping an arm around Eliza's waist. "I couldn't let you expose yourself, especially when you're going to be in close contact with seniors."

She didn't think of her parents as "seniors," and the word just pissed her off. "We're all healthy as horses, and he's going to come to dinner tomorrow anyway so—"

"No, he won't be well enough for that. He needs rest," Graham said—serious doctor voice.

"But if you wanted to move dinner to my place—"

"Better for everyone," Graham said cheerfully. "We'll stop by, have dinner so your parents can see Eliza and Britt, but we won't stay long."

She actually felt her jaw drop. "You're going to leave Zane alone? On Christmas?"

"He understands, and for today and most of tomorrow, he'll sleep in any case. But we'll be sure to add your chicken soup to his medication, and my care. I know what's best," Graham continued before she could object again. "I'm not only his father, I'm a doctor."

The thought, even the thought of Zane spending Christmas alone, sick, in bed, made her ache inside. "It's not right. Couldn't we, I don't know, wear masks? He's just a kid. It's Christmas."

"We're his parents." Eliza's tone took on an edge. "We decide. When and if you have children, you'll decide what's best for them."

"Where's Britt? At least—"

"In her room. A Christmas project." Graham tapped his fingers to his lips. "Top secret apparently. You'll see her tomorrow. Again, thank you so much for thinking of Zane, going to the trouble to make him soup."

He stepped away from Eliza, put a firm arm around Emily, and turned her around, walked her back to the door in what felt like a damn frog march. "Tell Quentin and Ellen we're looking forward to seeing them tomorrow."

"I—I can bring his gifts over tonight so he'll have them in the morning."

"No need. He's fourteen, Emily, not four. Drive safely now."

He didn't physically shove her out of the house, but it amounted to the same. Tears of anger and frustration stung her eyes as she walked back to her truck.

"It's not right, it's not right, it's not right."

She said it over and over as she got behind the wheel, drove out of the development.

But she was only the aunt. She could do nothing.

Zane's alarm clock read six-forty-five. At night, he knew that much. He'd spent more than twenty-four hours locked in his room, and his face and belly hurt so bad he'd only managed some patchy sleep. The pain wouldn't stop, and raw hunger added to it.

He'd eaten the other half of Britt's PB&J in the early hours of the morning. Just after eight, his mother brought in dry toast and a small pitcher of water, another ice bag.

Bread and water, he thought. Prisoner food.

Because that's just what he was.

She hadn't said a word to him, nor had he said a word to her.

Now it was nearly seven at night, and no one had come. He worried about Britt. Was she locked in her room, too? Sometimes he— Zane wouldn't think of the man as Dad anymore—locked them in. But only for a few hours, and they had TV or games or *something* to do.

He'd tried to read—they hadn't taken his books. But it hurt too much, gave him a terrible headache. He'd dragged himself into the shower because the hurt made him sweat, and he couldn't stand his own stink.

With the water running, his face throbbing, he'd cried like a baby. His face looked like Rocky's after a few rounds with Apollo Creed.

He had to get stronger. Micah's dad lifted weights. He had a whole room in their house for them. He could ask Mr. Carter to show him how to lift. He'd say how he wanted to build himself up some before baseball season.

And in three and a half years, he could go away to college. But how could he go away to college and leave Britt?

Maybe he should go to the police, tell them everything. But the chief of police played golf with his father. Everybody in Lakeview respected Dr. Graham Bigelow.

It hurt to think about, so he thought about baseball. He held a baseball under the covers, stroking it, feeling the stitching, like a kid cuddled a teddy bear for comfort.

He heard the lock click, and with hunger gnawing like a rat at his belly, felt relief.

Until he saw his father. He saw him in the backwash of the hall light. Tall, well muscled, carrying a tray and his doctor's bag.

Graham walked in, set the tray on the bench at the foot of the bed. He walked back to the door, flipped on the lights—God, they hurt his eyes!—shut the door behind him.

"Sit up," Graham said briskly.

Trembling again, Zane pushed himself to sitting.

"Any dizziness?"

Be careful, Zane thought. Be respectful. "A little, yes, sir."

"Nausea?"

"A little. Not as much as last night."

"Have you vomited?" Graham asked as he opened his medical bag.

"Not since last night."

Graham took out a penlight, shined it in Zane's eyes. "Follow my finger, eyes only."

It hurt, even that hurt, but Zane did what he was told.

"Headache?"

"Yes, sir."

"Double vision?"

"Not anymore, no, sir."

Graham checked his ears, his teeth. "Any blood in your urine?"

"No. No, sir."

"You have a mild concussion. You're lucky considering your behavior it isn't worse. Put your head back."

When he did, Graham pressed his fingers to either side of Zane's nose. Pain exploded, a nova burst. Crying out, Zane tried to push the hands away. Graham reached in his bag for tools, and fear sweat coated every inch of Zane's skin.

"Please. Please, don't. It hurts. Dad, please."

"Put your head back." Graham closed a hand around Zane's throat, squeezed lightly. "Be a man, for God's sake."

He screamed. He couldn't help it. He didn't see what his father did. Even if he'd opened his eyes, he wouldn't have been able to see through the red mist of pain.

Tears ran. He couldn't help them either.

When it was over, he simply curled into a shivering ball.

"You can thank me you won't have a deviated septum. You can *thank* me," Graham repeated.

Zane swallowed the bile that rose in his throat. "Thank you."

"Use the ice. You'll remain in your room until we leave for the resort on Boxing Day. You had an accident on your bike. You were careless. At the resort, you'll remain in your room in the suite. When we return home, you'll have had an accident while skiing. You were careless, not quite recovered from the flu, but stubborn. If you deviate from this in any way, it will go very badly for you. I will go to court and have you locked away with all the other misfits. Do you understand?"

"Yes."

Though Zane kept his eyes closed, he knew Graham loomed over the bed, tall, golden, smirking.

"Next week, you'll write to your grandparents thanking them for whatever gifts they had the poor judgment to buy you. Those gifts will be donated to charity. The gifts your mother and I selected for you will be returned. You deserve nothing, so nothing is what you'll receive. Do you understand?"

"Yes." It doesn't matter, doesn't matter. Please go away.

"Your computer will be returned for schoolwork only. I will check it nightly. If in a month's time you've shown proper remorse, if your grades don't suffer, if in my judgment you've learned a valuable lesson, the rest of your things will be returned. If not, they, too, will be donated to someone more worthy. If not, I'll rescind my permission for you to play baseball, not only this coming season but ever again.

"Do you understand?"

Hate. Zane hadn't known he could feel so much hate. "Yes, sir."

"I'll be looking into military academies as an alternative for your education if you don't straighten up. Your aunt sent the soup. Be sure to thank her for it when—and if—you see her again."

At last, at last, he left, locking the door behind him.

Zane stayed as he was until he thought he could ride over the waves of pain. He'd known his father could be mean, could be violent, that he could slide on the mask of the perfect husband, father, neighbor over what was under it all.

But he hadn't known, or hadn't accepted until that moment, his father was a monster.

"I'll never call him Dad again," Zane vowed. "Not ever."

He made himself get up, sit on the bench at the foot of the bed. He picked up the bowl of soup.

Cold, he noted. Just one more piece of mean.

But you lose, you fucking bastard, he thought as he ate. I've never tasted anything better in my whole life.

When he felt steadier, he took another shower since he'd sweated through his T-shirt. He made himself walk around the room, walk and walk. Getting stronger had to start sometime. He wished he had another bowl of soup, but settled for icing his face.

He heard Christmas music drifting up from downstairs, walked to the window. He looked out over the lake, saw the lights glimmering on the other side. He could pick out his aunt's house, thought of her and his grandparents celebrating Christmas Eve. Did they think about him?

He hoped they did. Sick with the flu, and isn't that a shame?

But they didn't know, didn't know, didn't know. And what would they, could they do if they did? Nothing against a man like his father. If Dr. Graham Bigelow said his son fell off his bike or hurt himself skiing, everyone would believe it. No one would believe a man like that would beat on his own son.

And if he tried to make them, what would they do anyway?

He couldn't go to military school. He couldn't stand it. He couldn't leave Britt.

So he needed to pretend, just like his parents pretended. He'd pretend he'd learned a valuable lesson. He'd say yes, sir. He'd keep his grades up. He'd do everything he had to do.

One day he'd be strong enough or old enough or brave enough to stop pretending.

Still, who'd believe him? Maybe his aunt would. Maybe. He didn't think she liked his father very much—or his mother either. He knew they didn't like her, because they said stuff about her all the time.

How she'd never amounted to much, how she couldn't even keep a husband. And lots of stuff.

He heard the piano, felt some relief. Britt was okay if she could play the piano.

Maybe he could get proof. He could get Micah to show him how to set up like a hidden camera or something. No, no, he couldn't pull Micah into it. If Micah told his parents, they might say something to *his* parents.

No baseball, ever, military school, another beating.

Not brave enough.

But he could write it all down.

Inspired, he went to his desk, found a notebook, pens, pencils. Not yet, he decided. One of them might come in again before they went to bed. If they caught him, jig up.

So he waited, waited, lay in the dark with his baseball for comfort and company.

He heard his father call out: "Sweet Christmas dreams, Britt!"

And she called back. "Good night."

Moments later he heard her whisper at his door, "I couldn't sneak in. I'm sorry. I heard you yelling, but—"

"It's okay. I'm okay. Go to bed before they catch you."

"I'm sorry," she repeated.

He heard her door close. He slipped into sleep for a while. His mother's laughter woke him. Coming upstairs, muffled words as they moved past his door. Staying where he was, eyes closed, breathing even, because he couldn't trust them.

And he was proved right when a few minutes later the lock clicked. The light from the hall reddened the back of his eyes. He kept them closed, but not tight—that's how they knew you faked it.

Even after the door shut again, the lock clicked again, he waited. One minute, two, five—he counted it off.

When he felt safe, he crept over to his desk, got the notebook, a couple of pens. Just in case, he took them and the little flashlight Britt had left him back to his bed.

If he heard the lock click, he'd have enough time to shove everything under the blanket, lie down again.

In the little beam of light, he began to write.

> *Maybe nobody will believe me. He says they won't. He's too important,*
> *too smart, so they won't believe me, but my English teacher says that writing*
> *things down can help you think and to remember stuff. I need to remember.*
> *On December 23, 1998, when my sister Britt and me—and I—he*
> *corrected—came home from school, my mother was on the floor. My father*
> *was hitting her again and when I tried to stop him he hurt me really bad.*

He wrote for more than an hour.

When he grew too tired to write more, he got a coin from his bank, used it to unscrew the air vent. He hid the notebook inside. Put the pens away even though he'd run one out of ink.

Then he crawled back into bed, and slept.

CHAPTER THREE

Zane followed orders. The pain eased; the bruises faded. No one at the resort questioned Dr. Bigelow's bike accident explanation, or his orders for Zane to remain undisturbed in his room during their stay. No one in Lakeview questioned Dr. Bigelow's skiing mishap explanation.

Well, Emily sort of did, wondering why Zane had been allowed to ski when he'd been recovering from the flu, but it didn't change anything.

Life went on.

If he'd learned a valuable lesson, it was to be careful.

He kept his room clean and tidy without prodding, did his chores without a murmur of protest. He studied, more out of fear than interest. If his grades dropped, he'd face punishment. If his grades dropped, he'd lose baseball. Baseball became not only his passion, his life's dream, but his future escape.

When he signed with the majors, he'd leave Lakeview and never look back.

Everyone acted as if December 23 never happened. Everyone inside the house in Lakeview Terrace lived the lie. He passed his father's tests—he was smart enough to know they were tests. The quick shoves or sharp slaps for no reason—and the satisfied look on his father's face when Zane kept his eyes on the ground and said nothing.

At night, inside the quiet of his room, he wrote the truth.

January 12. Graham shoved me into the wall. He said I sulked through dinner and didn't show my appreciation. I asked Micah's dad not to tell anybody he was showing me how to lift weights, that I wanted it to be a surprise. He doesn't talk to Graham anyway. I don't think he likes Graham very much. He said not to "sir" him every five minutes because it makes him feel like he's back in the army, and since we're working out together I should call him Dave. He's nice.

March 2. I'm getting stronger!!! I can curl 15 pounds, 12 reps, 3 sets. And today I bench-pressed 75 pounds and did 36 push-ups. I've gained 5 pounds. Dave says it's lean muscle mass. We have our first preseason game tomorrow, and Coach said my arm's a rocket! I think that's lean muscle mass, too. I got a single and a triple in practice, two RBIs. We're so totally going to trash the Eagles tomorrow! Eliza said to empty the dishwasher. I said sure. Graham slapped me. You don't say "Sure" you say "Yes, Ma'am," you Worthless Little Fuck. Then he slapped her because she didn't correct me and called her Stupid Bitch. I saw how Britt was maybe going to cry and gave her a look so she wouldn't. No point in her getting slapped.

He wrote every night, detailing his ball games, his progress in the gym, his father's abuse.

He wrote of his pride and the thrill when the Lakeview Wildcats took the championship. Of how proud his father acted during the game, and how casually he criticized Zane's base running, his fielding on the way home. Of how Dave Carter gave him a high five and called him champ.

By his fifteenth birthday that summer, he stood at five feet eleven, weighed in at 128. When Dave called him a lean, mean fighting machine, he didn't know that's what Zane aimed for.

On the night of December 23, he woke from a nightmare in a cold sweat. He'd dreamed his father found his notebooks and beat him to death.

But nothing happened, and the holidays came and went.

He got his first real girlfriend in Ashley Kinsdale, a laughing-eyed blonde, honor student, soccer star, and his first real date when he invited her to the end-of-school dance in May.

Since they doubled with Micah and his date—fellow gamer and

nerd-with-an-attitude Melissa—Mel—Riley—Dave volunteered to drive them to and from.

He had to get a new suit, new shoes, which he tried to pretend was bogus—but secretly he liked duding it up. Plus, he'd gained another two inches, not only in height, but in his feet.

He hated his hair—his father had decreed he wear it in a military cut, always reminding him military school loomed as an option. But otherwise, he thought he looked pretty damn good. He hoped to reach six-three by graduation, and maybe he would. That would put him eye to eye with Graham. Graham, who called Ashley "Zane's Mick slut" when she wasn't around.

His belly was still sore from the punch when he'd made the mistake of looking up the last time Graham had goaded him with that.

Two years, two months, he reminded himself. He'd be eighteen and free. They thought he'd go to UNC at Chapel Hill, study medicine. But no way. He aimed for USC. Not only was it on the other side of the damn country, but they had a solid baseball program.

He'd apply there, and at Cal State Fullerton, and Arizona State. Hey, if Arizona State was good enough for Barry Bonds, it was good enough for Zane Bigelow.

He'd use Emily's address, and when he got that close, he'd tell her. She'd keep it zipped—he was pretty sure. He didn't want to be a doctor; she'd understand. If he could get a scholarship, he could make it work. No way Graham would pay unless he toed the line, so he had to get scholarships.

He had a good shot. With the weighted courses he had a 4.2 GPA, and he knew his coach would get behind him on the baseball end. Math and science killed him, but he managed to hold the grades up.

He'd owe Micah for the rest of his life for that.

He'd gotten 190 on the PSATs. Only 50 in math, and the math score had earned him a backhand and a gut punch. He had to take it again the next spring, had to bring the math up, but he'd be better prepared.

He ordered himself to stop thinking about it. He had a date!

The knock on his door tensed his shoulders, then he remembered neither of his parents ever knocked. He opened the door to Britt.

"Jeez, look at you."

"Pretty smooth, right? Except for the dork hair."

"At least you don't have to wear it in a ponytail every day, or pin it into a bun for dance class. Chloe got to get hers cut and punked up. It's so cute. I'm thirteen now, and I have to wear it like I'm eight."

"Micah and Mel got matching blue streaks for tonight."

"Well, they're weird." She plopped down to sit on the side of his bed. "So . . . do you know Major Lowery?"

"Yeah, sort of. Freshman, basketball player. Made varsity. Why?"

She twirled the end of her ponytail around her finger. "No reason, just wondered."

"Give me a break." Zane snorted it out. "He's in high school. You're not."

"I will be next year."

"Aww, you got a crush on Maj." Now he snickered. "Gonna practice kissing the mirror so you—"

"Shut up."

As was his obligation as big brother, he made kissy noises. Then suddenly stopped, spun around. "Jesus, Britt, lay off there."

"It's none of your business."

When, chin up, she started to rise, he waved her down. "Major's black."

Her eyes fired up. "If you're going to be a racist, I'm—"

"Come on, Britt, you know better."

Her chin inched higher. "I thought I did."

"Do you hear how he talks about Ashley just because her grandparents came over from Ireland? Think about it, think about what he'd say, maybe even do, if he saw you hanging out with a black kid."

She dropped back on the bed again. "It doesn't matter. It's not like he even knows I exist."

If Graham even got a hint of it . . . . "You've got to be careful. Smart and careful. Five more years. I know it's forever, but it's really not."

"Mom's saying I have to do all this stuff so I'll be invited to the debutante ball when I'm sixteen. The ballet, the grades, how I dress, how I talk. At least you get to play baseball. White dresses and pearls—screw it, Zane."

She jumped up again, throwing her hands in the air. "It's not me. I don't want it to be me."

"You think this is me?" He tapped a finger on his hair. "Just be smart, be careful. When I go to college, especially." He glanced toward the door. "I've been thinking about telling Emily before I go."

"You can't." Fear jumped into her eyes, her voice. "He'd go crazy."

"That's just it. He's going to go crazy when he realizes I'm not going to Chapel Hill, when he realizes I'm out of here. He could take it out on you. You need somebody here. Emily would help."

"What could she do?"

"I don't know, but something." It gnawed at him, like a dog on a bone, constantly. "I'm not going to leave you without knowing somebody will help."

"You can't protect me forever."

"Sure I can. We'll talk about it later—not here in the house. We'll talk it out. Maybe Micah's parents, too."

"Zane, you just can't. They wouldn't believe us anyway."

"Dave's an EMT. He knows Graham, and I don't think he likes him. He doesn't say, but I can tell. We'll talk later," he repeated. "But I'm not going to let him hurt you."

She started to speak, then shook her head.

"What?"

"Nothing. We'll talk later. If they hear us . . ."

He'd read about POWs, about how they'd work together in secret to try to escape. He figured he and Britt were like POWs in their own house.

But for four whole hours, he was a free man. From the time he climbed into the Carters' SUV until he got out again, everything was normal. And fun.

Yeah, he had to go to Ashley's door, and go inside, and have his picture taken with her about a million times. Even her grandparents were there, taking *more* pictures, and talking in their cool accents.

And Ashley looked really good with her hair all ripply—she said her mom crimped it, whatever that meant. He told her he liked her dress, and he did because the blue matched her eyes.

The dance committee had the gym all done up in a beach theme.

Ride the Waves! Surf's Up! He didn't care about that, but the DJ and all the lights were cool.

And since Micah ranked as the worst dancer in the history of dancers, Zane knew his own moves came off pretty good. He especially liked the slow dances where he just had to sway, and Ashley pressed up against him.

She'd let him touch her breasts already—over her shirt, but he'd gotten his hands on them. He had hopes she'd let him get a real feel before too much longer.

And with the way she smiled up at him, he thought: Maybe.

She linked her arms around his neck, gave that little tug that meant she wanted to kiss. She tasted like gumdrops, smelled like flowers.

"This is the best night," she murmured. "One more week of school, then summer."

"Three and a half days," he corrected.

"Even better. But . . . I'm going to miss you so much when you go on vacation to Italy."

"Then you're going to Ireland." He held her close again. "I wish we were going over there at the same time. Then we'd be in the same part of the world."

"You have to write me. I'll write you. I wish you had a phone. I think we could text if you did."

"I'm going to try to get one. The parents won't go for it, but I think I could talk Emily into getting me one in her name, then I'd pay her for it."

And hide it really well, like the notebooks.

"That would be so awesome! I can't imagine not having a phone. You must feel so cut off from, like, everything. I mean everybody has one. Your parents are scary strict."

You have no idea. "Yeah, they are."

"Well." When the song ended, she stood with her body against his another moment. "We're going to be upperclassmen. Juniors. Maybe they'll loosen up."

"Yeah, maybe. Want to go outside for a while and . . ."

She smiled again. She knew what "and . . ." meant. "Let's do that."

Outside the night was lake spring cool so he gave Ashley his suit jacket. Other kids had come out to talk, to sneak a smoke, to sneak a joint. Or to "and . . ."

He stayed away from the smokers, the stoners. Not worth military school. And drew Ashley just far enough away, just enough into the shadows that they could get serious about kissing, enough so he could touch her breasts.

And just when he thought maybe, she pulled back. "We have to slow down."

Her heart had been hammering under his hands, and her breathing was unsteady. He thought if he only had another minute, maybe just thirty seconds.

"I don't want to." She took his hand. "But we have to."

"I really like you, Ashley."

"I really like you, too. But we should go back inside. Don't be mad."

"I'm not." Frustrated, yeah, with a hard-on so big he wasn't sure he could walk yet. "I get it. It's just . . . I think about you a lot. And I think about being with you."

Her eyes looked like the lake, he thought when she stared up at him. So soft, so blue, almost liquid.

"So do I, you know, about you. That's why we need to go in. My granny, she was my age when she got pregnant with my dad."

"Jeez!"

"I know. So, let's go back to the dance."

He hadn't thought about doing it—or hadn't thought of it in the maybe category yet. He wasn't sure what to think knowing she had.

And knowing she had didn't help with the hard-on.

"I just need to, ah . . ."

She glanced down, grinned. Her liquid blue eyes laughed. "Oh. Okay. Let's just talk about calculus."

"That would do it."

He had the best time. When he walked Ashley to the door, he got a totally serious kiss. And had to think about calculus so he could walk back to the car without embarrassing himself.

He figured when he wrote it all down in his notebook, it would be sort of like reliving it. Plus, he'd have a whole entry where nothing shitty happened, where he didn't write anything about tests, home-work, or Graham's put-downs.

"Thanks for the ride, man," he said to Dave, exchanged low fives with Micah.

He headed toward the door, half wishing he could just take a walk around the neighborhood, think about Ashley, that last kiss. But he'd miss his eleven-thirty curfew.

Maybe he'd risk making a snack—strictly forbidden after dinner—since after all the dancing he was completely starving. He thought about risking a sandwich, but he half believed Graham counted the slices of deli ham.

Better not—keep the head down, he decided. Graham had been especially hard-assed the last few days. Not slapping or shoving, but snarling. It was like waiting for a barking dog to bite.

When Zane unlocked the door and went in, those teeth flashed.

"You missed curfew." Graham stood in the foyer, a glass of scotch in one hand, eyes as cold as ice.

"Sir, it's eleven-thirty."

"Eleven-thirty-*four*. Did you forget how to tell time?"

"No, sir."

"Time matters. Adherence to the rules matter. Leaving this house for entertainment is a privilege granted, not a right."

"Yes, sir." Two years, two months, he thought, repeating it like a mantra in his head.

"*My* time matters. Do you think I have nothing better to do than wait up for my son because he can't be trusted to follow the rules?"

Instinct warned Zane to keep his gaze lowered because there was something here. Maybe it was the scotch, maybe it was whatever had been snarling under the surface for the last few days.

"I'm sorry. I guess it took longer to drop off the girls before—"

He'd expected the shove, or worse, so let the force take him back a few steps.

"Do you think I want to hear excuses? You should have been re-sponsible enough to factor in the time, respected the rules. But since, as usual, you're irresponsible and disrespectful, you're grounded for two weeks. No phone privileges, no gaming privileges, no outside activities, including baseball."

Now Zane's head snapped up. "Sir, we're going to States. We're going to take the championship for the second year in a row. We—"

Smugness coated over the snarling. "So by your lack of responsibility, you let your school and your teammates down. No glory days for you. You're a screw-up, Zane, always have been."

Zane saw it, saw it clear as a sign in neon.

"Is that what this is about? You don't want me to play, to be part of a winning team, maybe even to stand out. So you find any excuse to take it away from me. You—"

He hadn't expected the backhand, only because he'd lost himself in his own rage.

"And there's two weeks more." Tossing the drink aside, Graham gripped Zane by the shirtfront, rammed him back against the door.

And in that moment Zane knew he was right. The four minutes was an excuse to take away something he loved. His hands fisted at his sides.

"Have you been drinking?"

"No."

Graham slammed him back again. "Don't lie to me! Drugs?"

"No."

"You snuck off to the bushes and stuck it to that little slut, didn't you?"

"No! Ashley's not a slut."

"Just another slut, and you're too stupid to see she's trying to get her hooks into you for my money. Don't come in here late, half-dressed, and tell me you didn't fuck her."

He'd taken off his tie, his suit coat—like every other guy at the dance. "I didn't have drugs, alcohol, or sex. I went to a school dance."

The punch to the gut hurt and winded him, but he'd braced for it.

"Not much of a man then, are you, if you can't get in that little Mick slut's pants?"

"Graham!"

He didn't so much as glance around at his wife's frantic call. "Shut the hell up. I'm busy."

"Britt's sick. She's thrown up all over the floor."

"Deal with it!"

"Graham, she's throwing up, she's hysterical. Do something!"

"I'll do something, all right." He heaved Zane aside, charged up the steps.

He watched almost dispassionately as Graham used his fists, as Eliza shouted and tried to slap back. Let them bloody each other, he thought, like a couple of goddamn animals. He only needed to get past them to Britt.

He started up the steps, calculating, but the shouts, the fists, the curses, had Britt running out. Pale as a ghost, she covered her ears. "Stop, stop. Please. I can't take it. I just can't take it."

This time it was Britt who earned that vicious backhand. As he heard his sister cry out, saw her fall, something snapped in Zane. He streaked up the steps like fury, burning. Even as Graham spun to meet the attack, Zane's fists flew.

"See how you like it."

The muscles he'd trained for more than a year drove his fists, and the dark pleasure of seeing the shock on Graham's face, the blood he spilled on it, drove him.

Screaming, everyone screaming. He wouldn't stop, couldn't, until the man who made his life hell was down.

Somewhere, far away, he heard Britt shouting for help, shouting the address. He felt Eliza's nails rake down his face, but he didn't stop.

Then he was falling, flying, tumbling. His elbow hit a tread on the stairs like a hammer hits a nail. He felt something crack, break, shatter, and the pain bloomed red as his head hit another.

Dazed, he tried to stand, managed to get to his knees, lifted his shaking fists to defend himself.

But Graham didn't rush into attack. No one stood up the stairs. And Britt had stopped screaming.

Understanding that could be worse, he pushed himself up, fell again. Something wrong with his ankle, he realized, and began to crawl.

He'd made it to the base of the steps when Graham dragged Britt out—along the floor, by her hair. He had his doctor's bag in his other hand.

She didn't struggle, didn't cry, didn't move, and Zane feared, for the first time, for her life.

"Don't you touch her again, you son of a bitch."

"This is your doing." His voice flat and calm, Graham started down the stairs. "It won't be military school now. You'll wish for that, but it's too late."

He stood over Zane, angled his head as he studied him. "You take after your mother's side, in looks, in lack of ambition, in your poor attitude. I have serious doubts you're mine, biologically."

"I hope you're right."

The kick to Zane's gut was almost casual.

"But legally, I'm your father, and a well-respected leader of this community. Actions have consequences. You're about to pay the consequences for your actions."

"Fuck you and your consequences. What did you do to Britt, you bastard?"

"Oh no, *son*, it's what you did."

Sirens wailed. Zane thought, thank God, thank God. Britt had called for help. She must have called nine-one-one.

"They're going to lock you away."

Graham chuckled, shook his head as he set down his bag, started for the door. "No one as dull-witted as you could possibly be my blood.

"Eliza!"

"Yes. Yes, Graham."

"Do and say exactly what I told you."

He opened the door, took a deep breath, then ran out.

"Here! Here!" Outside, Graham waved his arms for the police cruiser. He made his voice shake, forced a few tears into his eyes.

It didn't surprise him to see chief of police Tom Bost leap out of the cruiser. After all, he'd cultivated the man as a friend. And considered him a useful idiot.

No reason not to play it up, Graham thought, and bent over, bracing his hands on his knees as if catching his breath.

"My God, Graham. What the hell happened? Your family—"

"Tom, oh my God, Tom. We need an ambulance."

"On the way."

"Zane . . . I don't—I can't—He attacked his mother. He struck her, Tom, with fists. Then our little Britt. I rushed upstairs to stop him. We fought. We fought. He fell down the steps. I had to give Britt a sedative. My boy's hurt, Tom. He's hurt. And I think he lost his mind."

"Hold on. Stay right here." He signaled to one of his officers.

Yes, indeed, a nine-one-one from the Bigelows brought out the force, Graham thought as he shook his head, and limped after Tom toward the house.

"Tom, Tom." At the top of the stairs, Eliza held a limp Britt in her arms. "We need an ambulance. My baby. My baby girl!"

"Coming now. Jesus, Zane." Tom crouched down. "What got into you? You on drugs?"

"No. No. He was hitting her again, and then he went after Britt. I tried to stop him."

"How can you say such a thing?" Weeping now, Eliza rocked Britt. "Graham's never lifted a hand to me or either of the children in his life! Oh dear God, Zane, what have you done?"

Stunned, Zane could only stare. "She's lying. She's lying for him."

"He came home from the school dance. I'd waited up—Britt was sick, throwing up. I was trying to take care of her, and told him I couldn't talk to him right now. He just . . . he flew into a rage. He hit me." She brought a trembling hand to her face.

Cradling his wounded arm, Zane felt something inside him die.

"What are you? What kind of a mother are you?"

"He's always been jealous of Britt, but I had no idea . . ." Eliza gathered Britt closer, began to sob.

A pair of EMTs rushed in.

"Look after them first." Tom pointed up.

Graham picked up his medical bag. "I want them transported to the hospital."

"And you with them," Tom said.

Graham nodded. "I need to talk to you, Tom. Outside. He says he hasn't taken any drugs, any alcohol," Graham told the EMTs. "I can't be sure. He has before."

"That's a lie!"

"Easy now, Zane."

Zane recognized the EMT—Nate, a friend of Dave's. "I didn't do this. I swear to God I didn't do this."

"Okay, son, we're going to take care of you now."

Zane just closed his eyes. "I didn't do this."

"You're not authorized to administer any pain medication," Graham said as he walked out with Tom. "You need to do a tox screen. He can't be trusted."

"I don't do drugs." No tears now, only hopeless fatigue. "I don't drink. You're off the team if you do drugs or alcohol. We're going to States."

It hurt, all over again it hurt, so he was thrown back to December 23. But he got some relief when they stabilized his arm, his ankle.

They got him on the gurney, started to roll him out. Tom came back in, face grim. "I need to cuff him."

"Jesus, Chief." Nate laid a hand on Zane's good shoulder. "He's got a broken arm, maybe a shattered elbow. His ankle may have a hairline fracture. Even if not, it's a major sprain. He couldn't put weight on it. He's concussed, he's shocky. Where the hell is he going to go?"

"It's procedure." With that, Bost stuck out his chin. "He's charged with assault, three counts."

Zane stared into Tom's eyes as Tom cuffed his wrist to the gurney. He saw no mercy there, no shade of doubt. Just as his father had always told him.

Still, he tried. "I didn't do this."

"Zane, both your parents tell me the same story. Your sister's sedated, but I'll be talking to her tomorrow." Bost closed a hand over Zane's as if that would comfort or reassure. "We're going to get you the help you need."

They rolled him outside. Neighbors everywhere—he could hear them. Who would believe him? None of them. No one.

He looked up at the sky. The same stars he'd seen with Ashley. But nothing was the same as it had been. Nothing would be the same now.

He heard running feet, started to cringe. His father, coming back to finish him.

No one would stop him.

But it was Dave who gripped his hand.

"Zane. It's going to be okay."

"I didn't hit Britt. I didn't hurt our mother."

"Of course you didn't. Why the hell is he cuffed?"

"You need to step back, Dave."

"What the hell, Chief? I dropped this kid off not a half hour ago. He and my boy went to the dance at the high school. They had a good time. How'd you get hurt, Zane?"

"He was hitting her again. He started on me first, then he started on her. And this time, he hit Britt. I couldn't let him. I tried to stop him."

In Dave's eyes he saw what he hadn't seen in Chief Bost's. He saw belief.

"Where the hell is Graham Bigelow?"

"On his way to the hospital, along with his wife, and his daughter. I don't like this any more than you, Dave, but Zane's charged with assault. He's going to get medical attention, then he's going to Buncombe."

"Good Christ, Tom, you know this kid."

Bost stood his ground. "I know his parents, too, and both of them gave statements. I've got no choice, Dave. He's charged, and Judge Wallace put through the order. You have to step aside."

"Hell I do. I'm an EMT. I'm going with him. Somebody's going to stand for this boy." Dave climbed in the back of the ambulance, helped load the gurney. "Give me his status, Nate."

Zane fumbled for Dave's hand. "He's a monster," he managed as the doors shut.

"Who is, champ?"

"Graham Bigelow. He's a monster. Eliza, too. Monsters. Don't let them hurt my sister."

"Don't you worry. You take it easy now. Let us take care of things."

"Emily." Someone believed him, Zane thought and closed his eyes again. Someone. It brought him a ray of hope that hurt almost as much as his arm.

"You need to tell Emily. You need to call Emily and tell her what happened. Please."

"I will. Don't worry now."

"She has to take care of Britt. I won't be able to protect her now."

He felt tears rising when Dave stroked his head, so turned his face away and let himself drift.

CHAPTER FOUR

Everything blurred. Sirens and lights, voices.

He kept his eyes closed; it hurt less somehow with his eyes closed.

More voices, talking fast, when they took him out of the ambulance, rolled him into the ER. He heard Dave's voice—Dave stayed with him—rattling off his BP and stuff.

He couldn't bring himself to care.

Man, he was cold. How did it get so cold?

He just wanted to sleep. He wished he had his baseball. Just something to hold on to.

They'd lied, his parents, the people who were supposed to love him, supposed to look out for him, had lied. He didn't even know where they'd gone. Maybe they were here, at the hospital—but not handcuffed to a gurney.

Maybe they'd come here because, for the first time in his memory, Graham had struck Eliza in the face. And Zane knew why. He'd hit her where it showed because he'd lie. They'd lie and say Zane had hit his own mother.

And Britt.

His eyes flashed open. His cuffs rattled as he tried to sit up. "Britt. He hurt Britt."

"Take it easy, Zane." To reassure, to monitor his pulse, Dave put a hand on his wrist. "We need to get you into X-ray."

"He hit her, he hit her. She called for help. I heard her, and tried to stop him. He knocked me down the stairs, then he dragged her out, gave her something. You have to find out how bad he hurt her. Where is she?"

"I'll find out," Dave promised. "I got a hold of Emily, called her on the way in like you asked. She's coming. And I called in a favor. We're going to have Dr. Marshall take care of your arm, your ankle. She's a hell of a bone doc. She's the best."

"We're going to States. He said I was four minutes late coming home from the dance. Grounded. No baseball."

"Oh, for Christ's sake." Dave scrubbed his hands over his face, took a long breath. "You have to tell the police everything you've told me."

"I tried. They don't believe me. Just like he said. He's important. I'm nothing."

"I don't want to hear that bullshit out of you." Dave leaned down so their faces were close. "You stay tough, Zane. You stay strong. Look at my face, look in my eyes. I believe you, and I'm going to do everything I can for you. First, we're going to deal with what we've got. We're going to get you fixed up."

"They're going to put me in jail. You have to look out for Britt. She won't have anybody but Emily. And they don't let her come around much."

"I'm on it."

Zane looked around the room, just a curtain to block it off, all the sounds of the ER outside. He kept his voice low. "You have to get into my house when they're not there. Take my house key. It's in my pocket."

"Why?"

"I wrote it all down. I've been writing it down for a long time. In notebooks. They're behind the vent over my desk. Maybe they'll believe it if it's all written down."

"How long has—" Dave cut himself off as the curtain was pulled back. "Looks like it's picture-taking time." But he slid a hand in the pocket of Zane's suit pants, palmed the key.

They took him to X-ray—with one of the officers lingering.

Afterward, they wheeled him back, but this time to a treatment room with a door. And the officer right outside.

The doctor came in. She made Zane think of a barrel—short, stocky. She had her hair, a lot of gray in it, tied back in a braid.

"Hey, Zane. I'm Dr. Marshall." She picked up his chart. "Let's have a look at things." Her eyes, dark as a crow's, narrowed, then she flicked them at Dave. "Do you know why Zane hasn't been given any pain medication?"

"His father said he might be on drugs. He's not, but they won't give him anything until they get the tox back."

"I've just looked at it. He's clean. Goddamn it—Sorry, kid."

She slapped open the door again, yelled for a nurse, started barking out orders like a general. General Barrel.

And in a few minutes, everything went light and easy.

"His fingers are numb," Dave murmured. "The skin at the elbow's cold."

"I'm reading the chart, Dave. Okay, Zane, here's the good news. Your ankle's not broken. You've got a nasty sprain, some torn ligaments. We're going to keep treating that with ice, rest, elevation, give you a nice boot for compression. I'm going to give you a list of what to do, how to do it. In a few days, we'll start some PT."

Floating on the painkiller, he smiled at her. "What's the bad news?"

"You've got three bones in your arm, and you hit the triple play. You've got yourself a broken elbow, kid. I'm going to splint it, and that's going to help with the pain, help keep it stable. You're going to keep it elevated over your heart as much as you can. In a few days, when the swelling's gone down, we'll hit those bones with sound waves, get you a cool cast. It may be you're going to need the extra cool pins and screws, but I'm going to take another look when you come back."

Floating, hazy, he smiled at her. "Doesn't sound so bad."

"That's the spirit! If you need surgery, well, I'm damn good. Plus, you're young and handsome, and got some really nice muscle tone going. We'll get you back in shape. Got it?"

"Yeah, okay. Will they let me out of jail for it?"

The smile in her eyes faded. "Doctor's orders. I'm just going to give you a going-over first. That handsome face needs a little help, too, right?"

"He didn't break my nose this time. I know how it feels."

Those crow's eyes went extra bright like, to Zane's thinking, a fire had blown up behind them.

"There's good news. So any double vision?" she began, and her hands, gentle as butterflies, moved to his face.

He heard shouting—Emily—and tried to get up.

"Stay down," Dave ordered. "Let the doctor do what she does. I'll be right outside."

"Tell her about Britt." Through the haze, it all tumbled back. "You have to find out about Britt. He hurt her. I tried to stop him. I'm stronger than I was, but he's still stronger."

"Who hurt her?" As she worked, Dr. Marshall signaled to Dave to go.

"Graham. That's what I call him in my head. Since December twenty-third. Not the last one, the one before, when he broke my nose and stuff."

Dave stepped out, found Emily shouting at the officer.

"Come on, Jim. You know Emily. She's Zane's aunt."

"I'm just following orders. I got orders nobody but medical personnel goes in. What am I supposed to do?"

Dave only shook his head, took Emily's arm. "Let's talk."

"What the hell is going on? How bad is Zane hurt? They wouldn't even let me see Britt."

"I'm going to tell you what I know. I'm going to tell you what your sister and brother-in-law told the cops, and what Zane told me. And I'm telling you I believe Zane."

He laid it out, no sugarcoating, watched her brace herself against the wall, go pale.

"I should've known. How could I not have known? My God, they're just kids. How long has—"

"I don't know. You don't doubt what Zane says?"

However pale her face, the eyes in it went ferocious. "Not for one damn minute."

"They're sending him to Buncombe, the detention center here in Asheville, after he's treated."

"They can't just—It's Graham." She set her teeth, breathed through them. "He'd make that happen, he'd find the strings to pull. Can I post bail?"

"I don't know. Em, Zane gave me his house key. He asked me to get into the house, to get notebooks he's got hidden. He's been writing it down. I don't know if it'll help, but I'm going to find a way to get them."

"Can you—It's a lot to ask."

"He's depending on me. He's a good kid, Emily. He's a good friend to my boy, and the way I see it, he's been kicked around by that son of a bitch for years."

She swiped at her face, stared down at the wet of tears. How could there be tears, she wondered, when she felt such rage?

"And Britt?"

"I don't know, but my impression is this might be the first time Graham went after her."

"They won't let me see her, won't tell me anything, not even her room number. Dr. Bigelow's orders. No visitors."

"Mild concussion, bruised cheekbone, a lot of bruising. I'm sorry," he said when Emily's eyes filled again. "He sedated her at the house. I know a lot of the nurses, and got the update on her. She's resting comfortably. Sleeping."

He glanced back at the officer, moved Emily a few more steps away. "I'm going to check, make sure Graham and Eliza are still here. She had some pretty severe facial injuries, so did he."

Emily balled both hands into fists, white at the knuckles. "I'd like to give them both a few more."

"I hear ya." He glanced back again. "I didn't want to leave Zane until you got here. I'm going to let him know you're out here, tell him Britt's okay, just sleeping. Then I'm going for the notebooks. They're going to take him, Em, nothing we can do about it. You have to go to the cops, tell them what I've told you. I'm coming back with the notebooks. We'll show them to the cops here in Asheville. Not the Lakeview cops."

"You're a good man, Dave."

"I'm a father. God knows that boy needs one. Try to reassure him when they come to take him to Buncombe."

Emily waited, she paced, she woke up an old friend, now a lawyer in Raleigh, for advice.

She took the names of two criminal attorneys he gave her, and reluctantly accepted his advice not to call them at one in the morning.

She made a mental list. Police, lawyer, maybe child services. And yes indeed, a conversation with her sister.

When the doctor came out, Emily all but leaped on her. "How is he? Is he okay? I'm his aunt. I'm Emily Walker, his aunt."

"I can't give you details. It's against the law. I'm going to tell you he's been treated, and he's as comfortable as I can make him."

"Ah, Doctor?" Jim the officer cleared his throat. "I've got to ask if he's cleared. The van to take him to Buncombe's outside."

Marshall fisted her hands on her hips. "And if I say no, he needs to stay here for observation?"

He shuffled, looked down at his feet. "Then I gotta tell you, ma'am, Dr. Bigelow said he'd come down and clear him personally. Look, I don't like it, but the kid went after his mom, his little sister."

"That's a lie, a terrible lie."

Jim's face toughened, but he didn't meet Emily's eyes. "That's the statement—from his parents. And the law says he goes to Buncombe until his trial. Now you sign off, Doc, or I'm ordered to let Dr. Bigelow know. It's going to happen either way."

Zane felt better. Maybe it was the drugs, or the weird splint, but he felt better enough he dozed off on the gurney.

And came around when a nurse—male—and one of the cops woke him to transfer him to a wheelchair. When they rolled him out, Emily rushed to him, dropped down.

"Oh, Zane."

"Emily, you're not supposed to—"

"You shut up, Jim, or I swear I'll tell your mama you manhandled me," she snapped back at him as she touched her hand to Zane's battered face. "I've known you since grade school, James T. Jackson, and I've never been so ashamed of you."

"I didn't—"

"You don't even have to say it." Still stroking, Emily cut off Zane's denial. "I know you, Zane."

"You have to look after Britt."

"I will."

"You have to promise. Don't let him hurt her."

"I swear it to you on my life, you hear me? I won't let him hurt her again, whatever it takes. You have to hang in for me, my man. I'm getting you a lawyer. Dave and I, your grandparents, and people who know you, we're all going to do everything to get you out of that place."

"It's just jail. That house, it's been jail a long time."

"We've got to take him out, Emily. You've got to move back."

"I believe you, Zane, and I believe in you. You believe me when I promise you, on my life, I'm going to fix this."

She kissed his bruised cheek, made herself straighten and move back.

When she watched them wheel him around the corner, she turned her face to the wall, wept. And weeping, fumbled her ringing phone out of her pocket.

Britt woke in the dark, moaned, lifted her fingers to her throbbing cheek. The light snapped on, and her father stood beside her bed.

Hospital, she realized. Her father's face had bruises, a blackened eye. His lip was swollen.

And his eyes peered out cold and mean.

"This is what's going to happen," he said. "When the police come to speak to you in the morning, you'll tell them your brother hit you. He hit your mother, and knocked her down. He hit you. You don't remember much after that. Your mother screaming for me, but you threw up and got dizzy. Do you understand?"

Be smart, Zane always told her. Be smart, be careful.

"Yes, sir."

"You saw me fighting Zane, were frightened. You ran to the phone to call for help. He got past me for a moment, struck you again. That's all you know. Is that clear?"

He did that to your face. I'm glad he did that to your face. "Yes, sir."

He leaned down close, and her heart beat like birds' wings in her throat. "Do you know what will happen if you say anything else? Do you think your face hurts, your head hurts now? It's nothing. Your mother and I have told the police what Zane did. They, of course, believe us. Zane should be on his way to prison very soon."

"No, please—"

He slapped a hand over her mouth, squeezed just a little. "Your brother is lost to us. Something's wrong with him, with his mind. He's probably on drugs. He attacked his family, and will remain in prison until he turns eighteen. He will be forbidden to contact you, or you him. He will not be allowed in our home again. Do you understand? Nod."

She nodded.

"Very bad things can happen to a young girl who disobeys her father. Especially if her father's a doctor. You don't want to find out what those very bad things are."

He let her go, took a step back, shot out a smile. "Cheer up. It'll be like being an only child. You'll get all the attention, all the benefits. Think about that."

He walked to the door. "Oh, and your aunt won't be visiting. I've told the nursing staff to keep her away. She's been a bad influence, I'm afraid. In fact, I wonder if that's where Zane picked up his drug habit. Rest now. You'll be able to go home in the morning. I'm going to go sit with your mother, and get some sleep myself."

When he closed the door, Britt lay very still. She could hear her breath panting, so quick and fast it made her ears buzz. She had to slow it down. Chloe's mom went to yoga classes, was always talking about breathing. Britt tried to get through the buzzing and remember what Mrs. Carter said when she and Chloe did yoga with her.

Because she had to get out, had to get away. She couldn't go home, not with him. She couldn't be alone, like an only child.

Her breath started to speed up again, and tears wanted to come, but she tried really hard. He said Zane was going to prison. She had to do something. But if the police believed her parents, why would they believe her?

And her face hurt. She just wanted to go to sleep until it all went away.

But it wouldn't, it wouldn't go away, and she couldn't go to sleep. Maybe the police wouldn't believe her, but Emily would. Maybe Mrs. Carter would. Maybe.

She got up slowly, crept and felt her way across the room until she found the bathroom. She turned on the light, closed the door except for a crack so she could see better.

She couldn't find her clothes, her shoes. She didn't have a phone in the room. He'd taken them. He would have thought of that. He thought of things.

But so did she, Britt told herself. And the thing she thought of first was: Find a phone.

She went to the door, opened it a crack, too. More light, a little sound, but not much. Mostly quiet. She didn't know what time it was—he'd taken her watch, too—but it had to be really late. Or really early.

Heart hammering, she slipped out of the room in her bare feet and hospital gown, dashed across the hall, slipped into another room.

Two beds, but only one person. Another kid, she realized. Younger than her. And a phone on the table by the bed where he slept. She took the phone as far away from the bed as she could, sat with it on the floor, and called Emily. Nobody answered, and she wanted to cry again when the machine came on.

But she had another number in her head. Emily's cell phone. If that didn't work . . .

"This is Emily."

"Emily." As she had countless times with Zane, Britt whispered. "You have to help us."

"Britt! Oh God, Britt. They wouldn't let me see you. Are you okay?"

"Nothing's okay. You have to help. Dad said Zane's going to prison. He said I couldn't tell what happened or he'd hurt me worse. It wasn't Zane, it was Dad."

"I know. I know, baby. Tell me your room number. I'll find a way to get in. I'm here. I'm in the ER right now."

"You're—you're here." Tears spilled then, shoved out of her by terrible hope. "You're here."

"I'm here. I'll come get you. What's your room number?"

"I'm not there. He took my clothes and shoes. He took out the phone. I went into another room where a kid's sleeping. Don't come up! Everyone will do what he says. They'll send you away, and they'll tell him. I'm coming down the stairs."

"Britt—"

"I can get to the stairs, and I'll walk down."

"Which staircase? Do you know?"

"This is room . . ." She turned the phone more to the light. "Room 4612. It must be pediatrics because there's a kid."

"Okay. I'll go to that staircase. If you aren't down in five minutes, I'm coming up."

"I'm coming down. I'm coming now."

She started to leave the phone on the floor and run, just run. But stopped herself, thought it through. If a nurse came in, the phone should be where it belonged. And just running out? She might get caught.

She put the phone back, froze when the little boy stirred and whimpered in his sleep. At the door she heard the sound of brisk footsteps passing by, waited, waited until they faded away before opening the door a crack.

Then wider so she could ease out enough to look up and down the corridor. She saw the sign for the stairs—so far away! She'd run, had to run. But quiet.

She heard a call bell ding, and like a runner off the mark, sprinted down the corridor. The stairway door, heavy, seemed to push back at her, but she got through, and kept running.

Somebody could come. He could come. They'd take her back, they'd tell him. He'd stick her with a needle again. Hit her again.

She got all the way down, breath wheezing, but Emily wasn't there. Drained, desperate, she sat shaking on the steps.

Maybe he'd found Emily. Hurt her. Stopped her. Maybe he'd—

The door opened; Britt's hands flew to her mouth to hold back a scream. And Emily rushed to her, gathered her up.

"Oh, Britt, oh, sweet baby." Pulling back a little, she looked at Britt's face, the black eye, the bruised cheek. "Oh, that filthy, fucking bastard. Put this on."

She stripped off her hoodie. "I would go for orange. Keep the hood up. We're going to walk—not run—walk, steady and direct, to the exit. There aren't many people around, and we're just going to walk out, keep walking to my truck. It's in the ER lot, but once we're outside, we'll be okay."

"You came. You came."

"Of course I did. We have to go. Hold my hand, keep your head down. Just walk. Don't talk, don't stop. Ready?"

Nodding, Britt gripped her hand.

They walked, Britt in the orange hoodie, bare feet, flowered hospital gown. And at one in the morning, no one gave them a second look.

Outside, Emily slid an arm around Britt's waist. The girl had shot up, she realized, and stood nearly as tall as she did. Growing like a weed. One she hadn't seen in weeks.

"I should've given you my shoes."

"It's okay, it's okay. Is it much farther?"

"Not much. We're fine. We're fine." But her voice shook a little, and Britt heard it. "We're going to get to the truck, and we're going to go to the police."

"No! They believe him. They put Zane in jail."

"Not the Lakeview police. The Asheville police. And we're going to make them believe us, Britt. Dave—Mr. Carter's going to help."

When her knees went weak, she staggered a bit. "Chloe's daddy? He—he's helping?"

"That's right. I'm going to call him when we get in the truck, tell him you're with me. He's getting Zane's notebooks."

"What notebooks?"

Doing her best to keep out of the light, Emily kept steering the girl forward. "I'll explain."

"Was he hurt really bad? Zane?"

"Yes. But he's going to be okay. And we're not going to let them keep him in jail. I'm getting him a lawyer, first thing in the morning. You're going to tell the police everything. Nobody's going to hurt you again, baby. I swear it."

"I'm so scared."

"Me, too. There's my truck."

Maybe her hands shook as she unlocked it, as she helped Britt inside. But her mind held clear and steady.

Graham Bigelow wouldn't put his hands on her niece again, whatever it took. She fumbled out her phone as she got behind the wheel.

"Dave. I have Emily. I'm taking her to the Asheville police."

"You—how did you—never mind. I have the notebooks. I'll meet you there."

Not much traffic, Emily thought as she kept carefully to the speed limit. And probably no one looking for them yet. They'd be fine, just fine, just fine. Unless they locked her up for kidnapping.

She reached out to squeeze Britt's hand as much to reassure herself as the girl. "I'm not going to ask you questions now, because I want you to say everything to the police. So it's not like we, I don't know, made it all up together."

Inside the orange hood, Britt's bruised face looked so small, so pale. "What if they don't listen?"

"We'll make them listen." They have to listen.

She drove straight to the police station, parked. Nobody else in the visitor's lot, she noted, and couldn't decide if that was good luck or bad.

"Okay, Britt, you just tell the truth. You tell all the truth, and it's going to be okay."

"He made us lie all the time. We had to lie to you all the time."

"He can't make you lie now."

Once again she took Britt's hand, and they walked to the station house. As they did, a man walked out. Britt's hand squeezed hers hard.

He looked tired, Emily thought, and his suit jacket looked as if he'd slept in it. A good day's worth of scruff gave his face a rough, tough sort of look. He paused, watched them come—the woman in red

Converse high-tops, with disordered dark hair, faded jeans. The girl with a battered face and bare feet.

She couldn't see the color of his eyes, but knew they assessed.

"You need some help?"

Britt spoke before Emily could. "Are you the police?"

"That's right. You got trouble?"

"We have a lot of trouble." Brown, Emily noted, his eyes were brown like his hair. "Do you have identification?"

His eyebrows lifted, but he reached into the inside pocket of his suit coat, took out his badge.

"Detective Lee Keller. Why don't you come in, tell me what the trouble is?" He gave Britt a look that had hope trembling inside Emily. "You look like you could use a soda. Let's go get you one."

CHAPTER FIVE

Detective Lee Keller assumed the exhausted woman was the kid's mother. But he set that aside. He knew it was better not to assume.

He didn't have to assume the fear. It was all over both of them. He didn't have to assume somebody had hit the girl, put her in the hospital. He could see her face, the hospital gown.

He led them through a lobby area, waved off a question from the officer at a counter, and kept going.

He stopped by a vending machine. "What kind do you want?"

"I . . . Could I please have a Sprite?"

"Sure." He glanced at Emily. "You want really bad coffee or a cold soda?"

"I'll take a Coke. I have change."

"Don't worry about it." He slid dollars in the bill slot, got the Sprite, two Cokes.

He led them down another corridor, then another, and into an area marked Criminal Investigations Division.

He pulled over a couple chairs from other desks, sat at another. "Have a seat. Why don't we start with your names?"

"I don't want to tell him. I don't want to tell him yet."

Emily shifted over to drape an arm around Britt's shoulders. "Honey—"

"It's okay," Lee decided. "How about we start with who hurt you?"

"My father."

"Has he hurt you before?"

"Yes."

"Oh." The woman pressed her lips to the top of the girl's head. "Baby."

"Just slaps before, or pulling my hair really hard. I didn't tell . . . my brother. I didn't tell him because if he tried to stop him, he'd get hurt worse."

"Where's your brother?"

When Britt shook her head, Emily cupped her chin. "Detective Keller can't help if you don't talk to him, if you don't tell him. Remember? All the truth."

"You left the hospital without your shoes," Lee commented in that same easy tone, "without your clothes. You must've been afraid."

"I called nine-one-one, and he grabbed the phone, and hit me in the face. He hit me before that because I threw up. I was scared because he was getting mad. I could hear him going off about Za— about my brother. He went to a school dance, and I don't know why that made my father so mad, but it did. My mother went to bed, but he stayed up. And I could tell he was going to hit my brother when he got home."

"Does he do that a lot?"

"He hits my mother and my brother."

"I'm not her mother, I'm her aunt," Emily said at Lee's narrowed look. "I didn't know about any of this before tonight. I should have, but . . ." She shook her head. "Tell him everything."

"When my brother got home, he started. He said my brother was late. Four minutes, do you get it?" Sudden passion spiked in her voice. "Four minutes, and he made it like Zane had done something criminal, right? He said he was grounded, no sports, and that means he couldn't go to States—the baseball championship. He started accusing him of drinking, doing drugs. He doesn't! And he said awful things about Zane's girlfriend. And she's nice, but he said things, started shoving Zane, hit him in the stomach."

She gripped the can of soda tight. "He mostly hits where it won't show. I don't know why I ran in to my mother. I knew she wouldn't help, but I did anyway. And I got sick, and she got mad, and she yelled for Dad, and he got mad. And he came up and hit me."

Beside her Emily sat silent, shoulders shaking as tears rolled.

"That's when Zane ran upstairs, and he hit Dad. He did it to stop him from hurting me. That's defense of others, right? You don't go to jail for that. They shouldn't put you in jail for that. And they had an awful fight, hitting and hitting, and Mom pushed and scratched Zane's face, but Zane didn't stop. And my Dad hit Mom in the face, and I ran to the phone and called nine-one-one, and I heard Zane yell, and thuds. Awful thuds. I think he fell down the steps. Dad came in, and hit me again, and he told Mom to get his bag—he's a doctor. He told her to hold me down because I tried to fight, and he got out a syringe, and stuck me.

"That's the truth. That's what happened."

She sat back, closed her eyes for a moment, then opened them, stared hard into his. Crossed her arms defensively.

"Okay." Careful, Lee only nodded. "Did the police come?"

"They must have, but he gave me something, and when I woke up in the hospital, he was there, waiting. He said what I had to say. That Zane had hit Mom, hit me, hit him. That if I didn't say what he said, he could hurt me worse than he had. No one would believe me if I said different, and Zane was already on his way to prison. I'd be like an only child. He took the phone out of the room, and he told the nurses no one could come in, and he went to get some sleep. I think they put Mom in the hospital."

Lee filed away the details, including the brother's name—Zane—the father being a doctor. The brother an athlete—must be baseball if he was going to States. And high school, older brother.

"Tell me about your mother."

"He never hits her where it shows, until tonight. Sometimes she hits back, but it's . . ." Color rushed into her face. She pressed her lips together, gave Emily a pleading look.

"It's all right. You just say the truth, and it's all right."

"It's that . . . I think they like it. I think she likes it. They have sex after most of the time, and then she acts like nothing happened. He buys her something, and she's like nothing happened."

She turned to Emily, burrowed in. "I couldn't tell you. I was afraid to tell you, but I was getting more afraid of not. Because when Zane goes to college, I'll be alone. Did Dad push him down the steps?"

Emily nodded. "But he's going to be okay. The boy isn't yet sixteen," she said to Lee. "He has a concussion, a broken elbow, a seriously sprained ankle. The doctor wanted to keep him in the hospital overnight, but . . . their father is a surgeon there, and the police where we live believed him and my sister, and he's friendly with important people. Like judges. They took that boy to Buncombe. He's fifteen. He's hurt. He's never been in trouble. You could talk to anyone and they'd tell you. His coaches, his neighbors, his teachers."

"Why did his doctor sign him out?"

"Because the man who put him in the hospital said if she didn't, he would. You can talk to her. She's Dr. Marshall, at Mercy Hospital."

Lee made another note. "Has he hurt your brother enough for the hospital before?"

"He didn't let Zane go to the hospital before. He locked him in his room. Christmas, Emily, you remember? Not last Christmas. The one before."

"Oh God." Emily closed her eyes. "Zane didn't have flu, and he didn't have a skiing accident when you were at the resort."

"We came home from school. The last day of school before Christmas. Dad was home early, and when we came in, we could hear Mom crying, and Dad yelling. Zane tried to stop me, but I ran back, and she was on the floor, and there was blood, and he was hitting her, and I yelled for it to stop. And Zane . . ."

She took a long sip of Sprite. "Before, he'd make me go upstairs, sit with me. Or if it happened when we were already in our rooms, I'd go to his, and he'd let me stay until it stopped. But this time, he tried to stop him from hurting her, and Dad . . ."

She let out a hiccupping sob. "I kept yelling to stop, and he— Dad turned and looked at me, and he was going to hit me. And Zane pushed me back and tried to stop him. He hurt him so bad, Mr. Keller. He kept hitting him, and he kicked him, and she just watched! And Dad picked Zane up, like over his shoulder, and took him upstairs, locked him in his room. I should've done something, but I was afraid."

"It's not your fault." Even paler than she'd been, Emily brought Britt's clenched fist to her lips, kissed it. "None of it's your fault."

"He broke Zane's nose, and his eyes were all swollen and black, and his lip was cut and swollen. I snuck him a sandwich when I could, a PB&J, but he could hardly eat.

"The day after, on Christmas Eve, I heard Dad go in, and in a little while Zane was yelling—screaming—like he was hurt again. And he said—Dad said—Zane had the flu. He was contagious and no one was allowed to see him, and spread germs. Even though Grams and Pop were coming for Christmas. And when we got to the resort, we'd tell the people there he'd been messing around on his bike and had a bad fall. He had to stay in the room while we went skiing. And when we got back, we had to say he fell when he was skiing."

She took the tissue Emily pressed into her hand. "You can call the resort if you don't believe me. You can call them. We go every year. They'll tell you he had the black eyes and everything when we got there. And you can talk to people where we live, to his teachers, and they'll tell you how we said he fell skiing."

"What resort do you go to?"

"High Country Resort and Spa. We go from December twenty-sixth to the thirtieth. We go every year."

"I went to see Zane Christmas Eve," Emily said. "My sister called, said he was sick, said we had to move Christmas dinner to my place because of germs. I went to take him some chicken soup, and a book I was going to smuggle in—on their do-not-read list. A Dark Tower novel, that's all."

When she felt her throat burn, she took a swig of Coke, breathed out the helpless rage. "They wouldn't let me go up, and they left him there alone on Christmas while they came to dinner. They've cut me off from the kids recently. I don't get to see them very often, there's always an excuse."

"They said you didn't want to spend time with us, that you had other things you wanted to do. We didn't believe them, honest we didn't, but that's what they said. Dad says you're a lazy slut."

Emily managed a smile. "Sometimes I wish." She kissed Britt's cheek. "We have more evidence. A friend—the father of my nephew's best friend is on his way here now. He's an EMT, and he heard Zane was hurt, he stayed with him at the hospital. Zane gave him his house key, asked him to go in and get some notebooks he'd hidden. He said he'd written it all down. They took him to prison, Detective Keller. They had to take him out in a wheelchair. If you became a cop to help people, help us."

"What's the name of the friend bringing the notebooks? I need to clear him with the officer on the night desk," he said when they both hesitated.

"Dave Carter."

"Give me a second."

He should call his lieutenant, Lee thought. Child services. He should call Buncombe and get the full name of the brother. But for now, he'd play it out.

The kid wasn't lying.

He came back to find the girl with her head on her aunt's shoulder. She looked so damn small, so beat-up.

"How'd you get out of the hospital?"

"I snuck into another room for the phone, and called Emily. She was already there, but they wouldn't tell her where I was because my father said not to. I went down the stairs, and she met me. Because she believes me, believes Zane, because she said we had to tell the police. My father will hurt her, too, if he can."

"You don't worry about that," Emily told her.

"If I'm going to help you, I need your names." It would take him about two minutes to find this Zane with a call to Buncombe, but he wanted the girl, the little girl with exhausted green eyes, to tell him. To trust him.

"Do you believe me? Will you believe me even when my father says I'm lying?"

"If I didn't believe you, I'd have made calls already. I'm a detective." He smiled when he said it. "I could find out your names, and your brother's. But I didn't, because I believe you, and I want you to believe I believe you."

Britt looked at Emily, got a nod. "You have to trust."

"I'm Britt Bigelow. My brother's Zane. My parents are Dr. Graham Bigelow and Mrs. Eliza Bigelow. We live in Lakeview Terrace. And I think he'll kill me if he can now that I've stopped lying."

"He's not going to touch you, or Zane, again. Didn't I tell you I wouldn't let him? The wrong Bigelow is in prison, Detective. And I'm Emily Walker."

"Got someone here for you, Detective." A uniformed officer led Dave in.

"Hey, Britt, let me have a look there." With a messenger bag over his shoulder, Dave crouched down by her chair. "Are you hurting?"

"I have an awful bad headache, Mr. Carter, and my cheek hurts a lot. My eye, too."

"Oh, Britt, why didn't you say? Damn it, I didn't even ask, not really. I must have some Advil or something."

"Let's not," Dave said as Emily started pawing through her purse. "I don't know what they gave her in the hospital. But I stopped on the way." He opened the bag, took out a bag of frozen peas. "Quick relief. You just hold that on your cheek, okay? How many?" He held up two fingers.

"Two. I'm okay, Mr. Carter. I feel better since we came here."

"Good to hear." Dave rose, held out a hand to Lee. "Dave Carter."

"Detective Keller."

"Well, Detective Keller, since I had Zane's key and his permission, I don't think going in the house, into his room qualifies as unlawful entry, but I'll take that lump if it comes."

He pulled several notebooks out of his bag. "I read the first entry in the one marked Number One. If you can read that and do nothing about getting Zane out of that place, about putting Graham Bigelow behind bars, you aren't human."

Lee opened the first book, read the first entry.

December 23.

When he finished, he picked another entry at random. Opened the second book, did the same.

"So, Britt, did your grandparents come to visit last summer?"

"In August, after we got back from vacation. They stayed with

Emily. It used to be their house, but they gave it to her and my mom. Mom didn't want it, so Emily paid her share. We had them over on the last day for a party on the sailboat. It was really nice. Then . . ."

She leaned into Emily again, carefully drank some Sprite. "Then after everybody left, my father got mad. He hit Zane in the stomach—he likes to hit in the stomach because it doesn't show. He said Zane embarrassed him because he's a bad sailor, and all he did was talk about baseball with Pop and he ate too much of the food like a greedy pig. And I don't remember all of it."

"That's enough."

Lee closed the book.

"If you had to go in front of a judge, and swear under oath, would you say everything you've said to me?"

"Will you get Zane out of prison if I do?"

"I'm going to work on that. Mr. Carter, do you remember Zane having a skiing accident?"

"Yeah, Christmas before last. Face-planted, he told me. Ah, shit. Shit." Dave pressed his fingers to his eyes. "He didn't come around until after the first of the year—and he and my Micah are usually joined at the hip. He had a broken nose, but it was healing up. I didn't question it. But it was right after that he asked me to help him get stronger. Learn to lift. Because of baseball, he said, and I didn't question that either."

"I told you."

"Yeah." Lee nodded at Britt. "You did. Now Mr. Carter corroborated your statement, your aunt's. And I'm going to wake somebody up at the High Country Resort and Spa, and nail it down a little more."

"We stay on the Executive level. They have twenty-four-hour butler service. But I don't know the number."

"I'll get it. I need to talk to the police chief in Lakeview."

Britt shook her head, cringed back against Emily. "He's a friend of my dad's. He'll—"

"He may be a friend of your dad's, Britt, but he's a law officer, and I've worked with him a couple times. He's not going to push this away. You have to keep trusting me, but another thing I have to do is going to be hard for you. I have to contact child services."

"They can't take her." Emily wrapped both arms around Britt. "I'm her aunt."

"I'm going to push as much as I can push, but if I don't contact them, it'll be harder yet. You took the minor child out of the hospital because both you and the minor child feared for her safety and well-being. Correct?"

"Yes."

"All right. You have to let me do my work, you have to trust I'm going to do that work with the safety and well-being of Britt top of my list."

"Zane."

"He's right up there with you, kid. I'm going to show you a place you can wait, maybe get some rest. Can you wait here, Mr. Carter? I just have a couple more questions."

"Sure."

"One more thing. The grandparents, not local?"

"Not anymore." Emily answered. "My parents moved to Savannah nearly ten years ago. You're looking for other family, in case they won't let me keep them. They'd come. They'd come without hesitation."

"Okay. Let me show you where you can wait."

When he settled them, he hit the break room, got coffee, brought some to Dave. "Being an EMT, I figure you can handle the coffee."

"Thanks. Jesus. Britt, she's tight with my daughter. Seeing what he did to her. What he did to Zane."

"You responded to the nine-one-one."

"No, I wasn't on, but word traveled, and fast. The kids are like family to me." Sitting, he rubbed hard at the tension in the back of his neck. "I went down to see what I could do, if I could help. They were bringing Zane out. And they had his wrist cuffed to the damn gurney, saying he was under arrest, three counts of assault."

Dave drank the cop coffee without a wince. "And bigger bullshit I've never heard. I'd taken him, my son, their dates to the school dance. And what, ten minutes after I drop him back home, he's attacking his mom? He wouldn't hit his mother or Britt. He was happy when I dropped him off, Detective. They'd had a great time."

"Any drinking?"

"Absolutely not. Kid's an athlete. He's serious about baseball, and damn good, too. He wouldn't risk getting benched for a beer, especially not before States. Jesus, you read the notebook."

"I'm getting details, Mr. Carter."

Dave held up a hand, drank more coffee. "Sorry. I'm wound pretty tight right now. Zane was sober, happy. It was their first big date, double date, Zane and Micah, my boy. And his tox came back clean. I was there when Elsa read it—Dr. Marshall, the orthopedic surgeon who treated him. He might still need surgery on the elbow, and he shouldn't have been taken out of the hospital, much less to Buncombe. Elsa didn't want to clear him—he should have had overnight observation. But Graham's not only his father, he's chief surgical resident. She didn't have a choice."

"You stayed with him?"

"Rode in the ambulance with him," Dave confirmed, "into the hospital, stayed. Neither of his parents came down. Emily came. I called her. They didn't."

"Tell me what Zane said to you."

Fueling himself with coffee, Dave went over everything he could remember, backtracked, added more detail.

"All right. I might need to talk to you again, but you can go home."

"I'll wait with Emily and Britt. I just need to let my wife know."

Lee angled his head. "Your wife? You and Ms. Walker aren't involved?"

"What?" Dave's face cleared for the first time with a quick laugh. "No. I've been married for seventeen years. Eighteen? One of those. I've got two kids. I used to work for the Walkers back when I was a teenager, and summers into my twenties. I've known Emily, and Eliza, forever. Emily and I—and Em and my wife—are pretty good friends."

"Not friends with Eliza Bigelow?"

Humor cooled out of Dave's eyes. "We don't run in the same circles as Graham and Eliza. She let that happen to her kids. Maybe she's a victim, too, but she let that happen to her kids. And her son is hurt, terrified, and in prison. She let that happen, too."

He got to his feet. "I'll wait with them."

Lee gave him directions, then sat back a minute. He'd been on his way home after a sixteen-hour day. Thinking he might have a before-bed beer.

Now it looked like more coffee with another long day to come.

He turned to his computer, did a run on Zane Bigelow, his parents, his aunt, Dave Carter. He got the phone number for the resort, and got to work.

When Zane looked back on the worst night of his life, small details stuck. The smell of the van—metallic covered with the sweat of fear and desperation. The sound of the wheels on the road sang misery. The impossible loneliness.

Whatever Dr. Marshall had given him for pain kept it under the surface. He knew it was there, knew it would come back, but he was too numb—body, mind, spirit—to care.

The guard had eyes like marbles, hard and cold. The driver said nothing. He was the only prisoner. He'd learn later his father's insistence and influence helped speed his transport, alone and at such a late hour.

"Looks like you got your ass kicked, didn't you? That's what you get for going at your mother, your baby sister."

Zane didn't respond—what was the point? He kept his head down.

And later, like so many things later, he'd learned the guard's marble eyes and the disgust in his voice were due, at least in part, to the fact that Dr. Graham Bigelow had performed surgery on the guard's son after a car accident.

He couldn't find his fear, couldn't even dig down through the numb for worry.

Until the misery music of the tires changed to a kind of threatening grumble. And he heard the sound of the gate clanging shut behind the van.

Panic bloomed in his belly, spread its tendrils into his chest. And rocks tumbled over it, sharp and heavy. He felt tears stinging the back of his eyes, and some instinct, some atavistic animal inside him warned that if they fell, if even one escaped, it would doom him.

"Welcome home, asshole."

The guard had to help him out of the van. If he felt any pity for the trembling boy with a splinted arm and ankle boot, he didn't show it.

He went through a steel door, a metal detector. He had to stand against a wall, bright lights in his eyes, his weight on his uninjured foot. He gave his name, his birth date, his address.

They took him to a room, took his clothes. He couldn't undress himself with his arm splinted, so suffered the humiliation of being stripped down, the unspeakable humiliation of the strip search.

They gave him clothes. Orange shirt, orange pants, orange clogs—or one clog because of the boot. They had to dress him.

They took him to a room—they called it a pod. It wasn't a cell like he'd imagined; it didn't have bars. It had a cot, a toilet, a sink. No window.

"You get up when we tell you. You make your bed, and wait till we take you in for breakfast. You eat what we give you. Since you got your ass kicked, you'll get a check at the infirmary before you talk to the head shrink, who's going to ask you about your fucking feelings. You do what you're told when you're told. Give me any shit, you'll pay for it."

Marble Eyes stepped to the door. "Your father's a great man. You're nothing."

He went out. The door locked with a click that boomed in Zane's ears.

And the lights went out.

He took one limping step, feeling for a wall, ramming his shin against the side of the cot. He crawled onto it as the trembles turned to shudders, as his breathing devolved into a kind of mewling.

He tried to curl up, just to hold on to himself, but he couldn't manage it. He wanted to sleep, just sleep, just sleep, but the pain broke through the surface.

He let the tears come now. No one to see, no one to care. The sobs racked him, hurt his chest, his belly, his throat. But when he'd exhausted them, the panic went with them.

He lay, body throbbing, spirit dead.

Hours before, just hours before, he'd kissed the girl. He'd looked at the stars and danced under colored lights.

Now, his life was over.

The dark, the solitude became comfort. He clung to them because he began to fear what his life would become once that door unlocked again.

CHAPTER SIX

Lee ran on two hours' sleep and black coffee. He'd made his case to his lieutenant, to the DA, to child services, and to the judge who'd signed Zane Bigelow's arrest warrant.

Now in Lakeview, he sat in Chief Tom Bost's office, a man he knew, and up until now had respected.

"This isn't your case, it's not Asheville's case, it's not CID's case. It's my case."

"It was." Lee spoke mildly, for now. "Now it's not. You shoved that boy through the system, Tom. You cut corners and bent the rules and shoved him through when he was hurt. You called in favors, pulled strings to get him slapped into Buncombe."

Red flags flew on Bost's cheeks.

"That *boy* put his mother, his sister, his father in the damn hospital. I did my job, and don't you come into my town and say different."

"I'm saying different."

"It's going to cost you, Lee. Graham and Eliza are half out of their minds about Britt. I don't know what the hell got into Emily Walker—I thought she had more sense. But she's going to face child abduction charges. And when Graham gets done, you'll lose your badge for being part of it."

Lee set a copy of the first entry of Zane's notebook on Tom's desk. "Read that. Zane wrote that—you can see the date. Read it."

"Every minute you hold that girl from her parents makes it worse."

But he snatched up the copy. "This is bullshit, Lee. That boy's sick."

"His parents are. I contacted the resort where they went on December twenty-sixth of that year. I talked to their butler, the housekeeper, the manager. You know what they all said, Tom, every one of them? They said Zane had a tumble off his bike, broke his nose, hurt himself. He came in that way. He had to stay in his room—they were ordered by Graham Bigelow not to disturb him.

"What did he tell you back then, Tom?"

"It's a mistake. Zane had a fall on the slopes."

"They told Emily and the grandparents Zane had the flu that Christmas. They wouldn't let anyone see him—germs, Bigelow said. I've got their statements, too."

Disgust in the motion, he pulled papers out of the file he held, tossed them on Bost's desk. "I've got Britt's statement." He tossed another. "Everything that boy wrote there is God's truth.

"You didn't begin to do your goddamn job on this."

"Don't tell me about my job," Bost hurled back. "I know Graham and Eliza."

"Do you, Tom?"

Chin jutted, Bost jabbed a finger at Lee. "You're trying to tell me Graham beats his wife, his kids, and they all lie to cover it? That not once until last night have we gotten a nine-one-one from that house?"

"That's right. Zane started writing it down that day, the day you've got there. And he kept writing it. The punches, the slaps, the fear, the threats. And the mother, she went along. I had her thirteen-year-old girl tell me how after her father knocked her mother around, they'd have sex. And he'd buy his wife something special. I had that kid look me in the eye and tell me she thinks her mom liked it."

"Britt's been traumatized. She—"

"Damn fucking right she has." Mild was done. "Look back, for Christ's sake. The kid calls for help, and when you get there, he's put her out so you can't talk to her. Zane's lying at the bottom of the steps, broken arm, concussion, torn ligaments. But you don't listen."

"The two adults gave the same story. Two people I know."

"I'll give you that. But you don't take a statement from the boy? You don't question the father demanding his son's arrest, how he pushed it through? How you *helped* push it through? How he wouldn't even give the kid a night in the hospital? Didn't arrange for a child advocate, a lawyer, nothing. Just lock him up? He said it was probably drugs, but the kid's clean. Did you bother reading the tox results?"

Lee yanked another paper out of the file, slapped it on the desk. "Clean." He snatched up one of the papers. "This is what Britt says happened last night. Read it. Put it the hell together."

"I've known Graham for over twenty years, for God's sake. Eliza even longer. I've had dinner at their house. I've been in that house, Lee, and never saw a sign of this."

"Read it."

When he had, Tom rose, turned to his window. "I believed him. You weren't there, you didn't see them. I believed him. If you'd asked me twenty-four hours ago to name the perfect family in Lakeview, I'd have said the Bigelows."

He raked both hands through his hair. "Most would've said just the same. Goddamn it, Lee, they'd have said the same. Now I think of little things, Jesus Christ. How he'd go on about how proud he was of Zane, but then cut that down just a little. How he had to keep on him to study because he had pipe dreams about playing pro baseball. How he had to be nagged to do chores, or how he talked back to his mother. Little things—you don't have kids yet, Lee. You expect some griping about kids, especially teenagers."

He turned back. "Eliza was president of the damn PTA. She— God."

"There's more you'll want to read. I'm leaving copies for your files." Lee got to his feet. "I'm going to Lakeview Terrace and arresting Graham Bigelow on charges of child and spousal abuse, on assault, on child endangerment. I'm arresting Eliza Bigelow on charges of child abuse and child endangerment. This was just a heads-up."

"I believed him." There was a plea in the tone now. "I believed Zane was a danger to them, and to himself."

"You were wrong. Zane's going to be processed out, and his record will be expunged. Emily Walker will have temporary custody of both minor children. I'm going to do everything I can do to make that permanent.

"Read the rest," he said, and walked out.

Ten minutes later, with his usual partner and four uniformed cops, Lee rang the bell in Lakeview Terrace.

He pegged the guy who answered as a lawyer, and held up the warrants. "Asheville Police."

"I'm the Bigelows' attorney. I have calls in right now to your captain, to Asheville's mayor. You're holding a minor child against her parents' wishes."

"Read the warrant." Lee muscled by him, into the big, high-ceilinged foyer, and straight into the living room, where Graham Bigelow surged to his feet.

"Graham Bigelow, you're under arrest for child and spousal abuse, child endangerment, assault." As he spoke, Lee spun Graham around to cuff him.

Graham spun back, punched out. "Add resisting and assault on a police officer. You have the right to remain silent."

"Graham, cooperate," the lawyer ordered while Lee read Graham his rights. "Don't say anything. I'll have this dealt with quickly."

But Graham ignored him, punched out again until two uniforms moved in to restrain him.

"You can't do this!" Eliza, her face bearing bruises, clutched her hands between her breasts. "This is insane. Zane—"

"That boat won't float, Mrs. Bigelow, and you are under arrest for child abuse, child endangerment, accessory to assault, for lying in a police report."

She batted him away as he Mirandized her. "Don't you touch me! Graham!"

"Eliza, try to stay calm, say nothing. It's not necessary to cuff her," the lawyer insisted.

"Disagree," Lee said, and did so.

It gave him enormous pleasure to perp-walk her out of the house, to see neighbors come out to stare, to put a hand on her head to load her into the car.

He had Graham loaded in a separate car. No more talking, no more coordinating stories.

No more making their kids' lives a living hell.

"We will have your badge for this," the lawyer warned. "And file a lawsuit that will bury your department, and you personally."

"Yeah, you try that."

"Don't attempt to speak to my clients. They have nothing to say."

"Fine. They can sit in a cell until you work that out. I've got somewhere else to be anyway."

Zane didn't have to make the bed when they told him to get up. He'd lain on top of the covers. He hadn't slept.

He tried to eat breakfast without thinking about it, without looking up or at any of the other prisoners. Some of them talked, some talked trash, some ate like they were starving, some barely ate at all.

The big room—like a dining hall, he guessed—echoed a lot, the dull beat of plastic spoons and forks against the plates, the scrape of chairs, the mutter of voices.

Somebody swiped the biscuit off his plate. He didn't care, and his lack of objection earned him a kick in his ankle boot under the table and a snicker.

After breakfast, they filed out as they had filed in. They took him to the infirmary.

The doctor there read a chart. He guessed somebody had sent one from the ER. He frowned a lot, then asked a lot of questions.

Blurred vision?

No.

Headache?

Yes.

He frowned more when he took off Zane's shirt and saw the bruises on his belly, his ribs.

Asked more questions.

He took off the boot, examined the ankle. Elevated it, put ice on it as he examined the splint.

More questions.

He probed, gently, at Zane's nose, his cheeks, under his eyes.

"Was your nose broken previously?"

"Yes."

"How?"

"My father's fist."

The prison doctor looked directly, for a long time, in Zane's eyes.

"Does your father beat you?"

"Yes."

"Have you reported the beatings to the authorities?"

"He's the authority."

He thought he heard a sigh.

A male nurse had to give him a sponge bath because he couldn't manage a shower.

"You should have been kept at the hospital overnight for observation, for pain management. I'm going to recommend you be transferred back under Dr. Marshall's care."

"They won't. My father's chief surgical resident. He wants me here."

He gave Zane a crutch—he could only use one because of the splint—but it helped. So did whatever he gave him for the pain.

"I'm going to have you taken back to your room, for rest. Dr. Loret, the center's therapist, will come to you later this morning. Keep your ankle and your arm elevated."

So he went back, to the solitude, the quiet. He could hear things through the door. Voices, movement, snapped orders, maybe someone dragging a bucket and mop.

He drifted a little. Not really sleep, but a zoning out, back in, back out.

When he heard the locks, he closed his eyes. He hoped the therapist would think him asleep, just leave him alone. He didn't want to talk about it. He'd exhausted everything he had to say already in the infirmary.

But he felt the bed give under someone's weight. Opened his eyes.

He saw a man who looked as tired as he felt, one who hadn't shaved in a couple of days. Brown hair and eyes, a suit and tie.

"Zane, I'm Detective Keller, Asheville PD."

A cop, he thought. Another cop. And closed his eyes again.

"Zane." He felt a hand on his arm—not restraining, just making contact. "I'm here to take you out."

"Out where?"

"Out of here. Zane, your sister came to see me."

His eyes flashed open again. "Britt. Is she okay? Is she—"

"She's okay. She's really smart, really brave. Your aunt brought her to see me last night."

"Emily. Britt got to Emily." Now he squeezed his eyes shut against the tears.

"And they got to me. Zane, Dave got your notebooks. I read them. I read every page. I'm sorry I couldn't get you out sooner. It took some time."

And in those brown eyes, the stranger's eyes, Zane saw what he'd seen in Dave's.

Belief.

"I . . . I'm going to get out on bail?"

"No. Just out. The charges are dropped. We can talk later, okay? Let's get you out. I've done all the paperwork so we can just get you dressed and go."

He started to shake, couldn't stop. "I can leave? I can just leave?"

"Try some good, easy breaths," Lee told him, and took his hand. "Just easy breathing. You should never have been here, Zane. Now, I've got some clothes for you. Or Emily got them for you. She got new—hopes she got the sizes right. She thought you wouldn't want to wear whatever you had on when you came in.

"We went for sweatpants," he continued, talking casually as he got the shopping bag off the floor. "A button shirt, boxers, sandals."

"I don't understand."

"I know. Let me give you a hand, help you change."

It wasn't so embarrassing because the cop kept talking as he changed the orange pants for sweats, the orange top for a blue shirt, slipped the sandal onto his good foot.

"Pants are a little short, but they work."

"They said I had to—they said I had to—"

"You don't. Come on." He got an arm around Zane, helped him stand, helped him with the crutch. He picked up the bag, walked Zane to the door, banged twice.

The door opened; the guard stepped back.

He smelled piney cleaner, maybe bleach. He knew he was shaking again, but the cop didn't say anything.

"Who are you?"

"Detective Keller. Lee. I'm Lee."

"Graham will stop you. He'll—"

"He won't. I arrested him, and your mother."

Both Zane's knees buckled. Lee just held him up, kept walking. Slow, but kept walking.

"Breathe now. Keep that easy breathing going. He's not going to hurt you or Britt again. You were smart to write it down, Zane. That was smart."

Nobody stopped them. Guards opened doors, let them pass through without a word. Then the sun was in his eyes. He saw the gate. And through the gate he saw Britt, saw Emily. He wanted to run, tried to walk faster.

"Easy. We'll get there."

"He hurt her. He hit her. Her face—"

"She's going to be fine. She's got a good story to tell you. She busted out of the hospital. You got a hell of a baby sister. Just a few more steps."

They called his name. Emily was sobbing and calling. But Britt didn't cry, not yet. She just kept calling his name.

The gates clanged open, and when he walked through, they surrounded him.

"Oh, baby, oh, Zane. I'm sorry. I'm so sorry." Emily lifted his face, stroked her fingers over him. "I'm so sorry." When he only shook his head, she held him again, held him and Britt close and tight.

"Let's go home," she said.

"I can't go back there. Please, please. I can't go back there."

"No, honey, no. To the lake house. Grams and Pop should be there by now. We're going home. Our home now. I'm going to take care of you now. Here, you and Britt sit in the back. I'll ride up front with

Lee. Lee, who I owe a really big home-cooked meal to, a really good bottle of wine, and, hell, sexual favors if he wants them."

He laughed, shook his head. "Just doing my job."

"They're my life now. You saved my life."

They helped Zane into the car, and Britt cuddled up against him. "Does it hurt?"

He gave the hand that held his a squeeze. "Not anymore."

Lee listened to the siblings talk, fill each other in. Resilience, he thought, thy name is youth. Both kids would have some hard bumps yet, need some therapy, he imagined. But they'd be okay.

Zane actually laughed when Britt told him about sneaking out of her hospital room in her bare feet. Lee noted she—for now anyway—edited out the part about her father being there, threatening her, when she woke.

Just as Zane did his own editing.

"Was it awful in there, in that place?"

"No, it wasn't so bad." For a second, Zane's gaze met Lee's in the rearview. "Not much different than being locked in my room back at the house."

"Lee took us to a shelter for the night. Well, it was really morning by then. It was sad, but not. A lot of women and kids in there who get hurt at home. Like us. But it gives them a safe place. They were nice to us. Emily said we're going to make a donation, in all our names. Like a thank-you."

"I guess she can't give them sexual favors."

With a big, rolling laugh, eyes sparkling with tears and that laugh, Emily looked back at him. "Smart-ass."

"Emily? Don't be sorry. Don't ever be sorry."

She reached back for his hand. "You either."

He settled back, his good arm around his sister. He had a bad moment when he saw the lake, but he pushed it away because the car didn't head toward Lakeview Terrace, but the other side.

The safe side.

He saw the water, the woods, the cabins, the flowers, the boats. And then the rental car in Emily's driveway. His grandparents on the front porch, already running toward the car.

They cried. Zane guessed everybody would cry for a while off and on.

"I'm going with Lee for a little while," Emily told him. "I'll be back. With pizza. I think it's pizza night."

"Could I—Detective Keller, could I talk to you for a minute first?" Zane asked.

"Sure."

"Okay, everybody in the house." His grandmother took over. "Let's make a picnic lunch. Come on, sweetie." She drew an obviously reluctant Britt toward the house.

"You didn't say what you arrested them for."

"For what they did to you and your sister."

"Eliza didn't hit us."

First name, Lee noted. Not our mother.

"She put those grooves in your face."

Zane touched the scratches with his fingertips. "I guess so. It's hard to remember."

"She let it happen, that makes her complicit. She abused you, Zane, just like Graham did."

Zane wanted to believe. God, he wanted to believe. "He knows a lot of people. He can get really good lawyers."

"Trust me." Lee gave him a steady look that eased the cramping in Zane's gut. "I'm pretty good at my job. Emily's going with me because I think she can help convince your mother to tell the truth."

"Then she won't go to jail. But—"

"A lighter sentence if she tells the truth, cooperates. But she's not going to be able to take you away from Emily or your grandparents. For one thing, both you and Britt are old enough to choose; for another, we're going to prove she's unfit. You don't need to worry about this."

"Will you come back and tell me what happens?"

"Yes. Are you prepared to go to court, to stand before a judge or jury and tell what happened?"

"Yes. I want to." It rushed through him, that want, like a wave of strength. "I want to look him in the face and say what he did. I want to."

"Good, because you're going to get your chance. I've got to get to it now."

"Sir? Thank you. Thank you for getting me out, for keeping Britt safe. I'm never going to forget it."

"You take care of yourself, Zane. Let's get you inside so your grandparents can fuss over you."

"They're good at it. Sometimes I'd imagine we could live here," he said as Lee helped him up to the porch. "After one of the times, I'd think what it would be like to live here."

"Now you will." He opened the screen door. "Can you make it the rest of the way?"

"Yeah. I can make it."

I bet you can. I bet you will, Lee thought.

"Tell Emily we gotta get moving."

They talked about it from every angle on the drive to the station house in Asheville, and while Lee's impression of Emily as a tough woman who handled herself only strengthened, he still hesitated at the door of the interview room.

"You're sure you want to do this?"

"Lee." Emily laid a hand on his arm. "I am doing it. It may not do any good other than getting it out of my own craw, but I'm doing it."

"When you're finished, or you've just had enough, bang on the door."

"Got it."

He opened the door, signaled the cop in the room to come out. Emily walked in, and the door closed behind her.

Eliza sat at a small table, back straight, cuffed hands folded on the table. Her face carried the night's violence, but her eyes, Emily noted, burned with angry pride.

"It's about damn time."

Her stomach hurt. Emily noted it with a detached interest as she sat across from her sister. "It really is, isn't it?"

"I've been in this hellhole for *hours*. I'm being treated like a criminal, and they won't tell me where Graham is, what's happening. I need you to find out. My lawyer assures me he'll have all these ridiculous charges dismissed, and at the very least we'll be released on bond until we can clear our names. But in the meantime, I need some of my things. I'll give you a list."

Fascinating, Emily thought. She's exactly the same as she's always been.

But I'm not.

"No, you won't. You're under the mistaken impression I'm here to help you. I'm not. And the fact you haven't asked about your children only cements that."

"My children—and they're hardly helpless babies—are conspiring against me, against Graham. Zane's dangerous, Emily. You have no idea what—"

"Shut up." Eliza's head snapped back when Emily lashed out with the two words. "Another word against Zane, one goddamn single word against that boy, and I walk away. You'll have no one. I know what happened last night, what happened over Christmas year before last. I know everything, so don't bother with the show, Eliza."

To help push her temper under control, Emily sat back. "They've allowed me to come in and speak with you. It's just you and me. They can't listen. It's against the law. I need to know why. Why you'd do this to Zane and Emily. Why you'd let Graham do this to them, to you. I need to know why."

"Stop being an idiot and do something useful for once! I need my skin care products. The fact that you'd take the word of a couple of recalcitrant teenagers over your own sister just proves what a fool you are."

"Cut the crap. I'm not getting anything for you, doing anything for you. Worried about your face, Eliza, your skin tone under the black eye and bruises? Just think what it's going to look like after a few years in prison."

"I'm not going to prison." But her lips trembled.

"You are, how long and what kind depends on what you do, what you say when the police come in."

"Our lawyer—"

"Stop right there." To push the point, Emily shot up a finger. "That's your first mistake, and it's a big one. You're not stupid, so think a minute about sharing a lawyer with the man who gave you that eye. You've got a chance—but it won't hold for long. You better get yourself your own lawyer, and the one thing I will do is give you the names of a couple of good criminal lawyers I found when I thought I'd need them to help Zane. He won't need them now."

"Zane needs to be locked up. He—Don't!" As Emily pushed to her feet, panic rang in Eliza's voice for the first time. "Don't leave me here."

"Then stop the bullshit."

"How do I know you're not recording this?"

Rising, Emily took off her shirt, turned a circle. "You and me, Eliza. Graham pays the lawyer, and who do you think he'll represent if it comes down to choices? Make yours, and when I walk out of here, I'll contact one who'll represent you."

She put her shirt on, sat again. "We were raised in the same house by the same people. We were raised to respect ourselves. Why have you let Graham abuse you, your children? Why didn't you come to me, to anyone, for help?"

"You don't understand anything, and it's *our* business. Our marriage. We love each other."

"A man who hits you doesn't love you."

"Oh, for God's sake." Eliza actually cast her eyes toward the ceiling. "Always so *ordinary*. Always." Face alive again, Eliza leaned toward her sister. "I am not ordinary. Graham and I have passion, something else you don't understand. You married a loser, then couldn't even keep him."

"His so-called passion put you in the hospital."

"Things went too far. He isn't allowed to hit me in the face, that's the agreement."

Honestly, Emily thought, she'd honestly believed she couldn't be shocked again. Yet she was.

"You—you have an agreement about where he's allowed to hit you?"

"And when we put this mess behind us, he'll have to make breaking the agreement up to me. But there were circumstances."

She hadn't believed it, not really, hadn't believed Britt, not in her heart, about that single, sick, sorry thing.

"You like it. You get off on it."

"Don't be such a prude. We have passion, even after nearly eighteen years we have real passion for each other. He has a demanding, stressful career, and he needs that passion at home. You think you can judge me? Look at what I have. The biggest, most beautiful house in Lakeview Terrace, vacations wherever I want to go, a husband who buys me gorgeous jewelry, an exciting sex life."

She tossed up her hands, looked at her sister with a kind of cold pity. "What have you got, Emily? An old house, a bunch of bungalows you have to rent out, and no man who wants you."

They sat, Emily thought, debated this with her battered-faced sister in prison garb, with a police guard on the door. And still Eliza saw herself as superior in every way.

And the single thing Eliza had that Emily had envied hadn't made Eliza's list.

"You know, Eliza, there's something else you have you didn't put on that list. Two children."

"I never wanted them." She shrugged them off, as she might an old sweater. "I kept my part of the agreement. Two children. And I did everything perfectly. They had everything—good clothes, a good school. Dance lessons for the girl, sports for the boy, music lessons for both—though Zane's pathetic there. Healthy meals, discipline, education, and the proper amount of recreational time."

Yes, yes, yes, she could still be shocked, Emily realized. "They're part of the agreement."

"How would it look if we had no children? A man in Graham's position needs to present the right image."

"So they're part of the image. It didn't matter to you when he hit Zane?"

"A disrespectful child needs to be punished. Zane's nearly grown in any case."

"So you've, basically, finished with him."

"He would have been sent to the right university, given every opportunity. He'd have studied medicine, become a doctor. Now?" She shrugged again, another old sweater discarded. "I have no idea what Graham will want to do. We'll have to discuss it."

"You and Graham will no longer have anything to say about either of the children. They're with me now."

"Please. As if any court would take them from two parents of our reputation and status."

"Exactly. Your reputation and status are shredded. The cops know everything."

"Teenagers' words against ours."

"There's also the statements from the staff of the resort, where you took Zane after Graham beat him. Didn't think of that, did you?" she added as she saw the flicker in Eliza's eyes. "Didn't consider that lie might come back to bite your sorry ass one day. And there's so much more, but I'll leave that to the police to tell you, and whatever lawyer you go with. You may have a chance to make a deal, to plead down some of the charges against you. Either way, when you go to court on this, I'll be one of the people testifying against you and against Graham."

Eliza's face went hot under the bruising. "You were always a bitch, always jealous of me. That's what this all comes down to. You've always been jealous. Because I'm prettier, popular, I married a doctor."

"No, Eliza, in fact I never was, and now I can't even feel pity for you. I came in here to try to convince you to tell the truth, to make some sort of deal so you only spent a few years rather then a decade or more in prison. But after this? I just don't care. I won't wish you good luck, Eliza," she said as she rose, "because I don't."

She read fear clearly, tilted her head. "I wonder, did you and Graham have an agreement on what you'd do if you ended up like this? Did either of you consider it might fall apart, and what you'd do when it did?"

Now she shrugged. "I bet he's thinking about it now."

Turning, she lifted her hand to bang on the door.

"Contact the lawyer."

Emily glanced back. "Which?"

"The one you have. I want my own lawyer."

"Okay, I'll do that. I'll do that, Eliza. It's the last thing I'll do for you."

She banged on the door, and when it opened, left without looking back.

It took time, but Lee didn't mind keeping Graham waiting. The DA pushed hard for holding him without bail, and used the two minors, seriously injured and in potential jeopardy, to good effect.

It hadn't hurt to have Chief Bost speak out.

So he bought a little time, time enough for Eliza Bigelow's new lawyer to catch up, to push for a deal.

By the time he walked into interview, his gut told him he had it solid. Just like it told him Bigelow probably hadn't been fully, what you'd call, forthcoming with his attorney.

He started the recording, sat.

"You'll address your questions to me," the lawyer told Lee.

"Sure. As you're aware, Mrs. Bigelow has her own attorney. I've just come from speaking to him, and her. She rolled on you, Bigelow. Got herself a deal."

"Spousal privilege—"

"Does not apply," Lee interrupted, "if the communication between spouses pertains to the planning or execution of a crime. Mrs. Bigelow opted for a reduction in charges. Can't blame her."

Graham leaned over to murmur to his lawyer.

"Mr. Bigelow wants to speak with his wife."

"You'll have to take that up with her lawyer, and the warden of the North Carolina Correctional Institution for Women, who'll be hosting her for the next five to ten. You know, she might've slipped by with three to five if it wasn't for her part in lying to have her severely injured minor son locked up. That and holding down her minor daughter while her husband pumped the kid he'd just knocked around with a sedative so she couldn't talk. That upped things.

"Your client on the other hand . . ." Lee opened his file. "He's going for the full ride."

"We will contend that Eliza Bigelow was coerced, and due to her own injuries, inflicted by her son, was emotionally and physically compromised."

"You can try that, but the shrink cleared her. Oh, she's got issues, but once she decided to tell the truth, a whole lot came out. One being striking his minor son in the stomach with the son's baseball bat after a game your client deigned to attend, and wherein the minor son had the nerve to strike out. He was eleven. That's what we like to call assault with a deadly."

"My client denies any and all charges. We've filed for another bail hearing."

"Yeah, I got that notice. Before you do, let's just move ahead a few years. I want to be sure your client's fully informed you about the events taking place from December twenty-third to December thirtieth, 1998."

Lee took papers from the file as he spoke. "How on December twenty-third of that year your client's two minor children came home from school to find their father, once again, hitting their mother. On this occasion, the minor son attempted to stop the assault and was in turn beaten unconscious."

"My client refutes that allegation, and in the strongest terms."

"The minor child, fourteen at this time, was subsequently locked in his room, initially denied medical treatment for his injuries. Which included a broken nose, bruised ribs, black eyes, a concussion. The nose, the good doctor here later set, without any pain medication. The child was also denied food until the following day."

"It's obvious Zane is suffering from some sort of mental breakdown," the lawyer began.

"You got kids, counselor?"

"That's hardly relevant."

"Humor me."

"I have two sons, eighteen and twenty."

"Keep them in mind when you read these. Apparently Dr. Bigelow didn't want to miss his holiday trip that year, despite his son's condition. I have statements from several members of the staff of the High Country Resort and Spa where the family stayed from December twenty-sixth through December thirtieth."

With his eyes on Graham's, Lee pushed them across the table.

"Kid was supposed to have the flu—that's the story they told the family when they kept him locked up over Christmas. What you're reading is the story they told the staff at the resort."

Graham leaned over again, but the lawyer held up a hand to hold him off.

"A boy, recovering from an illness, might easily fall off his bike."

"And here are the statements from neighbors, teachers, the chief of police of Lakeview, the minor's aunt. How does a kid get the flu, fall off his bike, get confined to his room at the resort, and manage to fall off his skis?"

Lee shoved over more papers. "Then there's Mrs. Bigelow's statement confirming the beating, the confinement, the conflicting stories. And this."

He laid a copy of Zane's first notebook entry in front of the lawyer. "Written by a fourteen-year-old boy, in fear and pain. The details all match. That's the night he started writing it out, *Doctor* Bigelow. The night Zane started documenting your systematic abuse."

"I need to consult with my client. This interview is over."

"You can consult with your piece-of-shit client all you want. I'm making it my mission in life to see he's put away for the maximum sentence allowed by law. My goddamn mission."

"I'll bury you. All of you."

"Be quiet, Graham. Don't say anything."

"You took their childhood, their safety."

"I gave them life!"

"You gave them terror and pain."

"They owe me for every breath they take, and it's my decision, *mine*, to decide how to raise them."

"Not anymore."

"That boy thinks he can defy me? He's lucky I didn't put him in the ground."

"Graham, enough! This interview's over, Detective."

"Your lawyer's going to start thinking deal, pleading all this down. Not going to happen." Lee jabbed a finger on the copy of Zane's notebook page. "My mission in life."

"I'll have your badge! You won't be able to get work as a fucking mall guard when I'm done."

"Yeah, yeah." Lee switched off the record, strolled out.

It took time—justice takes her time—but in just under a year, he lifted a beer and thought: Mission accomplished.

CHAPTER SEVEN

Lee drove the lake road on a spring day with the mountains greening, the wildflowers popping, and his mood high. He had a lot on his mind, decisions to make, moves to take—or not—but with the lake mirroring the happy blue of the sky, white boats, white clouds sailing, optimism was the name of his game.

Good didn't always win, right didn't always triumph—he'd been a cop long enough to know. So when it did, you fricking embraced it.

He rounded the turn for the lake house, pulled into Emily's drive just as she climbed out of her truck.

Even his timing was happy.

She wore jeans with holes worn through both knees, a T-shirt the same cheerful color as the sky. And that orange hoodie she'd put on Britt in the stairwell of the hospital a year before.

He'd heard Emily call it her lucky hoodie.

Her hair streamed, dark as midnight, out of the back opening of a fielder's cap.

He thought, with a quick jump of pleasure, she looked downright amazing.

She pulled off sunglasses, stood watching him get out of the car. Studying his face.

"It's good news. I can see it." Still she lifted a hand, rubbed the heel between her breasts. "But say it fast anyway, like you would bad news."

"Fifteen to twenty. He's being transported to Central Prison in Raleigh."

After bracing a hand on the side of the truck, she let out a long, wavering breath, held up her other hand. "I need a minute."

Taking it, she walked away from the truck, toward the lake. Hugging her arms in, she looked out over the water, that mirror blue. She felt the breeze, the warm balm of it blow light across her face. And breathed out again when she felt him walk up to stand behind her.

"I was going to come in for the sentencing hearing this morning, even though you said not to. I didn't want to see him again, told myself seeing his face when the jury brought back the guilty verdicts was enough. And still, when the kids left for school, I started to get dressed to come in."

"Why didn't you?"

"Lanny—head housekeeper—couldn't make it in. Her kid's sick. My backup couldn't make it in. Emergency root canal. Lois—you know Lois—emergency backup to the backup, had another cleaning job. We had two turnovers, the daily cleaning—and yay, we're full. Marcie couldn't handle it on her own, so . . ."

She let out a steadier breath, reached back until he took her hand, stepped beside her. "I took it as a sign I just wasn't supposed to go in, look at him one last time while the judge gave him his sentence. I even stopped thinking about it once I started scrubbing down bathrooms, changing bed linens."

She nodded, still looking out at the water.

"Twenty years," she murmured. "The kids will be practically as old as I am. Parole?"

"He does a minimum of fifteen. He won't get parole easy, Emily, and not likely on the first couple tries. Put that away," Lee advised. "He's locked up, where he belongs. The kids are safe."

"You're right, and I can tell them that when they get home. Couple hours. A little more," she added with a glance at her watch. "Do you have to go back to Asheville?"

"Not today."

"It's barely one in the afternoon, but . . . screw it. Let's have a beer anyway."

He went in with her. He liked the ramble of the house, and the fact it was never quite all the way tidied up. It held a lot of light and life. Throw pillows jumbled because somebody'd settled on the couch. A stray pair of shoes—Britt's, he identified.

Back in the kitchen, what was left of a bowl of fruit—not much—a vase of daffodils—fading already—a jacket tossed over a chair, the coffeepot holding the dregs from the morning.

"I might still have some chips left. Pretzels or something."

"Don't worry about it."

After pulling off her cap—and her hair, all that midnight, seemed to float up, then spill down—she tossed it and her sunglasses on the counter.

"I need to run to the store again. My God, those kids can eat. I'm still not used to it." She pulled a pair of Heinekens from the refrigerator, popped the tops. "It's been a hell of a year, Detective Lee Keller. One hell of a year."

She angled her head after they tapped bottles. "There's something else." She wagged a finger before he could deny it. "A hell of a year," she repeated. "Too many ups and downs to count, and you've been here for us, Lee, thick, thin, and otherwise. I've gotten to know you—even that cop face. Don't hold it back. I need to know if—"

"It's nothing to do with the Bigelows."

"Okay. Good. Why don't we take these out to the front porch, enjoy the view while you tell me what it is to do with. There's pretty much nothing I haven't dumped on you over this hell of a year. Your turn."

"Actually, yeah. I'd like to run it by you."

They settled on the porch in a couple of chairs she kept meaning to sand and repaint one day. The breeze sent the wind chimes Britt had given her for her birthday singing. The lawn Zane had mowed for her that Saturday smelled green and fresh.

"It's a good place, Emily. It's a good home you've made here."

"I hope so. I—"

"You don't have to hope. I've watched you and the kids over this hell of a year, seen them change, relax little by little. Lose that victim look in the eyes. It's been hard, with the trial, with having to deal with it."

"Counseling helped. It's still helping."

"You've done everything right, given them a safe place, and one that shows them what a home's supposed to be."

"I didn't do it alone, that's for sure. My parents, God, they're like oaks. To say this hasn't been easy for them is the understatement of all understatements. She's their daughter, too, Lee. Eliza's their child. But they stood up. My mama . . ."

Emily closed her eyes, shook her head. "She only once broke down, and that was when it was just the two of us."

"You come by your spine and your heart naturally. 'Oaks,' that's a good term for it. Walkers are oaks with good, strong roots."

"Well, I believe it. Zane and Britt are going through with having their name legally changed. They want Walker, so that's what they'll have."

"I think that's the right thing, all around."

"So do I. You know, Lee, friends, neighbors, they stood up, too, stood up, stood by us. We couldn't have stayed in Lakeview otherwise."

"It's a good place, Emily."

"It is."

And she knew she'd be forever grateful to look out at the lake, look out to the hills, and know that.

"The Carter family—the kids especially needed them. I needed them. They're always there. And you, Lee."

She laid her hand over his. "Especially you. I swear, I don't know what we'd've done without you. I'm glad we don't have to know. Now." Putting on a smile, she shifted to face him. "You tell me what's on your mind, so I can do a little payback."

"Okay. I had a meeting with Chief Bost. I've had a few actually, but we met again today after the sentencing. Bost, me, and a few others."

That smile began to fade. "You said it wasn't about Graham."

"It's not, or I guess you could call it a by-product. Bost is turning in his papers."

"His papers?"

"He's stepping down," Lee explained. "Resigning. He wanted to see this through, and now it's through. He and his family are moving to Wilmington once the school year's done. It's the right thing for him."

She rocked a bit, as if her whole body nodded. "That's good, from where I sit. I've harbored some hard feelings there. He came out, apologized to Zane, to all of us, face-to-face. But I've had hard feelings I couldn't let go of. I'm not going to be sorry Zane doesn't have to see him around."

"The position's coming open. They offered it to me."

"You?" She scooted around fully, smiling as she stared at him. "Well, that's a big surprise on a spring day. I don't mean to say we wouldn't be lucky to have you, but that's a serious sort of change for you. You're a city detective, major crimes. Would you want to be a High Country police chief?"

"Depends." Clearing his throat, he shifted a little. "I like the town, the people. Like I said, it's a good place. Might be I'm ready for a change. I don't want to put any pressure on you about that, or anything."

"On me?"

"It's just . . ." He needed a good pull on his beer. "I've got a little time to think about it, figure if it's best all around. Or not. If it'd be awkward."

She wondered if she'd ever seen him look nervous, and couldn't bring one instance to mind. "I'm just not following you."

"Because I'm not doing this right. Let's back up. Do you want to have dinner?"

"Sure. I just have to make that run to the store. . . ." She trailed off when she saw the slightest wince. "You mean like a date? You and me? I have to put down my beer."

She set the bottle down, pushed up, walked to the edge of the porch.

"I didn't mean . . . we can all go."

She turned back. Not only nervous, she realized, but at the moment he looked downright embarrassed.

Wasn't that the sweetest thing?

"You did mean, and I'm what Britt calls processing that. A year, Lee, just a few weeks shy of a year since Britt and I walked up to you outside the police station, and you've never made a move. Not even a little sneaky step."

"Of course I didn't. I wasn't going to muck up the case, the trial, you, or the kids with hitting on you, for God's sake."

"But you wanted to."

"I . . ." He drank more beer. "Well, yeah. Am I blind, deaf, stupid? You're beautiful, you've got brains. You're the strongest woman I've ever met, and you come with the biggest heart in the damn world to my mind."

She leaned back against the post as she felt places inside her she'd resigned to staying empty start to fill again.

And all sort of warm and trembly.

"I never got that read off you, Detective Lee Keller, not even once."

"You had enough to think about, to deal with. And the kids. The last thing they needed was somebody moving on their aunt when they needed her to steady their world."

"I owe you so much."

He set down his beer, a little harder than he intended, and pushed to his feet. "That's just what I don't want in this, just where we're not going. I'm not going to have you feel obligated to give me a shot. I'm not settling for that, and neither should you."

"You're absolutely right. Absolutely right about that."

"We got to be friends, and that's fine. If you're not interested in—"

She grabbed him by the tie, yanked him to her, and shut him up.

Just right, she thought. Oh God, just right.

When she moved her hand from his tie to his face, she smiled at him. "You're a detective. What do you deduce about my interest?"

"Seems piqued."

With a laugh, she wrapped around him. "I've thought about you, thought about this. Don't be needy, Emily, don't push in just because he's just right. So I didn't make a move either."

He pressed her back against the post so he could kiss her again, and fall into the kiss, the give of her body.

"So, that's a yes about dinner?"

"I'll cook tonight, you'll stay. The kids will need that when we tell them about Graham. Now, Saturday night, I'd like a genuine date."

"You've got it." He closed his eyes, held her. "I was afraid you'd start seeing someone else before this was done."

"Me, too—about you." Drawing back, she took him by the tie again. "Come on with me."

"I—now? Right now?" he said as she pulled him to the door, and through.

"Kids won't be home for some time. Instead of going to the store, we'll just make do with what we've got in the pantry. It's time, Detective Lee Keller, we both made our moves."

"Better make that Chief Keller," he told her, as they started upstairs. "I'm taking the job."

He not only took the job, but by June he moved into the house on the lake. In a few months, with the mountains flaming with fall, the lake shimmering under in the sunlight, they married.

When Zane entered his senior year in Lakeview High, he went as Zane Walker. It didn't erase all the years of Bigelow, but it made him feel better about himself.

He kept his grades up, his room tidy—both out of habit and a fear that would linger for years. He hung with Micah, worked out with Dave, teased his sister.

He did his chores, helped out with the family business, thought about girls.

He went to counseling.

If he sometimes woke in a cold sweat, he could get up, go to the window. And remind himself what side of the lake he lived on now. He could remember there was no one just down the hall who'd storm in, use fists on him.

All that was over.

So was his most cherished dream.

Zane Walker would never play professional baseball. Scouts would not come calling. He could play pickup games, town leagues if he wanted. But his arm was no longer a rocket, and never would be again.

More than his elbow had shattered the night he'd fallen down the stairs. His dreams, every one that really mattered, shattered with it.

He hadn't given them up, not right away. He'd dealt with the surgery, the recovery time, the physical therapy. When Dr. Marshall gave him the go-ahead, he started lifting again.

He built back the muscles, but he couldn't build back the full range of motion. Not what was needed to wing a ball from the hole to first, not in the majors.

Not even, he had to accept, in college ball.

All he'd ever wanted, for as long as he could remember—the one thing he was really good at and loved right down to his bones—poof. Over.

He'd even broken down in therapy over it—embarrassing. But Dr. Demar had understood, or seemed to. He didn't have to just get over it, like boom, oh well. He was allowed to be sad, to be angry.

Since he was both already, he didn't need permission. But it helped to have it. It helped that Emily didn't nag at him to stop sulking or bitching. And Dave let him sweat it out, or vent. And Lee—who knew Lee and Emily would, you know. Lee dug on baseball almost as much as Zane, could talk statistics, had a pretty good arm himself. He'd played right field with the cops back in Asheville.

He moved through it, though he often stretched out on his bed with a ball in his hand, rubbing the stitching.

He knew he needed a new plan, but it was hard to see past the shards of his dream. Still, he had to consider his options because college loomed.

Where it once represented freedom, college now stood vague and cloudy—a path cloaked in shadows, riddled with pits.

Medicine, never. Even though he admired Dave and his work as an EMT, he'd never go near being a doctor.

His grades would help him get into a good school. Maybe part of pushing himself there came from residual fear, but good, solid grades helped. When he thought about it, he guessed he liked his lit and history classes best. But where did that get him?

He didn't want to teach. Serious gak on that. He could write okay, but didn't want to try to go there either.

Military? No way. He already felt he'd lived his life regimented, under orders, in fricking uniform.

His thumb and fingers stroked the stitching on the ball, slowly caressing the waxed red thread.

He thought being a cop might be cool. Lee was cool, and he'd like, a lot, putting bad guys away. Without Lee, who knew if Graham would be behind bars? He wanted to put people like Graham behind bars.

So . . . maybe.

He started reading books about criminal justice and law and how it all worked. He had a lot of firsthand experience on that, too. The more he read, the more he thought while stretched out on his bed rubbing the stitching on his baseball, the more he began to see a path—not so shadowed and pitted.

Not just a path, he decided. A purpose.

He spent a lot of time working out the best way to hike the path, to reach the goal. He wanted a map of the twists, turns, potential pitfalls before he talked about it.

Talking about it made it real. If he made this his hope—no more dreams, but hope he could maybe handle. But if that cracked, he didn't know what the hell he'd do.

He took a chance, gathered up that hope, and walked downstairs. Britt had some after-school deal, and Lee would pick her up at the end of his shift. So for now, it was just Emily, and that's where he wanted to start.

She had something simmering on the stove that smelled like comfort on a cool rainy night. While its warmth drenched the air and that rain pattered outside, she sat at the counter with her laptop.

She looked so happy. Happy just shined over her like light. That was Lee, he supposed, because they fit together like they'd always been. He didn't know what to make of it, exactly. His parents had fit—rough, jagged, shiny pieces all dark and gritty underneath. But his aunt and Lee? That fit smooth and easy so the whole house worked like the stew on the stove. A comfort.

He'd owe them both for the rest of his life.

She looked up when he came all the way in, that happy all over her. Even as she beamed a smile at him, she flushed a little, closed the laptop in a way he recognized.

Secrets.

"Hey, pal, how's it going?"

"Okay. That smells really good."

"Chicken stew. Gonna make some dumplings to top it off. I had a yen."

"Do you need some help?"

"Not yet, but maybe at dumpling time. Something's on your mind. Sit down, let me have it."

He knew she meant it, knew she really wanted to know, knew she'd listen. And still nerves jittered up his back.

"Well, okay. Here's the thing." He sat, shifted, forgot his pitch altogether. "I've been thinking about college."

Was it relief he saw rush over her face; support he felt when her hand covered his and squeezed?

"That's good, Zane. What are you thinking?"

"My grades are good."

"They're several degrees up from good. They're stellar." When he hesitated, she gave his hand another squeeze. "Let's just put this out there. I know, I really know, how hard it is for you to lose the dream of playing pro ball. The doctor said you could try college ball, so—"

"I'd be second-rate."

"Oh, Zane, you're so hard on yourself."

"I'd never be good enough, that's just how it is. And I couldn't take not being good enough."

It hurt, more than he could tell her, to think of it.

"I have to put it away. I've thought about other things. You know they expected me to be a doctor."

"It's not about what they expected, ever again. It's about what you want. And what you want, Zane, I'm going to want for you."

"I don't want to be a doctor. I wondered about other stuff, but nothing really hit."

"You don't have to decide. College is about exploration, too."

"But I did decide. I . . . I want to go to law school. First you have to get the BA, and that takes like two and a half to four years, then it's law school, and that's another three."

She sat back, studying him—very carefully. "You want to study law, be a lawyer?"

"Yeah." And now that he'd said it, it was real. "I want to try. English and history are my best things, and that's a good foundation for it. I took that political science deal, and I was okay there. UVA—University of Virginia—it's in Charlottesville. That's only about three hundred and fifty miles away, so I could come home for stuff. And it's a good school for the foundation again. If I can get in."

"You've spent some time on this," she acknowledged.

"I needed to find out if I could make it work."

"First thing." She lifted her fingers, tapped them at her eyes. "Look right here. Is it what you want? Nothing else but that. What you want."

Man, he loved her, because he knew, bottom line, she meant just that. What he wanted.

"It really is. I mean, it's what I want to try. I want to be a prosecutor. I thought about cop, but it doesn't feel right. This does."

"Zane, this is great." Because he looked in her eyes, he saw the glimmer of tears. "You'll be great. A lawyer. My granddaddy was a lawyer. Town lawyer right here in Lakeview."

"Yeah, I guess I knew. There are a lot of scholarships I can try for, and I can get a part-time job now to start saving. Then there are student loans and all that. And I can work in college. It could take seven years, then I'd have to pass the bar. Sometimes you can get a clerkship, like with a firm or a judge, and if I can work summer courses or programs, I can maybe cut it down a year. Still—"

"Let's backtrack." Leaning forward, she brushed at the hair he'd let grow out. Dark as her own, it curled a bit around his face, over his collar. "Are you under the impression you have to pay for your education?"

"They're never going to turn over the college fund, and I don't want their money, even if we could make them. I can't take money from you. I just can't."

Now she sat back, crossed her arms. "You think you can stop me from helping you?"

"You help me every day."

She uncrossed her arms, took his face in her hands. "You need to stop worrying about this. Your grandparents already intend to pay for college for you and Britt." She shot up a finger to stop him before he could object. "That's what family does. We didn't tell you because it felt like pressure. What if you decided not to go to college, or take a gap year, or go to trade school? Now you've decided what you want. You'll call them, tell them. And you'll thank them."

She sat back again. "That said, I'm not saying you shouldn't work, pay some of your expenses. That's responsibility. You can work for me like you did over the summer, or do something else. As long as it doesn't interfere with school."

"It could take seven years. It could cost—"

She tapped a finger on his lips. "Stop. It's loving and generous of them, and that you'll remember. They not only can afford to do it, but part of them needs to. You'll let them, you'll give this to them."

Then she laughed. "Zane Walker, Es-freaking-squire. I love it!" She grabbed hold of him, hugged. "Let's make dumplings."

She started to jump up, wobbled, had to grip the counter as she went pale, swayed.

So Zane jumped. "Sit down. Are you okay? Jesus. Emily."

"I'm okay, I'm okay. Just got up too fast. Woof." She sat down, put her head between her knees.

"Something's wrong." He patted her back, then rushed to get her a glass of water. "You're sick. I'll call Lee."

"I'm not sick." But her voice was thin and muffled. "Just give me a second."

He set the water down, stroked her back, her hair. "I'm calling Lee."

"Lee already knows."

As the bottom dropped out of his world, he started to crouch down, but she straightened up—slowly. Her color had come back—thank God. She blew out a breath, then another, picked up the water for a few sips. "Better. Okay, well, you told me your thing, so I guess now I'll tell you mine."

He braced himself for the worst, the very worst as she lifted the top of the laptop, woke it up. She turned the screen toward him.

"Nine weeks . . . Pregnant? *Pregnant.*"

She let out a laugh, a whole roll of happy as his gaze automatically went to her belly. "I'm not showing yet. But I'm starting to have trouble buttoning my jeans."

"You're pregnant." He couldn't quite get the concept into his head, his body.

"We were going to wait a couple more weeks to tell you and Britt, but hey, you caught me. I found out about a month before the wedding. Surprise!" That laugh rolled out again. "We were going to try, you know, never expected it would happen so fast."

"You're really happy."

"Are you kidding? We're flying! It's been hard not to tell you—tell everyone. Friends, neighbors, total strangers. But we wanted to give you and Britt more time to settle in, school starting and all that. And to give this one a little more time to settle in, too." She laid a hand on her belly. "I get a little light-headed—that's normal. No morning sickness, which is nice. Are you okay with this?"

He had to sit down himself. "Britt and I can start doing more stuff. Around the house, the bungalows. And you can sit here, okay, and tell me how to make the dumplings. Just sit while I do it. That's my cousin. You're going to have my cousin."

"Another normal," she told him as tears spilled. "I got teary this morning when Lee said he'd pick up Britt after play practice."

"You really love him."

"I really do."

"Lee and Dave? They're the best men I know."

"Oh, there I go again." This time she dug in her pocket for a tissue. "Tell you what, before dumplings, let's call Grams and Pop. We'll give them a double dose of good news—yours and mine. I can have a good cry before I show you how we make dumplings in our house."

"Good deal. Emily?" His grin stretched ear to ear. "This is really cool."

In the spring, Emily gave birth to a healthy boy with a head of dark hair and a set of lungs that would have made Pavarotti proud. They named him Gabriel.

During that busy, blooming spring, Zane took a pretty blonde named Orchid to the prom—his romance with Ashley having faded—and had his first full-out sexual experience.

He decided sex, the real thing, ranked right up there with baseball.

Britt took on the role of Rizzo in the spring musical of *Grease,* fell briefly if madly in love with a gangly sophomore who handed her her first heartbreak.

Zane received his acceptance letter from UVA, breathed out in relief and trepidation.

He graduated, and though the whole ceremony seemed a blur of endings and beginnings, he found all he needed to find.

Micah, waiting for his turn to cross the stage. Dave giving Zane a fist pump. His grandparents looking misty-eyed. His sister, just grinning. Lee holding the baby so Emily could stand and cheer.

His world. His true foundation. He had to build something on it that mattered.

PART TWO

HOMECOMINGS

Home is where one starts from.
—T. S. ELIOT

You don't have to swing hard to hit a home run.
If you got the timing, it'll go.
—YOGI BERRA

CHAPTER EIGHT

February 2019

Darby hadn't stuck a pin in a map to choose Lakeview, North Carolina. She'd had a system.

She wanted South, but not Deep South. She wanted water, but not the ocean. No big cities, but not too rural. And she wanted to look out windows, wherever that might be, and see growing things, trees, gardens.

Eventually, she'd want to make connections, make friends, but no real rush on it.

And she wanted time. Needed time. She gave herself that—wherever she picked, she'd take at least two weeks before deciding to move on if it didn't suit. If it did, she'd move in.

She needed a place, a purpose, something to hold her down. For too long she'd felt as weightless as a balloon, one that once untethered could just float away.

She didn't want to float. She wanted to plant roots.

She'd studied maps, combed the internet.

North Carolina seemed to hit the marks. Good growing season, but resting time as well. And the High Country—something she'd known almost nothing about before those comb throughs—appealed.

She hadn't thought of mountains, and she liked the idea of seeing them rising up.

Lakeview seemed to check more boxes. She'd have the water she craved, those mountains she hadn't known she wanted, a decent-size town, and reasonable distance to good-size cities when she needed or wanted what they offered.

If it didn't work, well, she'd move on.

With that location in mind, she studied climate charts, rainfall, growing season, native plants, spread out to businesses, activities.

Where did people shop, where did they eat, what did they do? She shifted over to hotels, motels, B and Bs, rental homes. Then struck on the web page for Walker Lakeside Bungalows.

She liked the look of Emily Walker Keller, liked reading that the bungalows and business had been in her family for three generations. And she liked the look of them. Separate, private, but not lonely or really alone. Plenty of trees. Woods really, which struck some other previously unexplored interest inside her.

She'd stuck the pin in the map at that point, took the leap of making an online reservation. A month. If the two weeks proved enough, she'd just eat the rest of the cost, move on.

An adventure, she'd told herself as she'd packed everything she had left. She'd sold or donated the rest. Traveling light, she thought, and with nothing to hold her to the house that was no longer hers—in the pretty suburb of Baltimore—she loaded her car.

She turned once to study the lovely old brick house, its gardens sleeping under a layer of fresh February snow. The new owners had given her the afternoon after the morning settlement to, well, move on, and she appreciated it.

They'd appreciate the gardens, the dance of the weeping pear's branches when spring came. They'd mow the lawns, sit in the kitchen, sleep in the bedrooms. The house would live again.

It hadn't in nearly a year. It had just gone to sleep. Like she had.

It deserved to hold a family again, and now that it would, she could leave it without regret.

She got in the car, put on her sunglasses against the glare of sun, turned the radio up—loud.

She moved on.

The direct route clocked in at about eight hours. Darby took a week. The journey, in her mind, was about exploration, adventure, and in no small way freedom. On the road, she could be whoever she wanted to be, go wherever the urge struck.

Time out of time, she figured, so salt and vinegar chips and a cold Coke for breakfast worked fine.

She watched snow fall outside her window in a Motel 6 in the Shenandoah Valley, wound into West Virginia because why not? Took the back roads, climbing the mountains, cruising down them again. And wound back east.

Charlottesville earned an entire day. A tour of Monticello, long browses through art galleries, and an amazing ramp risotto with a crisp pinot grigio to cap off the day.

Out of Charlottesville, the back roads took her through farmland, vineyards, small towns, past old homes and new developments. Into the tentative hints of spring, the haze of green like a promise, the air like a cautious sigh.

Because she wanted to start her day crossing into North Carolina, Darby chose a motel near the border, ate southern fried chicken in a diner served by a cheerful waitress named Mae who called her sweetie-pie.

Or sweetah-pah in her lovely accent.

Mae had a fuzzy cloud of yellow hair, bright and bold against the hint of dark roots, an ample bosom, and a smile as comforting as the mashed potatoes and gravy on Darby's plate.

She spent the last night of her road trip listening to the couple in the next room have a whole lot of enthusiastic, vocal sex. As compared to other overheard motel sex along the route, Darby decided "Oh God, SuSIE!" and "Jack, Jack, *Jack*!" won top prize.

When her internal alarm woke her just before dawn, she rolled out of bed to shower. After studying her face in the mirror, she concluded that, since she'd show that face in Lakeview later in the day, some makeup wouldn't hurt.

She pulled on jeans, a T-shirt, a hoodie, laced on her battered and beloved Wolverines, and blew a kiss to Susie and Jack as she swung her duffle over her shoulder.

She hit the vending machines for a pack of Oreos and a Coke, sat a moment watching the eastern sky wake up, flirting back the night with its pinks and roses.

She headed south, crossed into North Carolina with the sun.

Driving through the morning, she let her mind drift. Not time, not yet, to think of the practical, the what-happens-next. This still spread as the whatever, and she could take any road, still detour, still turn north, or east.

She could opt to miss a day or two of her reservation, or cancel it altogether. Destiny rested in her hands, and no one else's.

But she wound west, saw the mountains. At first like shadows in the sun, then taking form and shape. Going with the pull, she headed toward them. Time to see, she told herself. Time to try.

Her first sight of Lakeview came with the sun, sparkling bright. Streaming down mountains, snugged into valleys, glowing on foot-hills. And casting diamonds on the blue lake.

Spring wasn't ready to dance here in the High Country, but from what she could see, it had begun to tap its foot.

She wanted the town first. Scenic had big points, but for whatever to turn into the what's-next, she needed those practicalities, a client base, a demand for her supply.

She saw quickly the lake itself held the center—and that made sense. Docks, a marina, shops catering to those who wanted the water—to sail, to swim or paddle, to perch on little strips of beach, or to fish.

Outdoorsy shops for the hiker, the sportsman. Arty shops, gift shops, restaurants, a couple of pretty hotels. Businesses, she noted, that looked as if they held their own.

People strolled the sidewalks or walked briskly. More wandered the marina docks. A few boats skimmed that blue lake.

And homes, for those who lived right in the center. More homes for those who wanted a little distance from the businesses.

Homes with yards, homes on sloping hills with shade trees and ornamental shrubs budded up and waiting, just waiting to dance into spring.

A quiet place, certainly compared to where she'd lived her life, but not sleepy. The lake, the hills, those mountains, the woods would draw tourists, and that was fine. But tourists weren't her target.

She weaved through a development—Lakeview Terrace. Big houses, fancy houses, the biggest and fanciest of them with a clear view of the lake from generous backyards.

It held its own little park, a small playground.

She drove out, began to round the water on the lake road.

Houses—some from what she'd read would have started their life as summer homes. She supposed a few still lived for summer or holiday goers. And some seemed built right into the rise of hill—lots of glass to bring in the view, jagging decks for sitting out on pretty days and nights.

What she could do if let loose on those fascinating, rocky, rising grounds!

Some traffic on the road, but not thick or impatient, and that was good, too. She saw a man in a red cap fishing off the end of a dock. A pier? Was there a difference?

A woman with a baby in one of those front packs—chubby little legs dangling out. She walked a big black dog on a leash. Darby glanced back at them through her rearview mirror as the woman unclipped the leash.

The big dog streaked to the lake, leaped into the air, landed with a splash. Charmed, slowing so she could watch the dog swim like an otter, she nearly missed the sign for Walker Lakeside Bungalows reception.

The road narrowed at the turnoff, went to gravel, and the woods snuck in closer. She had a moment to think it was its own private magic land—or the classic set for slasher murders—when she came to a neat bungalow, with the Lakeside reception sign.

It had a porch with a couple of rocking chairs, a table between, a walkway through a patch of front yard that looked more like weeds than grass, but neatly mowed.

She saw lights behind the windows and a curl of smoke from the chimney.

"Here we go," she murmured, grabbed her shoulder bag, and climbed out of the car.

She walked up the gravel path—slate, she thought, it should be slate with Irish moss growing in the joints—up to the porch, where she imagined azaleas in pink—very traditional—softening the foundation, and mixed pots flanking the doorway, with plantings to reflect the season.

She started to knock, saw the sign that read, COME RIGHT ON IN, so she did.

A woman sat at a long, glossy table working at a computer while a fire simmered in a stone hearth. She had dark hair layered nearly to her shoulders. Emily Walker Keller looked very much like the picture on the website.

Attractive, Darby thought, maybe late forties, dressed in jeans, a navy sweater, good boots.

She looked up as Darby closed the door. The big brown dog sleeping under the table opened amber eyes, thumped its tail.

"Hi. Darby McCray?"

"Yes."

"Emily Keller. Welcome to Lakeside."

She rose, walked over with a hand extended. Her eyes, sharp and green as a cat's, added welcome, and a quick appraisal. "How was your trip?"

"Oh. Illuminating."

Since the dog wandered over to sniff at her boots, tail still swinging, Darby reached down to pet its head.

"Rufus is part of the welcoming committee."

"He's beautiful."

"He's a good boy. How about some coffee or tea, or a soft drink, before we tackle the paperwork?"

"A soft drink would be great. Coke or Pepsi if you have it."

"I can handle that. Why don't you have a seat? I'll be right back."

"Actually, I've been sitting awhile. Is it okay if I look around, walk around?"

"Sure. You can come back with me if you want."

A hall led back from the front office to a storage room where sheets, towels, blankets lined shelves. Salt and pepper mills, coffeepots, teakettles, toasters, blenders, glassware, plates, flatware.

Another room held cleaning supplies—buckets, mops, brooms, vacuum cleaners, big jugs of cleaners, a neat stack of rags.

"You're very organized," Darby observed.

"Otherwise, chaos. We don't want that for our guests."

She led the way into a kitchen. On the small side, but fully equipped with another long table.

"This is our break room–slash–meeting room." As she spoke, Emily got glasses from a cupboard, filled them with ice from an under-the-counter machine. "Your housekeeper will service your bungalow between nine and eleven every morning. If you prefer earlier or later, just let us know."

"No, that's fine."

"We stocked your cabin with the supplies you checked off the list. We can take care of resupplying if you put in an order, give us three hours' notice. You'll also get information in your welcome packet on groceries, restaurants, activities, hiking trails."

Darby walked to the window overlooking a concrete patio as Emily poured Coke over ice. Slate, she thought again. It should be slate, mortared joints. Pots of flowers, maybe a trellis for a climber.

"Since you're here for a month, I imagine you'll do some exploring."

Darby turned back, took the offered drink. "Thanks. Yes, I'm going to explore. I saw a woman with a baby in one of those . . ." She juggled a hand in front of her. "And a big black dog. He jumped right in the water to swim. It was so happy."

"Well, how 'bout that? You saw my niece, Britt, and our baby girl, Audra, and their fish disguised as a dog, Molly."

"So you have family, right here."

"I do. Britt and her husband, Silas, the baby. And my nephew's coming home. Zane's lived and worked in Raleigh since college. It'll be good to have him home. And I have two boys—teenagers." She gave an eye roll.

"It's nice." The little twist in Darby's heart didn't hurt quite as much as it had. "It's nice to have family."

"It is, even though sometimes my husband and I end our day shell-shocked from teenage angst. And you're from the Baltimore area. Your family's there?"

"No. It was me and my mother. She died last year."

"Oh, I'm so sorry."

"So am I. It's beautiful here. I pored over your brochure, and soaked up all I could on the internet, but you still don't know exactly what to expect. It's beautiful."

"I couldn't agree more. You're going to enjoy your stay, I guarantee."

Pretty thing, Emily thought as she led the way back to reception. A little on the thin side but without any delicate air. Long-lidded eyes, blue and deep, and hair the color of the chestnut mare Emily had pined for at ten cut very short with a side sweep of bangs. Angular, both face and body, and the hands of someone who used them to work.

Other than that moment of sadness when she'd mentioned her mother, the girl seemed alive with energy.

They chatted easily enough while they finished the paperwork. Emily didn't ask the questions in her mind. Why Darby traveled alone, what she did for a living, what she would do for a month on her own in a strange place. If a guest wanted you to know the personal, the guest told you.

"You're set. You can follow me to your bungalow, and I'll walk you through."

She took the dog, who rode with his head out the passenger side window, ears flapping, tongue lolling as if tasting the wind. A short drive, no more than a quarter mile, behind Emily's truck. They passed a wonderful old house with a wraparound porch, lots of windows, a rambling roofline that—to Darby's eyes—desperately needed creative landscaping.

When she pulled up at the cabin, her heart skipped. After she got out of the car, she turned a circle, turned it again.

"Oh God, it's perfect! Perfect, just perfect."

"Music to my ears."

"I mean it. Oh, the views. I wanted water. Not the ocean, just something. And this lake is beyond what I imagined, even after seeing it on the website. And the mountains, the trees, this house just growing up right here. It's just exactly exact."

"Do you sail?"

"No."

"Fish?"

With a laugh, Darby shook her head.

"Well, you may before the month's up. You can rent a boat, a canoe, a kayak—no motors on the lake—in town. Or we can facilitate that for you. Same with fishing gear, the license. There's good hiking, and maps for that in your pack."

"I'm going to sit on that porch later with a big glass of wine and watch the sunset, watch the colors spread over the lake."

"Now, that sounds perfect. Do you paint?"

"Not at all. You must love living here."

"All my life." She led the way—gravel path again—to the porch, unlocked the front door. "Welcome to your home away from home."

It smelled of orange zest and polished wood. A fire lay, ready for the match in the stone hearth, with a big sofa covered in quiet blues and greens facing it. A deep chair for a guest and conversation, another tucked in a corner for reading.

A long table—it seemed the only kind here—provided eating space and the demarcation between living room and kitchen, a kitchen obviously updated in the last few years.

It gleamed with stainless steel, pearly white counters, deep, dark wood cabinets. On the counter sat a coffeemaker, toaster, a bright red kettle on the stove top, a blue bowl generous with fruit on the long table.

"I love it."

"More music. You have two bedrooms, and I expect you'll take the master. Second bath here."

She waited for Darby to poke in.

Smallish, but adequate with its corner shower, pretty vanity, the bud vase of Asian lilies, fluffy towels.

"Second bedroom."

That, too, would be adequate, with its white duvet–covered bed, the colorful throw artistically placed at the foot, the dresser, the closet space, the lamps with pretty white shades.

"It's adorable."

"It is sweet, isn't it? Now the master."

Her heart skipped again. The four-poster—thick posts—faced a wide window. The lake, and the mountains filled it.

"To wake up to that, every morning?" Darby let out a breath. "Amazing. Mrs. Keller—"

"Emily. We're neighbors."

"Emily, it's just wonderful. I may not make it to the porch. I might just lie here and gawk all day."

She wandered, skimming fingers over the duvet, the windowsill. And all but danced when she saw the bathroom.

"Pretty great?"

"Extremely great."

It held a big oval freestanding tub, a deep shower with jets, a long counter with double vessel sinks that gleamed copper. The stone tiles held tones of earth and sun.

A pretty basket of amenities stood on the counter along with more Asian lilies. Another long, wide window opened to the view.

"We updated a few years ago," Emily told her. "I decided to go for it."

"You got there. You definitely got there."

"You might want the fire in the evenings or the mornings. There's wood on the back porch."

She listed off other practicalities, operating systems. Darby tried to take it in, but she walked through a dream.

"If you need anything, or have questions, call the number in your packet. Why don't I help you bring your things inside?"

"Oh, no, that's all right. I don't need anything but my duffle for now."

"Then I'll leave you to settle in. But you call if you need anything."

"Thank you. So much."

Alone, Darby wandered, room to room, back again, walked out on the back patio (such as it was), did a little dance, walked out to the front, did another.

The hell with waiting till sunset, she thought. She got the wine they'd stocked for her, used the provided corkscrew, poured herself that big glass.

She carried it out, sat in one of the big porch chairs. She toasted the lake, toasted herself. And toasted what might just be her future.

It seemed reasonable to take a day or two to bask and absorb. Especially when the basking and absorbing included long walks, taking note—mentally and literally—of local flora and fauna, studying the topography, analyzing the soil, getting a sense of what both homeowners and landlords chose for landscaping, gardens.

It included walking tours of the town proper, chatty conversations with shopkeepers and their customers.

People tended to chat with her, often telling her details of their lives as if she already knew them. Her mother had called her an emotional magnet. Mostly Darby just thought she was a good listener.

But she learned, in that day or two, the area held lake people and hill people. Natives and transplants, summer people and year-rounders. And, to her mind, Lakeview and its environs had plenty of room for a new business.

She spent another day or two visiting nurseries and garden centers, starting with Best Blooms on the edge of town, owned and run by a delightful couple with three grown kids, five grandkids, and a pair of twins on the way.

They'd been married for forty-three years, had been high school sweethearts. He'd proposed after the romantic picnic he'd so carefully planned had been invaded by fire ants.

People did tell her things.

She hit every garden center within fifty miles, made more notes, ran more figures, drank more wine on the porch while she worked out details in her head.

Dreams were essential, creativity a must, but details, sweat, and a business plan made dreams a reality.

By the end of the first week, she had her plan nailed down, her details lined up. She wanted to sweat, and knew just where she hoped to start.

She walked up to reception—more time to work out her approach in her head. A lot of the working out came in mumbles of dialogue, which she managed to shut down as she spotted Emily standing outside with the woman who had the baby and the swimming dog.

No dog this time, and Emily bounced the dark-haired baby on her hip.

"Hey, Darby, come meet the prettiest baby in the history of babies—and her mom."

The mom had dark hair, too, worn in a sleek tail, and green eyes that blurred in just the faintest hint of blue. She wore a navy suit as sleek as the ponytail, low heels, and came off just a little frantic.

Darby crunched up the gravel path. "Hi. Darby McCray. I saw you and Audra and Molly taking a walk on my way in on Saturday. I gave Molly straight tens on the Olympic scale."

The baby, as babies often did with Darby, threw her arms out, gurgling, legs kicking.

With a laugh, Darby held hers back. "Is it okay?"

"Wow." Britt shifted the diaper bag on her shoulder. "She's friendly, but that's still a first. If you don't mind—"

"Are you kidding?" Darby took the baby from Emily, nuzzled her. "She already knows I'll sneak her a cookie whenever possible." As the baby tugged cheerfully at Darby's hair—what she could grab—Darby smiled. "I'm interrupting."

"No. Sorry. Nice to meet you. Sorry," Britt said again. "Our regular sitter's in urgent care."

"Oh no."

"Possible broken toe. Not serious, but not easy when she has a toddler. Emily—"

"We'll be fine. I'm emergency backup. You go, don't worry about us."

"I'm not worried, it's just—thanks." She passed over the bag, added a strong hug.

"You let me know when you find out how Cecile's doing."

"I will. You're a lifesaver. I have to run," she told Darby. "I have an appointment in . . . fifteen minutes," she added with a glance at her watch. "She may spit up on your shirt."

"I do that myself."

With a half laugh, Britt leaned in to kiss Audra's cheek, then jumped in her car. "If anything—"

"Go!" Emily ordered. She watched Britt pull out, waved her off. "She'll check on Cecile if she has time before the session. They've been friends since middle school."

"Oh, does Britt work at the medical center?"

"Yes. She's a therapist. Child and family therapy. You were coming to see me?"

"I was, but you're busy."

"Not that busy, and this one's an angel. I don't care how many grandmothers say the same, for my Audra it's pure truth. Come on in."

Grandmother, Darby noted, not aunt or auntie. Interesting.

She followed Emily in, where reception now held a baby pack and play area and a baby swing.

"You're prepared."

"When Britt called, I ran to the house for a few essentials, including several stuffed animals, stacking toys, banging toys."

"Softie."

"Oh, you bet."

She settled the baby in the swing, gave her a little stuffed lamb, set the swing to a gentle rock.

"I can't believe my baby's ten months old and starting to toddle. Now, what can I do for you?"

"It's actually what I hope you'll let me do for you."

Emily's eyebrows lifted. "Then why don't we sit down?"

"I should give you the quick background first. My mother and I ran a landscaping business in Maryland. After she died, I realized I just couldn't do it without her. It wasn't the work. It was the heart. I didn't have the heart to keep the business there, or the house, or anything really."

"What you did there, you did together."

"Yes, and without her I just couldn't find my balance, just couldn't see staying. I decided to sell the business, relocate, and come here."

"I didn't realize you'd planned to stay in the area."

"Well, I couldn't be sure until I got here. I did my research on the area, on the growing season, the native plants, the businesses—well,

I did my research, but I needed to be here, to see, to, you know, feel it. I intended to take two weeks to be sure, but, well, when you know, you know."

"You're hoping to start a business here?"

"I've already applied for the license, got the process started."

"My goodness." Emily let out a rolling laugh. "Girl, you're greased lightning."

"When you know, you know," Darby repeated. "I still need to look for the right location where I would set up, but in the meantime, I've talked to local suppliers. Joy and Frank Bestor at Best Blooms are just great, aren't they?"

"They are."

"I've talked to lumber suppliers, stone suppliers, and so on."

"Lumber and stone?"

"Fences, walls, patios, pavers—it's all part of landscaping. It's not just plants, though they're the heart."

"All right." While Emily didn't know much about it, she knew a lot about people. As she'd thought the first time, the girl was alive with energy.

"If you want me to spread the word—"

"Oh, not yet. I mean, I can give you a client list from Maryland, lists of references and all that, but it's not the same as seeing. So I'd like to offer you a proposal."

"Okay."

"I've got the bungalow here for another three weeks. I'd like to, at my expense, landscape its grounds. Time, material, labor—at my expense."

Caution flickered over polite interest. "What sort of landscaping?"

"I've got a drawing." Darby opened her pack, handed a computer-generated drawing to Emily, then got up to crouch beside Emily's chair to explain it.

As Darby bent her head, Emily saw the tattoo in deep, dark green on the back of her neck. An infinity symbol.

"You see the hardscape, the walkway, the back patio in slate," Darby began. "Rustic, but finished—and you won't have the expense of replacing the gravel every few years. A good, attractive, still rustic pole light—that adds welcome and security. For the plantings you want low-maintenance."

"The lowest. I have two black thumbs."

"Bet you don't. People just think they do. But we stick with native plants, and accents that are proven in this climate and zone. Mountain laurel, azaleas, soften the foundation."

Greased lightning, Emily thought again as she studied the drawing.

"You've got shady areas where I'd do some elderberry, some high bush blueberry—you get the flowers, then the birds get the fruit. And you could have some rosebay rhodos—they'll grow on the edge of the woods here, and so will some more wildflowers I'd coax in, some bulbs like daffs and lilies for naturalization. Your guest would have all that bloom and color in different seasons. And I'd do—again easy to maintain—pots of mixed annuals for the porch, the patio."

"But what about watering all this?"

"Drip hoses, self-watering pots. Low-maintenance."

"Honey, this is . . . ambitious to say the least. And even if I said yes, you can't take on all this expense."

Darby tracked her gaze up to Emily's. "We had a house. I sold it. And sold the business. Then there was my mom's life insurance. I've run a business already, and I have a business plan now. This is an investment in that. If you like it, you might hire me to do another bungalow. You'll tell your neighbors I do good work. They'll see it for themselves."

She sat back on her heels. "You run a business, so you know what goes into it. Yours came through your family, too, so you know the pride and responsibility of that. Worst case, you don't like my vision once it's realized. Best, you do. And there's a lot between worst and best."

So young, Emily thought, but good God, confident.

"You're taking all the risk."

"I'll be doing what I love, and what I'm good at. I have a degree in landscaping, and one in business management, and I've worked in the field for fourteen years. I'm confident in my skill, enough to offer this knowing you're going to be happy with the result. If you let me try."

"God, girl, you really know how to make a pitch."

Now Darby flashed a smile that danced into those deep blue eyes. "It's part of my charm."

"If I agreed, when would you start?"

Inside her head, Darby pumped fists in the air. "If you say go, I can have the slate and builder's sand I have on hold here this afternoon."

"On hold?"

Darby's smile only pumped up brighter. "Optimism's also part of my charm."

"I don't know why I'm more nervous about this than you are, but I am." There was something, Emily thought, something about the girl. "Okay, Darby, we'll try it out."

"I want to yell yay, but the baby fell asleep. I'll wait until I'm outside." But she gripped Emily's hand. "You won't regret it."

"Lord, honey, I hope you don't."

"Not a chance. I am really damn good at this."

"Aren't you going to need help? Stone has to be heavy."

"Stronger than I look, but I've got a helper in mind. Joy and Frank said Roy Dawson's a good worker."

"He is," Emily agreed. "Affable, too. He mostly does odd jobs. He's prone to wander from one to the next, when the whim strikes him."

"So they said. Anyway, I talked to him yesterday. He said he'd give me a hand, so I'll give him a call." Darby pushed to her feet. "Thank you, Emily. I'm going to send you my client list—you can contact anyone on it. I shut down our web page when I sold, but you can still get to some of it. I'll send you the URL."

She blew out a breath. "Now I'm going to go get started." She bolted for the door, stopped. "I'm going to make you a low-maintenance showpiece."

Emily sat, a little shell-shocked, and heard the echoing "YAY!" as Darby raced back to the cabin.

CHAPTER NINE

Roy Dawson proved a good and affable worker. He sang or whistled as he worked, didn't haggle about salary, and had no problem taking cash as payment as casual labor until Darby's business license came through.

A beefy guy with a scraggly beard, he wore more scraggly hair under a faded New Orleans Saints gimme cap. With his help, Darby removed the old gravel, widened the existing path, leveled it, poured the builder's sand.

Though she wanted the path to look organic, she rented a wet saw to trim some of the slate to suit her. The first time she used it, Roy had shaken his head.

"I've seen girls use saws before, but never seen one use one of those. You're a caution, Miss Darby."

He wouldn't drop the Miss, so Darby ran with it.

And since the man was as strong as a pair of oxen and didn't quibble about sweaty work, they had the path nearly done in two days.

"Here come the po-lice," Roy said as she laid the level on the next piece of stone.

Darby looked around when the cruiser pulled into the driveway.

The man who got out had a strong build, a lot of gray shot through his hair. He didn't wear a uniform, but jeans and a T-shirt.

Rising, Darby brushed off the knees of her own jeans, hoped she didn't smell too bad after a day of hauling and placing stone.

"Hey there, Roy. Ms. McCray. I'm Chief Keller, Emily's husband."

"Nice to meet you." She pulled off a work glove to shake. "I'm grateful for the opportunity here."

"I haven't had a chance to get down, take a look before this. You're damn near done with the walk. Looks—it looks good."

"Miss Darby says it won't have grass growing up in the cracks. She's gonna plant stuff there instead."

"Irish moss. You'll have Irish moss planted by somebody named Darby McCray—it's lucky. We'll finish the stone today."

"I have to say, it makes a difference."

"Oh, you ain't seen nothin' yet." She grinned at him.

"Well, what I see looks pretty good. I came down to take a look, and to let you know the town planner said your business license came in."

"It did? Oh my God. Oh my God, Roy, we're in business!" She threw her arms around him, made him blush bright red, then swung away to dance.

"She's a caution," Roy told Lee.

"I can see that."

It took most of a week to lay the patio, mortar the joints. Then she dug in, literally.

In Roy's truck—she'd trade her car in for one of her own when her first job was finished—they loaded her selected plants in the bed. For this job, she dealt exclusively with Joy and Frank. Nothing too fancy. She selected the pots, the annuals, and because it struck her as just right, a good-size wind chime she'd hang on a branch at the edge of the woods.

She ended each day filthy, sweaty, and blissfully happy.

After each completed project, she took pictures. She needed to build her website again.

She dug, planted, placed, pruned, edged, spread the yards of mulch Roy hauled in his truck.

He stood back as she placed a pot on the front porch.

"It looks a picture, Miss Darby. I swear I can't hardly believe I had a part in it."

"You sweat—and you bled a few times. You had as much a part as I did. That's why you're going to be my first official employee."

"Oh, now, Miss Darby—"

"I'm not going to take no." She knelt to fill another pot with the flowers she'd picked. "You already know I'm a good boss, I know you're a good worker. You've got a good eye for this work, too, which is why I'm giving you a dollar raise over what I've been paying you. Starting tomorrow."

"You said we're done here today. We got no work tomorrow."

"We will have." Please, God. "If we don't, you're going to go with me to look at that house I'm thinking about. If I buy it for the business, I'm going to need to build a greenhouse. And an equipment shed."

"You move so damn fast my head's in a spin most of the time."

"You can fill out the paperwork tomorrow." She looked up at him.

She knew he more or less worked when he pleased as a man-of-all-work, had a girlfriend of four years, a mother he visited nearly daily.

"I couldn't have done this without you. Not just the muscle, Roy. I needed the company, your eye, and your connections. So you be here at seven sharp, ready to work. You're High Country Landscaping's most valued employee."

"You ain't got but me."

"I will have, but you're the first, and the best. See you tomorrow."

"Don't you work too late, Miss Darby."

"Just going to finish the pots, give them a good drink."

"It sure looks a picture," he repeated, and got into his truck.

She planted in the quiet, just her and the breeze off the lake, the scents of the heliotrope, the dianthus, the sweet alyssum in her pots wafting up.

Once she'd finished, watered, wandered, cleaned up—because dear God she was a mess—maybe she'd call Emily, ask if she would come down and see how it all looked.

When she placed the pot, she sat, rested her chin on her fist, and looked out at the lake. Lots of boats now on this late afternoon as March moved in. So much green in the woods, on the hills, and wildflowers celebrating.

Yeah, she'd water, clean up, call Emily.

Even as she pushed to her feet, she heard the voices. Emily's laugh—pure and happy. A man's with it, warm and easy.

She looked down at herself, thought, Crap, then, Oh well. Then walked down to meet them.

The man—not the chief—had his arm slung around Emily's shoulders. They looked at each other as they walked, and the love, affection, mutual delight just shined.

Taller than Lee—easily six-three—and somewhere in his thirties by her gauge. A lot of dark hair tousled every which way by the breeze. Jeans covered long legs she imagined could eat up the ground, but he paced himself to Emily's stride.

Probably the lawyer nephew come home from Raleigh. No one had mentioned said nephew was gorgeous.

He glanced over then, spotted her, gave Emily a little nudge.

"Darby! Zane, this is Darby McCray. My nephew, Zane. He's barely gotten home, and I'm dragging him out. We were outside when Roy drove by. He called out you were done."

"Nice to meet you." She looked down at her hand, decided it was clean enough, and offered it to shake.

"You, too. She didn't drag me, but apparently Emily's been waiting until you finished to take a look."

"I know. First client I've ever had who never looked, peeked, changed the plan, or wondered when I'd finish. And now you're ten minutes early."

"Early?" Emily repeated.

"I still have some tools out, and I haven't swept up. But since you're here . . . Just—remember, if there's anything you don't like, I can change it. If you hate it all, well, I'll rip it all out, then kill myself. But that's on me."

"Pills, the rope, or the bullet?"

Darby couldn't see Zane's eyes through the dark lenses of his sunglasses, but decided they smiled. "The lake's right there. Might as well drown."

"Let's take a look, Em, see how long Darby here has to live."

"God, you two. Now I'm nervous."

But she rounded the curve in the road.

Darby didn't hold her breath—exactly. She only mentally crossed her fingers for luck as Emily stopped, stared.

"You see the—" And broke off whatever she'd wanted to say when Emily waved a hand at her.

Then Emily pressed both hands to her mouth as tears swam in her eyes.

"Oh God, please be happy tears."

"You did this?" Zane murmured.

"Roy and I did this. Emily—"

This time the words cut off when Emily threw her arms around Darby.

"Oh! I'm filthy, and sweaty, and smelly."

"Shut up." Emily just hugged tighter. "You have no idea. No idea."

So Darby hugged back, looked up at Zane over Emily's shoulder. "No idea's good, right?"

"Definitely."

Zane saw the bungalow, so familiar, transformed. The same structure, sturdy and simple, in a setting that turned the sturdy and simple into the charming, the welcoming.

The stone path meandered—the word that came to mind—as if to say nobody had to rush. Flowering shrubs swept along the porch, others kind of danced in and out of the woods. He spotted a pawpaw, one of the few he could name, and heard music.

He scanned, found the long copper tubes of a wind-chime swaying in the breeze. Flowers spilled out of pots on the porch. They just looked happy.

"You painted the porch chairs."

"It wasn't in the plans, but once things started going in, they looked a little dull. The lake can get that deep blue color, so I thought we'd bring it into the scheme."

Emily drew back, kept her hands on Darby's shoulders. "I got so used to seeing what was, always. We'd update the interior, you have to. But I never thought about this. My boys—you met my boys."

"Yeah, they're great. Gabe helped us out a few times."

"They'd start to tell me what was going on, and I'd shush them because I wanted to come to it finished. I knew it would look better. I never expected it to look amazing."

She turned to Zane. "You've got your phone on you. Can you take some pictures we can send to Grams and Pop? My parents are going to flip, just flip."

"You haven't seen the back patio."

"I forgot about it." Emily let out that rolling laugh, grabbed Darby's hand. "What's growing in the walkway cracks?"

"Irish moss," Darby said as they walked. "It's already taken a good hold. You can walk on it, it's easy to maintain, and it'll fill the cracks, add to the natural look of the walkway."

"Everything smells so good."

"I added some fragrants."

"Oh my God, Zane, look at this!" Emily broke away to step onto the slate patio.

"You laid the stone?"

Darby nodded at Zane. "Roy and I."

"Roy's no stonemason."

"He's a good worker, and a fast learner."

"You built a window box—I love it. For herbs." Still beaming, Emily brushed her fingers through basil, oregano, sage, parsley, thyme. "I know herbs even if I can't grow them."

"You can. I'll teach you. I thought, some of the guests will want to stay in, cook. It's a nice kitchen. So you can tell them to use the herbs if they want. And that rosemary against the corner of the house? It's sheltered there, and will grow to a nice-sized shrub. It'll smell great, and you can use it."

"You painted the chairs here, too," Zane commented.

"So it flows. I used bigger, vertical planters here because it's more open. They're all—like the porch pots, the window box—self-watering. They have a reservoir for water, a wicking basket to prevent root rot. Housekeeping only needs to check them every couple of weeks, fill the reservoir as necessary. And we can switch out the plantings seasonally."

"The little picnic table and benches."

"All Roy." It gave Darby pride to say so. "He sanded, stained, sealed. It doesn't look showroom new—we didn't want that. But it looks fresh."

"Get some pictures, will you, Zane? I'm just going to . . ."

As she wandered off, Darby took a step after her. Zane laid a hand on Darby's arm.

"She needs a little alone."

"Okay."

"She loves this place, all of it. We all do, but for Emily it's always been home, and legacy and pride and responsibility. You added to that. It looks great. More, it looks right, and—this is a compliment—as if it's always looked like this."

Darby felt a little misty herself. "That's a perfect compliment."

He pulled out his phone, then took off his sunglasses to frame in a shot.

Her heart knocked once. Silly, but there it was. "You have her eyes."

"Sorry?"

"Emily. You have Emily's eyes."

"Walker green."

"Brody has his mom's eyes in his dad's face, Gabe his dad's eyes in his mom's face."

Zane took a couple of shots, lowered the phone. "I never thought about it exactly that way, but you're right."

"The whole family's happy you're moving back."

"It seemed like time. And you're moving here. Bigger change for you."

"It seemed like time."

She liked his smile. It started slow, ended a little crooked. Like his nose, she thought. He'd broken it along the way—she knew how that felt.

Emily came back, heaved a big sigh. "Okay. Zane, I have to ask you for a big favor."

"Sure."

"I need you to go back to the house, get a bottle of wine."

"I have wine."

Emily angled her head at Darby. "Enough for the three of us to sit and have a conversation?"

"Conversational wine." Darby nodded. "I can handle that."

"Great. Zane, give her a hand. I'm going to sit here and bask while you do."

"I love that she's basking," Darby said as they went inside. "I like clients to kind of check things as we go, but she just wouldn't."

She got the wine, and didn't have to tell him where to find the glasses, the corkscrew. "You've put in some time in the bungalows."

"You don't live with Emily and not work the bungalows. Family business," he added as he pulled the cork.

Family business she understood. But the "live with Emily" came as new information.

What about his parents? And now that she thought of it, she'd heard not a word about any sibling of Emily's along her chatty journeys.

They took the wine and glasses outside where Emily sat with a dreamy smile at the picnic table.

"I'm coming back tomorrow—unless I'll be in your way—and taking some pictures for the website."

"You won't be in my way." After pouring the wine, Darby sat. "Plus, I'll have the potting soil swept up by then."

Emily took a sip of wine, studied the glass. "I know a little about wine, and this is nice. I know nothing about flowers that don't come in a vase. I know a little about trees and can recognize an azalea."

She took another sip. "I know business, customer service, raising kids. Adding business to what my eyes tell me, I know once I put photos on the website, add them to the brochures, I'm likely, very, to see an increase in interest and rentals for this bungalow. Considering that, and everything else, I'm not going to let you bear the expense for all of this."

Darby's shoulders went from relaxed to stiff. Zane saw the change from across the table.

"We had a deal."

"I'm changing the deal," Emily said easily. "And I have my lawyer right here. If you're as good a businesswoman as you are a landscaper, and I suspect you are, you have all your receipts and a good accounting of the materials, the time and labor that went into this project."

"We had a deal," Darby said again.

"Apparently," Zane tossed back, "we're renegotiating."

"We are. And here are the terms. I'll reimburse you for the materials. I expect you, being a licensed contractor, got them at a discount. I'll take the discount."

Those shoulders relaxed, just a little.

"Now, you'll also have an accounting of the cost of labor."

"No." Darby picked up her wine.

"Yes, you do. I'm willing to negotiate the bottom line on that."

"Roy's the first employee of High Country Landscaping. I pay him."

Zane held up a hand. "You hired Roy? Officially?"

"He's going to fill out the W-4 tomorrow."

"She performs miracles," Zane commented.

"We'll negotiate the cost of labor," Emily continued. "And if we come to terms, I'm going to contract you to do the rest of the bungalows."

Darby's mouth fell open, shut as she pressed her lips together, closed her eyes. "Oh. Oh, that's playing dirty."

"I play to win."

"You won't beat her," Zane commented. "Trust me."

"I want that so much." She pointed at Emily. "You know how much."

"I do. And I've got better, dirtier. I've seen the way you look at my house. You finish the bungalows, it's yours. I want you to do to my house what you've done here."

"Goddamn it!" Shoving up from the table, Darby circled the patio. She dragged off her cap, raked hands through her hair. "It's so beautiful, so perfect. So ridiculously naked. I've got a dozen different designs in my head already. This is so not fair."

She dropped down again, huffed out a breath. "Half. Half the labor. Fifty-fifty."

"I can agree to that."

"And the paint for the chairs—and that labor. The pots, the plants and labor, the window box, the wind chime. Those are gifts. They're gifts, and that's that."

"Done."

Darby stared at the hand Emily held out. "Really?"

"Really."

When they shook, Emily held on another minute. "You get me the accounting tomorrow. How soon can you start on the next bungalow?"

"Tomorrow."

"Tomorrow? Don't you want a day off?"

"No. No, I really don't. I've been working on designs in the evening. Optimism. Tomorrow."

When Darby's eyes filled, Zane sighed, looked skyward. "Not you, too."

"This means everything to me." Now she gripped Emily's hand in both of hers. "I made a difference for you here, and I will with all the others. But this is my life, and you've just made a difference in my life."

"Honey, you're going to need more than Roy once people around here see what you can do."

"Yeah, I know. I'm hoping to steal Gabe from you this summer."

"Gabe?" A smile flickered around Emily's lips even as surprise filled her eyes. "Really?"

"He's got an eye, good hands, an interest—and a work ethic I imagine he got from you. We'll talk about it. Meanwhile, I maybe need a lawyer, too." Darby shifted to Zane. "Do you handle real estate?"

He'd spotted the tattoo, found it nearly as fascinating as her eyes. "Not so far. But things change. Why?"

"I've got my eye on a place up for sale. If it works out, don't I need somebody to handle the property search thing, and the settlement, all that?"

"Wouldn't hurt."

"You're hired. I was going to take one more look, but I'm going to go ahead and make an offer tonight. I feel like all this is a sign."

"The Hubbard place, right? I heard you've been looking at it. You remember that place, Zane? This side of the lake, closer to town, and back down that steep lane."

"Yeah, vaguely."

"The house isn't much, but I don't need much there. What it has is five-point-eight acres, and I need that. Greenhouse, equipment shed, and so on. It'll work. Anyway, the bungalows. They won't look like this."

Emily jerked back. "But I love this. I want this."

"For this one. You don't want your bungalows—those homes away from home—to all look the same, to be uniform, like a development. Each one should be unique to its topography, its view, its setting. You'll have, we'll say, a look, a flow, but not cookie-cutter. I've got some designs worked up on my laptop. Why don't I get it, you can look? You could pick where you want me to start next."

"She always zero to sixty?" Zane wondered.

"In my limited acquaintance, yeah."

"Sorry, if you don't have time now, I can bring them to you tomorrow morning."

"I've got wine, got my boy. I've got time."

"Great. Be right back."

Zane frowned after her. "Does she ever wind down after hitting full speed?"

"Not that I've seen." Emily tipped her head to his shoulder. "I'm so glad you're home, Zane."

He brushed his lips over her hair. "Me, too."

Zane had the guest room in the rambling old house. His usual spot on visits. He knew Emily and Lee would be perfectly content to have him live there, open-ended. But he'd find a place. If he was back, he was back, and needed to reset his roots, so to speak.

Gardening terms, he thought as he tried to settle in for the night. Probably came from the landscaper.

He needed to start looking at houses. No condos like he'd had in Raleigh. Time for an actual house. Hell, he could hire the landscaper to do whatever with a yard if he ended up with one.

A view of the lake—an absolute must. Reasonable proximity to his family, to town, where he'd need to set up an office. It appeared the landscaper—again—would be his first nonfamily client in Lakeview.

She sure as hell made Emily happy, and that earned her major points in his book. Happy enough, after the family celebration meal—man, Emily could cook—that she'd dragged the whole family down to the bungalow.

And there, in the moonlight, they'd been treated to the lighting Darby had added. The quirky lamppost with its copper cap, the walkway lights, little lights under the eaves, front and back, that added charm and practicality.

She'd come out, of course. Cleaned up, and she cleaned up well. Of course, she'd looked just as interesting in a sweaty T-shirt and dirty jeans.

Interesting, he thought as he stared up at the ceiling, rather than a beauty like his sister, his aunt. The short, not quite red, not really brown hair exposed the little tattoo on the back of her neck.

An infinity symbol. Had to be a story there.

She had a wiry kind of build, and he figured it suited her, as she seemed wired altogether to him. Eyes so blue they read kind of purple in a face of sharp angles. And a nose slightly, just slightly, off angle.

Broken at some point, he thought. He knew how that felt.

Lost her mother in the last year, Emily had told him. Had sold off, packed up, and moved. That took either guts or a streak of recklessness.

So did the initial deal she'd made with Emily. Maybe she had both.

He had a feeling Lee knew more, but hadn't asked. He expected Lee would have run her background, just as a precaution—and since he'd watched Lee with her, had to assume Lee hadn't found anything to worry him.

The boys liked her, Britt liked her, Silas, too. The baby and the dogs apparently considered her their new best friend. So Zane decided he wouldn't worry either.

Plus, anyone who could talk Roy Dawson into a structured job had some sort of magic going. So he'd put all that to bed even if he couldn't seem to do the same with his brain.

He rose, went to the window.

He could see the lights across the lake, could pick out the security lights glowing on the house where he'd once lived in fear and misery.

Someone else lived there now. Not the someone else who'd initially bought it once Graham and Eliza had sold it, but another someone else. He hoped any residue from his life had long been banished.

Eliza had, to his knowledge, never come back to Lakeview. He knew where she was. Once she'd served her term, she'd moved to Raleigh, and there visited her husband in prison every week. Clockwork, never missed.

Zane had never run into her, something he was grateful for. Raleigh proved big enough for all of them. Or it had. In the last few months, he felt it closing in on him. Had begun to feel, however good his life, however satisfying his work, he'd never be fully shed of them if he could turn a corner one day and run into Eliza.

And more, Graham would very likely make parole the next time out—and that was coming right up. That had crawled under his skin and stayed there.

For a long time he'd believed he couldn't live in Lakeview again, live with the memories of that fear and misery. Then he'd come to believe he needed Lakeview, and the good memories, the people who made his real family.

He'd missed Audra's birth by an hour because he lived in Raleigh and couldn't get back in time. He'd played basketball with Brody, but had never been to one of his games. Only made it to a couple of Gabe's baseball games due to the luck of timing on visits.

The kid had an arm on him.

Standing, looking at the lights, Zane picked up the baseball he carried—a replacement for the one he'd long ago worn down.

They wouldn't come back here, he thought. There was nothing for them here. There could be everything for him here. All he had to do was take it, and make a life.

He went back to bed, the ball in his hand. Rubbing the stitching, he listened to the sigh of the breeze from the lake, the whisper of it through leaves gone green with spring.

And slept.

CHAPTER TEN

He didn't expect to run into Darby again so quickly. Lakeview wasn't Raleigh, but it held more than five thousand people, not counting visitors.

Still, within a couple of days he spotted her car on the lake road, slowed to give a wave.

She rolled to a stop, gesturing, so he stopped. Since he had the top down, he waited for her to lean out her window.

"Figured you'd be digging or something."

"I have been. I left Roy and Gabe clearing and leveling the walkway. Stone and sand coming this afternoon. I can't get some of what I want from Best Blooms, so I have to head out to one of the bigger garden centers. I want a good-sized weeping dogwood, for one thing."

He tipped down his sunglasses. "You're going to fit a tree in that car?"

"No, I'm buying a truck on the way there."

And just kept studying her over the tops. "You're buying a truck on your way to pick up a tree."

"I ordered it over the phone this morning."

"You ordered—I have to stop repeating what you say just because what you say is weird."

"It's not weird. They had what I want, they're starting the paperwork. I go in, boom, boom, drive off and get the tree, and so on. Anyway, are you still my lawyer?"

"I . . . could be."

"I need a quick minute. Let's pull over."

Since she did, he, baffled, followed suit. Got out as she did.

She wore brown cargo pants, strong boots, an unzipped red hoodie over a pale yellow tee.

"Okay, the Hubbards accepted my offer. I signed the contract this morning."

Zero to sixty, he thought again. "You've had a busy morning."

"Best kind. So, can you contact the Realtor? Lakeview Realty, Charmaine's handling it. And do what lawyers do? That's a really excellent car, by the way. I don't really know cars, but I can see that's a blow-up-your-skirt kind of car."

"Whose skirt?"

"Since I'm not wearing one, whoever."

She shifted to study his sleek, silver Porsche. "Yep. That's an excellent single guy's car."

"I'm a single guy."

"Yeah, I need a truck. But if I could also have an excellent car, that one would be top of the list. Anyway, can you handle this deal?"

"I can, conditionally."

Now she tipped down her sunglasses, peered over them with suspicious eyes. "Do you take after Emily?"

He'd liked her, Zane thought, because she'd made Emily so damn happy. Now, he realized, he just liked her.

"Maybe she takes after me. Here's the deal. I do it pro bono."

"I don't need—"

"I do. I've spent the last eight years as an ADA. I haven't done much general law. You'd be practice, and I need it. A simple settlement's an easy way to slide in. I just finished getting office space in town. Haven't even hung out my shingle, so to speak. I need the practice, kind of like you had to get your foot in the door with Walker Lakeside Bungalows. So it's pro bono."

"Maybe."

"And you can pay me back with a free consult."

Now those suspicious eyes—and they were kind of fabulous—showed some interest. "On what?"

"I'm figuring on buying a house. I'm also having a busy morning,

heading out to look at one. I looked at one already, and that's probably it, but I'm looking at a couple more first."

She held up a finger. "It's going to be the one way up on the ridge
on this side of the lake. The one that's like it's built into the hill. All
the glass, that sloped, uneven ground with the big drop-off in front,
the view people would commit murder for."

Well, he thought, son of a bitch. "Why?"

"Because, not unlike your car, it's amazing. I looked at it myself—
just to look, because it wasn't what the business needs. It may have
pulled at my guts, but I need the spread of land, the location nearer
town. Plus, there's the stickiness of the price. They're only selling
because he accepted a transfer to London, their kids are grown, she's
an artist who can work anywhere, and she has cousins in Brighton."

"How do you know all that?"

"They told me. People do that, tell me. Am I right?"

"Maybe. Probably. I'm thinking about it."

After tapping her sunglasses back up, she beamed at him.
Megawatt-style. "You should buy it so I can landscape the crap out of
it. It's got nice work now, but I could make it as magical as the view.
Anyway, consults are free all the time, for everyone."

"Do you make everyone dizzy?"

"I don't think so. I've got to go. Charmaine, the same one who's
handling the house you should buy. We'll figure out the rest later."

"Darby?"

She paused, one hand on the car door.

"How'd you break your nose?"

"Ex-husband. You?"

He usually lied if someone noticed and asked—a knee-jerk thing.
Said line drive or some other fantasy. But the word came out of his
mouth. "Father."

She let out a sigh of air. "You win that one."

She hopped in, drove off.

Apparently people did tell her, he thought. And more, she was
right. He should buy the house. Screw looking at a couple more when
that one had—right again—pulled at his guts.

It looked like he'd be handling two settlements.

He pulled out his phone, stood right there on the side of the road, and made Charmaine's day.

He went back into town, signed the contract, picked up some pizza, and took Britt to lunch in the empty office space of the building he'd bought right on Main Street.

They sat on the floor, drank Cokes, ate pizza.

"We can do this a lot more, at an actual table, once you're really in here. It's a good spot, Zane. Smack on Main Street, front entrance, the little porch. More than enough room for your office, a receptionist, a law library, and maybe a conference room upstairs. You even have the little kitchen."

"It'll work. We'll see if I will."

"Our great-grandfather was a town lawyer," she reminded him. "Another Walker family tradition."

Sitting in her bare feet, her quietly professional gray dress, she glanced around. "And you bought a building. And a house! That's the one I can't get my head around yet."

"Me either. I don't do that."

"Buy houses?"

"Go on impulse. The building, that's different. But I just bought an entire house, a fricking big-ass house, on impulse."

"It's a great house, or it looks great from down here. I've never been up there."

"It's amazing, but still. It's a lot of house for just me."

"It's not just you." Before she pointed, she licked sauce off her finger. "You come with a big family, and we expect you to entertain us lavishly and often."

"Ha. I don't think I'd have done it if I hadn't run into the landscaper."

"Darby? I like her. She's . . ." Searching, Britt circled her Coke in the air. "Infectiously appealing."

"That's one way to put it. Accurately," he decided.

"But what's she have to do with it?"

"Nothing, really, but she starts talking and you start seeing what she's saying. Or you don't but you're nodding along in your head. She bought the Hubbard place this morning, asked me to handle the deal for her, and before I know it, I'm telling her about this place, and the house, and she's convincing me I should buy the house. She's buying a truck on the way to buy a tree."

"Okay."

He snagged more pizza, wagged it for emphasis. "No, I mean, she ordered the truck over the phone—like I did this pizza—and she's buying it just like that, picking up a tree, and coming back. She's got Roy and Gabe working."

"Oh yeah, no school today. Well, if she convinced you, good for her. Because you're going to live on the tall hill, work in town, be right here. I missed you like crazy."

"I missed you, too, and all of this, more than I let myself admit." Reaching over, he laid a hand on hers. "He'll most likely make parole this time."

"I know. Eighteen years, Zane. It's a long time. Maybe not long enough for you and me, but a long time. She's never come back, not once. Lee would know if she had, and he'd have told us. There's no reason he'd come back."

"She still visits him, every week."

"She loves him." At Zane's instinctive sound of disgust, Britt pushed on. "She does love him. Remember the way—even after she'd rolled over to get a reduced sentence for herself—she testified *for* him at his trial? Swearing under oath what they had between them wasn't violence but passion. It's not healthy, it's not genuine, but it's real to her, maybe to them."

"It's obsession."

"Yes." As she spoke Britt turned her wedding band around her finger with her thumb. A gesture, Zane thought, he'd seen her make before when they spoke of their parents. "Yes, it is, and they have a terrible, destructive dependence on each other. We were just by-products, just status to them."

"It was always about them," Zane added. "About how they looked to outsiders, and their own sick connection."

"Oh yeah. I doubt they give either of us a thought."

"You're probably right."

"Did you come back, now, because you believe he's going to get out?"

"That's part of it."

"Protecting me again?"

"Always will."

"That goes both ways."

When Britt went back to work, Zane wandered around the empty office space. He could probably use some of his condo furniture, currently in storage.

His desk would work in the reception area. Once he hired a receptionist, or paralegal. Once he had actual clients.

Christ, what was he doing?

He'd worked as a prosecutor his entire career. Sure, he'd handled a few outside legal matters for friends, and he'd taken care of whatever Emily or Britt needed, but his focus had been making sure bad guys paid the price for bad acts.

And he'd been good at it.

Now? Wills, divorces, DUIs, civil suits. Well, there was a need. But who knew if he'd be good at it?

He walked to the window, looked out at the shops, the restaurants, the people taking advantage of a pretty spring day. Some he knew; some he didn't. He didn't know the guy on a stepladder over at the Breezy Café hanging baskets of flowers.

Did he need to do that? He had the nice little porch, so maybe he needed, what, a bench, a flowerpot, or something?

A good way for Darby to trade off the settlement work—then he wouldn't have to think about it.

Maybe he'd put his leather sofa in reception—or in what he'd use as the law library or conference room. He supposed most of his condo furnishings hit the same note as his car.

Single guy.

Maybe he'd buy himself a seriously lawyerly desk for his office, get some lawyerly art for the walls—walls he had to have painted something besides investment property off-white.

He'd worked in a tight, overworked space for so long, he wasn't quite sure what he'd do with so much room. Or time.

He'd just have to find the way to fill them both.

He watched a woman—really pregnant—with swingy blond hair push a kid in a stroller down the sidewalk. He started to turn away, get back to the business of figuring things out, when it struck him.

He rushed to the door, stepped out on the porch. And thought: Holy shit!

"Ashley Kinsdale!"

The woman glanced toward him, did a double take. Her version of Holy shit, he supposed. "Zane!"

He strode down to the sidewalk, and into her laughing hug. She smelled like baby powder, he realized, and weirdly, the one inside her gave him a little kick.

"Jeez, Ashley, look at you!"

"Baby boy coming your way this April."

"You look great. Seriously."

"I'm fat, but I feel great. And you, I'll just say mmm-hmm. You grew up just fine. Oh, Zane, it's so good to see you. I heard you were coming home."

"I didn't hear you were. Didn't you move to Charlotte?"

"Yeah, and it's been good. But I really missed home, missed my family, and realized I really, really wanted to raise my kids here. Nathan—that's my husband—got right on board."

Pretty as ever, he thought, her eyes still a laughing blue. "You're happy."

"Stupid happy. We just opened Grandy's Grill. I'm Ashley Grandy now. Nathan's a chef, and when we decided to move back, we decided we'd go for the dream of opening our own place. You have to come have dinner one night. Remember The Pilot?"

"Sure. I took you to dinner there once, before—" He broke off, winced, pressed a fist to his chest.

"Zane! Are you all right?"

"It just comes back on me now and then. My broken heart."

Her face cleared with a laugh, and she added a friendly swat. "Listen to you. Grandy's Grill took over The Pilot. New menu, new look, new, new, new. Got us a hell of a bar, too, good selection of craft beer. You come, Zane."

"I absolutely will. And who's this lovely lady?"

"That's my Fiona. Fi, say hi to Mr. Bigelow."

"It's Walker," Zane corrected as he crouched down.

"Oh, I forgot. I'm sorry, I—"

"No problem. Very pleased to meet you, Miss Fiona."

She smiled at him, a towheaded girl who couldn't have seen her second birthday, then wagged the doll she held in his face. "My baby."

"And almost as pretty as you." Still crouched, he looked up at Ashley, thought of a night, a kiss under a starry sky and swimming moon. "You're a mama."

"I sure am. And you're a lawyer."

"You don't happen to need one, do you?"

"As a matter of fact, we do." Her hand circled over the mound of her belly as he'd seen pregnant women do. "With a second child on the way, Nathan and I want to make a will, and name a guardian. We just don't want to think about it, but it's the right thing. If anything happened to us, we want to know our babies are looked after."

"That's smart and responsible, and simple. We can get it done, then you can forget about it."

"Can I make an appointment?"

He jerked a thumb toward the building. "I just got myself office space this morning. I'm not set up yet."

"How about this? Give me your phone, and I'll put my number in, the restaurant's, too. When you're ready, you can give me a call. That'll give Nathan and me more time to talk it through anyway."

After she added her contacts, she beamed at him again. "Are we your first clients?"

"Actually, after my family, you're number two. I bagged another a couple hours ago."

"No moss on you. Zane, come here." She cupped his face, kissed him softly on the lips. "You were the first boy I loved. I want you to meet Nathan. He's the last man I'll love."

"Seeing you just made my day, Ashley. That's the truth."

"Then you make good use of the rest of it. Now Fiona and I, and

Caleb, or possibly Connor, unless he's Chase," she added giving her belly another rub, "have to go earn our keep. You call me, you hear? And if you don't come into our place for a beer, I'll want to know why."

"Count on it. Bye, pretty Miss Fiona."

He watched her go, hair swinging, looked back at his little porch, his open door.

What the hell, he thought. It was all going to be just fine.

Within a week he'd made real progress. Since both Emily and Britt held very definite opinions about paint colors and decor, he let them pick, choose, debate over shades, form, and function.

Then went with what he wanted anyway.

He hired painters, bought furniture in Asheville and online, debated selections of art in local shops, and asked Darby to take a look at his porch, do something about it.

A few days later, he drove up to meet Micah—his IT guy for the office system—and found his porch decked out with a bench that looked as if it had been hewn from a sturdy oak and polished by elves, and a glossy blue pot full of yellow and blue flowers, trailing greens.

Somebody else didn't grow moss, he thought as he stepped out of the car. And damn if it didn't look just exactly right. He hoped to hell he didn't end up killing the flowers.

He walked up, pulled the folded note she'd taped to the door.

She'd listed the names of the flowers—which he'd never remember—clear instructions for how to handle the self-watering deal, and, as agreed, the cost of the bench.

Thanks for leaving me the key. The porch pot and flowers, the money tree with pot in reception, and the bamboo plant for your client restroom are pro bono. If you don't like the indoor plants I added, you're just wrong. You have that really tiny patio out the back. You should get a small umbrella table, a couple of chairs, add some small planters. Think about it.

Oh, and I like your paint colors. DM

He started to unlock the door, see what the hell she'd gotten him into plant-wise, then turned as someone called his name.

Not Micah, but Micah's mom. He'd had dinner at her house two nights before, really caught up with Micah, Dave, Maureen.

"Hi! Hey, do you want to come in, see what's what? Micah should be here in ten or fifteen."

"I would."

She wore a simple rose-colored dress, good heels. Her hair, shorter than it had been in his youth, waved around her face.

He remembered thinking as a teenager that she was pretty for a mom.

She still was.

"I love that bench. What a nice entrance."

"The landscaper."

"She's a clever girl, isn't she? I've been out to see the bungalow she finished, and the one she nearly has. I might have to have a talk with her myself. Oh, Zane, this is really nice."

She stepped in, scanned.

He'd done the walls in a pale gray. Though he'd yet to hang any art, he'd put his old desk so it angled in a way that whoever sat behind it could face both the door and the big window. Rather than the sofa, which he deemed better used in the law library, he'd used his living room chairs—oversize, dark gray.

The plant—note taped to the pot—grew about four feet tall with a thick, braided trunk. It stood in a corner where the light spread over it.

He pulled the note off. "It's a Mexican fortune tree, or a money tree. It'll like the light, is low-maintenance. Offices with plants are happier, have better air quality. And this one will bring me good luck."

"Darby McCray again?"

"Yeah."

"It's a nice touch. I know you're busy setting up, and when Micah gets here . . . So." She reached in her purse, pulled out a manila envelope.

"What's this?"

"My résumé."

"Your . . . really?"

"You're looking for someone to take that desk who has some office experience, who can handle a computer, and, hopefully, has some experience in a law office. I worked at a law firm in another life a million years ago."

"I didn't know that."

"A million years. In this life, I've helped Micah set up his IT and security business. And . . . it's all in the résumé. I didn't bring this up at dinner the other night because it wouldn't have been fair. Now it's just you and me."

"I didn't know you were looking for a job. How about you're hired."

"No, Zane, you sweet boy. You read my résumé, and you give it the same consideration you do any others you get."

"But I know you. I know you're steady just like I know that sitting at that desk needs steady. People come in or call, and they're trying to end a bad marriage, or sue the neighbor they're pissed at, or they just got really bad news from their doctor and realize they never bothered with a will. I know I can depend on you. I could always depend on you and Dave."

Her face took on a stubborn look he didn't know she had in her repertoire. "I don't want you to give me a job because you feel an obligation."

"Hell, I want someone I know I can depend on. Say yes, and we'll figure out salary and the rest."

"Read the résumé, contact my references. You can depend on me, Zane, so listen when I tell you to do your due diligence."

"Yes, ma'am."

"Good. I'll get out of your way. And that?" She gestured toward the money tree. "It really adds to the space."

He supposed it did, for now.

Alone, he carried the résumé back—glanced in the powder room, saw what he assumed was the bamboo in a little pot. The attached note proved that to be the case, and came with instructions. Low-maintenance.

He walked back to his office, saw yet another note on his new law-yerly desk. This one told him exactly what plant he needed for that space, why, and where.

Curious, wary, he looked in the attached full bath—full, he thought, if a closet could be considered full. But it had a skinny cor-ner shower so the space could be rented as an apartment.

No note.

But he found one in what would be the law library, another in the stingy kitchen. Frowning, he looked out the equally stingy window to what only an optimist would call a patio.

It was, to his eye, a square of concrete.

But yeah, it could hold a small table, a couple of chairs. Might be a nice place to break the day or end it.

Maybe.

But for now, he went back to his office—deeper gray there, digni-fied, because, you know, lawyer.

He sat at his newly purchased desk, back to the less stingy window, and opened his best friend's mom's résumé.

Ten minutes later, Micah wandered in. "Hey, man."

"Hey." Zane glanced up.

Micah wore his hair in a stub of a tail, sported a single tiny hoop in his left ear, and a little goatee that actually worked. He wore car-penter jeans and a faded Avengers tee.

Hippy nerd, and the look suited him.

"You got a tree out there. It's cool."

"Yeah, I guess it is. News? I'm going to hire your mom."

"Hire my mom? For like what?"

"For like my administrative assistant."

"No shit?"

"None. You know she worked in a law firm?"

"Yeah, sort of. Wow." He dropped down in one of the pair of wine-colored leather visitor chairs, shot out his legs, crossed his ankles over his red Nike high-tops. "That's cool. She didn't say anything."

"I just read her résumé."

"My mom has a résumé?"

"A damn good one. You're a reference."

"I am?" Micah's grin spread. "Kick my ass and call me Sally."

"She helped you get your business going, Sally."

"Damn straight. The Computer Guy wouldn't have gotten off the ground without her. Setting up the books and all that, helping me design the website. Does Dad know?" Micah waved the question away as soon as he asked it. "Sure he does. They're like a unit. This is totally cool news, man. I guess, now that I think, she's been rattling around some since Chloe got married last fall. All the wedding planning kept her way busy."

"How's she doing? Chloe, I mean."

"Good. She and Shelly dig the Outer Banks. You know, it's still weird how I dated Shelly a couple times in high school, and my sister ends up marrying her."

"Things change."

Micah put his fingertips together, bowed over them. "Wise words, my brother. I got a gander at the bungalow the new girl and Roy did, and the one they're working on. Man, the new girl is hot."

"Darby?"

"Superhot. Not like your sister hot—and you know I say that thinking about Britt like she's my own sister, only straight and married and a mom."

"Yes. Fortunately for both of us, I do."

"This one's different hot. Britt's like head cheerleader hot. The new girl's like kick-your-ass-if-it-needs-it hot. Like Black Widow, man—her hair's even sort of red. She's 'I can do what needs doing.' That's hot."

"Huh. It is, now that you mention it."

"I'm totally devoted to Cassie, right? My chick's the coolest chick in the universe of chicks. But if I wasn't, I would offer my ass up for kicking with the new girl.

"So, how about I set you up with some data, some communication, and some security?"

"Yeah, let's do that."

He hung with Micah awhile, answered questions about his needs, shot the bull, watched his old friend work his magic. Then he got his laptop and drafted a formal employee contract, with a full job description.

He fiddled with it awhile, let it sit while he took delivery on more furniture, some office supplies.

Went back to it, read it over, then emailed it to his new administrative assistant.

Now, if he could cop himself a summer intern, he'd be in business.

In business herself, Darby stuck her fists on her hips to check the positioning of the chairs—sanded, painted, dry—just placed back on the porch.

She'd sent Roy to the next bungalow on the list to start the grunt work of removing gravel while she finished the final touches here.

The only uniform element with the first was the lamppost. It gave the cabins symmetry, recognizability to her mind. And she hoped when she finished all of them, Emily would consider names instead of numbers, have signs added to the posts.

But the rest? Unique to the space, flowing, but unique.

Now she only had to finish the pots, sweep up, check all the lighting one more time, and voilà.

She turned at the sound of a car, waited when it pulled into the drive. A woman got out. Young, Darby noted, early twenties. A tough build in jeans, a soft cloud of hair around a face the color of good cappuccino.

"Miss McCray?"

"Darby McCray. Can I help you?"

"I'm hoping. I'm Hallie Younger. I heard you might be hiring."

"I might be. You're looking for work?"

"I might be." Hallie offered a smile. "I'm interested in this kind of work. I've got a résumé. There's not much to it that applies, but I added in how I gardened with my grandmother every spring and summer since I could walk, and helped my daddy build some fencing. I can do some stonework, too. I built a walk for my parents a couple summers ago. I'm not afraid of physical work."

"You couldn't be in this line. Are you working now?"

"I'm working at the Lakeview Hotel, in the office. I went to school for business, but, well, I just hate it. Not the people," she added quickly. "It's a good place to work, and a fair place, but I don't like being cooped up inside all day, every day. I gave it a year because I promised my daddy I would."

"So, you keep your word."

Hallie lifted her shoulders. The hair above them flowed in a cloud of curls. "Your word's no good if you don't. I saw what you did at the other bungalow, and now this one. It's what I want to do, too. I think I'd be good at it."

"Why don't you give me your résumé?"

"I appreciate you giving me consideration." She took it out of her bag.

"Before I do, why don't we have a trial. Tell me what you think, and why." Darby gestured to the bungalow.

"I'm going to say it looks beautiful. And I think you chose that turquoise blue for the porch chairs because you wanted them to pop along with that bright pink on the azaleas."

When Darby gestured to keep going, Hallie took a breath, dived in.

"I think you wanted a happy kind of look, and went softer with that weeper, the white dogwood. You're using native plantings, and they won't need a lot of fuss. You wanted them to look like they just grew up here on their own. I sure do like the slate and the moss. I used chamomile at our house."

"That's a good choice, too. Here, take my gloves, I've still got the pots and planters to do. You do the two for the porch."

"I'll be glad to. Which plants do you want me to use?"

"You choose. I'll read over your résumé."

Hallie bit her lip. "I reckon that's a kind of test."

"See what works for you, then we'll see."

While Hallie worked, Darby sat in one of the turquoise chairs, read the résumé. Business courses, solid grades, part-time office work during the school year and summers. She added pictures of the walkway—nice job—the fencing, some gardens.

She walked inside, called a couple of the references.

When Darby came back, Hallie sat back on her heels with a look on her face Darby recognized. The sheer pleasure of planting.

"They look good. A really nice mix of textures, colors, heights. Good thing, too, as the cabin's booked starting tomorrow. Why don't you help me do the patio planters, then we can clean up and be done."

"I'd be glad to."

"Great." Darby held out a hand. "Welcome aboard."

"I—I got the job?"

"You got the job. We can talk the details while we plant."

CHAPTER ELEVEN

Zane managed to push Darby's settlement up a full week, but her time still overlapped. To make room for incoming guests, she moved from her bungalow to another until the deal could be sealed.

With Hallie giving her two days a week until her two-week notice ran its course, and Gabe pitching in on weekends and after school—after baseball games or practice—they finished three more bungalows before she had her house keys in her hand.

With Walker Lakeside Bungalows fully booked, she switched her crew—she had a crew!—to reception, where she wanted to go a little bigger, a little bolder. It required her new Bobcat mini excavator, a lot of heavy lifting, loads of dirt, but she created what she considered an excellent rock garden.

"That looks a picture, boss," Hallie told her.

"And more of one after a few weeks. We should finish this tomorrow. Best plan is to shift to Bungalow Eight—no booking until next weekend. We can get the stonework done, so no stonecutter noise to disturb any guests. We'll wait on the painting, but should be able to get some shrubs in before it's occupied. Then we start on Emily's place, but go back and forth as other bungalows open, even if it's just a couple days."

"The woman works us to death." Roy shoveled dirt around the roots of a redbud. Wish I didn't like her so much."

"Maybe you wish you weren't so good at the work," Darby tossed back.

"I am pretty damn good at it. Always liked flowers and such well enough, but now I dream about 'em. And what happened just last Sunday? My own mama asked why I didn't plant her something pretty. Can't get away from it."

However he complained, Darby saw on his face that pleasure of planting time after time.

Hours later, after shoveling sand, laying stone, digging holes, she drove up her steep lane, parked her truck in front of her little house.

What she saw when she got out, stood, circled was potential. Land to clear, dirt to move, spaces to build, more to plant. A view of mountains going quiet with twilight, a stretch of woods swimming in shadows. And if she walked to where that land dropped off, hints of the lake below.

She imagined it, photographs in her mind, the retaining walls she'd build, the equipment sheds and greenhouse, the paved driveway, the color she'd add with shrubs, a cutting garden, a shade garden.

She had all the time in the world to plan, to make it happen.

Because she stood on her own land in front of her own house.

She danced her way back to the truck for the supplies she'd picked up.

Two trips later, she wandered the main floor. She could make the living room cozy—when she got some actual furniture. And the little powder room under the stairs could, with some work, transform from bare utilitarian to cute.

The kitchen . . . well, she'd never been much of a cook, so the ancient appliances would do. And she could paint the cabinets something cheerful or funky, find herself a fun table—or build one—a couple of chairs.

Stingy counter space, she admitted, and the dull yellow countertops needed serious help. Plus, the wallpaper—an explosion of yellow and orange daisies—had to go first chance.

But the windows throughout the house opened to the light, the views, and with no close-by neighbors, she intended to leave them undressed.

And she loved that the kitchen door led out to a good stretch of flat. She'd lay a pretty patio, plant a little kitchen garden. You didn't have to be a good cook to enjoy a little kitchen garden. Since she got plenty of sun, maybe a cute solar water feature.

Her house, she thought, and gave herself a hug. She could do anything she wanted with it.

She went upstairs. Two small bedrooms, one bath. She'd taken the front-facing bedroom, delegated the second for her office.

The office already held her computer and station, a desk chair, two visitor-hopefully-client chairs, and a money tree in a pot boldly striped in reds and blues.

Happily, very happily, she hadn't had to deal with wallpaper here, and had painted the walls a calm lake blue, and the trim a crisp white.

The bath? Well, wallpaper. This time fish, a whole lot of fish, bug-eyed and circling the walls. The sellers had left the shower curtain on the tub/shower combo. More fish.

It was downright creepy.

She'd take care of it, but for now she just had to live in the aquarium, and with the sad, peeling vanity and bucket-size sink, and the toilet that rocked just a little whenever she sat on it.

Better than camping, she told herself as she walked the few steps to her bedroom.

She had a bed, or at least a new mattress and box spring, and lovely new sheets and pillows. She had the view from the window, which was worth everything.

She just needed time to get to a furniture store and fill out the rest. And a decent chunk of time, more than decent effort, to rid herself of the wallpaper.

In here it ran red and gold, in what she thought they called flocked. She supposed some tastes might have deemed it elegant, but she found it creepier than the fish.

She showered off the day, dressed in the cotton pants and T-shirt she'd sleep in. In the kitchen, she stuck a frozen pizza in the oven.

Darby considered frozen pizza and microwave popcorn staples of life.

She carried her pizza and a glass of wine up to her office, turned music on—loud. And spent a very contented evening working on plans for her house and headquarters.

While Darby ate her pizza, Zane sat at a high-top in the bar section of Grandy's Grill. Ashley spoke truth about the selection of local brews, and plenty of locals, a good smattering of spring tourists kept the waitstaff hopping.

The place had the feel of a good Irish pub, a lot of dark, gleaming wood, quiet lighting, the long bar with an easy dozen or so draft beers on tap backed by a brick wall, shelves lined with bottles.

He hadn't ventured into the dining area as yet, but from what he'd seen through the wide opening between the two sections, business looked brisk.

Since the night's highlighted beer was Hop, Drop 'n Roll, Zane went with it. Dave, who sat with him, drank a Dark Angel.

The man, one Zane firmly believed had helped save his life, looked good. Time had threaded gray through his hair, but it suited him. Always the health and fitness guy, he now wore a tracker watch. The cotton shirt, sleeves rolled to his elbows, fit broad shoulders, strong arms.

Clearly, he still made good use of his weight room.

They talked lifting awhile, home gym setups. Once Zane moved into the new house, he had a whole lower level, and intended to install a home gym.

With the ease of longtime friends, they segued to town talk.

"I guess you know Grandy," Zane began.

"Yeah, sure. Nice guy. He and Ashley put a lot into this place."

"It works."

Dave cocked an eyebrow. "Not carrying a torch there, are you?"

"God, no. But I'm always going to have a soft spot for her, seeing as she was the first girl I thought I loved, and the first to break my teenage heart. It's good knowing she's married to a nice guy, and they've got a good place here."

"How about your place?"

"Getting there." Since they were in front of him he popped a couple of bar nuts. "On both fronts. I can't believe Maureen's working for me. I think of her running the car pool, making me and Micah Hot Pockets, telling us to wipe our feet, damn it. Now she's basically running the office."

"We've got ourselves an empty nest with Chloe married and living on the Outer Banks, and Micah with his own place."

Like Zane, Dave glanced toward the bar screen when a few cheers ripped out. March Madness.

"She'd been looking to go back to work for a while, just couldn't find anything that got her off the mark. Then, there it was. There you were. It's good to have you back, Zane."

"I wasn't sure I'd be able to say it and mean it all the way, but it's good to be back."

"How about that big, fancy house of yours?"

"You know, when I'm down here in town, or over at Emily's, at Britt's, I think about it and wonder if I lost my damn mind." Baffled at himself, Zane popped more nuts.

"Then I go up there? And it's freaking great. Everything about it just clicks. When I'm moved in, organized, I'm having all y'all up. We'll test out the killer grill that came with the place."

"Name the day, we're there."

"You know, Micah came up, went over the system—music, lights, TVs, security. I can do it all from a tablet, or my phone, how it's set up. Which meant I had to ask him to come back, run it through for me again. But I think I've got it now."

"If you don't, he's the man."

"Yeah, he really is."

"Now." Dave took another pull of his beer. "Why don't you tell me what's really on your mind?"

Zane studied his own beer, then studied Dave. The same strong face, Zane thought, the same eyes, both shrewd and kind.

"Graham's coming up for parole next week. He'll likely get it this time. I could go in, speak, and maybe hold it back, but it's just postponing."

"I'd go to the hearing again, Zane. So would Lee, Emily, Britt."

"I know it, just like I know how the system works."

After all, he'd *been* the system.

"He's served eighteen years," Zane continued, "stayed out of trouble, done the counseling, worked in the prison infirmary for six years now. The board's going to consider him rehabilitated. He's exactly the sort of inmate they want to move out, and I don't want to put Britt through another hearing. Or any of you."

"And what about you?"

He'd thought it over, hours of thinking, lying in bed, turning his baseball in his hand.

"It's going to happen, so there's no point. And sometimes you have to just close the book."

"Is that why you resigned from the DA's office, came back here?"

"Part of it," Zane admitted. "I don't have to forget, I sure as hell don't have to forgive. But it was time to, you know, close the book, open another."

"Okay. Okay then."

"Parole's not a cakewalk." Zane lifted his beer. "He'll never practice medicine again. He'll have to report in, submit to drug testing. He won't be able to leave the state. They may restrict him to Raleigh, slap him with mandatory anger management. He'll have to get a job." Zane shrugged. "He'll move in with Eliza. She's got a house, quiet neighborhood, works part-time in a fancy dress shop."

When Dave lifted his eyebrows, Zane shrugged again. "I felt better knowing where both of them were. Anyway, I'm closing the book, but I wanted to say something to you, something that'll move right from one book to the next. You've been more of a father to me than he ever was. You and Lee, but you as far back as I can remember. You're the one who showed me by who and what you were, how to be a man."

Dave took a moment, another sip of beer until he could speak. "That's a hell of a thing to hear. It's a hell of a thing to hear from a grown man I'm proud of."

"What you did for me—"

"Don't start on that."

"No, not just that night, Dave, and not just the days after."

And he needed to say it. Like writing it in a notebook, saying it made it real.

"Not just being there for me when I had nobody, fighting for me. Not just that. For all the time I spent at your house, or around you. You showed me what was real. Real family, real parents, even real husband and wife. Without that, without you . . . Abuse is a cycle. Without you, I might have become like him."

"Not in a million years, champ."

"Can't know. But the thing is, you, Maureen, Micah, Chloe, you added the weight to the other side of the scale. I'll never be like him, and that's the most important thing you've done for me."

"I'll tell you something back. You were never anything like him, or her. It used to puzzle me a little, how you and Britt seemed so different from them. I knew things weren't right at home for you, but I never saw what it was. I wish I had, but I didn't. What I did see? Graham was an arrogant prick, and Eliza, kind of a polished-up void."

"Jesus, that's good." After a breath, Zane took a pull on his beer. "That's good. 'Polished-up void' is exactly right."

"You and Britt? Just nothing like that, not the way I could see little bits of me and Maureen in our kids. Just little bits. Not even little bits of them in the two of you. What I saw in you? Heart. Neither of them had any."

Those clear, kind eyes held Zane's. "I don't forget either. I don't forgive."

"Then it looks like we're on the same page of the new book."

Dave smiled at him. "Looks that way. How about we order ourselves some of those loaded nachos and another beer?"

"Sounds good."

On a morning of April showers, Zane met Nathan Grandy at nine sharp when Maureen escorted him and Ashley into his office for their consult.

They looked, to Zane's eye, like a really upscale toothpaste commercial. Both of them blond, blue-eyed, and seriously attractive, Nathan stood gym fit next to Ashley's blooming pregnancy.

As soon as Nathan settled Ashley in the chair facing the desk, he stuck out his hand. "It's really nice to meet you. I'm going to say I'm also really glad things didn't work out between you and Ashley."

"Nathan Grandy!" came Ashley's laughing protest.

"Can't blame him."

"I heard you were in our place a couple nights back. Sorry I missed you. I think I must've headed home right before you came in. Ashley's getting close, so I try to get home in time to help put Fiona to bed."

"I like your place. Really like the loaded nachos."

"Can't go wrong with them. So, how do we do this?" Nathan asked. "It's the first time either of us made up a will."

"Why don't we talk about what you want?" As he spoke, Zane took out a fresh legal pad, started his notes.

"Simple, I guess. Right?" Ashley looked at Nathan. "We have the house, the cars, the business. It's all jointly owned. So if—you know—that would just go to the other."

"A good place to start. Let me get the information on all of that."

He asked questions, standard and simple, got their rhythm and a picture of their life, their holdings. Joint bank accounts, some investments. He gave answers and options, felt them both relax into it.

"Okay, now, if both of you went down in a zombie apocalypse, how would you want your assets handled?"

"Everything should go to the kids." By the way Nathan answered, Zane knew they'd talked about just this. "But our daughter's just a baby, and this one's still cooking."

"We can do a trust, then you decide who you want in charge of it, how you want it paid out. For their needs, their education, at what ages you'd want it turned over to them. Or if you'd want that spread out."

"Can their guardians be in charge?"

"Up to you," Zane told Nathan.

They exchanged another look that told Zane they'd already worked it out. Ashley took Nathan's hand, gave it a squeeze.

"We've decided we want to name my parents as guardians. We

want our kids raised here, and Fi loves my parents, knows them, trusts them. They'd take good care of our babies."

"Let's get that information. Full names, address."

As she answered, Ashley winced and pressed a hand to the side of her mound. "You know, Nathan, I think this one's fully cooked."

"Braxton-Hicks, Ash." He patted her arm with the casualness of experience. "You've got ten more days."

"He doesn't think so. He thinks today."

"What?" Zane dropped his pen. "Today, like, *today*? Let me get Maureen."

"No, no." Ashley waved him back down. "They're light, and that's only the third one. They're about twelve minutes apart. We've got time."

Still, Nathan rose, pulled out his phone. "I'm just going to call the midwife, let her know where we are. Give me a second."

"You have a midwife?" Zane asked as Nathan stepped out.

"Yeah, right here in the clinic in town." Placid as a spring morning, Ashley just smiled, rubbed her belly. "She's great. I'm fine, Zane. My mom already has Fiona, and we can be at the clinic in five minutes. I've done this before. So, what else do we need?"

"My mind's a little muddled."

She just grinned at him. "You said about education. My parents opened a college fund for Fi, and want to do the same for the new baby. I trust them to look after the kids, the assets, the everything. We just want this all put together, the best way, so we can forget about it."

"Yeah, that's the . . . You're really calm."

She sent him a sparkling look out of those pretty blue eyes. "About a possible zombie apocalypse?"

"No, about . . ." He gestured. "Happy birthday."

"I won't be in a couple hours, might as well be now." She glanced back as Nathan came in.

"Sandy's on alert. I called your mom. She'll call your dad and the rest, and they'll bring Fiona to the birthing room when we give them the go." He sat beside her, leaned over to rub her belly. "I let the restaurant know I'm going to be busy, and they're on it."

Now Nathan grinned at Zane as if a baby wasn't maybe going to pop out of his wife at any second. "So, what's next?"

It took another half hour—and three more contractions that made the spit dry up in Zane's mouth.

Maureen gave them both a hug, wished them good luck when Zane walked them to the door.

"I have to sit down," Zane decided, and dropped into a chair in reception. "She—my first real girlfriend—was in labor, in my office."

"Early labor."

"Labor," he repeated. "She's walking to the clinic to have a baby. Walking."

"Well, it stopped raining, and walking's good during early labor. You know what else would be good? For her friend and lawyer to pick her up some flowers on his lunch break, and take them by the birthing center before he goes home today."

"I can do that. It's just weird. She was the first girl I ever—" He broke off when Maureen narrowed her eyes at him. "Not that. We never—no. I meant . . . We'll leave it at weird."

He laid the legal pad on her desk. "What they want is pretty straightforward. You can draft it up, shoot it to me. If you can't read any of my notes, just let me know."

"You have very legible handwriting for a lawyer. You have Mona Carlson in about twenty minutes. The divorce—which she may actually mean this time. Then Grant Feister at eleven-thirty, DUI. Only two appointments this afternoon, but that's a good day, Zane, for your first full week up and running."

The phone on her desk rang. "And that may be one more. Good morning," she said into the receiver. "Zane Walker, Attorney-at-Law."

He got flowers, dropped them off about three in the afternoon. The cheerful woman who greeted him said she would take the flowers in, or she could ask Ashley if he could go in himself.

He told her to just take them. Please.

Since the rest of the day was clear, he headed over to Emily's with some paperwork she'd asked him to deal with.

He found her standing in front of the house, hands clutched together in her nervous pose as she watched Darby digging a trench with her little machine. Roy and Hallie planted some kind of tree on the other side of the front yard, now bisected with a flagstone path that ran to the front porch, where Gabe and Brody worked together to hang a porch swing the color of chili peppers.

He parked, and since Emily looked as if she might be sick, or run screaming, went straight to her.

Eyes a little wild, she grabbed his arms. "What have I done?"

"I don't know. What's happening?"

"She's digging a ditch. In the yard. It's for sprinklers or drip something, or—God. It's irrigation for a shrubbery."

"Like Monty Python?"

"Oh Jesus, oh God, it's like Monty Python. She says it'll have color from spring through fall, and texture all year, and balance the yard, and low-maintenance, and there's no such thing as a black thumb."

"If you don't want it—"

"You don't understand." She gave him a desperate little shake. "She starts talking and you just start nodding and thinking, That sounds beautiful, that sounds great. Why didn't I think of it in the first place? Then she starts doing it, and you're, What have I done? Look, look at the color of that porch swing."

"I did. It's what, red-hot chili pepper?"

"Oh sweet baby Jesus, it *is*! I picked it. I picked it myself—or did I?" Still gripping him, Emily turned her head toward Darby, narrowed her eyes. "Did I really pick it? I think she has some sort of mind control. I'm not kidding."

"Take a breath, Em." To help her out, he gave her a hug. "I can say one thing for certain. The stonework looks awesome."

She looked down at the walk. "It really does. She's a genius. I mean, I see it in every bungalow she's finished, but—"

"Keep breathing. You know what else? I like the swing."

Emily breathed. "Damn it, so do I. Somehow she always ends up being right. Distract me from my madness. How's it going with you?"

"Good. I've got a handful of clients. Maureen is pretty damn perfect, and I've got a line on a summer intern. If I pick the one I'm leaning toward, I'll be outnumbered by women. Oh, women," he remembered. "Ashley's having her baby."

"Now?"

"Now. She started having it in my office. It was beyond weird."

Emily tipped her head toward his shoulder. "We're having a day, aren't we?"

"You could call it that."

Her phone signaled, and after a glance at the readout, Emily kissed Zane's cheek. "I have to run down to the office."

"I have to get home anyway. Get some stuff done. But here's that paperwork you asked for."

"Oh, thanks. Come for dinner tomorrow night, when I'm less crazy."

"It's a date."

He started to walk up, say hi and bye to his cousins, when Darby stopped the machine, hopped off. So he crossed to her instead, studied the trenching.

"So. A shrubbery?"

"It's always best to appease the Knights Who Say Ni."

He had to grin. "So I've heard."

She took off her cap to swipe her forehead.

Just what the hell color was that hair? he wondered. Not brown, not really red. But more red than brown in the sun, more brown than red in the shade.

"You're just the man I wanted to see," she said as she put the cap back on.

"Need a lawyer?"

"Not right this minute, but I'm always looking for clients. How about I come take a look at your new place?"

He felt a little of Emily's panic. "You look pretty busy."

With a shrug, she pulled on work gloves. "You have to look ahead.

I've got some ideas, but I want a better look at things, with you factored in. I can come by in a couple hours."

She headed to her truck, called for the crew. He had a minute with his cousins before she pulled them in. He saw a lot of black plastic, a lot of black hosing.

And figured he should get gone before she tossed him a pair of gloves and sucked him into the work.

As he drove home he reminded himself he did want a few little things added to the exterior. And he wasn't a pushover, so he wouldn't end up with trenches and shrubberies.

Maybe a tree. He wouldn't mind a nice shade tree he could watch grow year after year. Maybe put a hammock under it for lazy Sunday afternoons. Or a couple of trees with a hammock slung between them.

He'd give her a tree, Zane decided, possibly two. Maybe a couple of bushes or shrubs—was there a difference? They didn't call it a bushery, right?

Anyway.

He'd hold the line on shrubbery/bushery. And that would be that.

CHAPTER TWELVE

Darby admired the drive up to Zane's. She knew just where the property line started, and knew she'd plant redbuds, or azaleas, maybe mountain or bay laurel. Scatter them up that drive so it looked as if nature put them there.

Not only would visitors have that "ah" moment as they ascended, but they'd show from the house, and from points below.

Gracious, lovely.

The house itself was, in her opinion, a kick-my-ass-sideways feat of architecture. All wood and stone and glass perched on the rise, just lording it over everything. Decks, porches, patios just begging for her touch. The big main entrance—and since they were in the South, that would be a veranda rather than a porch—screamed out for sleek stone urns—maybe concrete—filled with color and height.

Hell, she'd make friends with Zane just for the chance to spend some time up here as it was. But if she talked him into letting her get her hands on the place? She'd give him a mountain paradise.

She parked, looked up. The man didn't even have a chair on the deck—and she'd call that a terrace—off the master bedroom suite.

Clearly, he needed her.

He stepped out the big double doors onto the covered veranda, and she felt the click. He suited the house, to her eye, and the house suited him. That made it easier.

He was a tall one, so all those high ceilings, the soaring windows, the wide-open floor plan on the main level worked well.

She'd fix it so the grounds worked well for him, too.

Long legs that didn't have to hurry to cover ground, and a good, strong build that still hit the edge of lanky.

What woman didn't give an *mmmm* over a long, lanky, green-eyed man?

"You've got a hell of a place here, Zane."

"I'm not used to it yet." He stepped up to her, turned around, looked as she did. "I drive up here every time and think: Whoa, how about that."

"I have the same reaction to mine. Often add a little hip-shaking boogie. It's good to be home, isn't it?"

"You made the transition fast and smooth."

She turned, gestured to the view of mountains, the lake, the town, the everything. "Why not? I bet you stand in one of those gorgeous windows and think: Whoa, how about that."

"Every freaking day."

"It's a killer view. You know what it's missing?"

He felt his shoulders tighten. Hold the line, he reminded himself. "I figure you're going to tell me."

"You need a stone retaining wall, along here." She walked closer to where the ground began its long slope down. "Not only for erosion, but for structure—and safety. You might get married, have kids."

A tree, he reminded himself. Maybe a couple bushes.

"It feels like a wall would close things in."

"Not a high wall, nothing that would block the view from up here, or down there. Something to enhance. We'd go with man-made stone—I'll leave you a brochure. You pick the tones, the design. We'd add lights."

"Lights, but—"

"Not just for illumination, for magic." She reached in one of the pockets of her cargo jeans, offered him a small copper strip. "We'd use them—your choice of finish—on both sides. I've got some pictures to show you how they look at night. Just a nice, pretty glow.

"I get the previous owners wanted the house itself to be the wow, didn't want much else in the front. But they didn't have small kids."

"Neither do I."

"Yet. Plus, your sister has a little girl, and she'll be running around here. You don't want her to go tumbling down this slope."

He hadn't thought of it, but now he could see it. And the image moved his line, then and there. "Okay, a wall. Low wall."

"I'll leave the brochure, do some measurements, give you an estimate. So, let's stick with the front for now."

She talked about planting stuff along his drive—who'd have thought of that? Of finishing off his veranda with big concrete urns, chairs, a table, with stuff planted along the front.

He found himself doing just what Emily had warned him of. Nodding. Nodding even when they worked their way around the side, and there was talk of massing hydrangeas, peonies, lilies.

It was the waterfall that broke his trance.

"You've got to be kidding."

"I'm not talking Niagara. This house was built into the mountain, so it's already got the rise and fall and drop. Look here, Walker, this area's begging for a long, winding water feature. Natural stone, water tumbling down from the top grade, then meandering. We do plantings along that edge, sweeping them back into the trees. You put a stone bench here, some fragrant shrubs, do a loose stone walk, some pretty lights, mulch it, and you'd find yourself sitting here enjoying an adult beverage, the sound of the water, the view, the scents every single day."

Her hands moved as she spoke. Strong, ringless hands with long fingers, short unpolished nails. How did they manage to paint pictures in the air?

"But . . . a waterfall."

"Think of it as more of a spill," she suggested. "It would be a great use of this underused space. We'd maintain the pump. You'd just enjoy it. Otherwise—it wouldn't be my choice, but an option. Do you play golf?"

"No."

"A lawyer who doesn't play golf? I was thinking cute little putting green, but scratch that. Not a sports guy?"

"I used to play baseball."

"Hey, me, too. I love baseball."

It shifted his mind from waterfalls. "What's your team?"

Her look held pity. "Zane, I'm from Baltimore. I was born an O's fan, I live as an O's fan, and I'll die an O's fan."

He found himself smiling. "Me, too."

"Really?" She shifted away from landscape talk, hooked the thumbs of those interesting hands in her belt loops. "You ever get to Camden Yards?"

"A few times."

She sighed a little. "I wanted to live there."

It came out of his mouth before he censored himself. "I wanted to play there." It still brought a tug, one he made himself ignore.

"What position?"

"Short."

"Hey, second base here." She offered her fist to bump. "The town's got a league, but spring and summer are my high seasons, so no go for me. Are you playing?"

"No."

Something in the single syllable warned her to back off. "Well, I'm hoping to catch a couple innings of Gabe's game on Saturday. So I'm going to draw you up what I have in mind, give you a better picture. Meanwhile."

She talked about doing raised beds for herbs, for annuals, more shrubs, another wall to mirror the one in front.

He lost track.

"Now that I've given you a whole bunch to think about, I'm going to get some measurements. And I'll bring you some brochures to look through."

"Great. Need any help?"

"I've got it."

She walked back around to her truck, and Zane, more than slightly shell-shocked, went in the back through the kitchen.

He opened a beer, thought he should've offered her a beer. Decided he needed to recover from her first.

She smelled of earth and growing things, had strong, competent hands that drew pictures in the air. She painted them with words, too, so he could get a misty, mystical image of what she saw in her head.

But that didn't mean he'd fall for it.

The walls, those he could see. Safety mattered, and he hoped Audra would spend plenty of time visiting her uncle. And he liked the idea of the lights glowing on the stone, so good.

Maybe some of the plantings—some of them. But the waterfall? That was ridiculous.

Even as he thought it, he walked over to the big window of the great room, looked at the space she'd imagined the ridiculous waterfall.

No. Absolutely not. No. But . . . maybe he'd think about it.

She had a point about needing tables and chairs and so on outside. The veranda, the decks, the back patio with its pretty awesome built-in, big-ass grill—that all needed seating to make it a real outdoor living space.

So, okay, she had a point there.

He could grill—Lee had seen to that—and he wanted to have the family up for a cookout. So tables, chairs all around.

With his beer and his laptop, he sat at the big breakfast counter, began to see what the internet had to offer on outdoor furniture.

He left the glass wall accordioned open, and had earmarked a few choices by the time Darby tapped a finger on a panel.

"Come on in. Want a beer?"

"God, yes, but I'm driving. Half a beer?"

"Half a beer."

As he got up to pour her half a beer, she wandered in, circled the enormous kitchen. She admired the cabinetry, dark and rich, some with glass fronts, the acres and acres of counter in granite that flowed with sweeps of dull gold, rich browns, hints of woodsy green, bits of mica.

It had everything—the under-counter wine cooler and ice machine. The dishwasher drawers, a professional eight-burner range top with fancy hood, double wall ovens.

Plus, she knew from her lookie-loo tour, it boasted a butler's pantry with another dishwasher, a fridge, a big sink, more counters, more cabinets. And a storage pantry big enough to camp in.

"This kitchen almost makes me want to learn to cook—really cook."

"I'm happy to say it hasn't pulled me there." Zane handed her the beer. "Which is why I said a bed of herbs doesn't make sense."

"Herbs always make sense." She tapped her glass to his bottle, sipped, sighed. Then handed him brochures. "One of those is mine, just informal for now, but some of the work I've done may show you what I have in mind here. I'm still working on the web page, but it's up. Such as it is."

"If you want help with that, you should contact The Computer Guy."

"That's Micah Carter, right? He's been recommended."

"My oldest pal, and despite that, I can honestly say he's the best." Curious, he flipped a brochure open to one of her tags, saw stone walls in tones that reminded him of his kitchen counters, saw the night shots with those clever little lights glowing.

"Okay, wow."

"Right? You could have that."

"This is—what do you call it—terraced. You know, a couple of levels, with stone steps."

"You could have that, too, minus the steps. No reason for them. The terraced wall's not only doable, but I'd recommend it."

"You didn't mention that before."

She smiled over her beer. "Didn't want to scare you."

He looked up at her, deep green eyes full of cynicism. "You talk waterfalls, but don't want to scare me?"

"I'd lulled you a little by then. I'd recommend the two levels for aesthetics and more stability."

"But then you plant stuff like this one in the lower level, and that's—"

"Native plantings with an underground irrigation system. Heavily mulched. We maintain; you enjoy."

"That oughta be on your logo. Why don't you have a seat? I can flip through some of this while you're right here."

"Great." She pulled over a stool, then handed him some printouts she'd stapled together. "Take a look at this."

When she opened it to a damn waterfall, he felt himself sink.

"You built this."

"My mother and I did, yeah."

"It's amazing."

"I think so. It's a little bigger and more elaborate than what I'd want here, but it gives you an idea of what can be done. Working with the land, using the natural drop."

He studied the photos. This one spilled from several heights, had plants tumbling out of the stone, ledges big enough for someone to perch on.

"You're trying to make me want it."

She sipped her beer. "You already want it. I'm helping you get past your garden-o-phobia."

"What about winter?"

"Drain it, pull the pump. Then it's just a pretty feature until spring, when the pump goes back."

"Well, shit."

She didn't bother to muffle the laugh. "I'll draw you up what I have in mind, give you an estimate. Then you decide."

She angled, noted the page up on his laptop. "Checking out your outdoor living options."

"Yeah, you're right about that. I want to have the family up, but I haven't dealt with stuff for outside yet."

"You don't want to go too contemporary or too rustic. You—Sorry, can't stop myself. Do you mind if I just . . ." She circled a finger. "See more of how you're outfitting the house?"

"Sure."

"I really like what you're doing with the space. Big space, high ceilings, so the oversized chairs, the big-ass sofas, they really work. Mostly manly colors," she continued as she wandered, "but not dull. Comfortable, but not sloppy, nothing rigid when it comes to style. I hate when everything matches. And I love your dining room table."

"I just picked that up. They called it industrial rustic, whatever that means."

"Whatever it means, it's great." She trailed a finger over the long surface. "It's like barnwood, right? Man, you're really neat and organized."

A punch in the gut if you forgot to pick up your socks would do that, he thought. "I guess I am."

She wandered out to the living room, glanced through glass doors into a room he'd nearly finished making his home office. "What are you going to do with the lower level? Are you keeping the home theater?"

"I'd be crazy not to. I need to get some stuff for the guest suite down there. Right now I've set up my home gym, and that's about it."

Lips pursed, she walked back to him, curled her hand around his right biceps, squeezed. "I thought so. Very nice."

Then wandered off again, leaving him bemused.

"Okay, you obviously know what you're doing, what works for you and the space. I can, however, give you a list of places in the general area where you'd be able to see, touch, sit in, and so on the actual product rather than buying online."

"Okay."

"Why don't you give me your email, and when I work all this up, I'll send it to you."

"Sounds like a plan. I even have a card."

He pulled a case out of his pocket, handed her one.

"Impressive. 'Zane Walker, Attorney-at-Law.' It's a good name for an attorney. It's an even better one for an action hero. My card's in the brochure, if you have any questions." She handed him the glass. "Thanks for the beer."

"Half."

"Just right."

"Let me walk you out. Wait, I've got one of Micah's cards." He opened a drawer, ruthlessly organized, took out a card. "If you need a computer guy, call The Computer Guy."

"I actually should, so thanks."

"He thinks you're hot."

"He—hmm."

"And I have no idea why that came out of my mouth. He's in a serious, monogamous relationship, and crazy in love with Cassie."

"Good for him," she said as they walked to the front of the house. "And I am hot, so he's not wrong."

"He won't hit on you."

"Good to know. Man, I love your place." She stepped out on the veranda, breathed in the air, the view. "When I'm finished with it, the fairies will dance, the angels will sing."

"And the water will spill?"

She laughed. "If you're smart, it will. I'll talk to you later."

He watched her walk down the steps, walk to her truck. Yeah, definitely hot, he decided, in a strange, visceral, compelling way he couldn't quite get a handle on.

"Hey!" he called out. "Maybe I'll see you at Gabe's game."

"Hope so." She hopped in her truck, shot him a wave, and drove off.

And he realized as she drove away there'd been a kind of buzzing energy in the air that faded off.

He sort of missed it.

Zane supposed he started the email relationship with Darby when he sent her one with his choice for the stone for the walls. And adding he leaned toward the terrace deal. And the lights.

Within two hours, she sent him an acknowledgment, an approval on his choice, and a meticulously detailed pricing for labor and materials that included an estimate on time and an approximate start date (weather permitting).

The fact the cost came in somewhat under his fears didn't stop his quick wince. He wandered out on his bedroom terrace, looked at his grounds, currently lit by floodlights. Imagined that nice, soft glow against the stone.

Walked back in, emailed her instructions to send him a contract.

And she emailed him that within thirty. God help him, he printed it out, signed it, scanned it, sent it back. Received her acknowledgment thereof.

All of this before midnight on the very day she'd come to talk him into it all.

The next evening after dinner with his family, he checked his email, saw another from her.

This one had a drawing of the waterfall attached, complete with measurements. He studied it, coveted it, walked away from it.

When he got home, he walked outside, stared at the space, all but heard the water spilling against rock. Walked back inside and into his home office.

Do it, he wrote. You're starting to piss me off.

Her reply came moments later.

I get that a lot. Do you want a separate contract, or do you want to wait until I calculate the rest?

Figure out the whole damn thing. I'm not going to say yes to the whole damn thing, but figure it. I'll pick and choose. And I've decided you're not as hot as you think you are.

I should have full numbers for you by Gabe's game. Either way you go, if I see you there, I'll buy you a hot dog. And my hotness, unharnessed, is incendiary. Do you/can you set up LLCs?

I can. It'll cost you a million dollars. And a hot dog.

Great. We'll negotiate. I'll call your office for an appointment.

Zane found the rest of his week surprisingly full. He hired an intern, a sharp grad student with ties to the area. She'd been raised by her grandparents—father unknown, mother long gone. As her grandparents had retired to Lakeview a few years earlier, she wanted a summer position close by.

You didn't get much closer than smack on Main Street, and as she hit every mark he'd aimed for, Zane and Gretchen Filbert came to amicable terms.

Which meant he had to come up with another desk, and all that went with it.

He drew up an unhappy woman's marital separation agreement, talked his former US History teacher out of suing his own brother over what was, essentially, a family spat, took on a client who needed help settling her mother's estate as the attorney of record was also dead.

He couldn't claim a jammed calendar, but for a guy launching a private law practice in a small community, he figured he was doing just fine.

He returned from what he thought of as a house call frazzled, exhausted, and damp from the afternoon thunderstorm, and dropped into one of the chairs in reception.

Maureen swiveled around to study him. "You have the 'I've just spent two hours with Mildred Fissle' look. Eyes glazed, hair sticking up, as the electric charges in your brain shot through it, mouth slack from shock.

"Want coffee?"

"Will it have whiskey in it?"

"No. You have an appointment in thirty minutes. No booze for you."

"She—you know, I thought she was ancient and scary when I was a kid. Now she's really ancient and just plain terrifying. I had to sit in her parlor in this little rock of a chair—two hours with my knees up at my ears. I had to drink horrible tea that tasted like muddy flowers."

Maureen gave him a deliberately exaggerated sad face. "Poor baby."

"Everything smelled like withered rose petals and cats. She has five cats—that I saw. There may be more. One of them sat there and never stopped staring at me. It didn't blink, so I thought maybe it was dead and stuffed. Then it moved."

He shuddered. "I'm going to have to go back there, Maureen. I'm going to have to go back."

Enjoying him, adoring him, Maureen leaned forward. "She wanted to change her will again, didn't she?"

"She dragged out half a million previous wills, codicils, and all these little handwritten notes attached to them. Dozens of Post-it Notes, with cats on them."

Maureen rose. "I'm going to get you a Coke, sweetie. Just sit and breathe for a minute."

She came back with a cold bottle for him, and a glass of the ice water with lemon slice she preferred. "I'm friends with one of her granddaughters, went to school with her. Miss Mildred—even her grandkids call her that—changes her will more often than most change their sheets. Whichever one of her many children, grandchildren, great-grandchildren—and the building number of great-greats—happens to be in favor at the moment is told the numerous secret hiding places around the house where she stashes cash, jewelry, bankbooks, insurance policies, the latest will, and so on. Then that one falls out of favor. Miss Mildred writes her notes, changes hiding places, calls her current lawyer, and does it all again."

"She has six living children," Zane put in, "twenty-nine grandchildren, sixty-seven greats, and nineteen great-greats. Three more coming." He took a big glug from the bottle. "And she has specific bequests for every freaking one of them—except the ones she's decided don't deserve anything, and those she insists on leaving one dollar. It's like, these earrings go to Sue, this table goes to Hank, and Wendall gets a dollar because he couldn't be bothered to come in from Seattle to see me at Christmas.

"It went on like that for two hours."

"There, there."

"Funny. Remind me to give you a 'there, there' after you spend the rest of your afternoon turning my desperate notes into a legal document."

"Challenge accepted," she said when he opened his briefcase, took out a legal pad, a file. "It'll be easier next time, say, three months from now. Plus, she's, what, about ninety-eight? She can't live forever."

"She's ninety-nine, and don't be so sure of that."

He rose, shifted his briefcase to shoulder strap as his phone signaled a text. He pulled it out as he walked to his office.

Darby.

Are you sitting down? If not, text me when you are. And you might want an adult beverage handy.

He sat at his desk, wondered why he experienced twin tugs of anxiety and delight whenever he heard from Darby McCray.

I'm sitting. And since I'm a professional and it's only three in the afternoon—and Maureen said no—I have no adult beverage handy.

You might overrule her in a few minutes. I'm sending you an email now, with multiple attachments. I'm catching a couple innings of Gabe's game tomorrow, then have to work to make up losing this afternoon to rain and lightning. See you there.

He heard the email come in, glanced warily at his computer. How bad could it be? Plus, he wasn't going to do all the stuff she wanted anyway.

Pick and choose, Walker, he reminded himself. Just pick and choose.

He opened it, laughed out loud at the dancing hot dog GIF. Then downloaded and opened the attachments.

The first, showing just how clever and canny his adversary in this match was, featured drawings illustrating the projected work, completed.

"I'm not falling for it," he muttered. "Jesus, it's amazing. But I will not be lulled."

He moved on to her careful listing of trees, shrubs, plants, with pricing—all guaranteed with replacement at no cost for a year should they croak.

Fair.

Then there was stuff like fill dirt, topsoil, mulch, irrigation systems, pots, urns, planters.

Mostly that made him scratch his head. Why wasn't dirt just dirt—and shouldn't it be dirt cheap?

Then came the labor, and when his eyes uncrossed from that, the total.

"Holy fucking shit!"

Maureen ran in. "Language! What's wrong with you? We could have a client!"

He just pointed to his computer screen.

With the mother's glare still on her face, Maureen rounded the desk. "Oh good God!"

"See?"

"For landscaping? What are you landscaping, Disneyland? Emily's told me how reasonable Darby is, and I've been thinking about asking her to do a little something for me. But my good lord!"

"Don't let this put you off. It's a crazy bunch of stuff. And for some reason, she included the walls and waterfall I already contracted."

"Waterfall? You want a waterfall?"

"No. Maybe. No. It's crazy. I'm crazy."

He brought up the file, showed her. And she made a long, yearning sound.

"It's so beautiful. Oh, these walls—with the plants? Why, it almost looks like it's just part of the hill, doesn't it? Like it grew right there. Zane, it's wonderful. What else?"

Reluctantly now, he scrolled through the other drawings.

"This is fabulous, beyond fabulous. It's magic, but, I don't know, natural magic."

"You're not helping," he muttered.

"Well, bless your heart, I see what I see. Bring back that cost page again."

When he did, she rubbed his shoulder. "That's definitely amazing, too. Wait, there's another page."

"There can't be." But he noted it. "I guess I was too busy having a stroke to notice."

"Okay, okay," Maureen reassured, "you see where she's noted the previous contract and cost—because she's giving you what she's calling a Preferred Client discount on the work, including that. It's a good discount, Zane. Not to say that's not a lot of money, but it's a good discount."

He stared hard at the figures. "She's cagey—you ask Emily. She's cagey. She waited to do the discount until after my stroke or heart attack or coma. She waited, and didn't mention any possible discount when I fell for the wall and waterfall, but she includes them. She was always going to. She's lulling me. It's what she does."

Maureen scrolled back to the pictures, made that sound again. "If she can do all this, she can do a lot more than lull. Well, that girl's an artist. A magician. What are you going to do?"

"I'm going to stop looking at the pictures, the drawings, and burn that final figure into my brain so it reminds me why I'm going to stop looking at them."

He heard the quiet chime ring, something else Micah had installed to let him know when the front door opened. "And I'm blanking it all out." He clicked the file closed.

"I'll give you two minutes to recover, then bring your next appointment back."

She walked to the door, glanced back. "You have to admit, it would be something special."

"I don't need special. I like sanity."

CHAPTER THIRTEEN

Friday might have proven a stormy mess, but Saturday dawned beautiful. And Darby rose with it.

She downed coffee and a bowl of Cheerios with a handful of blueberries while she checked the short- and long-range weather forecasts.

She dressed in her spring uniform of cargo pants, T-shirt, and hoodie, pleased to top it off with the High Country Landscaping cap in dark blue, accented with a dogwood blossom. She figured using North Carolina's state flower hit the right note.

As she walked to the truck, she glanced back at the ground excavated for her equipment and tool sheds. With luck she'd have the concrete poured and inspected by early the following week.

She heard morning birds singing, saw trillium popping color through the trees that edged her little world. The wind chime she'd gifted herself caught a breeze, adding more music, more color.

What could be better than that?

Optimistic, she drove down to the lake, misty with the sunrise currently painting the eastern sky. A heron, bridal white, slid through the mist like a dream.

An early riser all her life, through wiring and career choice, she found seeing a new day dawn a perk of her job.

Alone on the quiet lake road, she went over the day's schedule in her head. It could all be done, with maybe some time in the evening to deal with her kitchen cabinets.

Doors off, she thought. Zane's glass fronts had inspired her. She'd remove the sorrowfully ugly doors, paint the rest, and be done.

Easier to see what she wanted anyway.

She let herself wonder about Zane for just a minute. He hadn't responded to her email, or the attachments. Unusual for him, she admitted. Normally he got back to her fairly quickly.

Probably still reeling some, and she couldn't hold it against him. Plus, she didn't expect he'd go for the whole shot. She just hoped he worked out his priorities carefully so she could give him what worked for him.

She pulled up at reception, pulled on her gloves, got her tools.

She had an hour in before Hallie pulled up, then Roy—a little hungover from a Friday night party. She'd given them the morning hour, as she intended to take an hour herself to watch a little baseball.

By the time Emily pulled up, they were down to mulching and pot planting. She walked over to where Darby gently wound tendrils of clematis around the hooks she'd screwed into the new lamppost.

"I'm getting used to it." Emily let out a sigh. "Used to thinking, Sure, go ahead with that. Moving into the panicked 'oh my God, what is she doing' stage, and into this 'it looks just perfect' ending."

"We aim to please."

"Well, you really do, even if I'm still in stage two at the house."

"We're heading there when we're done here. Final stage next week."

Still, when Emily looked around, Darby saw the worry line dig between her eyebrows. "I don't know how I'm going to keep it all alive."

"Low-maintenance," Darby reminded her. "And I'm going to teach you."

"Uh-huh. What's that tree again Roy's mulching?"

"Crepe myrtle. Perfect late summer bloomer. I'm putting one at your house, too."

"Okay, and good luck to it. I've got to get a couple hours in before Marcus takes over here so I can make it to Gabe's game."

Sitting back on her heels, Darby scanned the clematis, deemed it good. "I'm going to try to get there for an hour."

"I'll save you a seat. Darby, while I'm benefiting from your admirable work ethic, I also know the pressure of running your own business. Honey, you should take a day off."

"I had most of yesterday off, and it's going to rain next Wednesday, so that's another."

Emily crouched down. "And what do you do with your days off?"

"Plot and plan on how to make potential clients panic."

With genuine affection, Emily patted her cheek. "I bet you do. See you at the game."

She finished in time to take photos for her files, to get the crew started at Emily's, and to wash up with the garden hose.

"Back around one. Or one-thirty if you want me to pick up lunch. My tab."

"Hot and spicy sub!" Roy called out.

Hallie, her hair now in dozens of artful braids bunched at her neck with a band, leaned on her shovel. "I'll take a half ham and pepper jack with tomatoes—mustard not mayo."

"Got it."

"And chips," Roy added. "Jalapeño chips."

Darby liked the spicy herself, but Roy went for the flames. "One-thirty. Text if you have a problem."

She wound around the lake, admired all the bloomings, gave mental thumbs-ups to the home gardeners out at work in their yards, and continued through town already busy with Saturday shoppers.

And out the other side to the ball fields.

She had to hunt to park, considered that an excellent show of community support. As she walked the full block from her truck to the field, she listened to the crack of bats, the calls of fans, smelled the hot dogs and sloppy joes.

She paused to watch the little guys play, pint-size athletes learning the game and the value of teamwork. In the sunshine, she walked to where the older kids battled it out, spotted Zane, Emily, and Lee high in the long run of bleachers.

She'd only missed two innings, she noted by the scoreboard, and the home team had a run.

Top of the third, two outs, a man on first.

Gabe played the batter deep at third.

She waited to make the climb up until the batter—powerful swing—struck out.

As she threaded her way up, a number of people greeted her, and that was nice. Nice to live where people knew you, and took time to say hello.

Zane gave her a long glance from under his ball cap, behind his dark glasses, as she settled in beside him.

"How's Gabe doing?"

"Got the RBI, solid double in the first. Fielded a hot line drive and beat the runner to second, snagged a pop-up."

"Excellent. What do you want on your dog?"

"Mustard."

"That's it?"

"That's it."

"Got it. Hey." She leaned in front of him to speak to Emily and Lee. "I'm buying dogs at the end of this inning. How do you like yours?"

"Thanks. Just mustard."

Lee leaned past his wife. "Loaded."

"Now, that's a dog."

She watched the first batter fly out on the second pitch.

"So where's Brody?"

"Around here somewhere with his non-girlfriend girlfriend."

"Jenny? She's adorable. He's probably working up to asking her to the end-of-school dance. He wanted to do it casual, so a ball game works."

That pulled Zane's attention away from the next batter. "How do you know that?"

"He mentioned it. He knows she's waiting for him to ask, and probably knows he knows, but he doesn't want to make it a big thing. Gabe's on deck."

"Yeah."

They watched the first pitch to the batter, a called strike. Muttered together: "High and inside."

In solidarity, Darby gave him a light elbow to the ribs. "So have you worked through your sticker shock, figured out any priorities?"

"Maybe."

The second pitch brought the count to 1–1.

"You've got a chance for revenge Wednesday."

"Why Wednesday?"

"Forecast for rain throughout the day, so I called your office late on Friday afternoon, made an appointment. All right." She clapped as the batter took another outside pitch for ball two. "Good eye."

"Emily said you're nearly finished with reception."

"Am finished, looks awesome. We're back at the house the rest of the day. I'm going to hit Bungalow Six for a couple hours tomorrow between checkout and check-in."

Late swing, fouled back.

She turned her head so their eyes met briefly, shielded by sunglasses, shadowed by the bills of ball caps.

"Is that how you spend your Sundays?"

"Gotta dig holes while the sun shines, Walker."

Ball three. Full count.

People clapped, buzzed, stomped.

A kid of about three sat on his father's shoulders on the grass beside the bleachers and waved a little plastic bat. A trio of girls with yards of hair and legs strolled by a group of boys who pretended not to notice.

A couple of levels below where Darby sat, a woman plied yarn with a crochet hook and shouted, "Knock it outta here, Willy!"

"It's coming inside," Zane mumbled.

"You think?"

"You watch. Gonna try to crowd him, make him swing."

Darby watched. It came inside, missing the corner of the plate. Instead of knocking it outta there, Willy did the smart thing. He took the pitch, and his base on balls.

"Somebody else has a good eye," Darby commented. "Willy's got fast feet. He can stretch a solid single into a double."

Once again, Zane gave her a long look. "How do you know?"

"I try to catch a couple innings when I can. Maybe a practice after work. All right, Gabe!"

Gabe walked to the plate, shuffled, tested the bat, took his stance.

The kid had really good form, Zane thought. Excellent focus and instincts. He remembered standing in that same spot on a sunny afternoon with the smell of grilling meat, green grass, brown dirt, white chalk. How he'd blocked out the noise of the crowd, or used it.

How, in that moment, those smells, those sounds, the feel of the bat in his hands, the sight of the white ball winging toward him comprised the entire world.

Gabe didn't waste time, and banged the first pitch past the diving first baseman.

As Darby had predicted, the solid single put runners on the corners. She hooted, whistled, exchanged high fives with Zane.

"Bring 'em in, Luke!"

"Do you know all the kids?" Zane wondered.

"If you're going to live and build a business in a community, be the community. Plus, baseball."

The count built to 2–2 before Luke popped a one-hopper to left center. It brought in the run, advanced Gabe to second.

While the coach called time and walked to the mound with the catcher to settle down the pitcher, Darby turned back to Zane. "Depending on your schedule, we can stretch my appointment Wednesday if you want to go over options. Or you can come by my place tomorrow, or I can come by yours. Either way around ten in the morning, or after three."

She waited a beat. "Unless I've scared you off the whole thing."

"You don't scare me."

"Good. Just let me know when works for you."

Emily leaned forward. "You're talking about Zane's place. He showed me your drawings. It's like a movie!"

"But livable," Darby returned with a smile.

The conference at the mound worked. The pitcher worked the batter to a 1–2 count before crowding him into an easily fielded pop-up.

The next looped one to second, couldn't outrun the throw to first, and ended the inning.

"Two up." Darby slapped her hands together. "It's hot dog time."

"Zane, give her a hand."

Darby waved Emily off. "I'm good. A deal's a deal."

Darby worked her way down, then over to the cook shed to get in line. The woman in front of her turned.

"Hey, Darby."

"Laurie." Who worked at Best Blooms, and knew her stuff. "How's it going?"

"Going good. My husband's sister's boy's playing, and we're winning. I saw you in the bleachers." She gave a quick eyebrow wiggle. "I didn't know you were with Zane Walker."

"Sure, we're—Oh, no, not with-with. I wanted to see Gabe play for a bit. I'm just sitting with the family."

"Well, that's a genuine shame, because you sure look good together." Laurie shook back flyaway curls as she glanced back at the stands. "It's good to see him out here, at a game."

They shuffled up in line, paused as the crowd cheered a long fly ball snagged by the center fielder for an out.

"I was a few years ahead of him in school," Laurie continued, "but my sister was in his class. He was the star of the team, won State Player of the Year, two years running."

"That's big stuff," Darby commented.

"Oh, yes, indeed. He'd have won it again if it hadn't been for . . ." She seemed to catch herself, shifted her feet. "He had an injury that took him out."

"For the season?"

"For good, from what I know. Bad broken arm or something like that. Anyway, it's good to see him back in Lakeview, back at the field."

Laurie gave her order, leaving Darby to think it through.

Broken nose, father, she thought. Broken arm? The same source? Maybe. And maybe it explained why no one ever mentioned his father, or his mother, come to that.

And why he and Britt had lived with Emily and Lee.

Laurie gathered up her cardboard tray loaded with drinks, dogs, fries. "You come and see us at Best Blooms, now."

"You know I will."

Darby ordered the dogs, doctored them as specified. And thought of a teenage boy, star of the team, player of the year, one who'd dreamed of playing in Camden Yards.

Her heart broke a little.

She had to push it away as she carried the food up the bleachers. If he wanted her to know, he'd tell her.

She passed out the dogs, with napkins. "Down payment," she told Zane. "We still have to negotiate your million-dollar fee."

"Didn't I mention that's my hourly fee?"

"You did not. Will my LLC come gold-plated?"

"It's the only kind I do."

She ate her dog, stayed through the fourth inning.

"Gotta get back. Emily, be sure to take a look at reception. Good seeing you, Chief. Zane."

Once again she worked her way down the bleachers, started toward the road.

"Hey!"

And turned back when Zane came after her.

"Where are you parked?"

She pointed, tapping her finger in the air a couple times to indicate distance.

"I'll walk with you, stretch my legs."

"Well, you've got a lot of them."

The little guys had wrapped it up, and the next age group looked about to. Zane paused a minute, watched the center fielder misjudge a fly by about a mile and a half.

"Coach used to take us out for pizza, win or lose, after a Saturday game."

"Good coach."

"Yeah. So, I've given your staggeringly ambitious plans for what would have to be termed my estate considerable thought."

"As you should. But I think you need more acreage, a guest house, and an infinity pool to qualify as an estate. Possibly a tennis or squash court."

"I'm getting a freaking waterfall," he reminded her. "I've given it thought, started after my admin managed to bring me out of the fugue state induced by shock, and a little awe."

She shifted, hooked her thumbs in her front pockets. "I considered giving it to you in smaller bites, but it felt like cheating. Why don't you tell me what's an absolute 'no, forget it, are you crazy,' and I can adjust the plans and the costs?"

"Nothing."

She stopped dead. "You don't want any of it? It's your place, Zane, but I have to tell you, you need, at minimum, the foundation plantings, a couple of trees. With that, I could handle the work myself and give you a better break on labor."

"You misunderstand me, though that was exactly my first reaction. Absolutely no, forget it, she's crazy. Then I made a couple of mistakes."

"What kind of mistakes?" She wasn't entirely sure where he was going, even though she started to get a little buzz under her skin.

"First? I showed the plans to some friends, my family. Big mistake there. Next, I did a little tour of the bungalows you've finished. I even ran into a couple of guests outside one, a couple who've come every spring for the last three years. Emily gets a lot of repeats."

"Having been a guest myself, I can tell you why. Good accommodations, stunning view, exceptional and personal customer service."

"Which is pretty much what they said. Then they added that with the work done on the outside, they liked sitting on the front porch and looking out at the yard as much as the lake. Or having a drink on the back patio after spending the day on the lake. How everything looked so nice, how it felt like—I quote—their 'little private Eden.'"

"That's very nice."

"Then I still went home and thought: No, no, and no, maybe here, maybe, I'll consider that one. I got to the game today, after thinking more, with: No and no, maybe, okay, probably. And then . . ."

He stopped by her truck, looked around. He could see the mountains, shining under the pure blue of the sky, the houses, green grass, painted porches, flowers planted. He could hear the game—sound carried.

He knew the ground under his feet, the taste of the air.

"Then watching the game, sitting with Emily and Lee, saying hey to people I know, who know me. Who knew me. I thought, This is it for me. This is it. That's my house up there, this is my home, these are my people. That's why I came back. That's why I'm staying. That's why, fuck it. It's mine. And I want it all."

"All of . . . this."

"Of this," he agreed when she gestured around her. "And all of your staggeringly ambitious plans."

She held up a finger, turned away, walked a few steps away. "This is unexpected."

"Are you saying you can't do it?"

"Of course I can do it." She spun back. "I don't offer what I can't deliver. I didn't expect you to—I didn't expect. Well, hot damn." She came back, punched him lightly in the arm. "Hot, steaming damn. This is going to be great. You're not going to regret it."

"I better not. I just said yes to everything you wanted."

She shook her head. "You wanted it, too, or you wouldn't say yes."

"Regardless, I said yes, and all I get's a punch in the arm and I won't regret it."

"You're right. You are completely right. You deserve better. I can do better."

She threw her arms around his neck—that was unexpected—and did much better with a long, hard kiss, one she put a little punch into.

Enough of a punch to rock him back on his heels, to have his hands gripping her hips before he could stop them.

Then she pulled back, grinned at him. "There now. I've got to get back to work—and stop to buy subs for the crew on the way. But I'll be in touch."

He held on just another moment. "You *are* hot."

She laughed, kissed him again—light and friendly this time. "Told ya."

She pivoted to her truck, hopped in, then leaned out the window. "I'm still not paying you a million dollars."

With that, she started the truck, pulled out. She circled back toward town, and when she was well out of sight, pulled the truck over.

"Holy crap." Inhaling, exhaling slowly, she rubbed her hand over her jumping heart. "Holy double crap."

As if getting the job—the *whole* thing—wasn't thrilling enough?

She'd whacked herself silly with an impulsive kiss on the side of the road.

Anyone would need a minute to settle down.

Keep it light, she told herself. Keep it light, or try to. Who knew better the consequences of impulsive mistakes?

"Okay then, all good." She breathed out one more time, then ordered up her phone, the number for her stone company. Asked for her rep.

"Hi, Kevin, Darby McCray, High Country Landscaping. You can put that order through. How about we go over it, make sure we've got it right?"

By the time she parked at Emily's, she had her first deliveries confirmed. She hauled out the bag of subs and chips, stood studying the now completed shrubbery.

Perfect.

The foundation plantings, also perfect. And with the new stonework, the fresh paint, the clematis climbing up the new lamppost, the house had some serious curb appeal.

She had some great planters in mind for that fabulous wraparound porch. And since Emily actually cooked, there'd be a couple of tomato plants, plenty of herbs.

She walked around the back to where Roy and Hallie tested another section of irrigation.

She beamed at both of them. "We're going to need a bigger crew."

The following week, Graham Bigelow walked out of prison after eighteen years. His hair, shorn short, was steel gray with hints of white at the temples. Deep lines carved into his prison pale face, around his mouth, his eyes, in his cheeks, his forehead. He wore khakis and a pale blue golf shirt over a body, a bit thicker in the middle than it had been, but one he'd kept fit in the prison gym.

Eliza waited for him outside the gate. She wore a sundress in emerald green. Her hair, freshly colored and styled, swept dark around a face she'd spent a full hour perfecting.

Legs shaking, she walked to him, wrapped her arms around him, felt his wrap around her. She fought back tears as she lifted her face, and for the first time is nearly two decades, felt his mouth on hers.

He turned her to the car, the black Mercedes he'd approved her to purchase. Though his hands balled into fists for an instant—he had no license to drive—he opened the driver's door for her, walked around to take the passenger seat.

His eyes held hard on the prison gate, the prison walls, the prison guards, all that had kept him locked away and humiliated. Still shaking, Eliza drove away.

"Graham. Oh, Graham."

"Just drive, Eliza. I need to get away from here."

"Everything's ready for you, my darling. Your new clothes, your favorite foods. I sold the house like you said, rented the one you wanted in another neighborhood. The lawyer said we have to stay in North Carolina, but we can apply to move from Raleigh. I thought Charlotte. We can start fresh there."

The cars whizzed by, too fast. Too many. Too much sound, too much open, too much sky.

"Don't worry." She laid a hand over his. "Don't worry, Graham. You're free now. We're free, and we're together. We'll be home soon."

Finally, she pulled into the drive of a two-story brick home—smaller, much smaller than the one he'd left so long ago. But the old neighborhood with its cracked sidewalks meant room between houses, trees and fences forming borders and separation.

She drove into the one-car garage. And he felt a terrible relief at the sound of the garage door closing.

Inside again, away from too much open, noise, prying eyes. Inside with no bars, no locks.

They had sex first, fast and hard. Driving himself into her, feeling the bite of her nails, the rush of her breath, he began to feel like a man again.

They showered together.

She heated up the meal she'd hired a caterer to cook so it would be perfect, and set the table with candles, poured champagne.

They ate and drank together, went back to bed together, more gently this time.

They slept together and woke together, snuggled in bed with coffee together.

Began a new life together.

It took him nearly forty-eight hours to strike her.

CHAPTER FOURTEEN

As spring rolled toward summer, Darby hired Ralph Perkins as a part-time laborer. The squat barrel of a man with a mass of gray hair and bifocals came with experience as a stonemason and could operate the heavy machinery. What he knew about trees and plants wouldn't fill a bucket, but she wanted an experienced hand to help with Zane's hardscaping.

And to Darby's thinking, anyone could be taught to plant, from an oak to a petunia.

Ralph didn't use two words if a grunt would do, drank Dr Pepper like water, and had a delicate touch with the mini excavator Darby had invested in.

He'd also taken a shine to Gabe, and patiently taught the boy the art of building a retaining wall.

Zane watched the lower terrace take shape, move from a steep, rocky slope to a wide ledge formed from the bite of the excavator's claw.

He'd lost count of the number of times he'd stood on his bedroom terrace, drinking his morning coffee, and worried that damn machine would slide right over the edge.

But Darby appeared to know what she was doing, and so did the new guy. So disaster was averted.

He shot them a wave each morning as he headed to his office. Most days they'd knocked off before he returned. But he'd see little bits of progress—mostly bigger, wider holes.

One day he drove home and found trees lining the steep road, and the foundation or footers or whatever they called it for the front-facing wall.

As the wall began to take shape, actual stone rising, he'd catch himself slowing, even stopping on the drive up. He thought, every time, how it should have always been there.

He thought of Darby and her crew like elves who labored away when no one could see, then vanished like mists.

It surprised him to find her there one evening when he pulled up. Almost as much as it surprised him to see the spread of foundation plants along his veranda. Darby, in cargo shorts and boots, a T-shirt and cap, was on her hands and knees spreading mulch.

She stood as he parked, waited for him to walk over.

"What do you think?"

"It looks great. Scary great. Like 'I have to learn stuff' great, which isn't great."

"Low, slow growers, easy care."

"Those don't look easy. What are they?"

"Mophead hydrangeas, and they are easy. I love that variety with the intense green and blue, the touch of pink on each petal. Unique. The flowers grow on the old wood, so you don't want to prune at the wrong time of year. So don't prune. They're going to give you color until well into the fall. And you've got evergreens for structure year-round, more bloomers, good texture."

She dusted her work gloves against each other. "The wall's coming along, so I put Roy and Hallie on this to give you a nice little bang when you got home. You've been really patient, Walker, and deserved a splash."

"It's a splash. Seriously, it's beautiful. You're an artist."

"That's a lift to the end of my day. Thanks."

She had damn good legs, he mused. Long, toned arms. She smelled like cedar chips and grass.

"I haven't talked to you except by email since you were in the office."

"You give good email."

"So do you. Want a half a beer?"

"Absolutely."

"Come on in."

"Ah, grungy," she pointed out, spread her arms. "I'm not going to track through your house."

"We'll sit out here. I'll bring it out."

When he went in, she brushed herself off, stowed her gloves. After climbing up to the veranda, she settled into one of the deep, wide chairs with the thick navy cushions he'd chosen, let out a long, end-of-day sigh.

It felt damn good to just sit. Even better to just sit, admire the view, smell the fresh mulch.

When he came out, handed her a glass, she tapped it to his bottle. "You did good on the furniture out here. Comfortable, casual class."

"I like it." He sat in the chair beside hers, gestured to the view. "Now I'm king of all I survey."

"Damn right. How's the lawyering business?"

"Chugging along."

And satisfying, he mused. More satisfying than he'd expected.

"I've got myself an intern for the summer, and she's working out. She's smart. I don't have to ask you how business is going. I'm in the middle of it. You were right about the wall."

"Yeah, I was."

He just shook his head. "Not just the aesthetics, which have yet to be fully realized, but from the relief on my sister's face when they all came up for a cookout and she saw what was going in."

"Good. And how'd that go? The cookout?"

"All I had to do was provide the burgers, dogs, drinks. Since Emily and Britt made everything else, it went just fine. So, the ex-husband."

Brows lifted, Darby glanced over. "That's some segue."

"Inside my head, it was. What's the story, or is it off-limits?"

"If it was off-limits, I'd have said a line drive broke my nose." She shrugged. "Okay. I've just finished college, and there he is. Great-looking guy, a friend of a friend of a friend I meet at a party. Trent Willoughby."

"Willoughby. *Sense and Sensibility*."

"Points for you knowing Austen."

"Big readers in my family," he told her.

"Yeah, mine, too. So Willoughby—and he's just that handsome and charming and romantic. Trust-fund kid, but I don't hold that against him. He's started up his own advertising firm with two of his college buddies. We talk, some sparks, and since he's a friend of a friend of a friend, I figured sure, we can exchange numbers."

"I guess he called."

"The very next day. He hadn't moved on me at the party, kept it easy. So he says his family has a box at Camden Yards, and the O's are playing at home, would I like to go? I go, because who wouldn't? If you've never watched a game from a box, you're missing something. I also discovered he knew next to nothing about baseball, but I found that endearing, right? He'd made the date to please me. Sweet.

"One thing led to another, blah, blah, blah. I met his family, he met my mother. Everything was smooth. We dated for six months, and all I saw was this terrific guy, considerate, interesting, crazy about me, romantic. He takes me to Paris—I mean freaking *Paris*—for a long weekend."

With a half laugh, she sipped more beer. "I'd never been out of the country, never, in fact, been west of the fricking Mississippi, and now I'm in Paris. It's dazzling. And he proposes to me on the banks of the Seine, with the moonlight, and Jesus, I wasn't thinking about marriage—not yet, down the road—but Paris, moonlight. So, I said yes."

She took a moment and studied her beer. "I didn't really want a big, splashy wedding, but it got out of hand—or out of my hands. You could say his family sort of took over, and I got swept up. If I tried to throttle it back, he'd say how it would hurt their feelings. Anyway, more blah, blah, blah. I can say, looking back I can now see there were signs. But that's hindsight. Was he demanding, possessive, domineering? Yes, to all, but so subtle, and offset by that crazy-about-me, the romance, the little sweet things.

"I was stupid," she murmured. "And he was just so good at it."

"It doesn't take being stupid to get taken in," Zane corrected.

"Maybe, maybe not. Anyway, right before the wedding, he drove me out to this fancy gated community, pulled up to this monster house in a maze of monster houses. Our house, he told me. And I'm 'but—but.' His parents put down the deposit as a wedding gift. Done deal, not once consulting me. But he rolled over that. Surprise! Ten days before the wedding, and I'm a little sick. I don't want this monster house in Stepford Land, one that's a solid forty minutes from my mother, from our business."

"Did you tell him?"

"Tried. Not hard enough. I let him manipulate me, no question there. I thought, Well, I can make it work. I can landscape the yard, make it mine. I can just get up earlier to get to work. I loved him, didn't I? The important thing is we were starting our lives together.

"So we did. We had the big, splashy wedding his family somehow pulled off in six months because I should be a spring bride. Even though that's our busiest season. We had a honeymoon in Paris, where he started pushing for me to go off birth control so we could start a family."

"You didn't talk about kids before?"

"We did, and we'd agreed to wait a little. So I pushed back there, I want a year with him first before we talk kids. Hell, I was only twenty-three, I had plenty of time.

"We're barely home when he gets back on that again. He wants to make a baby with me, start our family. Don't I want to have his children? Then it's that I work too much, too hard. I'm coming home too late, and too tired. Owning a business should mean I don't have to work."

At Zane's quick laugh, she had to smile.

"Right? Owning means you work the hardest, but he didn't get it. And I'd already seen he didn't exactly put in tons of time and effort in his own firm. So it's around and around, up and down."

She paused, stared out at the view, the boats gliding on the lake. He waited, saying nothing.

"Six weeks and two days after I said 'I do,' I come home from a long, sweaty day that ended with me fighting ugly traffic, and he's sitting there, drinking a gin and tonic."

She had to stop again, let out a little breath. "He's laying down the law. Look at me, exhausted, filthy, and he's coming home to an empty house. A house he provided for me. I'm to sell the business and start behaving like a wife.

"I was so tired. It wasn't the work, you know, I loved the work. It was that horrible commute. I said no, I wasn't selling the business, and I wasn't going to talk about it because I needed a shower. The next thing I knew I was on the floor."

She shook her head. "In the year I'd known him he'd never shown any signs of violence. None. He could be demanding, yes, pushy, single-minded, and yeah, he could strike out with words. But that backhand shocked the hell out of me. It seemed to shock him, too. He was immediately contrite, appalled at himself. He cried. He made excuses—he'd had a terrible day, too much to drink, he'd been so worried about me, and more. He begged for forgiveness. I'd been married six weeks, and now the man I'd married was on his knees, weeping."

Zane said nothing. He already saw the end.

"I told him he had one chance, only one. If he ever hit me again, we were finished. Not only that, I'd file charges."

"How long did it take him?"

"Three weeks. By then I'd realized it wasn't going to work, that I fell for the man I thought he was, not the man he actually was. I'd been freaking Marianne Dashwood, and that was just mortifying."

He couldn't help himself, and put a hand over hers. "She turned out just fine."

"Yeah, it took her a while. Me, too. The man I had married was so damn needy and . . . just not altogether right. If I spent time outside of work with my mother or a friend, I was taking time from him. If I disagreed about the smallest thing, I was attacking him. Didn't love him enough. Any time, effort, affection I gave to anything or anyone else was stealing it from him."

Stupid, she thought again. She'd been incredibly stupid.

"I came home from work, and he went right at me. Verbally first. He even accused me of having an affair with one of the crew—a guy I'd known forever who was happily married with two kids. My mistake was to laugh at that one. Then he went at me physically."

She paused for a moment, studied the view until she felt settled again, able to finish.

"No backhand this time. The first punch broke my nose, and he was raging, pounding. You can't think when someone's beating you like that. You just try to get away, make it stop. Basically, he beat the crap out of me, tearing at my clothes, screaming all the time, and I couldn't make it stop, I couldn't get away. At some point we must've knocked a lamp over because I got my hand on it and hit him with it, hard enough to stun him. I ran outside. There were neighbors out in their yards, thank God. I just ran screaming for help. I couldn't even see where I was running. People came over to help me, even when he came charging out of the house, they helped me. Somebody called the cops, and they helped me. Even when he tried to spin it that I'd attacked him—that didn't fly.

"I filed charges, I filed for divorce, and moved back in with my mother. She was a brick, an absolute brick. He got a really good lawyer, but I had the medical records, the police report, the witness statements. He got three to five."

"Should've been more."

"Well, really good lawyer. He got out in three. I had a restraining order, but come on."

"Did he come after you again?"

"He caught me when I got home one night after seeing a movie with some friends. But he got the surprise this time. I'd taken self-defense courses, and martial arts. Kung fu."

"No shit? Kung fu?"

"Bet your ass. I'd earned my brown belt by then, so he got worse than he gave. Mostly because it caught him off-guard. I called the cops, and they picked him up. He did the full five."

"Should've been more.

"Shoulda-coulda. My mom and I talked about moving when we knew he'd get out, but damn if I wanted that. We had a home, the business, and he had to know if he came after me again, he'd do more than five. But when she died, there wasn't any point staying. So fresh start."

She finished the beer. "And that's my story."

"Has he bothered you again?"

"I haven't seen or heard from him. I don't see how he'd know where I am now, or, after all this time, why he'd come down here to mess with me. So that's that."

"You wouldn't have been his first."

She tapped a finger toward him. "Smart guy. With a little digging we found out he'd smacked around a couple others. Nothing as violent as my experience, but it was a pattern. Moral of the story is don't let a good-looking guy with a cool name charm you into marriage. Though it seems like since the actual marriage lasted about three months it shouldn't really count."

"You could get it annulled. I happen to know a lawyer who could help you with that."

"Thought about it, but it doesn't seem worth the trouble. Finished's finished."

Like closing the book, he thought. But he knew it always stayed inside you. Always.

"Are you hungry?"

"Yet another interesting segue. I could be hungry. What have you got?"

"The only thing I'm sure I have is frozen pizza."

"Pizza is never wrong. And I could probably have the other half of the beer if I had pizza."

"Let's eat."

"I'm going to take my boots off out here, and wash up in your powder room."

"That works." He rose as she bent over to deal with her boots. "Kung fu?"

"I've got a black belt now. Second degree. I'm ditching the socks, too. They're sweaty."

"You're a really interesting woman, Darby."

"You're a good-looking guy with a cool name, so don't try to charm me into marriage."

"I'll refrain."

He opened the door, and she walked into the house on bare feet. With toenails painted the same dark green as her tat.

Which reminded him.

"What's the story with the tat?"

"Oh." She lifted a hand to it. "I got it the day they found Trent guilty. Life goes on, right? My mother liked to say that no matter how bad or good things were at any given moment, it moved along. Life just cycles."

Now she looked around. "You've got more stuff," she noted.

"Yeah, I've been picking up this and that now and again."

"That is nice." She pointed to the painting over the fireplace. The lake at sunrise, misty and secret, taking hints of color from the blooming eastern sky.

"Yeah, it caught me. Local artist."

"It captures the moment. I'd have expected, you being a man, to see a big-screen TV up there."

"I've got that in the great room."

"It's looking good, Walker, seriously good. Is it starting to feel like home?" she asked as they walked back to the kitchen.

"It is. Yours?"

"I'm concentrating on the outside work right now. The interior needs a lot of help, but it can wait until winter when work slows down. Or rainy days."

He pulled a pizza out of the freezer. "Pepperoni okay?"

"Pepperoni's been okay since the dawn of time." While he pre-heated the oven, she slid onto a stool. "I like watching a good-looking guy with a cool name slave over a hot stove."

"Ha. You should see me create my amazing PB&J." He got out a beer, a fresh glass, split it with her. "So are you doing the interior work yourself, too?"

"It's mostly cosmetic. There's scary wallpaper almost everywhere. So pull it off, no doubt sand the walls, paint. I've been picking up some this and that now and again, too. And your kitchen inspired me."

"It did?"

"Yeah, the glass fronts. My kitchen cabinets are crap. Absolutely crap. Eventually I'll replace them, but I figured on painting them for now. Then I thought about your glass fronts. I took the doors off instead. I mean, what am I hiding? I painted the rest, got some pretty dishes and glassware. Done. Well, I had to paint the lower cabinets."

She sipped her beer when he unwrapped the pizza, slid it into oven, set the timer.

"Okay, so you got my broken nose story. Do I get yours?"

He lifted his bottle to drink, studied her over it. "I'm surprised you haven't heard it already."

"I would be, too, because people tend to tell me stuff. All kinds of stuff. But what I've found is people around here are very careful and respectful of the Walker/Keller family. I can be, too, if you'd rather not tell me."

"It's not a secret. I'm surprised and kind of touched the whole thing isn't low-hanging fruit on the gossip vine. Do you want the condensed version or the full narrative?"

"I like long stories. Details matter."

"Well, it might take a while. To start, my father knocked my mother around as long as I can remember. Graham Bigelow. Dr. Graham Bigelow, admired, respected, prosperous, important. On the outside, he and Eliza, his wife, were perfect. They had two perfect children and lived in the Lakeview version of Stepfordville."

"Lakeview Terrace."

Intrigued she'd nailed it, which likely meant she saw it as he did, he nodded. "That's the one. He was chief surgical resident at Mercy Hospital in Asheville. She played hostess, charity chairwoman, PTA president. We had a housekeeper/cook three times a week. Groundskeepers, a couple of Mercedes in the garage. Your polished upper-class family."

"But there were undercurrents. That's what I call them, like what was in Trent."

"That's a good term for it." Idly, he picked up the baseball he'd left on the counter, rubbed the stitching. "Yeah, plenty of undercurrents. You never knew when he'd go off. Never in front of anyone, always careful where he hit. The other—we'll use it—undercurrent, one I didn't understand for a long time, was Eliza, my mother, liked it."

"Oh, Zane—"

"I know what you're going to say. I know the pathology of a battered spouse, the many reasons for not leaving, for taking on the blame. That's not this. That'll come clear as we go along."

"All right."

"I don't remember, not clearly, the first time he hit me. I don't mean a swat on the butt. He favored gut punches, kidney punches, the ribs. He knew just where to hit. He didn't hit Britt, not back then. He belittled her, all of us, but that was his main abuse for her. Verbal and emotional abuse. We, Britt and I, were never, never good enough."

"That's a horrible way to grow up. You didn't tell anyone?"

"He was terrifying, and they were a unit. We were afterthoughts, status symbols. Even, in a way, their beard. If he started on her at night, Britt would usually come to my room. We'd just sit there until it stopped. When it stopped, the sex started. That was almost as disturbing.

"Anyway, that was our life, the pattern of it. That changed December twenty-third, 1998."

He laid it all out, coming home with Britt, the blood, the shouts. How he'd snapped and tried to stop Graham. The beating that followed.

"So," he finished, "I understand getting the crap beat out of you."

When the timer went off, he got a round platter, slid the pizza onto it. He pulled a cutter out of a drawer. "I suppose you want a plate for this."

"I . . ." She had to breathe out, to breathe away the fist squeezing her heart. "I insist on a plate. In fact, I'll get them, as I can see them through the handy glass fronts."

"Knife and fork?"

She managed a haughty look. "Don't insult me. How about I take the plates out back to your excellent new table? It's a nice evening for eating outside."

"Works for me."

She took the plates out, gave herself a moment. She couldn't think past the two children, living in cruelty and fear and violence. And somehow surviving it, not being dragged down by those ugly undercurrents.

He came out, sat across from her, slid a slice onto her plate.

"You have an actual pizza server. I'm impressed."

"Well, it's a staple around here. Do you want the rest?"

"Yes, but only if you want to tell me."

"We got this far. They told everybody I had the flu. My grandparents were coming in from Savannah, staying with Emily. We were supposed to all have Christmas dinner—catered—at our house. But they switched that up. They wouldn't let anybody come up to see me. Emily made me chicken soup, brought it over, but they wouldn't let her come up. Britt told me Em really tried, but they made her leave. What could she do?"

"I'm glad. I want to say she's about my favorite person in Lakeview. I'm glad she tried to help you, to stand for you."

"She did more than that—that part's coming. We went to this ski resort on Boxing Day, family tradition. He loaded me in the car, in the garage, left really early. He told the people at the resort I'd had an accident on my bike. When we got back, he told everybody I'd had an accident on the slopes."

"Did that actually work?"

"For a while. I healed up, and I went to Dave—Micah's dad. I asked him to teach me how to lift. I said I wanted to build myself up for baseball."

"You wanted to get stronger." His version of her martial arts.

"And I did. They'd decided I'd go to medical school, and I'd decided I'd apply for baseball scholarships when the time came. I wouldn't tell them. I'd earn scholarships, save my money, get a job, whatever it took. And when I turned eighteen, I could get out. He'd never hit Britt, and she just had to get through a couple more years. I'd do whatever I could to look out for her. But he was never going to beat me like that again."

He bit into a slice. "And, of course, when I played college ball, the Oriole scouts would be amazed at my skill and scramble to sign me on the spot."

"I heard you had amazing skill. State, Athlete of the Year."

"It's all I wanted in the world. But things changed again."

He told her about the dance, Ashley.

"Ashley Grandy? Grandy's Grill Ashley?"

"That's her."

"She's terrific."

"First love." He patted a hand on his heart. "It was a great night, a sweet night. Until I got home—four minutes after curfew—and he was waiting."

Darby listened with growing horror. The viciousness, the ugliness, the desperate boy trying to protect his sister. Fighting back only to have his own mother attack and betray him.

"But, my God, how could they believe you'd attacked your family that way?"

"Because Dr. Bigelow said I did, and Eliza stood right with him and said the same."

"No one believed you?"

"Dave did. He believed me, he stayed with me. He stayed the whole time, on the way to the hospital, in the hospital. I'll never forget it. He called Emily. He argued with the officer, but the officer had his orders from Graham's friend the chief."

Shock jolted her. "Not Lee!"

"No, not Lee, he wasn't in Lakeview back then. My arm was pretty fucked up, I'd have surgery later. But the bone doctor stabilized it. And she fought, too, but they had orders. I asked Dave to take my house key, get my notebooks from where I'd hidden them. And they hauled me to Buncombe."

"What is that?"

"Kid prison. Want another half a beer?"

"No." She felt a little sick. "No, thanks."

"Coke? Actual Coke's what I've got, not the southern term for soft drink of any kind."

"I . . ." Maybe he needed a minute, too. "Yeah, Coke's good."

When he went inside, she thought of her mother, and her absolute certainty her mom would have stood up for her against anything, anyone. How she had. How she stayed with her in the hospital, stayed with her while she talked to the police, to lawyers. Always there.

When he came back, sat, she leaned forward. "Your mother let them do that to you?"

"Without a qualm."

"Then you're right. She wasn't a victim. She was as much an abuser as he was. You must have been terrified."

"Numb by then mostly. Can't say I spent an easy night. What I didn't know was while I was being locked up, Britt was sneaking out of her hospital room. He'd been there when she woke up, threatened her, had her basically in isolation. No phone. She got into another room, used the phone to call Emily. Emily was already at the hospital trying to get some answers."

As he spoke, she imagined the little girl, hurt but making her way down the stairwell in bare feet and a hospital gown. And the woman who loved and believed her getting her out. Getting her to the police.

"And there was Lee. Detective Lee Keller of the Asheville PD," Zane continued.

"That's how they met?"

"Yeah. He listened. I don't know how much he believed at first, but he listened. Dave got my notebooks, drove back to Asheville, to the police. Lee believed enough to do what cops do. He made calls, asked questions. He talked to the resort, found out I'd come in that December already injured. Oh, and Graham had tried the 'he must be on drugs' gambit, but my tox was clean. Lee knew the old chief, and he went at him, cop to cop, laid out the evidence. The ski accident story fell apart just like the bike accident story. Lee came to see me at Buncombe, got me released into Emily's custody. And he arrested Graham and Eliza."

"He deserves someone as terrific as Emily. He's a hero."

"He's one of mine."

"Did they go to prison?"

"Eliza did a few years. He did eighteen and change. He's out on parole now."

Darby heard Zane's earlier comment echo in her head.

Should've been more.

"How do you feel about that?"

"There's nothing for them here but humiliation. He lost his medical license, and won't get it back. Eighteen years inside. I feel pretty good about it."

That was the lawyer, she supposed. She wasn't as convinced the boy inside the man felt the same.

"Have you ever been to see them?"

"What for?"

"I think that's a very healthy attitude. I'm not a therapist like your sister, but I've been to one. After Trent," she explained. "But I think severing all ties is healthy. They're toxic. Plus, your family's here, and they're terrific. I love that Emily and Lee fell in love. It gives it a nice dusting of goodness. She's your mom."

"She is, in every way that counts. Let's get all the hard stuff over with. How'd you lose your mom?"

"Hit and run."

"Ah, Jesus, Darby, I'm sorry. Did they get the driver?"

Darby shook her head. "She liked doing this three-mile run on Sunday mornings. It's quiet, there's a bike path to run on. They figured the car just mowed her down, kept going. They said she died on impact, and I hope that's true. They found the car abandoned about a half a mile past. Stolen."

She paused to drink. "The guy who owned it—classic '67 Mustang—had been refurbishing it with his son. It was in their driveway when they went to bed, gone when they got up. They figured kids hot-wired it sometime during the night. Joyriding, drinking, smoking weed. The car reeked of both, but they'd been smart enough after they'd hit my mother to get rid of the cans or bottles, empty the ashtray, wipe down the doors, the steering wheel. No prints, no DNA."

"Did they look at friends, classmates of the son of the owner?"

"Yeah. They looked at a lot of people, but they never found anything. Worst day of my life. She was a great mom."

"What about your dad?"

"He left when I was about four. It was the—you know Springsteen? 'Got a wife and kid in Baltimore, Jack. I went out for a ride, and I never went back.'"

She shrugged it off. "He was a decent guy for all that."

"How do you figure?"

"Well, they had savings, he didn't touch them. He didn't take the car—left it at the bus station—didn't take anything but his clothes and his Gibson guitar. He just couldn't hack husbandhood, father-hood, familyhood."

"As Britt would say: How do you feel about that?"

"I'm okay with it. I hate that he hurt my mother. She loved him. I barely remember him. I remember he was never mean, and I wonder if he left because he was afraid he would be if he tried to stay in a life that didn't make him happy."

"You've got a pretty healthy attitude yourself."

"We're a couple of healthy individuals."

"We should—First." He angled his head. "It occurs to me that outside of family, which includes Micah, Dave, and Maureen, I've never told that long saga to anyone. I have to think about why I told you over beer and pizza."

"People tell me stuff."

"Maybe. Anyway, now that the hard stuff is done, we should have dessert."

"Dessert?" She wiggled her eyebrows. "This is turning into quite the event. What have you got?"

"I have Swiss Rolls."

"Little Debbie?"

"Of course."

"Classic, I'm in."

CHAPTER FIFTEEN

They ate Little Debbies while dusk crept in and the sky over the western mountains burned.

"That's another painting," Darby pointed out. "Imagine sitting here, eating classic snack cakes, watching the sunset, and listening to the water spill melodically over rock and into its pool."

"You've already sold me that."

"But imagine anyway. You need a hummingbird feeder."

"Why?"

"Hummingbirds," she said simply. "Some of what I plant out here will attract them, and songbirds, butterflies. But they'd appreciate a good-looking feeder. This is so nice. I could play with your grounds for pretty much ever."

"I bet you could."

"But that's it for tonight. I'm going to load your dishwasher as a thank-you for food and drink."

"I could say you don't have to do that, but why would I?"

She rose, stacked plates, cleared the table. He followed her in, watched her deal with the dishes.

"You know," he began, "we haven't talked about that outside-the-ballpark kiss."

"Should we?"

"Here's what I'm thinking. You're a client of mine; I'm a client of yours. I think that washes the client deal out."

"I can agree with that."

"We've established we're healthy individuals. I'm a good-looking guy with a cool name, you're a hot woman who really knows how to wear cargo shorts."

"This is all true."

"Maybe we should go out for a drink, or dinner, or the movies. Or."

She turned around, leaned back against the counter. "You've already bought me a beer and a half, pizza, and Swiss Rolls. That covers drinks and dinner."

"I appreciate you acknowledging that. Movies then."

"I could be interested in a movie. I could be interested in 'or.'"

He stepped closer, watched her eyes. Yes, interest, with a good dose of amusement. "I have Netflix and all the premium channels. I can find a movie in two minutes."

"Do you have popcorn?"

"Newman's. Microwave."

"This is tempting." Especially when he laid his hands on her hips, as he'd done during that outside-the-ballpark kiss. "I'd enjoy a movie, and have a strong suspicion I'd enjoy 'or.' But—"

He paused on his way in to seal the deal with a kiss. "I'm not going to like this part."

"I'm grungy," she reminded him. "I'd like to embark on 'or' when I'm clean, and perhaps more appropriately dressed."

"You can use the shower. And I like your shorts. I especially like them when you're still wearing your boots."

"Thanks, and that's very generous of you. How about this? If you're not doing anything tomorrow night, I could shower at my own place after work, come over about nine for a movie. Then if we're both in the same frame of mind, we try 'or.'"

He believed in negotiations. "Eight-thirty. We'll have cocktails first."

"Oooh, cocktails. Fancy. I definitely need to clean up for that."

"Okay. What kind of movie?"

"Since the movie is basically foreplay, nothing weepy. I can go for a solid rom-com or action adventure."

"You're a really interesting woman."

He went in for the kiss, and she met him, rising up on her toes, linking her arms around him. He felt himself slide into it, into her, just slide like he would into the lake on a hot summer day.

The need washed over him, drew him deeper until his hands ran up her body, down her back, testing her shape, etching it into memory.

He felt her give just a little more, just a little more.

When he drew away, a breath away, her hand rested on his cheek, and her heart thudded in time with his.

"Maybe I like my women grungy."

"Oh boy." Her breath, wonderfully unsteady, fluttered against his lips. "It was such a sensible plan, too. If I'm going to change plans, convince me."

His mouth took hers again, let the heat flash, let the hunger out. This time when his hands took her hips, she boosted herself up, wrapped her legs around his waist.

"Convinced." On a throaty sound she nipped at the side of his neck. "You smell so much better than I do. Maybe I should take that shower."

"After."

"After," she murmured as he carried her through the house. "I'm supposed to be doing paperwork."

"Me, too." He paused at the bottom of the steps, gave her an extra dose of convincing, then carried her up.

"I love your house. I'd probably have had sex with you just to see what you've done with the rest of your house."

"Now she tells me."

She laughed, nuzzled his neck again, then her head popped up as he carted her through the open double doors of the master.

"Oh my God, look at this space!"

"I'll give you a tour later."

"Oh, don't put me on the bed. My clothes—"

"You won't have them on long. And I have more sheets."

He tumbled her on the bed, tumbled down right after her. And gripping her hands, dived into the kiss like a man starving.

Maybe he was. She'd stirred his appetite almost from the first glance, intrigued him from the first conversation. Then she'd flattened him at the ballpark.

Now he could feast.

Her hands, hard, strong; her mouth, smooth, soft. The sharply defined angles of her face, with the skin under her jaw, down her throat as delicate as silk. Tough, taut muscles, yielding breasts.

He found her a series of fascinating contrasts.

He tugged off her shirt, and she wasted no time returning the favor. More flesh, more muscle. She ran those firm hands over his chest, breathed out.

"Mmm, yes."

He wanted to look at her, just look, but he couldn't stop his hands. When they worked off the simple white sports bra, he thought, *Mmm, yes,* as he captured her breast with his mouth.

As she arched, he fought with the buckle of her belt, with the button of her shorts, riding on the urgency for more.

Breathless, struggling for some sense of control, a little finesse, he eased back. "I should slow down."

"No," she said, very definitely, and wiggled to help him strip her down. "No, you shouldn't."

"Thank God."

"Let me . . ." She worked her hands between them, quick, capable hands, loosened his belt. "Let me."

As she dragged at his pants, they rolled so he could kick free of them, rolled again, greedy to take.

Slow could wait. She wanted fast and fierce and free. Here, with him, she wanted the loss of control, for both of them, wanted to steep in the mindless desperation of mating. To be touched, to be wanted, to feel the need pulsing in him just as it did in her.

When he plunged into her, at last, at last, the pleasure struck sharp as an arrow.

Her hips pumped; her fingers dug into his as she reveled in the power and speed. Release ripped through her, leaving her trembling, gasping.

Grateful.

And still he drove her, building it all again.

She held on, held on, matching him beat for frantic beat. When she fell again, when the hands that gripped him slid weakly away, he fell with her.

After a moment where they both lay wheezing for air, he flopped over on his back so they lay, hip to hip, staring up, dazed as two survivors of a shipwreck.

"It's confirmed," he managed. "I like my women grungy."

Her laugh, still a little wheezy, ended with a sigh. "It looks like I like my men built. Not scary built." She reached over, patted his abs. "That can be intimidating. I'm going to get a better look at you once I stop seeing double."

"I guess we'll call that one the lightning round."

"We both won."

"Yeah, we did. It's been a while for me, so lightning round."

This was nice, too, she thought, that they could lie here, sated from sex, and have an actual conversation.

"What's 'a while'?"

"I guess about nine months, maybe ten." Staring up at the high, coffered ceiling, he decided his brain was too buzzed to accurately calculate.

"I had a sort of relationship. Not serious, but steady. When I decided to come back, she supported that, she got it. And we both decided to break off the sex."

"Nine or ten months?" Darby made a *pffft* sound. "That's nothing. I've got more than double that."

"Why?"

"Psychotic ex, time spent questioning my own choices, time to focus on self and business, losing my mother, deciding to uproot and replant. All of it."

"That could do it."

"Anyway, I think that worked out, too. We hit the-time-is-now button in sync."

He shifted, looked down at her. "Any thoughts about hitting it again?"

"Well, it worked the first time. But I absolutely want that shower. It's a really big shower, as I recall. Plenty of room for two healthy individuals."

"And plenty of hot water."

"Excellent. But I'm not putting those dirty clothes back on after a shower. I've got spare clothes in the truck, because you never know."

Russet, he thought, at the moment he'd call her hair russet. "If you're going to have sex?"

"If you're going to get covered with mud, or rip something." She rolled out of bed. "I'll run out and get them. Be right back."

"Wait. You're going outside like that?"

She shoved a hand through her hair. "Like what?"

"Naked. And by the way, *you're* ripped."

"The truck's right out front, and there's nobody around but you, who's already seen me naked. Two minutes."

As she dashed out, Zane pushed himself up. He didn't consider himself overly modest, but she was going outside naked.

The woman he'd left behind in Raleigh wouldn't have walked out of the bathroom naked.

She also wouldn't have stepped out of the house without doing her makeup, styling her hair. He didn't think he'd ever seen Darby wear makeup.

If anyone had asked, he'd have said she wasn't really his type. And yet, he was looking forward to getting her in the shower.

Rising, he walked to his terrace doors, opened them, stepped out to watch naked Darby pull a gym bag out of her truck. She looked up, laughed, spread her arms.

"I'd have gotten arrested for doing this in Baltimore."

He'd have sworn something shifted in his chest. "You look like a sylph, wearing nothing but moonlight."

"A sith?"

"No." Now he laughed. "Not one of the Dark Jedi. A sylph—mythological fairy type."

"I like that better. Is it okay if I stop off in the kitchen? I can bring up some water."

"I've got a minifridge in the dressing room up here."

"Of course you do. Coming up."

The alarm clock in her head woke Darby just before dawn. She lay still, thought about the fact that she woke in Zane's bed.

She hadn't meant to stay, and she didn't think he'd meant her to stay. Sex between healthy, willing individuals equaled one thing. Sleeping together added another layer of intimacy.

But shower sex had led to a craving for more Swiss Rolls, then the snack cakes had somehow led to yet more sex. And that round—call it the slow dance round—had enervated both of them.

So when he'd mumbled, "You should just stay," she'd managed an "Okay," before she'd dropped straight into sleep.

Now the problem. She had to get up, get dressed probably a full hour or more before he did. It had been a long time since she'd slept with someone, and she hoped she hadn't lost her ninja skills.

While her eyes adjusted to the dark, she put the room, the furniture placement in her head. Terrace doors to the right, master bath, walk-in closet, and dressing room to the left. That put the chest of drawers at about four o'clock, the love seat and coffee table at about eight.

And the bench at the foot of the bed—where she'd dumped her gym bag. She couldn't remember where yesterday's clothes had ended up, but she'd find them.

She eased out of bed, inched her way toward the bench, feeling with her foot for any stray clothes. She found yesterday's bra, T-shirt, rounded to her gym bag.

"Why are you sneaking around in the dark?"

She didn't jump, exactly, but her breath hitched at the mumbling coming out of the dark. "Damn it. Ninja failure. I'm sorry I woke you. The point of sneaking was not to wake you."

"I'm a light sleeper."

"Obviously. Go back to sleeping light. I'm going to get dressed in the bathroom. But since you're at least awake, you don't happen to have an extra toothbrush, do you?"

"Second shelf, linen closet. What Emily calls a hospitality basket. It's got spare everything. It's still dark."

"Actually, day's just breaking. Shh. Sleep."

She closed herself in the bathroom, opted for another quick spin in the shower. Following routine, she slathered herself with sunscreen from her gym bag. Once dressed, she found the toothbrush just where he'd said.

Now she needed to find yesterday's pants, which included her belt, her phone, her multi-tool, and loose change.

She'd intended to sneak out, but she opened the door to light, and to Zane standing in his boxers at the open terrace doors.

"It is a break between night and day," he said. "I never really thought about it before."

"I love how the birds wake at first light, get so excited." She crossed over, kissed him on the back of the shoulder. "But I'm sorry I woke you up."

"There was a woman in my shower, so I started thinking about the wet, naked woman. Who could sleep?"

"Since you can't, do you trust me to make coffee?"

He turned, studied her. "You'll make coffee?"

"I'll make coffee, especially if you have any kind of cereal. Not that a Little Debbie isn't perfectly acceptable breakfast food, but I try to save that for weekends."

"I have Cheerios."

"Excellent. Any fruit?"

"I think I have bananas."

"Then I'll even fix breakfast." She gave him another light kiss, started out, scooping up the rest of her clothes on the way.

By the time he came downstairs, she'd opened his great room doors to the morning. She'd set his outdoor table again, unearthing place mats he never used, actual napkins, even a small vase now filled with what he assumed were colorful weeds. She'd put out bowls, a sugar bowl and creamer, a pitcher of juice, glasses.

If you took away the box of Cheerios, the table looked like the setup for a casual yet sophisticated breakfast alfresco. He noted her boots now stood by the open back door, and she walked in barefoot.

"Hey. I wasn't sure how long you'd be so I held off on the coffee. I also needed a couple minutes to figure out your fancy machine."

She walked to the fancy machine as she spoke, placed one of his oversize mugs. "Go ahead and sit down. I'll bring it out."

Still blurry, he did as he was told while the machine whirred and finally that life-giving scent hit the air.

She brought out mugs—one no more than two-thirds full. When she set the other in front of him, he lifted it, inhaled the first dose straight into his brain.

"You drink it black. I'm always amazed at people who drink black coffee. I don't actually like coffee."

As he watched, she flooded her mug with milk, showered it with one, two, dear God, three spoonfuls of sugar.

"That is no longer coffee."

"Exactly. But it still has that punch I go for in the morning."

Shaking his head, Zane dumped cereal in her bowl, then in his own. She doctored hers with milk, rapidly sliced half a banana over it. Held out the rest.

"You want?"

"I guess."

Before he could take it from her, she sliced banana over his cereal.

"No sugar?" he asked as she spooned up a bite.

"I like Cheerios. And I see you've combined the Honey Nut with the Very Berry."

"Yes, I have."

"I find that brilliant, and see myself emulating your style in my own home."

They ate in easy silence until he gestured toward the vase with his spoon. "Aren't those weeds?"

"Wildflowers," she corrected. "Native wildflowers. Yours, as your pretty clump of woods is alive with them. Trillium, Johnny-jump-ups, cranesbill. I can see I need to get you a book so you can identify your own treasure trove."

He drank more coffee. "You look good in the morning. And you smell like the beach."

"Thanks. That's sunscreen, and it won't last. The beachy scent, I mean. I slap it on every few hours, but the beach loses to sweat, dirt, and whatever. Which I need to get started on."

"The crew's not here."

"They will be." She rose, started stacking dishes.

"I'll take care of that. You cooked."

"I did set the table, and what I don't know about cooking I make up for in presentation. I'll take these in because I'm going to steal a Coke for later."

He carried the rest in behind her, got a Coke out of the fridge, handed it to her. "Are we still on for movies and popcorn?"

Her smile hit her eyes first. "Sure. Eight-thirty, right?"

"Eight-thirty." He cupped her hips, drew her in, drew her up. Kissed her in a way he intended to have linger in her system until he saw her again.

"Well." Her fingers trailed through his hair. "If I came over at eight, you could give me that full house tour."

"Come at eight." And kissed her again.

As the days rolled on, the wall neared completion. Darby juggled jobs, pleased the work she'd done attracted interest. She spent more nights than she thought either of them intended in Zane's bed.

She didn't look toward the future there. For now, the future was her work, her place in Lakeview, the life she built for herself.

Still, the day she looked at the completed terraced wall, the lower level full of good, rich dirt prime for planting, she thought of Zane.

Whatever happened, he'd have this, and he'd remember.

"It's freaking beautiful." Gabe stood beside her, beaming in a way she understood. "I've never had a part in building anything like this. And it's freaking beautiful."

She hiked an elbow on his shoulder. He had a few inches on her five-seven. "It's going to be even better once we plant it."

Hallie wrapped an arm around Gabe's other shoulder, gave him a quick squeeze. "Let's get it done."

"Roy, why don't you go back and work with Ralph on the back wall. I'll get Hallie and Gabe started."

He took off his company cap, waved it in front of his face, settled it on his straggly hair again. "Miss Darby, you work me to death."

"You look lively enough to me. Besides, we need to finish what we can this afternoon. It's going to rain tomorrow."

Roy frowned up at the sky, tipped back his cap. "Don't look like rain's coming."

"Trust me. Or the National Weather Service. We're getting boomers tonight, and a soaker tomorrow. You can sleep late."

He brightened right up. "Maybe sleep all damn day."

She helped wheel over the plants, jumped down so Hallie could pass them to her, to Gabe. It took all three of them to muscle down the crepe myrtle she wanted for the far end.

When she'd placed them, she boosted herself back up, studied the effect. "Gabe, switch the mountain laurel, that one, with that azalea. Yeah, yeah, better balance. It's going to look great. Man your shovels, team. I'm going to check on Roy and Ralph."

She could see the good, solid bones of the wall as Roy and Ralph worked, communicating with grunts while Roy's iPod played country rock.

There she'd plant Bloomerang lilacs for the all-season color, the wonderful scent, one on either end as anchors to all the flow of texture and color between.

And when Zane sat out on his pretty patio, with those scents, those colors, with the little kitchen garden she'd already started in pots, he'd remember.

She took a good glug from her water bottle, dived into the work.

When Hallie called out, "You want to take a look, boss, before we start hauling mulch?" Darby stepped back, checked the time.

"Yeah, let me take a look. We can get that done, then you can knock off." She gave Roy a poke in the ribs. "All of you."

"I'm ready for that!"

"Zane'll be home before much longer," Hallie commented as she started back with Darby.

"Won't he get an eyeful?"

"Are you going to hang around till he does?"

"Depends."

Hallie stopped, out of earshot of Gabe in front and the men in the back. "You know, mornings when he wanders up to watch us working before he leaves for town, you can't help but feel the . . ." She wiggled her fingers in the air.

"The?" Darby mimicked the gesture.

"I know how to keep quiet, girl, but I'm telling you it's probably not as big a secret as you think that you and Zane are . . . spending time."

Darby honestly hadn't thought about it one way or the other. "It's not a secret, it's just, ah, discretion."

"That's a word." Hallie gave her a pat on the shoulder. "Anyway, he's what my granny would call a prime catch."

"I'm not playing catch."

"Boss, we're all playing catch. It's just nature."

Darby thought about that as she cleaned up, as the crew left. Maybe, just to test things out, she needed to push discretion a bit.

She hopped in her truck, drove home. Pausing on the road below, she looked up. And seeing that long curve of wall, the plants rising, fanning, she sighed.

"That's good work," she said aloud. "That's damn good work."

She'd barely showered off the day when the text came in from Zane.

Wow. Seriously wow. I owe you a beer, a bottle of wine, half my take-out lasagna. Come back.

Oh, she wanted to, maybe a little too much. But she looked around at so much in her own space she'd neglected.

Wait until dusk when the lights come up. Even more serious wow. Must pass on the beer or wine and lasagna. Gotta catch up on paperwork. Take a walk outside for me after dark.

I will. Don't work too hard. See you tomorrow.

Didn't anybody check the weather forecast? But she only typed back:

Night.

The storm crashed in with a flash and a boom. A solid sleeper, Darby slept right through the war of it. Then popped out of a dead sleep a full hour before her internal alarm. She lay in the dark, watching the electric slaps, listening to the echoing bangs and the thunder of flooding rain.

With sleep a fond memory, her mind circled from waterfalls—couldn't wait to start on it—to paperwork—all nicely current—to Zane. Was he awake, too?

If she'd gone back as he'd asked, she'd have company right now through the big, bad storm.

And her paperwork wouldn't be all nicely current.

Trade-offs, she supposed, as her mind continued to wander.

When lightning lit up the bedroom like a Broadway stage, she decided to get up. In the kitchen, she made coffee and drank it in the open doorway, absorbing the wrath of the storm.

Something to see, she thought, all that energy rolling and pounding, the cracks over the sky like shattered glass, the rocket flashes that threw the mountains into eerie relief before plunging them into the black again.

Still, it brought home to her just how isolated she was. She might be on an island somewhere on a raging sea.

With plenty of food, she reminded herself, a solid roof over her head, and power. At least she had power for the moment.

Thinking of that, she gathered up flashlights, checked the batteries, filled a couple of jugs with water, and thought about getting a small generator.

And a dog. Dogs were good company, she mused. She should definitely consider getting a dog.

But right now seemed a great time to attack ugly wallpaper.

By midday the storm had long since turned into a steady, soaking rain and the air to a steam bath. After breaks to vent frustration, Darby scraped off the last stubborn strip of kitchen wallpaper.

"Eur-fucking-reka," she muttered, and shoved her cap back to swipe at her face. "I won, you bastard."

Maybe her kitchen resembled a war zone, but she'd won. Now all she had to do was wash down the walls, which revealed themselves in a hideous shade of moldy green, wait for them to dry—probably sometime in the next century—prime, and paint.

She stepped over a pile of defeated wallpaper, crouched down to get a bucket from under the seat. And lost ten years of her life at the rap-rap on her open kitchen doorjamb.

There stood Zane, hair a little damp and wearing a dark suit.

"God, you gave me a start. I didn't hear you drive up in all this rain." A dog, she thought again. She needed to look into getting a dog. "You're wearing a suit."

"I was in court this morning."

"You look different. Good, but different."

He glanced around her war zone, smiled. "Housecleaning?"

Straightening, she jabbed a finger at ragged strips, piles, scraps of wallpaper. "I killed it."

"From what I can see, it looks like self-defense. I'll get you off."

"They wallpapered over wallpaper. Who knew?"

He studied the walls. "That paint color might be worse."

"I know it. I know it. I may have to get a priest, a shaman, a white witch, whatever, to come in here and exorcise the spirits of evil decorating."

"Are you doing this and lots of laundry? It smells like lots of laundry."

"Fabric softener. One part to one part really hot water equals a good, nonchemical wallpaper solvent."

"How do you know that?"

"Internet. Don't get any of this crap on your shoes. They look like really nice shoes. Is there food in that bag?"

"You were on my way back, sort of, from court, and I've got a couple hours before I need to be in the office. I picked up Chinese."

"You picked up Chinese." She may have fallen at least a little bit in love as he stood in her steam bath of a kitchen with its horrible walls in his lawyer suit and excellent shoes, holding a bag of Chinese takeout.

"I wanted to make sure you were okay. That was one bitch of a storm this morning. Branches and limbs all over the place. Plus, I wanted to see you."

Straight-up honesty, she decided, on both sides. "Hallie mentioned she—and people—are speculating about you and me."

"You're not in Baltimore anymore," he began, then angled his head. "Is having people speculate a problem for you?"

"No. I thought it might be for you."

"Why?"

She puffed out her cheeks. "I don't know, exactly. I'm out of practice, Zane, on how this all works. Plus, I'm the new girl around here, and you're the returning son."

And, he thought, their relationship, so far, almost exclusively consisted of evenings, nights, mornings at his house.

That he could fix.

"What are you doing Saturday night?"

"I'll have to check my busy social calendar."

"How about you squeeze in dinner at Grandy's?"

"I think I can juggle that in."

"For now, how do you feel about sweet and sour pork?"

"I feel really good about it. Why don't we eat out on the front porch. It's probably cooler out there than in here. And it's certainly less ugly."

"Sounds perfect."

"Just let me wash up—No, no, don't touch me. I'm disgusting."

"I think there's a clean spot right here." He continued in, cupped her chin, kissed her.

PART THREE

FROM ROOTS TO BLOOMING

Kind hearts are the gardens,
Kind thoughts are the roots,
Kind words are the flowers,
Kind deeds are the fruits.
—HENRY WADSWORTH LONGFELLOW

The earth remains jagged and broken
only to him or her who remains jagged and broken.
—WALT WHITMAN

CHAPTER SIXTEEN

The following evening, though she discouraged it, Zane came to her place to partner up in the battle of the wallpaper.

"You have no idea what you're getting into."

"You think I can't handle it. I have my own scraper." He held it up.

"Oh, it's all shiny and new. Not for long. All right, come on up. I'll show you the battlefield. And I'm letting you know right now, if you decide to back out at any time, I won't hold it against you."

"Obviously you doubt not only my skills, my endurance, but my . . . Holy shit." He gaped at her bedroom walls. "What is it?"

"It is the beast. It's what slouched toward Bethlehem to be born."

"It's . . ." Cautiously, he ran a hand down it, felt the weird texture. "It's somewhere between abandoned bordello and fresh hell. How do you sleep in here?"

"With my eyes closed."

"Even then. Maybe we need reinforcements. Or napalm."

"I figured we'd start with the bathroom. It's smaller."

He followed her across the hall, stared at the fish. "It's sort of oddly amusing."

"You wouldn't say that if you're in the shower and they're all staring at you."

"Bad, but not as bad. No, we go for the gold—and red and black. We take on the beast. Show me what to do."

Thirty minutes in, Zane looked at his partially stripped wall—and the screaming blue paint uncovered. He glanced over to check Darby's progress. Slightly better than his, but she'd had practice.

"Reinforcements," he announced. "I'll draft Micah."

"Zane, I can't ask him to—"

"You're not. I am. You got beer, wine, snacks?"

"Yes."

He pulled out his phone, so Darby swallowed objections. Especially when she looked at the walls, the room, and estimated hours before they'd eradicate her bedroom nightmare.

"He's in. Cassie's coming, too. She's actually done this before." He pocketed the phone. "She still has the tools."

She liked Cassie, who taught yoga, made pottery, and added a kind of bouncy, New Agey touch to Micah's laid-back geek.

"That's beyond nice of them. I'm just a little worried."

"What? They know you bought the house this way."

"Not that. It's . . . What if, in these close quarters, Micah's distracted by my hotness and hurts himself?"

"Funny." Zane grabbed her, pulled her in.

While Zane and Darby stripped wallpaper with the affable Micah and the chatty, cheerful Cassie, Eliza cleaned the dinner dishes.

Graham had actually complimented her attempt at chicken and rice, had eaten well despite the sticky rice and dry chicken.

No wonder she adored him.

She felt he'd adjusted very well. When he'd first gotten his driver's license reinstated, he'd insisted she accompany him everywhere. But he'd gradually regained his confidence.

She knew he disliked his job. Working in a medical supply store was lowering, but it fulfilled the terms of his parole, and now that he could drive to and from the strip mall, he'd gained some independence.

She hadn't cared for her job at first either—terms of her own parole. But now that Graham was back, and he'd insisted she quit, she found she missed the interaction.

She had no social contacts, and since he took the car, nothing to do all day but stay home.

Her old life, the parties, the club, the lunches with friends, all of it lived inside her like a dream.

Calculating his mood, the timing, Eliza mixed them both an after-dinner drink. The dishes could wait. After all, she'd have the entire next day, alone, to deal with them.

After carrying the drinks to the living room, she sat beside him. He kissed her cheek as she curled her legs up.

"Thanks, lover."

"It's such a nice night. Maybe we could take a walk."

"Too many nosy neighbors."

"I guess you're right." She tipped her head to his shoulder. "Graham, I've been thinking I should get a car."

"What for?"

"To shop, run errands."

"You do all that on my days off."

"Yes, but sometimes I think of something in the middle of the day, and I know how you dislike me asking you to pick something up on your way home."

The lines around his mouth only dug deeper. "You should be more organized. It's all you have to do, Eliza. You don't have to get up every morning and go to a humiliating, menial job, do you?"

"No." Instinctively, she rubbed a hand on his thigh. "I hate that you do. I hate it for you, but it won't be forever. When this is over, we'll be able to go wherever we want, start a real life together again. It'll be like it used to be, Graham. We'll buy a lovely house, join the country club. We can travel. We can—"

"Are you just stupid?"

"Graham."

"How are we supposed to pay for all that? Goddamn lawyers took nearly everything."

"I know, I know." She rubbed his thigh. "But we still have some money, and I have my trust. We—"

He threw the drink in her face, blinding her so she didn't see the first slap coming.

"Don't. Please. You promised after the last time you wouldn't hit me anymore. It's not like it used to be, Graham, and I can't—"

"Nothing's like it used to be." He slapped her again. "*Your* trust, you stupid, selfish bitch." He shoved her to the floor, hitting her again when she tried to scramble up and away. "You want a big house, the country club, a goddamn car so you can go wherever you please while I'm humiliated selling blood pressure cuffs?"

When he dragged her up, pushed her against the wall, she tried to twist away, but he wrenched her arm, shooting pain through her that buckled her knees.

"What do you do? What the fuck do you do? Sit around all day thinking of what to complain about? You can't even make a decent meal. You useless cunt."

"Stop, stop, stop."

"You want a car? You want a car so you can drive to some motel with whoever you were fucking while I was locked up like an animal?"

"I never—not with anyone. I waited for you."

"Liar." The gut punch would have doubled her over if he hadn't pinned her to the wall. "You could never go two days without sex. Who knows better?"

"With you. With you."

"With me." He shoved up her skirt, yanked down her panties. It hurt, it hurt. When he raped her against the wall, there was only pain, no thrill, no deep, dark excitement.

And when he'd finished, when she dropped weeping to her knees, he stepped back, zipped his pants. "You're not even good at that anymore."

He kicked her, but put no real force behind it. That glorious, energizing rage had faded. He walked into the kitchen, glanced with disgust at the dishes yet to be washed.

And mixed himself another drink.

After his clients left, Zane sat at his desk. Clint and Traci Draper had given him a bad feeling. The consult had been odd enough, a boundary dispute, with the potential clients' desire to sue a neighbor over what amounted to about twenty-five square feet of land.

Seeing as Draper claimed the land after a self-conducted new survey, his case was shaky at best. But what concerned Zane were the clients themselves.

The fact that Draper—down to the rebel flag belt buckle—appeared to put the red in redneck didn't bother Zane. His assertion that his neighbors had a faggot for a son did, considerably.

What had troubled him even more than Draper's brash, bigoted bullshit was the fact that his wife spent most of the consult with her eyes cast down and her mouth shut.

He knew the Draper family—hill people who kept to themselves. They'd had a reputation as hard-assed, bigoted troublemakers even when he'd been a kid. It struck him that Clint, the youngest of them, wanted to keep that rep going.

Rising, Zane circled the room, picked up his baseball, rubbed the stitching as he paced.

He remembered Traci's older sister, a little.

And wasn't it odd, when Zane had mentioned her sister, or asked any question of Traci directly, she'd glanced at her husband—as if for permission—before answering.

Not odd, Zane corrected.

Telling.

He put the ball back on his desk, walked out to reception.

"The Drapers didn't look happy when they left," Maureen commented.

"They wouldn't be after I pointed out that doing his own survey—one that two professional surveys dispute—wasn't going to fly on his claim for a foot-wide strip of land. Added to it, his neighbors have used said foot-wide strip of land, maintained it, have a hedge planted on it, for over twenty years. Pointing that out, suggesting if they wanted to pursue this boundary issue he hire a reputable surveyor made me, in Draper's opinion, an asshole city lawyer who didn't know shit about shit."

"Did you see the bumper sticker on his pickup?" Gretchen, a trim, petite streaky-haired blonde with a sharp legal mind, spoke up from her desk. "Sorry, interrupting."

"No, that's okay, and I didn't. What about it?"

"It said: You won't get my guns, but you might get my bullets."

"Charming." Zane sat. "What do you know about Traci, Maureen? I don't remember her at all, but I knew her sister a little."

"Not much. She's younger than my kids. Her dad's a mechanic. We still take our cars to his garage. Nice guy, friendly enough."

"Right, right, I forgot. Mr. Abbott, sure."

"The mother's a little shy, but affable. Works at the bakery here in town. The Drapers, now, they're more hill people than lake people."

"That I remember, too."

"Well, it seems to me the kids—four boys—were mostly home-schooled. I'm stretching my memory and talent for gossip," she added, "but I think one of them went into the service, another one just took off and ended up in jail for cooking meth. One's married, lives out there with his wife and kids on the Draper land. Clint would be the youngest, I think, and he and Traci got married about a year ago."

"Okay."

"If you want to know more, you might ask Lee. I know he's had the two youngest as guests—in jail—a time or two. But I'm wondering why you're asking if you're not taking them as clients."

"She never looked me in the eye, not once. She couldn't have said as much as ten words."

"She might be shy, like her mama."

"It wasn't shy. I've got some time, right?"

"You're clear for the next hour."

"I'm going to take a walk."

He walked straight to the police station. Of course, straight in the small-town South meant stopping half a dozen times over the three-block walk when someone called out to him, having conversations about the weather—hot and humid—how Emily was doing, how he liked living up in the fancy house.

When he finally got there, he found a couple of officers, including his brother-in-law, working at their desks, the dispatcher at her station.

More conversations, thankfully brief.

"I was hoping for a few minutes with Lee. Is the chief in?"

"Yep, in his office," Silas told him. "Go right on back."

He found Lee at his desk, scowling at his computer screen. The scowl cleared when Lee looked up. "A distraction, just what I need. Budget—pain in my ass. Come on in."

The office suited Lee—small, spare but for a few family photos. It held a couple of creaky visitor chairs, a bulletin board, a whiteboard— both covered—a coffee maker holding dregs, and a stack of files on the desk.

Though Lee's door was rarely closed, Zane closed it behind him.

Lee lifted his eyebrows. "Problem?"

"I don't know. I just turned away a client. Clint Draper."

"Ah." Nodding, Lee gestured to a chair, leaned back in his. "Boundary line. Doesn't matter how wrong he is, how many ways he's told he's wrong, he won't let it go. I guess he wants to sue Sam McConnell."

"On the strength of a survey he and his brother conducted themselves. He didn't like being told it wouldn't wash."

"Are you worried he'll take a swing at you?"

"Should I be?"

Lee puffed out his cheeks. "I wouldn't think he'd come at you. You're young and fit and he's a coward under it. We did answer a call a few weeks back. Mary Lou—Sam's wife—called nine-one-one when Draper started a pissing match with Sam over the line, tried hacking at the hedges. But then Sam's older than me, and not what you'd call robust. Those properties are just inside my jurisdiction. The rest of the Drapers belong to county, and I can't say I'm sorry about that."

"Maureen said you've had him here, as your guest, a couple times."

"Drunk and disorderlies, pushy-shovies."

"Have you ever been called out to his place for anything other than the border business?"

Once again, Lee lifted his eyebrows. "Such as?"

"He brought his wife—Traci—with him. I know the look, Lee, the attitude, the signals. I know when I'm looking at abuser and abused."

Now Lee let out a sigh. "We've never had a domestic disturbance call out there. I'm going to say despite the border bullshit, the houses aren't within spitting distance. And Clint's brother Jed, who he runs with, is on the other side. Old man Draper's land's behind Clint's place."

Zane nodded slowly. "So, she's surrounded."

"You could look at it that way. I know about a month after they got married, Traci took a fall, had a miscarriage. They both say she felt light-headed, tripped, and fell down the stairs. Her mother came to me, swore he'd done it somehow, but Traci stuck to the story, and there wasn't a sign that's not what happened."

"But it's not what you think happened."

"I know the signs, the attitude, the look, too. But she never budged from the story. I pushed it as far as I could, even slipped her Britt's card."

"All right. I wanted to see if my instincts on this hit the mark. Thanks, Lee."

"Nothing you can do," Lee said as Zane rose. "Nothing the law can do unless she changes her story, unless she comes to us for help."

"I know. I hope she does, because you could and would help her."

Maybe, Zane thought as he walked back to his office, she needed to hear that from someone who knew the fear, the helplessness.

He kept it to himself, but two days later, Zane drove out to the disputed property line. He took a casual walk along it, and up to the Draper house. He knew, because he'd asked around, the family had built the little two-story place.

He could see the windows sparkled, and someone had tried to spruce it up with a small, struggling flower bed. He could see a clothesline, a vegetable garden in the back—and Traci hoeing weeds.

When he wandered back, he knew, *knew*, by the look of alarm on her face he'd been right about her life here.

"Miz Draper." He gave her an easy smile, kept his distance. She wore a straw hat and a long cotton dress with the sleeves rolled to just below the elbows.

She had to be roasting.

And though he knew the answer, had made certain of it, asked, "Is Mr. Draper home?"

"He's at work. He's working with his brother at the feed and grain outside Asheville. You have to come back after four-thirty if you want words with him."

"Oh, that's all right. I just thought I'd come take a look at the line, maybe give y'all the name of a surveyor."

"He doesn't need a surveyor. He and his brother did it themselves. I need to get my weeding done."

"You've got some nice tomatoes going there. Pretty land."

It wasn't, but he could see she tried to make it so. "That foot-wide strip won't make any difference to you."

She kept her eyes down, wouldn't meet his. Her hands gripped the hoe like a weapon. "Clint wants what's his."

"Pretty sure he's got what's his. Miz Draper—Traci—I've been where you are."

Her eyes wheeled up, then down again. "I don't know what you mean. I need to get back to work now."

"I think you do know. Your sister was only a couple years ahead of me in school. She'd have heard the story. I was afraid, too. Afraid to tell anybody. Afraid he'd hurt me worse if I tried, or that no one would believe me. We can help you."

"You need to go. Clint doesn't like people coming by when he's not here."

"So he can keep you isolated, cut off. Under his thumb, with his family close and yours not. You can trust Chief Keller. You can trust me and my sister. All you have to do is ask for help, and you'll get it. He'll never hurt you again."

"My husband doesn't hurt me. Now you best leave."

"If you ever need help, you call." He took a card out of his case, laid it on the stump he imagined they used to chop wood. "It's all you have to do."

Almost certain she wouldn't call, Zane left her, walked the line back, then cut over to the McConnell home—a study in contrasts.

Though it might've started out about the size of the Drapers', they'd added on nearly that much again, with large windows, wide porches.

And now that he knew how to recognize it, some very nice land-scaping.

Like Traci, he found both the McConnells in their back garden. The woman, sturdy in knee-length shorts and floppy-brimmed hat, straightened, pressed a hand to her lower back.

"Well, look here, Sam. It's the young Walker boy. Come on back here, Zane. You won't remember me. I taught at the middle school, but I never had you. Had your sister one year, though."

"It's nice to see you." He shook hands with both of them. "That's a garden and a half."

"Always plant too much." Sam, a bandanna covering his balding head, knobby knees jutting out from his shorts, shook his head. "The grandkids put up a roadside stand to sell some of it, and we still give bags away."

"It's time for a breather," Mary Lou declared. "How about we sit in the shade of the porch, have some lemonade?"

"I wouldn't say no."

He walked back with them, took a seat with Sam while Mary Lou went inside.

"A lawyer now, aren't you?"

"Yes, sir."

Sam pulled out another bandanna, wiped his sweaty face. "That Draper boy hire you?"

"He tried. He hasn't got a case, Mr. McConnell, and I told him as much. I expect, considering, you've been to your own lawyer and been told the same."

"We have. And that if he keeps on at us, we can sue him for harassment. I'd rather avoid that kind of thing."

"I don't blame you." Zane got up to take the tray of lemonade from Mrs. McConnell.

"I heard enough to know you've got the good sense not to take a fool and bully on for a client," she said, pouring the lemonade over ice.

"Yes, ma'am, I do. The boundary issue isn't why I'm here. It's an excuse. I wanted to ask, and I know it's not my business, but I need to ask if either of you know of any trouble next door. Between Clint and Traci."

He noted the quick exchanged look. "We stay out of their way," Sam began. "As much as we can. They aren't what you'd call friendly."

"She won't say boo," Mary Lou continued. "I had her in school, two years. She had a good brain, did well, had friends. Was a little shy, but not timid. I took them over a cake when they moved in. She took it politely enough, but wouldn't ask me inside. Even said she didn't remember my classes, though I could see she did. I tried again when that poor girl lost her baby. He wouldn't let me in, though he took the casserole I took over quick enough. Never returned the dish."

"Oh, now, Mary Lou, it wasn't your best one."

"It's the principle, Sam. Chief Keller asked us what you're asking. We had to tell him what we're telling you. We've never heard or seen anything that looks like he's physically abusing her. But I've looked out the window upstairs, seen her out hanging wash, crying while she did.

"She's not the girl I knew back when she was ten, twelve. She's not that girl. It's breaking her mama's heart. Her mama, as good a woman as I know, isn't welcome over there. Her sister either. Not since she lost the baby, and not much before that either."

"The Drapers are hard people," Sam added. "We steer clear, and never had any trouble to speak of until the boy built that house. I'd give him the damn land at this point, but Mary Lou won't hear of it."

"I will not. You give in to a bully, they find something else to bully you over."

"You've got that right," Zane agreed.

He stewed and chewed over it a bit longer, then found himself telling Darby. She listened over a beer on his back patio.

"I met Traci's sister at Best Blooms. Joy introduced us. Allie was in there looking for a hanging basket for her mom for Mother's Day, and Joy asked how Traci was doing. Apparently she used to work for Joy in the busy season."

"I didn't know that."

"Allie just said she didn't see much of her. It struck me she would've said more if I hadn't been there, so I wandered off. They talked for a while. It sounds to me like the classic separation tactic."

Shifting, she looked at Zane directly. "So this is what's been on your mind. I figured it must be some legal wrangle you couldn't talk about, but it's not. Why didn't you tell me before?"

"They're not clients, so there's no privilege, but . . ." He waggled a hand in the air, and she pointed at him.

"Not it."

"Not altogether."

"Some elements are similar to what happened to me. The separation gambit, for instance. Did you think it would upset me to talk about an abused spouse? Because you're right, she's being abused. If it's not physical, it's certainly emotional."

"I had concerns there, yeah. It's always under there, right? And those memories, the feelings are so easily triggered. I didn't want to trigger yours."

"You, obviously, look to protect. It's your nature. I object to being protected. I have to. It's a survivor trait. On the issue of abuse and triggers, I'm solid. My experience was, thankfully, short-lived, and I came out of it smarter and stronger."

"Can't apologize for my nature."

"Nope, me neither. But if we're in a relationship . . ." Tipping her head, she gave him a long look. "Would you say we're in a relationship?"

"It has all the earmarks thereof."

"'Thereof'—lawyer." She smiled, sipped. "In that case, this is just the sort of troubling event we should be able to talk about. Now, would you like my take on the troubling event?"

"I would."

"From what you've said, it sounds as if Clint was raised to believe men are in charge, and superior. Women are meant to do what they're told, tend the house, have children. She was pregnant—probably why they got married in the first place. Now she's not. Whether or not he had anything to do with her losing the baby—and my money's on he did—she failed in one of her duties. She's cut off from her family and surrounded by his and their particular culture."

"She could walk away," Zane pointed out. "Her family's right here. So's the law. I know it's not as simple as that, but—"

"It's not, it's not, it's not. Yes, she's an adult—you weren't. Yes, she has family, she has support if she reaches for it. But—"

She sighed, heartfelt and long.

"After Trent, part of my therapy was group sessions. Jesus, Zane, the stories I heard. Women who'd stayed for years. Women who got out, then went back, again and again."

"Revolving door," Zane said. "That's what we called it."

"But it wasn't because they wanted to be hurt, not because they were weak. It was because they'd been beaten down emotionally, spiritually, mentally. Because they were caught in a cycle. Abused by a parent, now a spouse. Or because they believed he'd changed, convinced by him or themselves it wouldn't happen again. Or if it did, they deserved it. And some, because they had nowhere else to go."

"I know it. I prosecuted my share of batterers. Just like I know I can't help Traci Draper, Lee can't help her, her family can't help her, until she steps across the line and asks."

"And you want to help," she concluded. "Even need to help. So it pisses you off you can't help."

"Oh yeah. And since it does, let's put it away. Put it the hell away. Let's call Britt, have her bring Silas and Audra and Molly up, hang out."

Darby cocked an eyebrow. "And what do you plan to feed them? It's unlikely they've had dinner yet."

"Uh . . . delivery?"

Darby shook her head. "Big, beautiful grill right there. And if you wait until tomorrow, you could ask your whole family, use that grill—having picked up red meat. And your back wall will not only be finished, but planted."

"Not as spontaneous."

"No. But . . ." She rose, skirted the table, straddled his lap. "We could try a different kind of spontaneity."

"We could." He watched, a little stupefied, when she peeled off her shirt. "Here? But it's—"

"A really pretty evening," she finished, and took his mouth with hers.

CHAPTER SEVENTEEN

He hadn't hit her that hard, and God knew she deserved it. And more. She'd barely lost consciousness after her head struck the floor—with a satisfying thud.

He hadn't bothered to hit her again, and certainly hadn't bothered with sex. She'd lost her appeal in that area.

It amazed him now how much passion he'd once felt for her, how perfectly she'd suited him, in every way. My God, he'd even forgiven her for betraying him, accepted her sobbing apology, her excuses about being weak, afraid, being manipulated by the police, her own family.

But now, stuck together in this ugly box of a house, coming home from humiliating work to find her putting some disgusting excuse for a meal together night after endless night?

She reminded him, every day, every hour, every minute, of all he'd lost. Her fault, too. If she'd handled the little brat upstairs, he would have dealt with the disappointing, disrespectful son she'd given him.

Then she'd turned on him, betrayed him, told their secrets in exchange for a lighter sentence.

He'd done eighteen goddamn years due to her weakness.

It was past time she understood she'd cost him everything. Past time she accepted the punishment for it.

If she'd done what she'd been supposed to do, he'd still be Dr. Bigelow. Still be someone important. Still have his life, and not wake up in the middle of the night in a sweat as he dreamed of prison.

Yes, she'd cost him everything, and he should never have let himself forget that. She and the children they should never have had were responsible. She'd cost him nearly twenty years, and she had the nerve to whine to him—again—about getting a car, a job, moving.

Then that sad, sad look she'd given him when she'd come to.

Still, she'd done the dishes—he hadn't had to tell her *that* a second time—while he'd watched TV, because what else was there to do with the endless evenings in this shack they rented like a couple of losers?

He hadn't noticed her slurred speech immediately—he hadn't been listening to her endless whiny chatter. Then she'd said his name, like a question, before she'd collapsed, before she'd seized.

He'd watched for a moment or two, more fascinated than alarmed before he'd gone to her, dealt with her. But he knew, made his diagnosis, as he watched her slide away.

Subdural hematoma. A brain bleed. Head blows were tricky that way, with all those tiny veins in the meninges. When she died in his arms, he stroked her hair, even wept.

Then the truth struck. Walking out of the prison gates hadn't given him freedom. But this did.

He had cash in the house. He'd instructed her to withdraw cash every week, every week for all these years. Some instinct, he decided, must have foreseen this very day.

He could get more, would need more, as credit cards left a trail. He'd need two days—report to his probation officer on Friday, report to work on Saturday. He had Sunday and Monday off.

He could—as he'd yet to take a day—call in sick Tuesday and Wednesday. He doubted his supervisor would report him right away, so he would have as much as a week's head start.

He had a car, and would keep to back roads, to the speed limit, use cash. As steps and purpose ran through his mind, he realized under it all that he'd planned for this all along.

He knew not only what to do, but what had to be done.

He'd spent years saving lives, and they'd taken that from him. Wasn't it true justice for him to now take lives? To take the lives of the people who'd stolen his?

"You freed me, Eliza." He stroked her hair, her cheek. "Be happy for me."

Rising, he went to the bedroom, took a blanket, a pillow and arranged them in the tiny second bedroom. He carried her in, laid her carefully down on the floor, then covered her with a sheet.

He wasn't an animal.

Darby consulted with a client at the woman's pretty lakeside cottage. Noting the dock, the boat, the slope and rickety wooden steps leading down to both, Darby already had ideas.

"I bet when you're not out on the water, you're sitting up there looking at it," Darby mused.

"You'd win that bet." Patsy Marsh, a cheerful woman in her fifties, just smiled. "My Bill and I love living on the lake. Our kids are both in college now, but when they're home, they're right out there with us. Do you like to sail?"

"I haven't tried it yet. Busy season for me."

"So I see and hear. I'm hoping you can help us out, even though it'll make you busier. You can see," Patsy said as she gestured at the slope. "We just can't keep mowing that. Bill kept saying leave it be, then he had a fall with the mower, and I put my foot down. He wasn't hurt, but he could've been. He finally threw up his hands and said to call that girl who did Emily's place."

"I'm glad he did, because you're right, he could've been hurt. You said you were thinking ground covers."

"Something that we don't have to mow, but isn't unsightly, doesn't get too tall."

"I can give you some recommendations there, but—"

"Uh-oh!" Now Patsy laughed. "Emily told me to watch out if you said 'but.'"

"She knows me too well."

"I'm willing to listen."

"I like to think about what I'd do if a client's place was my place.

And what I'd do here is, first, replace those steps with stone. Widen them another foot."

"I've been telling Bill somebody's going to go right through one of them and break an ankle. Keep going."

"On the slope, I'd continue this really nice patio by doing a couple terraces of raised beds, matching the stone on the steps. Curved terraces to mirror the curve of the lake, low shrubs and perennials. And at the base, I'd do river rock."

"I've seen that wall you built up at Zane's place, and it's gorgeous. But it's so structured. It feels like it wouldn't work for the cottage."

Ah, Darby thought, a woman who can see what's good, what's not. Excellent.

"You're right, it wouldn't. You want something pretty, but a little more, well, cottagey—like the soft, sand brown of your patio. I'd want that same look."

"I've never been able to plant anything on this damn slope."

"Your front garden's beautiful, and so are your patio planters. You do it yourself?"

"I do, and I love to garden. I'd love plants out here. Curved," she murmured. "Wouldn't that just look sweet?"

"It would—from your house, your patio, and from the water. I could do a rough sketch for you to show your husband."

"Why don't you do that? We're going to need some numbers."

"I can work that up. Let me get some measurements."

"Emily told me you'd have ideas."

She had a million of them, and dispensed more to another potential client in Lakeview Terrace.

Darby walked the lake-facing backyard—enormous yard—with the pert and perky Charlene. "Your house, your view, your gardens are absolutely stunning. Why do you need me?"

"I really want to keep the gardens stunning. I can't take credit for them. We just moved in this winter, but Joe and I've done our best to keep them up. The thing is we both work full-time, have an active two-year-old—who's with his grammy today—and we're expecting our second in November."

"Congratulations."

"Thanks. We're excited. The thing is we need someone to do fall maintenance, spring cleanup, and, at least for a while, help us with what we've got here every couple weeks. The owners before us did a hell of a good job, but she was retired and an avid gardener. Before them, the owners had, I'm told, groundskeepers."

"And that's what you're looking for."

"More or less. But, both Joe and I want to work at it, too. It's relaxing and satisfying—and it's our yard. It's just we sure need to learn more than we know now. We figure, when we can, to sort of shadow you."

"That's what I like to hear. If the goal is to have a beautiful landscape and have someone else deal with it? Nothing's wrong with that. But better, to my mind, to take real ownership."

"You have busy lives," Darby added. "That's where we come in. I can put you on a schedule for the twice-monthly maintenance, and we'd follow the weather for the spring and fall."

"Perfect."

"Can I ask how you heard about us?"

"Britt Norten. She and I both work at the clinic. I'm an urgent care doctor. And coincidentally, Britt used to live here."

"She, oh . . ." Where Zane grew up. Darby turned to study the house again; all that beautiful glass made it seem so open. But it hadn't been. The grounds, blooming, graceful, made it seem so gracious. It had been anything but.

How would he feel about her working here?

"You know Britt, right?"

"Yes, yes, I know Britt. I know the family. Why don't I give you a price list, and if you want us to go ahead, I'll send you a contract."

"Perfect. While you're here, there are a couple of plants I just can't figure out. I tried books, internet. Maybe you can tell me what they are."

"Sure."

She walked around with Charlene, identified a few mystery plants as Charlene looked over the price list.

Surely Zane had walked here as a boy, maybe hit some fungoes, tossed up a baseball to snag. Had he wandered out to the dock to sit dreaming by the water?

Dreamed of pulling himself out of the grip of those undercurrents churning so violently inside the handsome house.

"This is exactly what we need."

"I'm sorry?" Darby yanked herself back. "I was distracted."

"I said this is just what we need. Why don't you email the contract and Joe and I will look it over tonight?"

When they came to terms, Darby walked back to her truck torn between the elation of signing a twice-monthly client and worry over how Zane would feel.

She might not have noticed the Mercedes across the street—luxury cars peppered the development—but its engine turned over just as she reached her truck. She had a vague impression of a man behind the wheel in a ball cap and sunglasses before he pulled away from the curb and drove off.

It struck her as slightly odd that she hadn't seen the driver walk to the car or get in, but she dismissed it. Still distracted, she thought.

She had a couple more stops to make before joining the crew. They'd finally squeezed in a full day's work between guests at the next-to-last bungalow.

But the nursery came first, and since Joy of Best Blooms had already talked to her good friend Patsy Marsh, she wanted to talk about the planned terraces, the plantings.

The stop she'd estimated at ten minutes took closer to thirty, but she got what she needed. She hit the hardware store and another conversation. It was the South, after all, and she'd learned to roll with it.

Though she'd intended to go straight to the bungalow, when she saw Emily's truck outside of reception, she pulled in. To check the rock garden, she took a winding route, gave a nod of satisfaction before winding back to the front door.

Inside, Emily crunched her phone between her ear and shoulder while she keyboarded. "Happy to, and I've got you booked, party of four, for tomorrow at eight a.m. That's right. Yes, they'll take good care of you. You're welcome. Bye now."

After pulling the phone free, she rolled her shoulders, tick-tocked her head.

"You should get a headset."

"I keep meaning to."

"Emily, your hair!"

Biting her bottom lip, Emily lifted a hand to her newly shorn bob. "Is it awful?"

"I love it. Seriously. It looks fun and breezy, and . . . you got some highlights," Darby added as she moved closer.

"A few, just to perk it up."

"It perked. It's a great cut. Who did it? I've been trimming my own since I got here because, well, it's hard to trust somebody with your hair. But I'd trust whoever gave you that cut."

"Sarrie Binkum, down at Reflection Salon."

"Do they do pedicures? I'm doing my own there, too. My work's hard on the feet."

"They sure do."

"I'll try them out. And I'm holding you up."

"You're not. In fact, you're just in time, because I need a break. Come sit outside on my very pretty patio."

"Five minutes."

"That's about all I've got, too. Time enough for a cold drink and a breath."

Back in the kitchen, Emily poured tea, making the ice in the glasses crackle. "I was going to head over to Bungalow Eight, just to let you know the guests coming in tomorrow asked if they could check in at noon. Any way you can be finished?"

"I'll make sure we are."

"You're a wonder, Darby."

After carrying out the tea, Emily sat at the little table with its cheerful striped umbrella. "I'm taking part of our five minutes to repeat what I told you up at Zane's the other night. I love what you've done, and you were right. I do look out the window and smile. Plus, bookings are up."

With a sigh, she looked around. "I needed to get this place, and myself, out of the rut. You kicked us out of it."

"And I'll repeat my appreciation for the referrals. I got two new clients today."

"Well, congratulations."

"One of them is the family that lives in Zane's old house."

Emily paused, then nodded slowly. "I see. You're worried that's going to be a problem for Zane, for Britt, for the rest of us."

"Yes. Well, I don't think Britt, as she's my referral. The client's Dr. Charlene Ledbecker. She works at the urgent care at the clinic."

"Good for Britt," Emily stated.

"It couldn't have been easy for her to make a connection with the woman who owns the house where so much happened to her."

"Britt's got spine. So does Zane."

"I know it, but—"

"It's a house, Darby. It wasn't the house that hurt those children. Do you want my advice?"

"It's why I'm here."

"Talk to Zane, get it off your mind."

"I will. I wanted to talk to you, too."

"It's a house." Emily patted Darby's hand. "I think of Eliza in it once in a while. Those moments when you can't sleep, and your mind starts roaming to dredge up every mistake you ever made."

"I know those moments."

"I can wish I'd made more of an effort to be close to her, but then, would it have mattered? Would that have changed anything? I think of her now, once in a while, wonder if I should reach out to her. Our parents aren't getting any younger, and there's been no contact in nearly twenty years. Should there be? I'm never sure if that would matter or change anything.

"But I know Zane and Britt deserve my unwavering support and loyalty. So I don't reach out."

She shrugged it off. "I like seeing him happy. You make him happy."

"I think we were both ready, both at a point where we were ready to be happy. Being happy with someone's like a bonus. Now I'm going to go finish your bungalow."

"I'll come down and look as soon as I can."

"Sit," Darby said as Emily started to get up. She came around behind, rubbed Emily's shoulders. "Finish your tea, smell your flowers."

"Five more minutes." Reaching back, Emily squeezed Darby's hand. "Stay happy."

"That's the plan."

Zane wasn't sure what he was in for when Darby texted she planned to cook dinner. Especially since she put cook in scare quotes.

Still, he figured if it bombed, they had frozen pizza or canned ravioli.

When he walked in after a pretty damn good day, she stood in the kitchen chopping a bunch of stuff he assumed meant salad. And whatever she had in the oven smelled really okay.

A bottle of wine stood open on the counter with two glasses.

"This here's what I'm talking about. My woman making me a hot meal." He exaggerated the southern, gave her a light slap on the butt to punctuate it.

When she just rolled her eyes and laughed, he bent down to kiss the infinity symbol on the back of her neck. "What's the occasion?"

"Besides being Tuesday? We finished the next-to-last bungalow and started prep work for your water feature, and I signed two more clients."

"Big day. Sounds like I should make you a hot meal."

"Your turn next. But you sure could pour that wine."

He liked coming home, finding her there. Maybe he got some twinges about just how much he liked it, but one look at her and they died away.

He supposed he could work up some twinges over how easily the twinges died away, but that edged into paranoid territory.

"So, what are we having?"

"This very healthy salad, which includes some of your own nasturtium."

"I have nasturtium? What is it?"

She tapped her finger at the bold orange and yellow flowers on the counter.

"Flowers?" That one set him back. "We're eating flowers?"

"They're not only edible and pretty, but very tasty—as are their leaves, which are already in the salad."

"Okay, but you go first."

"Coward." She plucked a petal off a flower, popped it in her mouth. "Yum."

"Uh-huh. What are we eating besides flowers?"

"The amazing mac and cheese I made—not from a box, but from scratch."

"Get out. How is that even possible?"

"I asked that question when Hallie and Roy started arguing about which of their mamas made the best mac and cheese in the history of mac and cheese. I made some comment about those handy microwave packages of same, and was met with serious disdain. I mean serious. Anyway."

She picked up her wine, drank, gestured. "After my humiliation came inspiration. I went with Hallie's because she called her mother right then and there, rattled off the recipe—adding any fool could make it. I am that fool."

She gestured again, drank again. "And let me point out right now, there was nothing easy about it. You'd think, mac and cheese, how hard could it be? I can't even talk about it."

The oven timer buzzed. "Well, here we go."

She went over, opened the oven door.

"It smells good," Zane said over her shoulder. "It looks good."

"It does. It does." She slid on mitts, took it out to set on the counter, where they both studied it.

She took out her phone.

"You're going to take a picture of it?"

"Don't judge me, Walker." She picked it up again, carried it outside. "Bring the salad, and the wine. We'll start with the salad while it cools down some," she told him. "And I'll drown myself in the wine if the mac and cheese sucks."

She had flowers on the table again, different ones in a blue Mason jar she must have brought over or picked up somewhere. He looked at her while she served the salad, the short cap of russet—he'd decided to stick with russet—hair, the depthless blue eyes, the diamond-edged cheekbones.

"I could get used to this," he decided. "Coming home to a pretty woman, a pretty table, a hot meal."

"I wouldn't get used to the hot meal. I swear to sweet little plastic Baby Jesus, digging a hole in rocky ground with a pickax is easier than cooking. I can say that because today I did both."

"Renaissance woman. The salad's good. Even, strangely, the flowers. So, new clients?"

"Yeah. Patsy and Bill Marsh."

"I know them. They're friends with Emily and Lee, serious boat people."

"That they are. I'm giving them lakeside appeal—versus curb appeal, because lake. And I've been promised—or threatened with—a day out on their boat."

"Don't like boats?"

"I like them fine. I've been out on one with an engine, even kayaked a few times. But I've never been on a boat with a sail. I love watching them, the way they just seem to glide along. Like magic. I guess you know how to sail."

"Yeah. I grew up with boats. I haven't been sailing in years. Probably a trigger." Which he hadn't realized until that very moment. "I should test that out. I could rent one, take you sailing."

"Seems like I ought to try it eventually, since lake. Are you ready to risk the main event here?"

"More than."

"Okay, here goes." With some trepidation, she dished up the mac and cheese. Watching Zane, she took a forkful. "Together, on three. One, two . . ."

He ate, angled his head, then holding up a finger, forked up another bite. "It's freaking great."

With obvious surprise, she studied the next bite on her fork. "It's really good. Who knew?"

"Got a nice little kick, too."

"Tabasco. Still harder than digging holes, but ultimately, just as satisfying." She wiggled her eyebrows. "So, what was your plan if it did, indeed, suck?"

"I was working on brutal yet sympathetic honesty with a bolstering hey, you tried, since if it sucked, you'd know, and any attempt to pretend it didn't would be seen, rightfully, as patronizing bullshit."

"I think that's acceptable. I need to tell you about my other new clients."

"Sure."

"They moved here last winter, moved into Lakeview Terrace. They bought the house you grew up in."

He said nothing for a moment, but stopped eating, topped off both wineglasses. "Okay."

"She knows Britt. They both work at the clinic. Charlene Ledbecker. She's a doctor. He's an engineer, works in Asheville. They're expecting their second child next fall. I wanted to give you a picture of them."

"All right."

"I didn't know, until Charlene mentioned that Britt used to live in the house, what house it was. They want help with the grounds, a couple times a month, and seasonally. They want to learn how to take care of the grounds. They . . . you don't care about any of that."

"Not really. So you made me mac and cheese."

"Inspired by Roy and Hallie's argument," she reminded him. "What's more comforting than mac and cheese? I had to tell you even knowing it would stir up bad memories."

"Food as a security blanket?"

She caught the tone, recognized irritation. "It wasn't meant to be patronizing, Zane. I wanted to do something to balance out having to upset you. And instead I've pissed you off."

"What pisses me off, Darby, is the fact you clearly felt you had to tiptoe up to telling me you landed a client who happens to live in that house."

She actually felt her spine stiffen, her temper simmer up toward boil. "It wasn't an insult to your manly balls. The tiptoeing was as much, maybe more, for me. I felt guilty, right or wrong, I felt guilty profiting over something that hurt you."

"It doesn't hurt me, and my balls are insulted. I wouldn't have come back to Lakeview if I couldn't handle it, and both my balls and my brain are aware someone lives in that house. And if the people who do came to me on a legal matter, I'd handle that. Why wouldn't I?"

Darby took a moment herself, then said two words. "Traci Draper."

He started to speak, felt the pin jab the air out of his righteous insult. "Yeah, well, you pointed out I was stupid about that, so you should've known you were being stupid about this."

"Sounds like a wash to me, and you got mac and cheese out of it. I don't mind fighting, but if you want really stupid, it's fighting because somebody had concerns for your feelings."

"We're not fighting." At her long, slow stare, he blew out a breath. "We were disputing, and apparently we've settled the dispute."

She smirked. "Lawyer."

"Guilty. Look, I spent some time hating the house. I even drew a picture of it—and I can't draw for shit—in my journal back then. Drew it surrounded by the nine circles of hell."

"You read Dante as a teen?"

"I read everything. It was one of the most surefire ways to go somewhere else for a while. I got over hating the house, or mostly. You working there isn't going to bother me. Don't let it bother you."

"Then I won't."

"See? Dispute settled. I'm having more of this." He piled more mac and cheese on his plate. "You?"

"Half that."

"How would you feel about leaving some of your stuff here instead of hauling your clothes in and out in your duffle?"

It took her off guard, shot her off balance. One minute they're "disputing," and the next he's making room in his closet.

"I . . ."

"And I could leave a few things at your place," he continued in the same easy tone, "for those rainy days when I bring takeout after work and give you a hand with painting."

"I really thought, that first time, this was just going to be about good, easy sex."

"It is, just not only about."

No, she thought, it wasn't just about. He'd already given her a key and the security code. For convenience, and leaving some clothes ranked the same, didn't it? Convenient.

Why make a big deal?

"Who does the laundry?" she demanded.

"Hmm. I could say you do it at your place, I do it here, but you're here more than I'm there, so those aren't equitable terms. We take turns."

"I can agree to that. I'll bring some stuff to leave tomorrow. God." She shoved her plate away. "I don't care how good it is, I can't eat any more."

"Tell you what, we'll get these dishes out of the way, then walk this off. We'll stroll around here and you can tell me the names of stuff that's blooming even though I'll never remember."

"You'll remember eventually."

He smiled, polished off his mac and cheese. "It's sweet you really believe that, darlin'."

Sipping wine, Darby considered. They'd had their first fight, sort of, resolved it. They'd agreed to leave personal items at each other's places.

And he'd called her *darlin'* for the first time in that gorgeous High Country drawl.

No doubt, absolutely none, they'd just entered the next phase, whatever that turned out to be, of their relationship.

CHAPTER EIGHTEEN

Graham paid cash for his motel rooms on his careful trip from Raleigh to Lakeview. He used the free Wi-Fi and Eliza's tablet to search for information about Emily, about Detective Lee Keller, about his own—obviously inept—defense attorney, the prosecutor, the judge who'd presided over his case.

All of them, every one, had played a part in ruining his life, in humiliating him. He would ruin theirs, every one.

Unfortunately, the judge had died six years before. So Graham could only gain satisfaction from imagining him rotting in hell.

The prosecutor had retired and moved to Solomons Island, so he would have to wait. His own attorney, also retired, still lived in Asheville.

So, soon for him.

He knew, because Eliza had told him on one of her visits, that his whore-bitch of a sister-in-law had married the dirty cop. He knew the cop was now chief of police in Lakeview, and they had two sons.

So many ways to hurt them. As he sat in his motel room, with the TV on to alert him if and when his own face flashed on-screen, he imagined all of them.

He thought setting that old relic of a house on fire, with all of them inside, would serve.

He considered Dave Carter, the busybody asshole neighbor. Oh, he'd played a part. You play, Graham thought, you pay. In careful block print, he added Dave Carter to the list in the notebook he'd bought at Walmart.

Maybe a terrible accident. Cut the brake lines on his car. He could look up how to do that—you could find out anything on the internet.

Then, of course, most importantly, there were the spawn who'd betrayed their own father. The father who'd put a roof over their heads, clothes on their backs, food in their bellies.

The father who'd given them life. The father who would take those lives, take them with his own hands.

He read over the list of names, again and again. Meticulously wrote down any and all information he remembered or could find about each and every one.

He detailed every grievance he had against them, and those filled line after line after line.

Before he slept, he whipped himself through fifty push-ups, a hundred crunches, rotated to squats, lunges. Every morning he repeated the routine, using the long list of grievances to drive his body through.

When he slept, he dreamed of himself in surgery, performing miracles only God could match. Like God, he'd bring judgment against those who'd betrayed him.

When he woke, he didn't shave. He hadn't shaved for three days now, and felt the deepening scruff helped mask his face. He'd combed product through his hair to cover the gray, and would continue to do so as he let it grow.

Along with the notebook, he'd bought a ball cap, sunglasses, cheap tennis shoes, jeans, T-shirts. He'd learned a few things in prison—and blending, not bringing attention to himself, was key. Just as switching the license plates—twice now—on his car was key.

Driving into Lakeview had him shaking with anxiety and excitement.

They'd changed things. A stoplight where none had been. Different stores, restaurants. It infuriated and disoriented.

He had to pull over to get his bearings, to breathe through what he recognized as—he was a fucking doctor after all—an anxiety attack.

Sweat popped out on his face; his heart hammered. His vision blurred, doubled for an instant. Then it snapped clear when he saw Zane striding down Main Street as if the son of a bitch owned it.

He'd let his hair grow to faggot length, broadened in the shoulders, put on more height, but he knew his own goddamn son when he looked at him. And it took every ounce of willpower not to leap from the car then and there and beat the bastard to the ground like he deserved.

That had to wait, he reminded himself. That had to be a private moment.

He watched Zane climb steps to a porch, walk into a building. He considered going in after him—it could be a private moment—but he saw movement at the large front window. A woman, vaguely familiar, Zane joining her so they were framed in the glass.

His offices. Thought he was a big shot now, but Graham knew the truth. Spineless bastard couldn't make it in Raleigh so he'd come slinking back to Lakeview.

And in Lakeview the betrayer would finally meet justice.

Calmer, he drove into Lakeview Terrace. Changes there, too, he noted. They'd put in a playground for people who couldn't keep their children at home where they belonged. He saw kids on swings, slides, kids biking—many without parental supervision.

Disgusting.

He drove to his home—no longer the largest in the development, as several status-seeking neighbors had added bonus rooms over the garages, or sunrooms, covered decks.

Again he pulled over, this time to consider the house. His house. The strangers who lived in it were nothing more than squatters. Back when the world was sane, he could have had them evicted with a snap of his fingers.

Now he'd become the interloper. Because of Zane.

He thought about breaking in, seeing what the squatters had done to his home. He'd find out their names, add them to his list.

As he considered how he would deal with them, a woman came around from the back, walked toward the truck in the driveway.

Dressed like a man, he thought. Hair short as a man's. Probably a lesbian. Intolerable! He should march right over to *his* house, drag her to the ground by her dyke hair.

But when she glanced his way, nerves flooded through him, shook through him as he punched the ignition, hastily drove away. Not the time, he consoled himself. It wasn't nerves, but willpower.

He locked himself in his motel room, poured a glass of scotch to settle himself again. But only one. He had work to do.

He sat down with Eliza's tablet and his list of names, began to search social media. He found the website for Zane's law offices, for Emily's creaky old bungalows easily enough. As he studied them, minutely, his rage bubbled hot. Emily's had a Facebook page for the business, but her personal one she'd kept private. Though he'd learned a thing or two in prison, he didn't have the skill to hack through it.

Neither of her brats had public social media, nor did Britt or Zane. But he found what he wanted thanks to Eliza's idiot mother.

A treasure trove of photos, of family news for all to see.

Everything he needed spread out and posted by the chatty old bag. He studied a photo of the pathetic family billed as Zane's first family cookout at his new house. Another one of Emily's brats and Zane.

Grandsons Zane and Gabe in front of Zane's house, with endless vomit-inducing commentary on Gabe's interest in landscaping, his summer job. He read every revolting word in case he could use any of her blather.

He studied the house. He'd seen that house on his careful drive around the lake, the ridiculous one high on the hill.

Now he knew just where to find Zane for that private moment.

Zane shot awake when his security lights flashed on. When he rolled out of bed, Darby didn't even stir. He knew from experience the woman could sleep through cannon fire until her internal alarm went ping.

On his way to the terrace doors, he grabbed pants, jerked them on. He caught the red glow of taillights heading down his long drive.

Somebody made a wrong turn, he decided, and realized it when the motion sensors turned on the lights. Satisfied, he went back to bed, where Darby slept like the dead.

He'd never known anyone who so perfectly fit the cliché. Once she hit the off button, she barely moved or made a sound until morning. Which made her an excellent bedmate for a chronically light sleeper.

He drifted back off only to be awakened again about an hour later by his phone. His heart leaped—another cliché, but calls at four in the morning meant trouble. So did the readout from his security company.

"Zane Walker."

Though it was hardly necessary for Sleeping Beauty, he walked out of the bedroom while he talked to the security company about a break-in or attempted break-in at his offices. Though they assured him the local police had been notified, he went back to the bedroom, turned the lights on low to find clothes.

His phone rang again.

"Zane, Silas."

"I just talked to my security company."

"Yeah, somebody heaved a rock through your office window. Look, we've had three calls tonight like this. Must be some asshole kids."

"Son of a bitch."

"I got a good look through the window here, and that's the only damage I see. You're going to want to come in, but there's no rush. Nobody got in. I can see the damn rock lying on the floor in there, and your doors are secure."

"Okay. I'm coming in, but I'll pull it together first."

"Take your time. We've got this."

He dressed, got his insurance file out of his home office. Downstairs he made coffee, then made a second cup—one that wasn't coffee, but oversweet, coffee-flavored milk. He took both up to the bedroom. He could leave a note, but hell, her eyes would pop open in about twenty minutes anyway.

The fact they did now surprised the hell out of him.

She said, "Coffee."

"The smell of coffee wakes you out of your coma, but lights, ringing phones don't make a dent? What are you?"

"Coffee," she repeated, and took the one he held out. "Who called?"

"Somebody threw a rock through my office window."

"What? No." Her eyes blinked clear. "Oh, Zane."

"Apparently the somebody's having a spree doing that around Lakeview tonight. I'm going to head down, take a look."

"Do you want me to come?" She shoved her sweep of bangs aside. "I can be dressed in like two minutes."

"No, but thanks. It's like Silas said, probably some dumb kids. I'll get it sorted out, have breakfast in town."

"Okay. Sorry, this sucks."

"Me, too, and it does." He leaned over, kissed her. "See you later."

"Text me," she called out. "Let me know what's what."

"Sure."

She drank half the coffee in bed—an indulgence—while her brain woke up. Hell of a way for him to start his morning, she thought. Vandalism never made sense to her. Creative tagging on abandoned buildings she could see as urban art, but out-and-out vandalism made no damn sense.

What satisfaction or thrill did someone get from destroying someone else's property?

She got up, and since she'd showered the night before—with Zane—pulled on work clothes. She'd top off the coffee, have some cereal, check the weather forecast.

And get an early start on the waterfall.

As she wandered downstairs, she switched on lights. After setting Zane's coffee maker for half a cup, she checked his kitchen tablet for the weather.

Hot, humid, probable late afternoon or evening thunderstorms. Typical. Yawning the night off, she poured cereal, got out the blueberries she'd stocked for overnights.

As she started to doctor her freshened coffee, the security lights went on. Her first thought: Deer.

She sprayed regularly with her homemade organic repellent, ordered Zane and her male crew members to pee around the shrubs—another fine repellent in her estimation. She'd planted plenty of deer-resistant plants.

But you just couldn't trust Bambi.

She disengaged the alarm, pulled open the accordion doors, and started out with every intention of chasing off the invaders.

It hit her like a guided missile, knocking her back, crashing her against the kitchen island and onto the floor.

For a moment, dazed, she imagined a ten-point buck charging in. Then she saw the man.

"So, Zane's got himself a little whore. One built more like a boy. Figures." He pulled the doors shut behind him. "Saw your truck. I just needed you to let me inside while he's down in town. Thanks for that."

He started toward her, fists curled tight. "Now, you're going to stay down, stay quiet."

The hell she would.

She jumped up, spun, planted a hard kick in his midsection. Instinct had her running when he stumbled back. She could get outside, lose him in the woods.

But how would she warn Zane with her phone still on the charger?

So she whirled back, heart racing, and dropped into a fighting stance. She'd stand her ground.

Eyes glinting, he charged. Fast, she thought, he's fast, and she used his momentum as she pivoted aside, followed up with a kick to his kidneys. He pitched forward, went to his knees.

"Now you stay down."

He came up fists flailing. She blocked a punch with her forearm, felt the force of it scream straight to her shoulder. Ducked, and came up with the heel of her hand. Felt the crunch as she broke his nose.

He got one past her, landed a blow on her still singing shoulder, aimed for her face with his left. She batted his arm away, shot a kick higher, struck his jaw. And when he reeled back, planted her boot— two hard, fast kicks—in his crotch.

This time he went down, stayed down.

And she ran.

Zane stood in his office, hands in pockets. Just broken glass, he reminded himself. Nobody hurt, easily repaired. Insured.

But it upset and disturbed him that anyone would deliberately destroy what was his.

"The only person I've had any trouble with since I got back would be Clint Draper," he told Silas.

His brother-in-law, dark blond hair still a little bed-rumpled, his raw-boned face still carrying the night's stubble, nodded.

"I know it. We'll be talking to him. But like I said, we got three calls for broken windows, all within about fifteen minutes."

"All on Main Street?"

"I don't think so. I need to check on that. Ginny was on call tonight, and contacted me when your office got hit. She handled the first two, but figured I'd want in. I'm two minutes away, and family. Speaking of, I felt like we had to let the chief know."

Silas shook his head at the rock, at the shards of glass. "It's just not the sort of vandalism we get around here. Some mailbox bashing along the lake road, kids TPing houses now and then, keying cars, and the like."

"Well, if you catch them, and they want a defense attorney, they can count me out."

"Can't blame you." His radio signaled. "Hold on." Silas paced away, paced back after a brief conversation.

"The chief's on his way. He wants you to stay put. He needs to talk to you."

His brother-in-law had a good cop face, but Zane knew him too well to miss the worry. "What is it?"

"He's contacted the local LEOs in Raleigh, just to make sure Graham Bigelow's where he's supposed to be."

"Why?"

"Dave Carter's place got a rock through the window. And so did your old house in Lakeview Terrace. That makes a connection, Zane, so let's make sure."

"Why the hell would he—Darby." Fear chilled him straight down to the bone. "She's alone at my place."

He rushed out before Silas could stop him, and screamed away from the curb just as Lee pulled up.

"Get in," Lee shouted at Silas. "We just got a nine-one-one from Zane's house."

"Darby's there."

"I know. She made the call."

The Porsche hit eighty before the town limits, and Zane didn't ease up. He hit the hands-free to call Darby, to tell her to hide, lock herself in and hide, and the phone rang.

"Darby. I need you to find a safe place, lock yourself in. I think Graham's going to try to get in the house."

"Too late. I'm okay. I called nine-one-one first."

"I'm nearly there."

"I'm okay. I'm all right. I—I can see you. Slow down. Jesus, don't wreck the car. I'm okay."

He could see her now in the wash of security lights, sitting on the steps of the porch. Her face so white the blood on it shined like neon.

She started to get to her feet as he screamed to a stop, wobbled, sat again.

He lifted her straight up. "Where are you hurt? What did he do to you? Which way did he go?"

"I'm not hurt. He tried, but I'm not really hurt. He didn't go anywhere. He's inside."

Everything in him went hard and cold. "That's Lee coming. You hear the sirens? You stay right here, wait for him. Stay out here, Darby."

He went inside, ready, even eager now, to take on the man who'd put blood and bruises on what was precious to him.

And found Dr. Graham Bigelow on the floor, unconscious, his arms and legs restrained with . . . bungee cords.

"I had some in the truck," Darby managed from the doorway.

"You did this?"

"I . . . I feel a little sick." When she stumbled back outside, Zane scooped her up again, sat her down.

"Head between your legs. Breathe slow, darlin'. Just breathe."

He waited for Lee to pull up behind his car, for Lee and Silas to leap out. "He's inside. He won't give you any trouble. Darby saw to that."

"Is she hurt? Does she need an ambulance?"

"I don't think so." He kept rubbing her back, slow, steady strokes. "Just shaky. If she needs to go to the clinic, I'll take her. You can decide if he needs one."

"I'm all right," she said again, but kept her head between her knees.

Silas came back out, crouched in front of her. He used the same gentle tone Zane had heard him use with Audra. "Sweetheart, did you hog-tie that son of a bitch with bungee cords?"

"It's what I had handy."

"How about we get you inside, get you sitting down with some cool water. If you don't want to go to the clinic right off, I can call Dave Carter. He'll come look you over."

"Do that, Silas," Zane told him. "I should've thought of that."

"I'm not really hurt," Darby began, only to have Zane pick her up. "And I can walk."

"No," he said, and carried her inside.

He walked straight past Graham and Lee, who was switching out bungee cords for cuffs, carried her back to the great room sofa.

"Sit."

"Do I get a Milk-Bone?"

"Knock it off." He walked to the kitchen, got her a bottle of water, walked back, dampened a cloth, and unbalanced her mood by gently wiping the blood from her face. "It's not yours," he murmured, and kissed her cheek.

"No. It's his. I broke his nose. That was for you."

That broke him. He gripped her free hand, pressed it to his lips, just held there. Then he looked into her eyes. "I don't know what to say to you."

"Nice work?"

"Ah, Jesus, Darby."

"Here." She held out the water. "I think you could use some, too. Then maybe we just sit here a minute and pull ourselves together."

Lee found them like that, sitting, passing the water bottle.

"Dave and Jim are on their way. Silas is on Bigelow, and I've got another couple of officers coming. He's going to need some medical attention, so we'll get him out of here. Honey, are you hurt?"

"Not really."

"There's blood on your shirt."

"That's his. I broke his nose, and I kicked him in the face. And the balls. I—I've got a black belt. Kung fu."

Blowing out a breath, Lee sat. "Are you steady enough to tell me what happened?"

"Yeah. I was just shaky before. I never actually . . . training and competitions aren't the same. I was down here, in the kitchen, and the security lights went on. I figured deer. I use repellant but they're tricky. So I turned off the alarm, opened the back door to go out and chase them off. I didn't even see him coming. He charged me—that was his mistake."

"Mistake?"

"If he'd punched me, he'd probably have put me down, maybe knocked me out, but he just barreled in, knocked me back against the island—I think—and I fell. I was a little dazed, but not out. I think I saw him yesterday, parked across the street from the Ledbeckers' place."

"Did you notice what kind of car?"

"Black, four-door sedan. I don't really know cars, so I don't know the make, but I think a luxury car. It looked new, but I'm not sure."

"Okay, he knocked you down, then what?"

"He called me Zane's whore, said something about seeing my truck."

"The lights came on just after three," Zane put in. "I saw taillights heading back down when I got up to check. He must've driven up here, seen I wasn't alone."

"He'd have seen me and the truck at the Ledbeckers', put that together. Wait, he said he'd needed me to let him in while Zane was in town. The broken window at the office."

On a hiss, she tapped a fist to her head. "I played right into it. Well, he didn't get away with it, did he? He was going to make sure I stayed quiet, stayed down, and he came at me. I got up. I have to say he seemed amused and pleased I was going to fight back. But he didn't know I could kick his sorry ass."

Tears trickled out, had her pressing her fingers to her eyes. "Sorry."

"Don't you be sorry," Lee ordered. "We can do this later."

"No, no, I'm good. He doesn't really know how to fight, just how to punch and hurt. I hurt him first, but he kept coming. I knocked him down, and started to run, but I realized I didn't have my phone, and maybe I could lose him in the woods, but I couldn't warn Zane, call the cops. So I decided to finish it."

She took a minute to swipe away tears, drink more water.

"He got up, and I did—finish it. When he was out, I ran out to the truck. The bungee cords were handy, and I wanted to get him restrained in case he woke up before I could call for help. And that's about that."

She started to get up; Zane pressed her back.

"I want a Coke."

"I'll get it. Sit down."

When he walked to the kitchen, he saw Dave rush in with his partner, Jim, behind him. And Graham sitting up, hands cuffed behind his back, his face a mass of blood and bruises.

"Good to see you, Graham." Dave paused to give him a sneering look. "Good to see you just like this. You take him, Jim. I'll take the lady."

He started back, his eyes meeting Zane's for a long moment. Then he crossed over to Darby, crouched, smiled. "How's it going, champ?"

"I'm okay."

"I'll be the judge of that. Any dizziness, nausea?"

"No. I had a little of both right after, but it was just reaction."

He opened his kit, took out a blood pressure cuff. "Your knuckles are swollen and bruised. You've got some bruises coming up on your left arm."

"I blocked a punch. He's strong."

"He likes to gut punch."

"He didn't get one in. He only got one by me—I think—adrenaline blur. In the shoulder—and it was feeling it from the block. I'm a little rusty or he wouldn't have gotten one by me."

"If that's a little rusty," Lee commented, "I'd like to see what you can do when you're all in."

"I'm with you," Dave agreed. "I need to see the shoulder."

When she started to take off her shirt, Lee pushed up.

"Sports bra," she said. "You see more at the gym—don't worry about it."

Her shoulder protested, but setting her teeth, Darby peeled off her T-shirt. Twisting her head, she got her first good look. "Okay, shit. He got one by me all right."

"Her back's bruised and scraped." Zane's voice came out deadly calm, in direct opposition to the blood rising hot under his skin.

"It's a little sore, that's all." To prove it, she lifted her elbow, then her arm, rolled the shoulder back, rolled it forward. "Nothing's pulled or broken. Full range of motion. I know what it feels like when it's really hurt. It's not. A couple of Motrin will handle it."

"After a visit to the clinic," Lee said.

"I don't—"

"I'll take her," Zane interrupted.

"It only adds to the case against Bigelow if you're under a doctor's care for injuries he inflicted," Lee pointed out. "It would help us out."

"Okay, okay. But I need to get the crew started. They're probably here and wondering what the hell.

"Give me a minute."

When Dave went out to consult with Jim, and Lee walked away to answer his signaling phone, Zane got a bag of peas out of the freezer. "Never eat them," he said as he handed Darby the Coke, laid the cold bag on her shoulder. "Always have them."

"Hey, me, too. It's just bumps and scrapes, Zane."

"I know." Still he stroked her hair. "But you're going to the clinic."

"We're taking Bigelow into Asheville," Dave said. "Jackie Chan here did a number on him. Broken nose, black eyes, a few loose teeth. Jaw may be broken. His balls are nicely black-and-blue. Lee's having two officers ride with us.

"And you." Dave walked over, framed Darby's face, kissed her on the mouth. "We'll let the clinic know you're coming in shortly."

He walked over to Zane, gave him a hard, one-armed hug. "Don't worry about this. We've got him."

When she stood up, Darby felt some twinges, a lot of stiffness she wasn't ready to admit. "I need a fresh shirt. I need to talk to my crew."

"I'll get you a shirt."

"Moving's good, otherwise you stiffen up."

He worried he'd snap, just snap. "Let me take care of you."

"You have been, from the second you drove up at light speed. Believe me, it made a difference. But okay, you can get me a shirt, then drive me to the clinic after I talk to the crew."

"Zane." Lee stepped back in. "I need a minute."

"What?" He could see it, see something coming.

Darby took a step back. "I'll just—"

"No." Zane took her hand, held her in place. "What is it?"

"I got a call from Raleigh. The locals gained access to the Bigelow residence. Eliza's dead, Zane. Probably a few days dead. They'll do an autopsy to determine that and cause of death."

Darby edged in closer, took a harder grip on Zane's hand.

"I should feel something, but I don't. Maybe later."

"I don't want you to worry about this. I'll handle it."

"Emily. My grandparents."

"I'll handle it. You take care of your girl, and leave this to me." He put a firm hand on Zane's shoulder. "Leave it to me."

Dulled, numb, Zane just stood where he was. "I want the details when you have them."

"You'll get them. You get checked out now, Darby, and I want the details on that. I need to take some pictures of your injuries."

"Sure. Fine."

"I'm going to go up, get her a fresh shirt."

Nodding, Lee took out his phone. "You let him take care of you now, you hear? It'll help him."

She'd seen Zane's eyes go blank, felt the absolute stillness in him.

"We'll take care of each other."

CHAPTER NINETEEN

While, in odd synchronicity, the doctor who lived in his old house treated Darby, Zane walked over to Britt's office. He caught her before her first appointment, and her surprised smile of greeting faded when she got a good look at his eyes.

"You need to sit down."

"Grams." As she did, she pressed a hand to her heart. "Pop."

"No, it's not that." Fast was usually best. "Eliza's dead."

"Oh." As her hand dropped to her desk, Britt's breath came out long, shaky. "I'm not surprised. How could I be surprised? He killed her."

"That's not official yet, but of course he did. There's more."

While he told her, she stood up, walked to the window, and circled the room, her hands clasped tight.

It shouldn't have surprised Zane how strong she was, but it constantly did.

Her voice held just a touch of pity when she spoke. "He could have lived his life. They could have lived their lives. But it wasn't enough for him. We took everything that mattered away from him—that's how he saw it. The only way he could see it. We had to be punished. He meant to kill you this time."

"And Darby just because she was there. Because she was with me. He'd have come for you if he could."

She didn't flinch, only nodded in agreement. "Yes, you first, then me. Then Emily, Lee, Dave, very likely Charlene and Joe because they had the house he'd see as his."

She leaned a hip on her desk. "I'll tell you he'll have a list, either written down or inside his head. Everyone he deems responsible for what he lost. Lee should check, make sure, he came here first. I think he would—you'd be priority one—but Lee should check on his lawyer, the judge who sentenced him."

"Christ." In opposition to her admirable calm, Zane raked his hands through his hair. "I should've thought of that. Lee probably has."

"I'm surprised you can think of your own name with the morning you've had. You'd have stopped him, Zane. He doesn't know the man you are."

"Darby did stop him. He didn't know the woman she is."

"Darby, God." Britt scrubbed her hands over her face. "Charlene's a good doctor. If it's any more than bruises and scrapes, she'll find it, treat it. I want to see her, but damn it, I don't even know what to say."

"You'll think of something." He found himself able to smile, at least a little. "It's what you do."

"I should reschedule my appointments. Emily might need me. She was Eliza's sister. And Grams, Pop. No matter what, she was their daughter. Oh God, Zane, what are we going to do for them? What can we do for them?"

"We'll figure it out." He drew her in, held her. "We'll figure it out," he repeated. "We came out okay, didn't we, you and me? We got through worse. We'll get through this, and so will they."

"I'm so glad you're here. I'm so glad you came home." She squeezed hard, drew back. "I thought of something. I have something that may help Emily, Grams, Pop. Something good."

"I'll take it."

"I peed on a stick this morning."

Baffled, he squinted at her. "Why the hell would you—" Then his brain clicked. "Oh. Seriously?"

"Positively, you could say. I haven't even told Silas yet because he was . . . Well, you know where he was. I wasn't going to say anything to anybody but him for a few weeks, but hell, if not now for happy news, when? We wanted our kids close, and we rang the bell."

"This is great. Britt, this is just amazingly great."

"It shows who we are. We're making our lives, living our lives, both of us, Zane. Yeah, we're okay. They couldn't take who we are away from us. We're who we are despite them."

Despite them, Zane thought. And in some ways, because of them. He worked his way back to urgent care, and while he waited, contacted Maureen.

She'd have heard plenty over the grapevine, but he filled in some details, let her know he was fine, Darby was being looked after. And asked her to handle the insurance claim, reschedule his appointments.

He'd get in when he could.

Darby, looking mildly annoyed, came out along with the pretty, pregnant Dr. Ledbecker.

"You're Zane. Charlene. And you're in charge of this one today?"

"Hey."

Zane overrode Darby's objection. "That's right."

"No breaks, no torn or pulled muscles. She has some substantial bruising, and her shoulder's going to be tender for a few days. Ice, ibuprofen should do the job. No lifting anything over five pounds, and no digging for forty-eight hours."

"Got it."

"The same for her back, her hip." She handed Zane a bag. "Some samples of medication for her knuckles, and a list of instructions. We'll follow up in two days."

"She'll be here."

"My number's on the instruction list. Any other issues, call."

"Thanks. I'll be fine," Darby said.

"No digging!" Charlene warned as Darby dragged Zane out of urgent care.

"Jesus, she's thorough. I was half-afraid she'd bring out the leeches. Did you see Britt?"

"Yeah, we're good."

"Okay then. You drop me off, then go see Emily."

"That's the plan." Not the whole plan, but the first part.

When he dropped her off, he annoyed her all over again by relaying the doctor's restrictions to her horrified, angry, fascinated crew.

With the addendum if they didn't make sure she followed same, he'd kick some asses himself.

Then he went to Emily.

She sat alone on her back patio, staring off at nothing, but jumped up when she saw him.

"I should've come to you. I—"

"Stop. I'm fine."

"Darby."

"Checked out by Dave and the doctor. She'll be fine, too." He saw she'd shed some tears, was struggling with them now. "You've talked to Lee."

"I told him to go on. He has so much to do, and nothing he could do here. I need to call my mama and daddy, but . . ."

"It can wait." He folded her in.

"Oh God, my God, Zane, that he would come back here after all these years. Try to hurt you again. Worse. I think worse. He killed Eliza, you know he must have killed Eliza."

"I know." He stroked her back, tried to soothe the trembling, and finally just pressed his lips to the top of her head. "Let go, just let go."

When she did, the strongest woman he knew clung to him, let loose a torrent of sobs. So he held and stroked and swayed, and said nothing.

"I don't know why I'm acting like this. You're not hurt. Both you and Lee told me Darby's going to be okay. I need to go see her, but . . . And that bastard is in custody. In the hospital thanks to that amazing girl, and in custody. We're safe. We're all safe. My family's safe."

"Your sister's dead."

"Oh, Zane." She drew back, swiped her hands at the tears. "I can't even bring her face into my head. I can't see her."

"Sit down. I'm going to get you some water, some Kleenex."

He brought out water for both of them, nudged the box of tissues in front of her. She pulled some out, blew her nose, wiped her face.

"We never bonded," she said at length. "We always seemed to be at odds. A lot of siblings are at odds at various times. Jesus, Gabe and

Brody went through a couple periods where they weren't happy unless they were bickering or picking on each other. But there's a bond between them. Eliza and I never, never had one."

"You're opposites," Zane put in. "You never had anything in common."

"I never loved her. At least I don't remember a time I loved her. I'm not ashamed of that. It's not my fault."

"No, it's not. So why are you feeling guilty because you didn't love her?"

Emily let out a sigh. "I don't know. Honestly don't." She reached down to pet the dog that sat loyally at her feet. "But I am sorry I didn't love her, couldn't love her. I'm sorry she's dead, and sorry her own choices most likely led to her death. I'm sorry for the grief my parents will feel because they did love her."

He took her hand. "We'll be there for them. That's who we are."

"And we'll do our duty. Have you talked to Britt?"

"Yeah, she's all right, too. In fact . . . I should probably let her tell you, but I'm going to spring it. She's pregnant with your next grandbaby."

"She . . ." The tears spilled again, but Emily shook her head, pointed at her face. "Good ones. Really good ones. It's not just life moving on, Zane, it's life thriving."

She laid a hand on his cheek. "And that's just what we'll do."

Zane would move on, and he hoped like hell to thrive. But he had business to finish first.

When Zane arrived at the hospital in Asheville, Lee was waiting for him outside the ER.

"I figured there was no point telling you not to make the trip."

"No point," Zane agreed.

"I'm going to let you talk to him—after I do. Right now they're putting him in a room. They want him here a couple hours before we transport him back to Raleigh."

"That's time enough."

"It is." Lee put a hand on Zane's shoulder. "Let's walk a bit. It's a lot more peaceful out here than it is inside. Don't know how much he'll have to say."

Zane stuck a hand in his pocket, gripped it around the baseball he'd put there. "Has he asked for a lawyer?"

"Not yet. But seeing as they wired up his jaw, he's not doing a lot of talking. Fixed his nose, from what they tell me, did their X-rays and whatnot. Seems like she bashed his balls real good, too."

"I need to buy her flowers. A lot of flowers."

Lee smiled, then let out a sigh. "I can't be sorry she did a lot more damage to him than he did to her. So while we're walking here I'll tell you what we've been able to piece together."

"He killed Eliza. There's no question of it."

"I'm not arguing, but we need the autopsy results. I can tell you he had a job at a medical supply store, and called in sick a couple days. Statements from neighbors say they saw him, in and out up to Saturday, but hadn't seen her since last Thursday. Next-door neighbor saw her step out into the backyard Thursday afternoon, before he got home. Not since."

"So he killed her Thursday night."

"I expect so, but we'll wait for confirmation. I've been in contact with the detectives in Raleigh. It seems his supervisor didn't report him when he didn't show up to work yesterday, as he called in sick. Sundays and Mondays are his days off."

Zane nodded. "So he likely left after work on Saturday, took his time getting here, probably used back roads, paid cash for rooms, for gas, whatever."

"They're working on tracking him. So are we. We've got him staying two nights at a motel off 40. Confiscated an iPad, some cash from the room, a notebook—the paper kind. More cash in the car he parked at the scenic pullout below the road to your place."

Lee scratched his chin. "A lot in the notebook, starting with a list of names."

Britt nailed it, Zane thought. "His revenge list."

"I'd say. Lots of details on just what he held against the ones on the list, what he knew about them—where they lived, what they did. Ideas for how to pay them back."

"Me, he'd want to beat to death. You?"

Lee walked on a bit more. "I'm not telling this to Emily or the boys. There's no need for it. His top choice there was to set our house on fire, with us inside."

"Jesus Christ, Lee. He lost his mind." Zane held up a hand, shifted to the lawyer, the prosecutor. "Whoever takes his case will try for that—try an insanity defense, but I'm telling you it won't wash. Calling in sick to buy time, the broken window to draw me away, the cash, the careful planning—because you bet your ass he planned every step. He won't meet the bar for legal insanity."

Zane worked it out in his head. "He left the stuff in the motel because he wasn't done with it. He planned to go back, check out, after he took care of me, of Darby. Unless he . . .'"

It wouldn't have been enough, Zane thought, ignoring the sound of oncoming sirens as an ambulance pulled in.

It wouldn't have been finished.

"He's always been an arrogant son of a bitch, Lee. He would've planned to go after Britt, Emily, and your family. Dave and his—anybody in Lakeview on his list. We're all to blame, and he'd have wanted to deal with all of us before he moved on."

"I'm not arguing there either, but he'll never get the chance now. Crazy or sane, he's going back in, Zane, and he won't be coming out again."

"Let me sit in on your interview. I won't say anything," Zane continued quickly. "And if he objects to me being there, I'll leave. I don't think he will. You want a confession to wrap this up right and tight? Let me sit in."

Lee paced back and forth a minute, fought a brief internal war. "Here's what I'll do. You sit in, you say nothing till I'm done with him. He wants you out, you go out. You mess up my interview, you and me, we're going to have a long, unpleasant conversation."

"Won't be necessary. I appreciate it, Lee."

"Well, come on then. Let's see if they've cleared him to talk—such as he can."

They'd made some changes to the ER over the years, and this time Zane walked in unharmed and free. But the memories rolled back on him, the pain, the fear. His arm ached in response; his throat went burning dry.

He said nothing while Lee cleared them through, nothing in the elevator.

"I've got an officer on the door," Lee told him, "and Silas inside with him. No chances."

Zane merely nodded.

Lee showed his badge at the nurse's station, kept moving.

"You go on, take a break, Donny," he told the officer on the door. "I'll let you know when we're done."

"Sure thing, Chief."

Silas stood when Lee and Zane walked in, set aside the magazine he'd leafed through.

This time, Graham lay cuffed with his face a symphony of bruises and bandages. The beeping monitor took a jump, telling Zane that Graham's heartbeat spiked when he looked Graham in the black and swollen eyes.

"How about you turn on that recorder, Silas, so Mr. Bigelow and I can have a talk."

Graham's response came harsh and clipped between clenched teeth. "Doctor."

"Not anymore and not for some time. You can go on, get some coffee, Silas." Lee pointed to the chair Silas vacated.

Zane sat.

"This is Lakeview chief of police Lee Keller interviewing Graham Bigelow after he's been medically cleared to talk. You've been read your rights, Mr. Bigelow? We've got that on record, too, but it's good to ask, right?"

"Know my rights."

"Good. Now, you're charged with trespass, breaking and entering, assault and battery. There's the little matter of stealing a license plate, illegally displaying it on your motor vehicle. You've violated your parole six ways to Sunday, so you'll be serving out the remaining two years on your sentence before we even get to the other charges I just mentioned."

Lee eased a hip on the foot of the bed in what might have been mistaken for a friendly gesture. "And all that doesn't address the up-coming murder charges. The local cops found Eliza's body, Bigelow. Found it just where you left it, on the floor, the head on a pillow, tucked up in a blanket and covered with a sheet. And with clearly visible signs of physical assault."

"Accident."

"Is that gonna be your line? You *accidentally* beat your wife to death, left her on the floor, then drove here to attempt to, what, accidentally beat Zane to death?"

"She fell. Eliza fell, hit her head. Subdural hematoma."

"Did she fall on her face first? They sent me a picture." Lee drew out his phone, kept speaking as he brought it on his screen. "Did she manage to fall on her face, then crack the back of her head? That's some trick."

He turned the phone around, shoved it in Graham's line of vision. "You hit her, and more than once from what they've already determined, and she hit the counter in the kitchen—her blood's on it."

"Fell. She fell. Subdural hematoma."

"So you just let her die?"

"Nothing to do. Too late."

"You didn't call for help?"

"I am a doctor," Graham gritted out.

"No, you're not. You're a violent criminal whose assault on the woman who, for reasons I'll never understand, stood by him, waited for him, betrayed her own children for him, led to her death. We found your motel room, Graham, your car. Your tablet. Two minutes on that iPad showed you've been stalking Zane, Britt, Emily, and more."

Graham turned his head to meet Zane's stare. "What're you look-ing at? Think you matter? You're nothing. Were nothing, are nothing, always nothing."

Rather than respond or react, Zane just let his gaze bore into Gra-ham's. In his pocket, his fingers rubbed against the stitching of the ball.

"He mattered enough for you to leave your dead wife on the floor, come all the way back here, push your way into Zane's house, and assault a woman," Lee pointed out.

"Nothing. Big house? Nothing. Bullshit lawyer? Nothing. Sit there, too afraid to speak."

Zane kept the stare hard, and smiled.

"Wipe that fucking smile off your face!" Graham winced as he said it, tried to shout it with the wires holding his jaw in place. "Weak, useless fuck. Should have killed you in your crib, you and your whiny bitch of a sister. You destroyed my life. You destroyed your mother."

Lee caught Zane's eye, gave him a slight nod.

"How'd I do that?" Zane wondered.

"Disrespectful punk. I couldn't make a man out of you. I gave you life, and you ruined mine. I should've killed you that night, you and your little bitch of a sister. Eliza would still be alive. We'd be happy."

"You just couldn't stop hitting her, could you? All those years in prison, all those years she waited for you, and you still couldn't stop."

"She wasn't the same. She'd lost herself. Your fault."

"So after you hit her this last time, watched her die, you came back here to make me pay."

"You need to pay, you, all of you."

"Rocks through windows, to get me away so you could get into the house." Zane filled his tone with derision, with mockery. "You figured hey, there's just a woman alone in there. And you're so good at beating on somebody smaller, weaker than you. Then you could lie in wait for me, make me pay."

"You take my life, I take yours."

"You broke into my home, attacked Darby intending to wait until I got back so you could kill me."

"I gave you life. I have a right to take it away. I have a right to make you suffer first for every minute of every day I spent locked away like an animal."

"You killed your wife."

"I ended the empty woman she'd become. Taking that empty life was mercy. You stole her from me. You should be dead."

Zane rose, crossed to the bed. "I'm sorry I missed the chance to take you on one-on-one, old man. But a woman beat me to it, and she kicked your ass. That must be really humiliating for someone like you, and knowing that is incredibly satisfying. Here's something for you to chew on while you're doing life without parole. A tough, smart little girl ruined your plans for me nineteen years ago. And a tough, smart woman ruined them today."

He started for the door, stopped, looked back one last time. "If any part of where you ended up before, and where you're going now, is my fault? That's just one more cause for celebration."

Silas walked over when Zane stepped out. "You okay, man?"

"I'm just fine. From my experience, there's enough on record for the DA's office to charge him with second-degree murder along with the rest. He'll get a lawyer and they'll work on pleading it down to man one, but he's gone. He's done, and whatever time he has left in the world he'll do on the inside."

"Well, he earned it. Listen, if you need to hang out, have a beer, I'll be there."

"I know it. Tell Lee I'll talk to him later. I need to get home, make sure Darby's behaving herself."

And he needed some good, clean air.

He didn't think someone like Darby had a favorite flower, so he bought a bunch of everything that looked colorful and happy, that smelled good. Then realized the couple of vases he had at home wouldn't do the job, so with the help of a delighted salesclerk, bought small vases, big vases, square vases, tall vases, and a big galvanized bucket to hold all the flowers until he got home.

Since he was in that deep, he decided what the hell and bought a couple bottles of champagne.

He rarely bought jewelry, didn't intend to now, but a charm caught his eye, seemed predestined. Rather than a bracelet he figured she wouldn't wear, he had it put on a chain.

When he drove the rest of the way home with the top down, the wind blowing the scent of flowers, the mountains green against the blue of the sky, he realized something had changed inside him.

The hook Graham and Eliza had lodged in his guts had pulled free. Done, he thought again, really done now.

He pulled over by the lake to get out, just to look at the sky, the hills reflected on it. Maybe there were undercurrents and always would be, but they'd never drag him down again.

He'd keep building his law practice, and he'd take Darby sailing. Maybe, shit, yeah maybe he'd play some baseball.

And put the past where it belonged. Locked away, like Graham.

He cruised up his drive, saw the solidity of his house—he'd done that—the charm of the terraces, the new trees—Darby had done that.

He wondered if, like him, she'd begun to see this place, this home, as a blend of them. And what that could mean to him, what it might mean to her.

For now he parked in the front, hauled everything inside. He watched through the door, studying the way Darby placed stone, how she and Ralph used the elevation in that placement, in the design, with Gabe doing the hauling.

He couldn't follow it yet, but figured if he didn't trust her vision by now, it made him an idiot. And a man smart enough to have Darby McCray in his life was no idiot.

He opened the doors, left them wide, and walked out into the backbeat of rock and roll.

Ralph spotted him, lifted a hand. "She ain't lifting over the limit, boss. We're sitting on her good there."

"Glad to hear it. Where's everybody else?"

"Maintenance job." Darby swiped sweat. "Are you checking on me? Haven't I got enough keepers?"

"She's a little pissy," Gabe told him.

"Who wouldn't be?" She muttered it, jabbed a finger where she wanted Gabe to set a stone so she could arrange it.

"It's coming up on time for her to pop the pills."

Darby sent Ralph a stare from under her ball cap. "I know what time it is."

"Hot work," Zane observed. "How about I make a big pitcher of lemonade?"

Darby shifted her stare to Zane. "You know how to make lemonade?"

"Sure I do. You get the can out of the freezer, open it, dump it, add cold water, stir."

Some humor leaked through. "Funny, that's my family recipe, too."

"I'll do that, then y'all can take a break, Darby can pop the pills."

And he thought as he went inside, he'd call his office afterward, do some work from home. Later he'd grill up some chops and sweet corn, put some potatoes on with them.

Because like it or not, he intended to take care of her.

CHAPTER TWENTY

Sweaty, sore, and satisfied, Darby took a couple pictures of the water feature in progress before she knocked off for the day.

She knew Zane sat at the back patio table with his laptop, a Coke, and one of the baseballs he tended to cart around. She'd tolerated Ralph's ribbing.

"Somebody's keeping an eye on you, boss."

Just as she'd tolerated having a teenager hand her a fresh ice pack every hour or so and remind her to take a break and ice her shoulder.

She wasn't an idiot, Darby assured herself, and she was perfectly capable of doing her job *and* being pissy while still appreciating the concern.

Now the workday done, her crew gone, she prepared herself to tolerate Zane's fussing over her.

So she walked over to the table, picked up his Coke, gulped some down. "You know, you didn't have to stick around and sit out here. I already had Gabe and Ralph on my case about doctor's orders."

"Uh-huh." He finished up a last email. "Actually, I was enjoying an afternoon working at home and outside while surrounded by the landscape my lady created. A nice change of pace for me."

He lifted a chin toward the progress of the water feature. "Coming right along."

"It is. And if you go away, go to work the rest of the week like you're supposed to, you should see the finished product by end of the day Saturday. Barring rain delays."

"Yeah? That's great because I'm figuring, if you're pretty much done with the works by the end of the month, I'm going to throw a big, bust-out Fourth of July party."

"Really?"

"We'll have a hell of a view of the fireworks on the lake from up here."

"Hmm." After tipping down her sunglasses, she narrowed her eyes on his face. "You look like a man in a pretty good mood."

"I'd say that's accurate."

"And unexpected."

"I'm in a good enough mood to fire up the grill in a bit. Interested?"

No fussing, she concluded, and didn't know quite what to think about it, or his good mood.

"I could be. I'll grab a shower."

She walked inside, then nearly straight back out again. "Are you opening a sideline flower shop out of your kitchen?"

"What? Oh." Shaking his head, laughing, he got to his feet. "Slipped my mind. They're for you."

"For me? Walker, there has to be seven or eight dozen flowers in there."

"I couldn't decide, so I got a bunch. And the vases," he added as they walked back in. "I thought about sticking them in vases, but then I decided you'd do a better job of it."

"Well." She searched for a word, settled on "Wow."

"I didn't get a card because I didn't think they made one that covered all of it. Like thanks, I'm sorry, heal up soon, maybe a congratulations thrown in there. And the overall important you matter. You matter, Darby."

"Wow" didn't measure up, she realized, to what he made her feel at that moment. The words, the way he looked at her, the glory of scent and color surrounding them.

"I'm really dirty, but too bad." She went to him, wrapped around him, and hoped what she felt in that moment came through the kiss.

"This is ridiculously beautiful, Zane. Insanely thoughtful." Before stepping back, she pressed her hands to his cheeks. "I'm going to have the best time arranging all these."

"We can have some champagne while you do."

She blinked. "Champagne."

"I picked up a couple bottles." He got one out of the fridge, started to open it. "I didn't think to ask if you liked champagne."

"I'd be crazy not to. Zane, where did you go when you left here this morning?"

"We'll talk about it." He opened the bottle with a cheerful, muffled pop. "Meanwhile, open this."

He handed her a small, wrapped box, then pulled out champagne flutes.

Overwhelmed, even a little anxious, she stared at the box. "Zane, I've got a few bruises. For all this I should be in a coma."

"If you were, you couldn't drink champagne. Open it. If you don't like it, I'll keep it myself because it made me think of you."

Anxiety didn't erase curiosity, so she pulled the ribbon, ripped the paper. And had to smile when she opened the box to a book-shaped charm on a chain with its flowing script quote.

"'Though she be but little, she is fierce.'"

Holding it up so it dangled in the light, she looked at him. "I'm five-seven. That's not so little."

"Comparatively. And God knows the 'fierce' works."

"Well, I love it, so you don't get to keep it for yourself." She slipped the chain over her head. "Now I might start milking every bump and scrape I get on the job to see what I can get out of it."

He didn't smile. "This was personal."

"Okay. Why don't we sit outside and drink this fancy wine, and you can tell me why you left here angry and upset, and came back in a damn good mood."

"We'll do that, get it done. Then I'm going to fire up that grill while you do something with these flowers."

He sat out with her, dived right in because he wanted this part of their evening opened and closed. "You know I talked to Britt this morning, then I went to talk to Emily—and I'm going to round back to that. Then I drove into Asheville to see Graham."

"I figured you would."

"He looks like he did ten rounds with the champ, which he did.

Pair of black eyes, broken nose. They wired his jaw. Can't say I saw his balls, but I'm told they're busted up pretty good. Don't look distressed. Don't."

"I've never hit anybody, hurt anybody like that. It's different in training. Even that time with Trent, it wasn't like this."

Zane reached over, tugged down the shoulder of her T-shirt to expose the bruising. "Do you think he'd have stopped there?"

"No. I know I did what I had to do."

"Lee let me sit in while he interviewed him in the hospital. They tracked down his motel room, found his car. There's evidence, plenty of it, on what he planned to do. And eventually, like I knew he would, he couldn't stand me being in there. Couldn't stand me just sitting there, looking at him, and all that hate, that rage, took over."

He told her, not softening any of it, just cutting through to the meat.

"He confessed." Shocked, appalled, Darby gripped her hands together under the table. "To killing his wife, to coming here to try to kill you."

"I want to say he changed since I saw him last, but it's not really true." He picked up the ball, studied it, turned it in his hand. "I think prison and life after it stripped away the veneer. He isn't able to polish himself up, to hide behind that layer now. What he is, it's just there."

It helped to sit here with her, smelling flowers, feeling the air while he emptied himself of the day.

He set the ball down again.

"Lee got the preliminary report on Eliza about an hour ago. Graham had the cause of death right. Subdural hematoma, resulting from the blow to the head. She had fresh bruises, old bruises. I expect they'll plead it down to man one before it's finished."

"But—"

Zane waved a finger. "Due to the circumstances, the pattern, the evidence, he'll get twenty years for it. Add in the aggravated assault and battery on you, breaking probation, and so on, his past history with violence, he won't get out again. He'll die in prison."

Pausing, he looked out at what was his, what she'd made of his, the blooming where he'd never have thought to put it, the young trees, the pots spilling with color.

"I never confronted him after that night. I was the one in the hospital then, in cuffs then. After, I testified in court, but I didn't confront him face-to-face. I did that today, for myself. For Britt and Emily. For my grandparents. For you.

"And I realized, when I walked away, that it's over—and it hadn't been, because I had it buried inside me all this time. Now I don't. I ripped it out, like . . . a poisonous plant, root and all. It's gone."

"It took courage to do what you did."

"He couldn't touch me."

"Not physically. Emotional wounds run deeper, we both know it. It took courage, and smarts. Serious smarts there, Walker. You knew just what to do to push him. I bet you were a hell of a prosecutor."

"I wasn't bad." He flashed a grin. "Not bad at all. Now let's round back, end this on a high note. Emily's going to be fine. It's rough on her, and my grandparents, but we'll get through it. Britt, too, because they're all—we're all—going to be focused on something good and positive. Britt's pregnant."

"She's— That's great!" With a quick chair dance, Darby lifted her glass, tapped it to his. "The best of the best kind of news. When's she due?"

"I don't know. It's really new. She wasn't going to announce it yet, then figured she would. She's good at knowing how to balance things out."

"I'll say. You should've taken her flowers."

"You're right. I'll do it tomorrow. You can deal with yours, get your shower, ice your shoulder. I'll deal with dinner. And we'll get seriously buzzed on champagne."

"I can get behind that plan." She reached over for his hand. "The day may have started on a really shitty note, but we're going to end it happy, well-fed, and a little bit drunk."

While her bruises healed, Darby talked to the Asheville police, the prosecutor, dealt with reporters from the *Lakeview Weekly* to reporters from Asheville, from Raleigh, and from the Associated Press.

The original case against Dr. and Mrs. Graham Bigelow had generated considerable media at the time. The current one dredged all of that up while layering on the new.

She knew Zane dealt with reporters, too, just as she knew both of them breathed a sigh of relief when the news cycle switched to some other scandal.

As June wound down toward July, she finished up work at Zane's, squeezed in the stonework between guests at Emily's last bungalow, started the Marsh job on the lake.

With the help of her crew, and the surprise that Zane knew his way around a nail gun, she had her equipment shed under roof, and a sweet little garden shed completed and stocked, and the skeleton of her greenhouse erected.

Maybe she'd neglected the interior of the house for now, but she built her business, client by client.

She worked with two of those clients on a pretty Saturday afternoon while their little boy took a nap in the shade.

"When you deadhead?" She demonstrated to both Charlene and Joe. "You not only tidy up the plant or bush, you encourage new blooms. And your herbs there? You want to pinch off the flowers."

"Oh, but they're pretty," Charlene objected.

"But the plant's energy's going to the flower instead of the vegetation, and once they flower, your leaves can get bitter. You also want to pinch back the plant to encourage it to fill out. Look here at the branch point, now count up a couple leaves, pinch off the stem. You're going to use that in something you cook, and your basil's going to be stimulated at the same time. It's going to grow back even better."

"We've just been taking off a few leaves here and there," Joe explained.

"Yeah, so I see."

He studied the plants through his horn-rim glasses. "And that's why they look a little straggly?"

"Yeah. Try this way, and by the time you want to harvest, you're going to have tons."

"If we do, I'm going to make you pesto."

Darby angled her head at Joe. "I'll take it."

She moved around the yard with them, giving advice, delighted that they both took notes.

"Uh-oh. The boss is waking up. I've got him, babe." Joe tucked away his notebook as he went to his little boy.

"We really appreciate you coming over just to talk us through some of this, again. Your crew is so helpful."

"It's what we're here for."

"Your bruises are healing. Any trouble with the shoulder?"

"None. It's down to that ugly yellow stage, maybe still a little stiff first thing in the morning, but not as much. And it works out quick."

"The advantage of being active and in shape," Charlene declared. "We were surprised to get an invitation for the Fourth."

"Why? You and Britt are friends. You're basically my doctor at this stage."

"Now that we know the whole story of what happened in this house, we thought Britt and her family would want to keep their distance."

"You had nothing to do with it. Neither did the house."

"When I think he might have broken in that night. The baby. Babies," she said, with a hand pressed protectively to her bump.

"Don't. He's back where he belongs, and he's going to stay there."

"Joe keeps telling me exactly that. I wonder—Even in a friendly, safe community like this, there can be trouble. I wonder if you'd consider teaching a self-defense course."

"Oh, I'm not qualified."

Charlene let out a wide-eyed laugh. "Are you kidding me? Think about it. Maybe over the winter when your work slows down."

"I'll think about that if you and Joe think about getting a composter."

"I know we should." Charlene let out a sigh. "It feels like another chore."

"You'll be amazed how it pays you back. I've got to get to Zane, and I have one more stop to make. Party planning in full swing. We'll see you on the Fourth."

"Wouldn't miss it."

She glanced across the street before she got in her truck. Even knowing there would be no brutal man in a Mercedes, she couldn't break the habit.

Yet.

She swung by the Marsh job to check on Roy and Ralph, then spent an hour working with them to finish the new stone steps.

In their boat, the Marshes tacked over. "They're beautiful!" Patsy called out. "Absolutely beautiful!"

"And safe!" Darby called back.

"How about a ride around the lake?"

She shook her head at Bill's offer. "Wish I could, but I've got to get on. I'm late already. See you on the Fourth."

She turned, saw that Roy had walked down the dock, sat with his legs dangling over.

"What's that about?" she asked Ralph.

Ralph gave his usual grunt and shrug. "Probably sulking 'cause he's working on Saturday."

"Well, you can clean up and knock off now. We'll work on the terraces on Monday."

Though she rolled her eyes, Darby walked down the dock, sat by Roy.

"Workday's done. It's a dumbass time to sulk about it."

"Not sulking. I like looking at the water. Don't go on it because I get seasick, which blows."

"That does blow."

"But I like looking at it. And I like looking back from here and seeing those steps I had a part in building. They look damn good."

Darby looked back herself. "Yeah, they do."

"I'm sitting here, looking at the water, looking back at those steps, and damn if I don't see in my head just what you're going to have us do on that slope. I can see it. You ask me to see it last year, even a few months back, I'd've said, What, I see a damn steep slope mostly weeded up. But I see it just like we're going to do it."

He knocked a fist on her thigh. "And I know how to go about it, too, or a lot of it. So I'm sitting here, taking in the water and the pretty nice breeze off it, and it hits me. I've done got myself a trade. Ain't that a hell of a thing?"

"You've got a strong back, Roy. You've also got smart hands and a good eye. The hands and the eye are better than they were, and they weren't bad to start. If you think about going off and starting your own business, I'm going to punch your lights out."

He ducked his head, grinned. "Believe you could do it, too. No, I'm thinking I've got a good job. I've got a trade. I'm making a regular, decent living. And I'm thinking, well, hell, I might just ask Adele to marry me."

"Holy shit, Roy!" She punched his shoulder, then grabbed him, kissed him, making him duck his head again and laugh. "She's terrific!"

"You know what's most terrific? She's never tried changing me. She loves me like I am. And I guess I changed me some, and you did, and she still loves me like I am."

"You better grab on to that, my man."

"I think I'm gonna."

"Clean up, knock off, go get the girl. I'll see you Monday."

She gave him another punch, scrambled up. "I'm so late!"

She took the new steps, pleased at how the stone felt—sturdy, level—under her boots. And grinned all the way to Zane's.

She found Emily and Britt with him on the patio. "Sorry, sorry. Stuff. I am totally in party mode now. What do you need me to do?"

"They want me to string lights," Zane complained. "And they say I need at least two more tables for food, with canopies over them."

"Sure, we can do that."

He just closed his eyes. "And to think I actually believed you'd be on my side of this."

"We've hired a local band for music," Emily said definitely.

"Live music? This is so cool."

"I've got outdoor speakers," Zane reminded them. "I've got an endless playlist."

"Not live." Britt patted his hand. "We're going to set up a few games for the kids. With little prizes."

"I'm loving it. I've got some old plywood at my place. We cut a hole in the middle, paint it up, and you've got a beanbag toss. We could do a water balloon toss, a little scavenger hunt. There's tons of stuff."

"And here I figured I'd throw a bunch of food on the grill, buy a truckload of drinks, and pick up sides."

The three women just stared at him with a combination of derision and pity.

"So," Darby continued, "I can make a big green salad, but if you let me out of the actual cooking, which everyone will thank you for, I'll take care of the kids' games and prizes."

"Deal, but I'll give you a hand with that," Britt added. "It'll be fun. And we'll probably need you on board for the lights."

"I'll pay for the band."

"Emily, you're not paying—"

She cut Zane off with a look. "It may be your house, Zane, but this is a Walker-Keller-Norten-McCray operation. Now, as I was saying before, people will bring food because that's what they do, but we'll finish up our menu, our supply list, then hand out assignments."

Outnumbered, definitely outgunned, Zane retired from the field of battle.

After the women in his life rolled over him, Zane sat with Darby on the patio. He contemplated his beer.

"What was I thinking in the first place?"

"Kick-ass party," Darby reminded him.

He gave her a long look. "My definition of 'party' doesn't seem to be in the same universe as the rest of y'all's."

"It's going to be great. You can't have a house, grounds, a view like this and not throw an awesome party." She smiled as he brooded. "How about I make mac and cheese?"

He gave her another long look, this one considerably less broody. "From scratch, like before?"

"You look like you need a little comfort."

"I do. In fact . . ." He tapped his list of assignments. "I need more than a little. It calls for an appetizer."

"My two no-fail appetizers are opening a jar of olives or spraying

Cheez Whiz on a Ritz. If I go all out, I put an olive on the Cheez Whiz on the Ritz."

"We can do better." He rose, tugged her to her feet.

As he backed her into the house, her smile turned sly. "My Spidey sense tells me you're not thinking about food."

"I don't know. You're pretty tasty."

"That's true. I am." Willing to prove it, she shifted, began backing him toward the great room sofa. "And it's a good thing I am, because dinner's going to be late."

He started to mention the patio doors were wide open, but then he was on his back on the sofa with Darby straddling him.

He decided a man's home was his castle.

"We're going to find out if sex whets your appetite or sates it." With that, she pulled off her work tank.

Before she curled down to him, he trailed his fingers over the fading bruises on her shoulder. "Still sore?"

"Not enough to worry about." But since the look in his eyes clearly said worry, she cupped his face. "Don't go there," she murmured. "Come here instead."

She laid her lips on his, taking the kiss deeper, still deeper, degree by degree.

Just us, she thought as his hand slid over her. Just you, just me while the late evening breeze slipped over the skin, with the light a gilded sparkle.

What she'd intended as a quick bout of fun turned slow, turned tender as they comforted each other.

Even as pulses quickened, they took time to give, to let the moments spin out as they touched, as they tasted.

She unbuttoned his shirt, spread it open to glide her hands over his chest. Then to press her lips to his heart.

A good heart, she thought, generous and open despite all he'd been through. Or maybe because of it. She wanted to tend that heart, to help the deep, underlying scars heal.

He rose up to meet her, to watch her eyes as he slowly, carefully peeled her bra away. He skimmed his lips over the bruises. He, too, wanted to heal.

She was strong and fierce, but he understood the hurts buried inside her. He needed to show her, above all, he'd always protect her, always defend her.

And now, in this moment, he'd give her peace in pleasure.

He cupped her breasts, thumbs whispering over her until those depthless eyes closed. Her body moved against his, slow, sinuous, as sensations layered and built with the stroke of hands, with the brush of lips.

She shifted, moaning, as he slipped her clothes away, as he paused to take her mouth. Her breath caught as she took him in, as their eyes met, then again their lips.

He filled her, body and heart, so beautifully she wondered how either of them could bear it. They moved together, riding slow, undulating waves. Giving and taking in equal measure while the light sparkled and the air spilled over them warm and sweet.

And holding fast to each other, caught in each other's eyes, they crested.

Tears stung the back of her eyes. She couldn't say why so she lowered her head to his shoulder until she'd fought them off. She tried to think of something fun and flippant to say, but couldn't, and stayed curled to him while his hands stroked up and down her back.

"It's different." He spoke quietly. "It's different between us." When she didn't respond, he traced a finger over her infinity symbol, thought of her reasoning for it. "Does that scare you?"

"Maybe. Some. Yes. I made such an incredible mistake before."

He drew her back enough for her to see the quick flash of anger in his eyes. It mirrored in his voice. "This isn't a mistake. I'm not Trent."

"Zane, you're nothing like Trent. You're pretty much his opposite. And that, stupid as it sounds, is part of what scares me a little." To soothe them both, she rubbed her cheek to his. "How could I have believed I loved him, how could I have married him and now feel what I feel for you? But I did, and I do."

"I want to say it does sound stupid, but it doesn't, at least not entirely. But this is you now. This is me. I wasn't looking for you, for this. But here we are, Darby."

"I like where we are."

"So do I. That's one of the reasons I want to ask you to move in here, with me."

"Oh." She wrapped hard around him, squeezed her eyes shut. "Don't ask me yet. I know it's more stupid. I can hear how stupid especially since I'm here more than I'm there. But I need my own place for now. I went from my mother's house to Trent's—because that place was never mine—then back to my mom's. I just need my own for now."

"I can swallow that for now. You know, when for-now's over, it's still your place. Just like I'm going to be in love with you whether you're ready for it or not."

He filled her up again so her heart swelled, thudded. "So much stupid coming out," she murmured. "Can you give me a little time? I need to feel like I'm solid, steady on my own."

"Are you kidding me?" Sincerely baffled, he drew back again. "Not about the time—we've got time—about the rest. You're about as solid and steady as they come."

"Not much more than a year ago, I was barely able to go through the motions. We're both rebuilding our lives, and we're doing a pretty good job of it. Let's just get a little farther along."

"I can work with that." Lightly, he trailed his fingers down her back. "Especially since you'll cave."

"Will I?"

"Guaranteed. You're crazy about me."

She laughed, nudged away. "Listen to you."

"Crazy about me," he repeated as she reached for her clothes. "Then I have the winning ticket with this house. You'll cave."

She stood holding her clothes, dressed only in the boots he hadn't been able to get off—and the necklace he'd given her. And made him want all over again.

"The house is a draw, I give you that one. Maybe that's the reason I have sex with you."

He just smiled. "Crazy about me."

"Yeah, yeah. I'm going to grab a shower."

"Good idea."

The look in his eyes as he got up had her backing away.

"Just to clean up. Do you want to eat tonight?"

That look stayed in his eyes. She found herself laughing as she dashed away. He scooped her up halfway up the stairs.

Dinner was very late.

CHAPTER TWENTY-ONE

Darby got in most of a day's work before afternoon storms banged and boomed over the mountains. Rain meant switching from outdoor, client work, to indoor, personal work.

After a trip to the hardware store for paint.

She'd gone bright and cheery in her kitchen with canary yellow walls, bold blue shelves and cabinets. Because she accepted she wasn't quite that handy, she'd hired a local to replace the ugly countertops, opting for pure white to pop her colors.

Eventually, she promised herself, she'd replace the hideous flooring. But when she let herself into the kitchen, out of the rain, she could look around with considerable pleasure.

She'd found a cute little bistro set at the flea market just outside of town, had painted it the same blue as the cabinets with some yellow trim. All that color after the gray rain said happy.

She stripped off her wet hoodie, her work cap, hung both on one of the three sunflower hooks she'd screwed into the wall, then took off her boots. Her herbs—mostly for looks and scent rather than cooking—sat in their little white pots on the windowsill over the sink. After testing the soil, she gave them all a drink.

She started to grab a Coke out of the fridge, stopped, frowned. She'd have sworn she'd had four bottles, but only three stood next to her quart of milk. With a shrug, she took out her phone, added Cokes to her shopping list.

After sticking her bottle in the cargo pocket of her pants, she carried the paint and primer to the living room. Or what would be the living room one day.

At the moment it served as storage for paint and painting supplies, household tools, some planters and other garden accessories she'd picked up on sale, all organized by category.

She grabbed her painter's tape, a tarp, then stood baffled.

Why in the world would she have put the fairy statue—one she intended for a fairy garden she'd plant the following spring—over with paint supplies? And what was the wind chime, still in its box, doing in tools?

More annoyed with herself than disturbed, she put things where they belonged, then hauled the tarp, the tape upstairs.

She still had to deal with the short hallway, but her bedroom, like the kitchen, hit the more-than-acceptable level.

She'd chosen a soft, misty blue there with a creamy trim. No actual bed yet, she thought, but the white duvet and lots of colorful pillows made it all homey and inviting. Sooner or later she'd paint the flea market dresser, but she'd scored with the big mirror over it with its iron frame of twining vines.

Probably needed a rug, and she'd get to that, but she loved the trio of watercolors—the lake, the mountains, a fanciful garden—she'd hung on the wall.

She stepped into the tiny bathroom. When she'd killed and stripped off all the fish, she'd found dingy white walls. She intended to use the palest of pale greens, walls and ceiling, with the same trim color as the bedroom.

Once she'd taped off the trim, she tarped the room. With the rain drumming, the occasional strobe flash of lightning and rocking boom of thunder, she dug out what she'd designated as paint clothes. As she changed, she considered her painting playlist. Maybe classic rock, a good, hard beat.

She opened the top drawer of the dresser to get a bandanna to protect her hair from paint splatter.

And froze.

"That's not right," she murmured, took a couple careful breaths. "No, that's not right."

Carefully, she backed away from the dresser, and heart hammering, body braced, yanked open the closet door.

Nothing but clothes, she noted as the blood roared in her brain like the thunder outside.

But not right. Not quite right.

She dug her keys out of her pocket, slipped one, point out, between her clenched knuckles, and did a search of the house.

When she'd finished, assured she was alone, she pulled out her phone.

"Lee, it's Darby. I think someone's been in my house. Yes, I'm here now. No, I've been through it. No one's here, but—Thanks. Yeah, thanks."

She slid the phone back in her pocket, and while she waited for the police, began a more thorough search.

Lee arrived in minutes, but she already had a list going in her head. She let him in the front with the rain drumming at his back.

"Thanks for coming, and so fast."

"That's what we're here for. Are there signs of a break-in?"

"I didn't find any."

"I'll take a look." Standing on the inside mat, his black slicker dripping a bit, he scanned her living room. "What makes you think someone's been inside?"

"Some of this is going to sound silly, but . . . Well, we can start right in here. I'm using this for storage right now. I've got things together by category."

"I can see that right off. You're a tidy soul, aren't you, Darby?"

"Yeah, plus, time management. If things are in their place, you don't waste time looking for them. But some of the things in here weren't in their place. I came home to paint the bathroom upstairs, so I was getting the tarp and tape before I came back to get the pan, the roller. And some of the garden stuff was mixed in with the paint stuff. I don't do that. I know it seems like anybody could do that and forget, and I initially brushed it off, but . . ."

She could hear herself, the nerves in her voice, so worked to steady it. "When I came down to look again, I realized a couple of tools were in the garden section. And that box? I know I didn't open it yet—it's the shower curtain and all that for when I finish the bath. I hadn't opened it, but it's been opened."

"Okay, honey. Did you notice anything missing?"

"A Coke. And I know how that sounds, but I *know* I had four in the fridge, but there were only three."

"There's one in your pocket," he pointed out.

"That's one of the three." Taking it out, she twisted the cap off, twisted it on to keep her hands busy. "Lee, when I go below four, it goes right on my shopping list. It's habit. I brushed that off, too. I just shrugged it off, but upstairs . . ."

Shoving the bottle back in her pocket, she let out a breath. "I'll show you."

As they started upstairs, she continued, "I wanted a bandanna for my hair before I started priming the walls because I didn't want to get paint on the logo cap. But when I opened the drawer . . ."

She gestured to the one she'd left open. "Here's the thing. I keep underwear, socks and bandannas in the top drawer."

He walked over, looked in the drawer. "That's what I'm seeing."

"I have eight pair of underwear, eight sports bras, two dress bras—one black, one white—eight pair of work socks, eight pair of regular socks, eight bandannas. I'm a laundry-once-a-week type, and keep the spares for when I miss laundry day. I have one of everything in my truck, in case. I keep two of everything at Zane's. Well, not the dress bras because I hardly use them."

"Okay, I'm following you."

"I'm wearing underwear, a sports bra, work socks. That means there should be four of those items in the drawer. Nothing's in the hamper but today's work pants and tee—I haven't been here for a couple days, except to run in and out. There are only three pair of underwear, and what's there isn't folded right."

He nodded, looked at her. "Anything else?"

"In the closet. Everything's there, but things have been shifted around some, like somebody was going through it. I have a box on the shelf in there. Some of my mother's things. Nothing valuable, just keepsakes, I guess. Like her reading glasses, her work gloves, this bead necklace I made her when I was about twelve, sympathy cards people sent me. It's all there, but someone's been through it."

And God, God, that upset her more than anything else. Her mom's things touched by a stranger.

"Do you keep any cash in the house?"

"What? Sorry, yes. I keep two hundred in fives, tens, and twenties in the drawer of that table by the bed. It's down to a hundred. Why would they leave a hundred, why not take it all?"

"Hoping you wouldn't notice, I'd say."

Relief spilled through her. He believed her.

"They went through the medicine cabinet. It's just over-the-counter stuff, but it's shifted around again."

"Did you have the place locked up?"

"I did. That's habit, too. I came in the back, through the kitchen. I used my key."

"When's the last time you were here?"

"I didn't get here at all yesterday, but the day before I was here for a while after work. Just a quick in and out. I wanted another sheet of plywood for the beanbag games we're doing at Zane's, and I had this bird feeder I picked up and wanted to use on a job—so I came in for that. I'd have noticed, I think I'd have noticed if things had been out of place."

"All right. I'm going to take a look at your doors, your windows."

"I'd appreciate it."

She went down with him, peered around him when he opened her front door, studied it. "See these little scratches?"

"Now I do. Someone picked the lock?"

"I'd say a credit card would do it. It's not much of a lock."

"Crap, crap, *crap*! I'll get better ones. A hundred bucks and a pair of panties? I've got tools right over there worth more than a hundred, and the little TV in the kitchen? You could walk out with that under one arm."

"Might be kids."

She felt another wave of relief, quickly gone. "You don't think so. Kids would've taken all the money, and wouldn't have been so careful."

Lee let that ride. "I'm going to take a good look around outside. And we'll see if I can get any prints off this door, some of the other surfaces. Were you planning to stay here tonight?"

"Not anymore. I think I'll paint the bathroom another time."

"We're going to do regular drive-bys for the next day or two. And I'll have my ear to the ground."

No prints, Darby thought later as she drove through the rain. None at all on the door handles, the drawers rifled through. She didn't need Lee to tell her the intruder had likely worn gloves, and gone the extra step of wiping surfaces down.

Awfully careful for someone who only took a hundred dollars and a pair of panties. And awfully creepy.

She couldn't dig down for real anger, or even genuine fear. What she felt was sharp disappointment that the community she'd embraced so wholeheartedly held someone who'd violate her home, her privacy.

For nothing.

She circled the lake, slate gray and gloomy behind the curtain of rain. The thick sky smothered the mountains, dulled all the color.

It suited her mood.

She told herself not to be naive. Every community had its bad side, its sad side, its ugly little secrets. After all, Lakeview, for all its easy southern charm, had once harbored a pair of horrific abusers.

Undercurrents, she reminded herself.

And still, one creepy break-in couldn't and wouldn't overpower all the rest it offered.

She reminded herself to be grateful she had a safe haven in Zane's house, she had friends, people she trusted.

When she turned up Zane's road, she felt a trickle of optimism slip back inside. The lights on the terrace walls glowed against that heavy gloom, shined warm through it. The accent lights she'd placed to showcase the water feature glimmered quiet and steady.

Whatever lurked under the surface, she'd handle it. And she'd keep building.

More settled, she took off her boots on the covered veranda, un-locked the door, reset the alarm. After carting her boots back to the mudroom, stripping off the hoodie, she got down to the serious busi-ness of pouring herself a glass of wine.

Then in the quiet, empty house, sat at the counter with her laptop to look up local locksmiths. And though the optimist in her hated to do it, the practical woman took a look at security systems.

The pelting rain masked the sound of Zane driving up, and she didn't hear the door open and close, so she jolted when she heard footsteps, swiveled around to jump off the stool.

"Jesus, Jesus, Jesus." Slapping a hand on her heart, she settled back down. "You're not supposed to be here."

"I live here."

"Yeah, and you're supposed to have dinner with Micah and Dave tonight."

He walked to her, skimmed a hand over her hair, kissed her. "And you're supposed to be painting your fish room. Plans changed." Sliding his hands down to her shoulders, he rubbed gently. "Are you okay?"

"I take it word got back to you about the panty thief."

Now those hands on her shoulders gave her a little shake. "There's no point pretending you're not upset."

"Of course I am. Nobody likes to imagine somebody invading their home and messing around with their things. But that's what happened, and taking the classic step of closing the barn door after, I'm calling a locksmith in the morning, and I'll look into a security system."

She patted the hand still on her shoulder in hopes of dimming the angry light in his eyes. "You didn't have to change your plans."

"Yeah, I did. And I have to wonder why you'd think I'd sit around tossing back a beer and some wings after you had a break-in." Now he cupped her face, firmly. "Don't do that."

"I don't want to be one of those needy women."

He let out a half laugh, walked over to get a glass to join her with the wine. "You're the least needy person I know. In fact, you could use a little needy in there."

"The needy's why I ended up with Trent."

He sat, considered her. "Is that what you think?"

"It's what I know. My father leaves me and my mother, and I want—need—someone to love me, a guy who'll stand by me, stick with me. Thick and thin. He saw that, played on that, and, well, it didn't work out very well for me. Maybe I've overcompensated," she admitted. "I'm working on finding the balance."

"Wanting someone to love you, stand, and stick isn't needy, darlin', it's human. I'm here right now, standing by you."

"I know it." She did know it, and it made the back of her throat ache. "And under all the I'm fine, no big deal, I'm really glad you are. I mean, what kind of perv steals plain cotton underwear? They're not even sexy."

"They are when you wear them. So just that and half your house cash?"

"Panties, a hundred bucks, and a bottle of Coke. What I figure is most people wouldn't have noticed any of it. Even the cash you might dismiss as being forgetful, you know? It's creepy, and disturbing, but basically harmless. Mostly I'm pissed because I didn't feel comfortable staying there tonight and getting that bathroom painted."

"We'll paint it tomorrow after work."

"Tomorrow's the third. We should spend it in party prep."

"That bathroom has about ten square feet of wall space. How long could it take? After, we can prep our asses off."

He settled her down, she realized, when she hadn't really understood she'd needed to settle down.

"We could start now, working on your list. Like did you rent the extra tables and chairs?"

The sulky came back to his face. She thought it was adorable.

"I bought the damn tables and chairs. Micah and I are picking them up tomorrow. We're having pizza," he decided and rose to switch on the oven.

"You bought them?"

"Don't play innocent with a lawyer. We know. You and the other women decided this bash would be an annual event, so I bought the tables, the chairs, which I'll now have to haul in and out of the storage room every year."

He poured more wine. "Along with the ridiculous red, white, and blue tablecloths Britt demanded, with coordinating plates, napkins, cups, flatware, and some dumbass serving pieces. And the stupid lights, lanterns, and God-all, including arranging for half a million hamburger patties, hot dogs, buns, gallons of beer, wine, soft drinks, and the gargantuan Hefty bags we'll need to haul all the debris away when it's over."

She sipped her wine, smiled when he got the pizza out of the freezer. "You didn't shop for all that."

"Shopped for some, paid for all."

"Grumpy."

"One moment of weakness, and I'm throwing a crazy-ass party every Fourth for the rest of my life."

"It's probably not a good time to mention you're going to want to throw a crazy-ass party around Christmas every year."

He narrowed his eyes. "Who says I want to do something like that?"

She rose, wrapped her arms around him.

"That won't soften me up."

"It's not for that—I have other ways to soften you up. It's for being here when I didn't want to need you being here."

"Get used to it," he replied, and brushed his lips over her hair. "Here's what we're going to do. We're not going to think about panty-stealing perverts or crazy-ass parties. We're going to eat pizza, drink wine, then put a bag of popcorn in the mike, drink more wine, watch a movie. Then we're going to have some wild sex."

"What kind of wild sex? Our definitions may vary."

"We'll find out."

But he did think about perverts and just how isolated and vulnerable her house was. Zane thought about it enough to leave shortly after Darby in the morning to drive over and catch Lee at home.

"You after breakfast?" Lee asked him. "I sweet-talked Emily into making French toast."

"Nobody turns down Em's French toast," he said, and kissed her cheek.

"Then you're in luck." She returned the kiss before he bent down to give Rufus a full-body rub. "Gabe's already gone, and Brody's still in bed. You're up early."

"It's getting to be a habit. Darby's up at dawn." At home, he poured coffee, got out another plate, then sat with Lee.

"I expect you want to know where I'm at with her break-in."

"I'd be surprised if you're anywhere on that, considering."

"You'd be right. It wouldn't take much to figure out she's not home some nights, and she's got flimsy locks."

Zane gave himself one more mental kick for not so much as thinking of either of those facts beforehand.

"She's taking care of that part today, and she's going to talk to Micah about a security system."

"I'm glad to hear it, both counts."

Emily brought a plate piled with French toast to the table, sat with them.

Now that the family had settled, Rufus curled himself under the table to join them.

"How's she doing?" Emily asked.

"Not pissed enough if you ask me. Mostly baffled because the whole thing seems stupid."

Lee slathered on butter, poured syrup. "I'd agree with her if it wasn't for the door, the drawers being wiped down. Not a print on them. Now, it may be some asshole, hormonal kid who watched enough TV to worry about leaving prints, but it strikes me some asshole kid's going to take all the money."

He wagged his fork in the air. "Taking part of it, that's smart. Most people are going to say, well, I'd swear I had two hundred in here, then figure they forgot taking some cash out. And I don't know anybody who knows just exactly how many pair of underwear they've got, or Cokes in the fridge, or the rest."

"She would," Zane said. "It's how she operates."

"I got that, so I'd think asshole kid getting a little rush. But it doesn't feel quite right. I'd like her to get that security system ASAP. I'd feel some better knowing if somebody tried to get in while she was there, they'd be in for one hell of a surprise."

"Problem is she sleeps like the dead. Seriously."

Lee smiled a little. "Is that so?"

"First few times I actually checked to make sure she was breathing. Once she's out, she's out. I swear, the proverbial bomb could go off and she wouldn't so much as twitch."

"Then she ought to stay with you at least until Lee figures this out, and she gets new locks and that security." Emily got the worry line between her eyebrows. "I don't like thinking of her alone up there after this."

"Neither do I. I asked her to move in with me before this happened. She's not ready."

"You . . ." Emily put down her fork. "That's a big step, Zane. A big one for you, but apparently you're ready."

"Yeah, surprise. I am."

"Then ask her again."

He shook his head. "She's not ready. She's got more issues in there than she shows."

Lee poked a finger at him. "What're you going to do about it?"

"Wait until she's ready. And give her a few nudges along the way. She'll stay with me until she gets her house secure. She can handle herself, knows it, but she's not stupid. And she'll want her place secure when she moves in with me anyway. She'll want to keep the house, the land."

"For another kind of security?" Emily asked.

"Maybe for a while, but primarily because it's hers, and it's where she can keep her equipment, maybe hold meetings, experiment with plants."

Reaching over, Emily gave his hand a squeeze. "You've given this a lot of thought."

"I've given her a lot of thought. She's who and what I want in my life. I can wait a little while for her to be sure I'm who and what she wants in hers."

Zane gave a quick shrug, a quicker grin. "Because I am."

Once Darby had her crew set for the morning, she headed to her place to meet the locksmith and consult with Micah.

Rochelle, the locksmith, turned out to be Ralph's second cousin on her mother's side. She wore a thick braid the same color as her steel-rimmed glasses and lipstick as red as a fireplug.

"My mama says Ralph sure likes working for you. Retirement didn't suit him a whit."

"I'm glad to hear it. I'm lucky to have him."

"He's a quiet sort, our Ralph, so when he says you've got a head on your shoulders and aren't afraid of hard work, you take that as gospel. Cousin Lydia—that would be Ralph's mama—she wasn't certain how Ralph would do working for somebody so young, and female to boot. But he's pleased as Sunday punch."

"It's a good thing. I'm hoping to get older, but I'm most likely to stay female."

Rochelle let out a guffaw, gave Darby a hefty slap on the back.

"We got that in common. So, you had some trouble here, I reckon."

"Somebody got in. Didn't take much or do any damage, but I need better locks."

"You're not wrong about that, Ms. McCray."

"Darby."

"Still not wrong. I can take care of that for you, and will, but I'm gonna have to tell you—you being young, female, and a good boss to Cousin Ralph, I could bust this door in here with one half-assed kick."

"Yeah, I thought of that." Darby puffed out her cheeks. "I might replace the doors, front and back, over the winter, but for now good, solid locks. And I've got Micah Carter on his way out to see about an alarm system."

"There's that head on your shoulders. That boy knows what he's do-ing, even if I can't understand what the hell he's talking about half the time. You're pretty isolated up here," she added as she looked around. "Though I heard you can handle yourself just fine. Heard you're going to be doing a self-defense course at the community center."

"Oh, well, I didn't—"

"I'd sign up for that. I'm not what anybody'd call a delicate-type flower, but I'd like to learn some real self-defense. No telling where my work takes me. And my daughter, Reanne? She's got her real estate license now, just started working with Charmaine. You know Charmaine."

"Yes, I do. She helped me get this place."

"Well, my Reanne's hardly as big as a minute and as pretty as strawberry shortcake. I wouldn't worry so much if she knew how to defend herself."

When Darby finally steered Rochelle toward locks, they agreed on dead bolts, front and back. Then Micah arrived and set off another spate of conversation.

Thinking of the work still on her plate, she managed to nudge him inside when Rochelle started drilling.

"Okay, well, what I figure is I just need a basic alarm deal. Something to scare off anybody who tries to get in."

"I could do that." Micah scratched at his goatee. "And Zane would have my ass. He's pretty freaked, Darby, so you gotta cut him a break." He held up both hands before she could object. "First that asshole Bigelow goes after you, and now some other asshole breaks into your house. The guy's entitled to a break, right?"

"Maybe."

"What I'm going for here is a nice compromise." He added a winning smile. "That's what life's about, am I right? My man Zane, he'd like to see you with the works, like video surveillance, a motion detector—"

"Oh, come on."

"I get it, I get it. You just want noise to scare off the assholes. So I'm saying, let's meet in the middle. I can give you the noise—somebody tries to compromise the locks or breaks a window, tries to bust in the door, alarm starts screaming. Zane says, if you were sleeping, that might not wake you up."

"I don't sleep that solid! I . . . crap. Maybe, maybe not."

"So I add a couple bells and whistles. I can fix it up so the alarm triggers the lights. House lights up. And the alarm signals Lee's phone."

"I don't want to bother Lee with—"

"Compromise. Odds are word's going to get around you've got a system—in fact it's gonna get around 'cause I'm going to mouth off about it. I can't see anybody trying to get in again. So it's compromise time. Otherwise, Zane's going to badger you until you cave to shut him up. Lawyer, right, they'll argue you brainless."

She rolled her eyes. "I want a Coke. Let's get a Coke."

She walked back to the kitchen, opened the fridge.

"Hey, it looks good in here. Man, if these colors don't wake you up in the morning, nothing will. I like it."

"Me, too." She handed him a Coke. She'd calculated a ballpark for the basic she'd aimed for. Now she studied Micah as she chugged Coke. "What's the estimate for the compromise?"

When he named a price, she sighed. "Micah, that's under what I figured for the basic deal. Come on."

"You get the friends and family discount. It's how I roll. Plus, I need one of those trees like you got Zane for his office. It's cool. Cassie's gonna make us a nice big pot for it."

She let out another breath. "Looks like we've got a deal."

"Solid." He gave her a fist bump. "You know what else I'd do, living back up here?"

"What?"

"You ever thought about getting a dog?"

She poked a finger in his chest. "Yes! But then getting the business going, and I spend a lot of time at Zane's."

"We had a dog when I was a kid. I think Zane loved that dog more than I did, and we were all crazy for Betsy. He wanted a dog, but that was a big no in his house, so he'd come over to hang with Betsy as much as hang with me."

"Really?"

"He made some noises after he came back about getting himself a dog, but said since he was gone all day, it didn't seem fair. You getting one? That sounds like another compromise. So happens I got a friend who fosters dogs and cats."

With another winning smile, Micah drained his Coke.

PART FOUR

HEALING TRUTHS

Healing is a matter of time,
but it is sometimes also a matter of opportunity.
—HIPPOCRATES

This above all:
to thine own self be true.
—WILLIAM SHAKESPEARE

CHAPTER TWENTY-TWO

Zane drove up the long, winding road toward home figuring he deserved a very large drink, considering not only the day he'd put in but the evening he'd have to spend on insane party preparations.

Even as he made the last turn, the wild, deep-throated barking tore through the quiet. Something bounded around from the back of the house, a blur of black-and-white speed.

And teeth, Zane noted as it bared them when he parked.

He took a good long look from the pathetic safety of a convertible with the top down as Darby came on the run.

"Zod! Stop." And clapped her hands twice.

The thing that might be a dog stopped barking, looked back at Darby with a face that appeared to have been smooshed together by a strong, jagged vice.

"Sit!" she ordered, and it did, sort of wagging a stub of a tail. When she leaned down to give it a pet, it stared up at her with huge, protruding eyes full of adoration.

"Is that a dog?" Zane asked as he—slowly, carefully—got out of the car.

"Yes. He doesn't bite. He was just letting me know someone was coming. I didn't mean to do it," she continued in a rush. "I swear on all that's holy I only meant to take a look, then depending, maybe we'd have a conversation. Then he . . . hell."

"You're sure it's a dog?"

"Of course it's a dog. He's General Zod."

"From the Phantom Zone by way of Krypton?"

"Vicky's kids named him."

"Vicky."

"You went to school with her. Micah—it's really his fault."

"Okay." Crouching, Zane took a longer look. The smooshed face was mostly white, like the stubby tail. The rest of him, about twenty-five pounds of compact muscle on legs slightly less stubby than the tail, was a streaky mix of black and white. The bulbous eyes gleamed like saucers full of oil.

"This is one homely dog."

"I know. I thought, barking dog, another security measure, and I'd been thinking about getting a dog once I had time to train one. A puppy maybe that I could train from the ground up not to dig or run off. Then Micah brought up dog, and how he had this friend who fosters. I was just going to check it out."

"Zod." Watching the dog, Zane patted his knee. The dog trotted right over, licked his hand with a wide, wet tongue. "Security measure?"

"Well, yeah. I mean, as you've already seen, he barks like a maniac—but stops when you tell him to stop. That was a key. And he doesn't bite, he's good around kids—Vicky has two sets of twins. "

As Zane scratched Zod's pointy little ears, the dog moaned as if in deep, desperate pleasure. Those weird eyes gleamed as he rested his chin on Zane's knee.

"See! He does that! Looks at you like you're the center of the world. And Vicky said he's never dug in any of her flowers. He's house-trained, good with other dogs and people. He sort of tries to herd them, but he's gentle. He likes riding in the truck. That was another requirement because he'd go to work with me. He did really well when I took him on the job today—and I should have talked to you first."

"We weren't allowed to have pets when I was a kid."

"Micah told me."

"I couldn't get a dog in Raleigh, living in a condo, at work more than I was home. I figured when I got one, maybe a Lab or retriever. You know . . ." He opened his arms to indicate size. "A *dog*."

After rubbing his way down the strange muscular body, earning more grateful moans, Zane rose. "General Zod," he muttered, and had Zod wagging all over.

"Vicky's had him about three months. The people who owned him decided they didn't want a dog after all. He was about a year old, so they took him to the pound. He was on, you know, death row when Vicky rescued him. It's what she does. I'll take him out and feed him and all the stuff when I'm here."

Zod plopped down, rolled on his back in the grass.

"Why should you get all the fun?"

"You're not mad?"

"Why would I be? Jesus, he's what my grandmother would call ugly as homemade sin. I kind of like that about him." He bent, rubbed the wide head. "Kneel before Zod!"

With a laugh, Darby threw her arms around Zane, had the dog worming his way between them, then Zod lifted his head high, let out a long howl.

"What the hell kind of dog is he?"

"She wasn't sure. Maybe some bulldog, maybe some beagle, maybe a bunch of a lot more. I was just showing him around, trying out the woods for his personal business."

"Good idea. Let's get a drink and walk the dog."

"He has a quirk," she warned as they walked around the house with Zod between them.

Amused, Zane watched the dog manage a kind of prance on those weird legs. "Darlin', he is a quirk."

"He steals any article of human clothing that ends up on the floor. He doesn't chew them, just hordes them in his dog bed. He likes to sleep with a sock or a T-shirt that smells like people. He'll even get something out of the hamper if he can manage it. If you try to take it back before morning, he howls until you give it back."

"I can handle that one." He looked down at her and the dog between them, and felt pretty good about it. "Anything else?"

"Well, you don't want to say t-r-e-a-t unless you've got one handy because he goes a little nuts."

"Have we got any?"

"Vicky gave me a bag. I put a couple in my pocket in case I needed to lure him off the lawn into the woods."

"Okay then. Treat."

For an instant, Zod froze—the world's homeliest dog statue—then to Zane's complete delight bounced a good foot in the air like a dog on springs, his eyes wild and wide with mad glee. When the treat didn't magically appear, he continued to bounce, managed an ungainly flip in midair.

"Circus dog. Let him have it."

Obliging, Darby tossed one. Zod snatched it, ran in circles, then gobbled it.

"He's ugly," Zane decided, draping an arm around Darby's shoulders, "but he's sure entertaining."

And the boy inside the man reached into Darby's pocket and, grinning, said, "Treat!"

Just after dawn, with a day of party preparations ahead of her, Darby headed to the job site. A couple of hours, she calculated, would finish up most of the work ahead of schedule, give her canine companion more experience on the job, and get her back to Zane with more than enough time to set up for the evening festivities.

Zod sat beside her in the truck, his pointy little ears vibrating in the air blowing through the open windows. As she turned away from town, took the quiet road beyond the lake that led into the hills, she decided she and Zod made a pretty lucky pair.

They'd both found their place.

Behind them, the sun rose up, shedding light on what promised to be a pretty damn perfect summer day.

"Lots of kids later, Zod, and dogs, too. We're going to have one terrific Fourth of—"

She slammed on the brakes. As Zod yipped in surprise, she swung to the side of the road. She'd seen the woman, bruises covering her face, rush into the trees in a limping run as the truck approached.

"Wait," Darby said as much to Zod as the woman, and jumped

out of the truck. "I won't hurt you! You need help. I could see you're hurt." Pushing back her instinct to rush forward, Darby stood beside the truck.

She'd only gotten a glimpse, but she'd seen fear in the blackened, swollen eyes.

"Let me help you. I'll take you wherever you want to go. I'm Darby. Someone hurt me once, and I needed help. Let me help you."

She heard the rustle, made herself stand still. "Or I'll call someone for you. I'll call whoever you want, and stay here until they come."

She caught another glimpse—thin, bruised face, long dishwater blond hair. "I can't go the way you're going. They might see me."

"We'll turn around and go the other way. Anywhere you want. Look, how about if I turn the truck around now? I'll turn it around so we're going in the right direction. You're hurt. I can't leave you here alone. I'll just turn the truck around, okay?"

With her heart hammering, she got back in the truck.

Don't run, she thought, please don't run, as she made a slow, careful U-turn.

"I don't know you."

"I'm Darby. Darby McCray. I moved to Lakeview last February. I can call someone and wait right here if you don't want me to drive you somewhere."

She came out cautiously, with those battered eyes tracking from Darby to the dog.

"His name's Zod. He's awfully sweet. He won't hurt you."

To make sure he didn't bark, Darby stroked him while the woman's eyes darted back up the road. With that limping run, she dashed to the truck, pulled herself inside.

"Can you drive away from here?" The words poured out in a shaking rush. "Just drive away?"

"Sure." Nice and easy, Darby thought. Keep it nice, easy, calm. "I can take you to the clinic," Darby began as she drove. "Or the police, or—"

"No, no, no."

"Okay, don't worry. We won't go anywhere you don't want. Do you have family?"

"I can't go there. They'd find me there."

"All right." As Darby spoke, her voice soft, Zod licked at one of the woman's shaking hands, then laid his head in her lap.

She began to weep.

"You can go home with me, or . . ."

With that shaking hand, the woman reached in her pocket, drew out a creased business card. "Can you take me there? To him?"

When she scanned the card, Darby let out a breath. "Are you Traci, Traci Draper? Don't be afraid," she said quickly when the woman grabbed the truck handle as if she'd fling open the door and jump. "I know Zane. He's a friend. He told me he was worried about you, and why. I can take you to him. He's—we're . . ." How to say it? "We're together. He won't let anything happen to you."

Traci gathered up Zod, rocked, and clung to the dog. "I don't know what to do."

"You're doing it. You're getting help."

"If they find me . . . Why are you turning here!" Panic pitched her voice high. "This isn't right."

"It's where Zane lives. He's not at the office in town now. It's too early, and it's a holiday so he's still home. I just came from here. He's at home. It's all right. No one's going to hurt you."

Reassure, connect, and take it slow, Darby told herself.

"I met your mom, and your sister. They're awfully nice."

"He said he'd kill them, kill them and me if I tried to go to them. He'll kill them."

"We won't let that happen, Traci. We'll stop him. We're going to stop him. See, that's Zane's car. We're going to go inside, and you can tell him what happened."

Clutching the dog tighter, Traci twisted to look behind the truck. "Clint will try to kill him if he finds out I came here."

"Don't worry. Nobody knows you're here. We're going inside," she said after she parked. "And we're going to figure out the best thing to do."

She got out, hurried around to help Traci out of the truck. "Zane may not be up yet, but I have a key. I stay here sometimes."

With Zod leading the way in his happy prance, she guided Traci to the front door, unlocked it, dealt with the alarm.

"That was quick." Wearing only cotton pants and carrying a mug of coffee, Zane wandered out of the kitchen. "Christ, Traci." He rushed forward, slowing when Traci cringed back against Darby's supporting arm.

He gentled his voice. "It's okay. It's going to be okay. Let's get you back, get you some water. Maybe some coffee."

He walked ahead of them. He'd not only survived physical abuse, but had prosecuted abusers, interviewed their victims. She might not want a man to touch her or come too close.

Relieved that Darby seemed to understand, he split off to get the water, to grab a T-shirt out of the mudroom while she guided Traci to the great room sofa.

Zod, eyes full of love, laid his head on the sofa next to Traci's leg.

"He—he's a nice dog."

"He really is. Do you want some coffee?"

"Just the water please. Thank you. I don't know what to do."

"We're going to figure that out," Zane told her as he brought the water, offered it. Then offered an ice bag. "Where else are you hurt, Traci?"

"He hit me in the stomach a lot, and when I fell, I banged up my knee. It hurts, and my arm where he grabbed me. He got mad last night. He was drinking and he got really mad. He didn't like what I made for dinner, and his mama said I only worked in the garden for an hour. They watch me."

Even though she gripped the glass with both hands, it trembled as she brought it up, took slow sips.

"He said I was lazy and no good, and he started beating on me. And I thought this time he might just kill me. And he made me have sex with him and it hurt, everything hurt, and he hit me again because he said the sex was bad and how I was just a whore anyway."

When fresh tears began to spill, Darby put an arm around her.

"I thought if I don't just die I gotta get out."

"Is he home now?"

Traci lifted her blackened eyes to Zane, shook her head.

"I couldn't've gotten out if he'd been home. He left real early to go hunting with his brother and his daddy. If I'm not out in the garden working in an hour or so, or hanging out the wash, his mama or his sister-in-law will come over looking for me. They watch me from their houses, and they tell him if I don't do what he says, or if I talk to anybody.

"They saw you come," she told Zane as tears dripped again. "But he didn't get too mad because I made you go pretty quick. He only slapped me a couple times for that."

"I'm so sorry, Traci. I'm sorry for that. We're going to help you. We're going to make sure he doesn't hurt you again, but there are a couple of things that have to be done. You need to file charges."

Her head dropped, her shoulders bowed. "He said he'd kill me if I tried, and nobody believes a lying whore. If they did, he'd kill my mama, hurt my sister."

"We're not going to let that happen. You need a doctor to examine you, Traci."

"I can't. I can't! He'll go crazy like he did when I fell down the stairs and lost the baby. He hit me and I fell down the stairs and lost the baby. He went crazy 'cause I had to have a doctor."

Darby and Zane exchanged a quick glance.

"How about if we have a doctor come here?" Darby kept that soothing arm around her. "A woman doctor. She's a friend. And you know Chief Keller, Traci. He's a good man. He wants to help you. He'll help you if you tell him what happened last night, what happened when you lost the baby."

"I lied to him before. I had to!"

"That doesn't matter now," Zane told her.

"I just need to get away. If I could get far enough away, he won't find me."

And go where? Darby thought. Do what?

"I was married to a man who hurt me like you're hurt." Darby paused as Traci turned her head to meet her eyes. "If I hadn't gotten help, if people hadn't helped me when I needed it, he'd have hurt me even more than he did. I was awfully scared. But people did help me. And the police locked him up so he couldn't hurt me again."

"What did you do that made him hurt you?"

"Nothing, and neither did you. People like that hurt you because it's who they are, not because of anything you did."

"Why did you come to me, Traci?"

At Zane's question, she dropped her head again, and her nervous hands tugged and twisted in the long skirt of her cotton dress.

"Clint said it was all a lie how your daddy beat you so bad when you were a boy, but my mama said it was true. My mama doesn't lie. Clint lies. You can help me get divorced maybe, but I've gotta get far away."

"There are places that are safe that aren't so far away. My sister works with people who need safe places. We can get you into a shelter. I can help you get a restraining order, and help you get into that safe place. I can help you get a divorce."

"I don't have the money to pay you. Maybe Mama—"

"You don't need to pay. You need to talk to the chief, tell him what happened. Tell him what's happened before. What happened when you were pregnant."

"He said he'd kill me and my whole family if I did that."

"That's what you tell Chief Keller. You tell him everything, and I'll be right with you, as your lawyer, okay? You let the doctor examine you, so she can tell the chief how he hurt you."

"If I do, can you keep my family safe?"

"We're going to make sure of it."

"I can call the doctor, Traci, and your mother. They can both come here."

She froze, her hands going limp on her skirt. "My mama can come here? Can she go with me to the safe place?"

"We're going to work that out." Zane rose. "I want you to tell me if it's okay to call Chief Keller. You tell Darby if it's all right to call the doctor, and your mama. We don't do anything unless you say it's all right."

"I'm so scared. I'm so tired." Putting her head back, she closed her eyes. "I half hoped he'd just kill me last night, so it'd be over with. I can't live this way anymore. I don't want to live if it's this way. If you call them, it'll change. I need it to change, so you can call them. But please call my mama. I just want my mama."

Putting her face in her hands, she sobbed.

It shook Darby down to the bone, brought back with crystal clarity the fear, shock, utter helplessness of being beaten by a man who'd vowed to cherish her.

More than the attack by Graham Bigelow, she realized, witnessing Traci's exhaustion, despair, and terror shot her back to her own.

And that need, that desperate, visceral need for a mother's comfort.

Lee came first, so Darby busied herself making coffee while he spoke quietly with Traci and Zane in the great room. Gentle voices, she thought, a gentle way as she served the coffee, then went outside to wait for the others. To give Traci privacy.

And remembered her own interview with the police, how calm they'd been and, yes, gentle. Patient, she realized, guiding her back through the nightmare so she could document it for them.

All she'd wanted? Her mother.

She watched the car coming fast up the steep road, walked down to meet Traci's mother, and, she noted, her sister as she got out of the car.

She saw that Traci's mother still wore her house slippers. Tears burned at the back of Darby's eyes—her own memories, her relief.

She fought them back, reached out a hand for Lucy Abbott's.

"She's inside, with Chief Keller and Zane. She doesn't want to go to the clinic, but Dr. Ledbecker's coming here."

"How bad is—I need to—"

"He hurt her, Mrs. Abbott. It's not the first time, but we can make sure it's the last."

"You go on in to her, Mama. I need a second here. Can she go right in?" Allie asked.

"Sure. Straight back. Mrs. Abbott . . ." Darby hesitated, then went with her gut. "She's going to need you to just hold on to her for a while. That's what she'll need."

With a nod, Lucy rushed to the house and inside.

"Okay." Allie's jaw set like iron. "Where is the son of a bitch?"

"Traci said he left early to go hunting. That's when she got out."

"About fucking time. Sorry—Mama hates that word, but it just keeps pushing out of me. How'd she get here?"

"I had a job I wanted to finish up out on Highpoint Road, and I saw her when I was driving out, saw she was hurt, talked her into getting in the truck. She wanted to come here. She had Zane's card with her."

"Good sense at last." When tears swirled in Allie eyes, she blinked them away hard, then put her arms around Darby. "Bless you."

"No, I didn't—"

"Bless you," Allie repeated. "Let me thank you. I've been sick with worry and mad as all hellfire with Traci for a long time, so let me thank you and pull myself together before I go in."

"He threatened you and your mother."

Allie jerked back.

"If she left or said anything about the beatings, he'd hurt you. She believed him, so maybe don't be so mad at her."

With her lips pressed tight together, Allie stared out toward the lake, the hills. "I tell you this, I tell you this right now, my Tim and I can take care of ourselves, our babies, Mama, and Traci, and damn Clint Draper and all the rest of them. She's coming home if I have to drag her there this time."

"She shouldn't go home yet."

Fire flashed the tears dry as Allie whirled back to Darby. "If you're saying she's going back to that bastard, I'm going to pop you right in the mouth."

"I'm not saying that. Zane called Britt, and Britt's making arrangements for Traci to go in a shelter in Asheville. Your mother can go with her if that's what she wants. She'd do better at a shelter for now, until Lee makes sure Clint's locked up, until she feels safe. And she'd get counseling there, be able to talk to other women who've been through what she has."

"All right, as much as I want her home, maybe that's good sense, too. She was always so bright and sweet, my baby sister. I want my sister back."

"They spied on her, Allie—the Drapers—watched to make sure she toed the line. He threatened her family if she crossed that line. It took courage for her to leave."

"You're right." Heaving out a cleansing breath, Allie shoved her dark blond hair back from her face. "Okay, you're right, and I have to get rid of some of this mad. I'm going to go on in."

"I'm going to wait out here for the doctor."

"I'm not going to forget what you did today. Nobody in Lakeview will forget what you did." Allie squeezed Darby's hand. "Neither will the Drapers, so you have a care, Darby."

When Charlene arrived, Darby took her inside. While Zane showed Traci—with her mother glued to her side—and Charlene to a guest room, Darby grabbed a Coke and took Zod outside for a walk.

"You stayed right with her, didn't you?" she murmured to the dog. "You have a good heart."

She wandered into the trees while Zod sniffed, pranced on his stubby legs, and eventually squatted.

"That's the way, and here's the place. No pooping on my nice lawn or in my most excellent gardens."

When she walked out again, she saw Zane sitting at one of the tables, making notes on a legal pad.

"There you are." He got to his feet, walked straight to her as Zod danced, and wrapped his arms around her. "Don't be sad. It's a good day. Don't be sad."

"It threw me back. Not like when I faced off with Bigelow—that was the flight-or-fight instinct, and remembering how I didn't know how to fight with Trent. This took me all through the afterward. It was one horrible night in my life. How many horrible nights has Traci lived through?"

"It ends now. We'll help make sure of it. Lee's already got a warrant. He's called up a couple of officers, and they're heading out to the Drapers'."

"He won't be there if they went hunting."

"That's the next thing." Giving her arms a rub, Zane stepped back. "It's not hunting season, for anything, so Lee can slap all of them on that one. Clint's going to come home eventually.

"Meanwhile, Britt's heading over. Emily put some cabin amenities together, so she'll pick those up, then take Traci to the shelter, help her settle in. That's saying Charlene clears her for it. If not, Britt'll take her to the hospital in Asheville first."

"You were so calm with her," Darby acknowledged. "So calm and kind. You knew just what to say, how to say it."

"Just part of the job."

"No. No, no." Agitated, she paced away as she spoke. "It's not. It's who you are. And whatever you said to her before, when you gave her your card, that had to be the right thing in the right way or she wouldn't have kept it, she wouldn't have wanted to come to you."

"I was in her place once."

"Worse. Worse, and look who you are." She turned back. "You could've turned bitter, you could've turned mean, or had the spine beaten out of you. But you didn't. You're kind and caring, and you've built a purposeful life. Damn it, you've screwed things up for me."

He let out a half laugh as his eyebrows shot up. "How's that?"

"I came here because it suited my list of requirements. It could've been any of dozens of other places, but I ended up here. My mother always said there's a reason for everything. And I guess there is. Lakeview was away—that was number one. The growing season, the size of the community, the topography, and so on. Suited."

"It's hard for me to screw up a growing season. Any of that Coke left?"

She pushed it at him. "Not that. I also had very specific goals. If, after living here for a few weeks, it felt right, I'd start building my business. Again, number one. A very close second? Finding my own place, buying a house, some land, making it a home. Building good connections in the community, working my way into it, making friends."

"Seems to me you've done a good job all around there. Can't see where I screwed it up for you."

"No? Well, I'm not finished. I like sex."

"And for that I'm grateful."

Agitated, she stuck her hands in her pockets, pulled them out again. "Not a damn thing wrong with finding somebody—unattached, trustworthy, interesting who I'm attracted to—to have sex with. Add on he's great-looking, fun, smart, and all that? Bonus round."

Zane rested a hip on the table, rubbing the happy dog with his foot. "Just not seeing the screwing-it-up part here."

She pulled her cap off, began to slap it against her thigh.

"Did you hear 'relationship' in there? 'Serious relationship' on my list of requirements? No, you didn't. The sort where I end up all but living with him and not really turning my own place into my home."

"We got the scary wallpaper down, got the walls painted."

"That makes it habitable, not home. Just now? I'm taking Zod back in the woods, and congratulating him for not pooping on *my* lawn or in *my* garden. Not Zane's, not his, my. Personal pronoun, because you've screwed things up and this is home."

"Look at it." Zane spread his arms. "You made it one, darlin'. That's not me screwing things up."

"You let me," she pointed out, though that was weak, and she knew it. "Then I see you with Micah, a friend you've kept close since you were kids. I see you with your family, and they're just goddamn terrific, I see you with every-damn-body, and you're this *person*."

"I am a person. I can't deny it."

"Oh, don't be so damn funny. I'm irritated. I'm agitated. I see you, and you're kind and caring because at the core, you have honor."

"Well, that might be stretching it some."

"I say you have honor," she snapped back. "I see it, I feel it, I hear it. And why the hell couldn't I have met you a couple years from now after I finished crossing off everything on my completely sensible list?"

Now he smiled. "Kismet? I wasn't looking for this either. I wasn't looking for you, but I love you, Darby."

"I know it," she said on an annoyed huff. "And as if that doesn't screw things up enough, I love you."

"I know it. But it's sure nice to hear you say it. Come home, Darby. Come all the way home."

She already had, she thought with a sigh. "I'm keeping my place."

"Why wouldn't you? You'll make the grounds spectacular, put in the greenhouse you talk about, store equipment and Christ knows what other big-ass machine you'll want. Your place is essential for High Country Landscaping."

She jabbed a finger in the air as he strolled toward her. "See, you get me. That's another way you—"

"Screwed everything up?" he finished.

"Yeah." Surrendering, she framed his face with her hands. "I guess I'll just have to live with it, and you."

CHAPTER TWENTY-THREE

Zane waited with his sister while Charlene finished treating Traci's injuries.

"I can go with you," he began. "Help you get her and her mother moved into the shelter."

"No, you've got a ton to do here, plus, it'll give me some time to talk to Traci. It's a big, scary step she's taking."

"Text me when you get her there." He glanced at his watch. "I was hoping to hear from Lee by now."

"Let Lee do his cop thing. I'll do my counselor thing, and you do your lawyer thing. Add on host thing for a really big party." She pulled his wrist over to check the time herself. "I'll be back to pitch in there in a couple hours—and Silas, too, when he's wrapped up the cop business. Emily'll be over, too—with Audra. We'll get it all done."

"I'm thinking of it as Traci's Independence Day."

"It's a good thought."

But Zane knew his sister. "You're worried she won't stick."

"She's got plenty of support, but she's also got a hard road ahead. We'll be hopeful."

He led with that hope as he helped Traci into Britt's car, reminded her to call him, anytime, if she needed him. After thanking Charlene, assuring Allie he'd stay on top of things, he stood a moment on his hill. Quiet now, peaceful now, the lake below shining in the sunlight.

A perfect summer day, he thought, echoing Darby's earlier assessment. The kind of day for taking a sail, eating potato salad, drinking a beer in the shade.

The kind of day where it seemed nothing hard or mean existed.

But it did, always would. Life meant you navigated the hard and mean, rose over it, pushed it back.

So he would.

After using the warrant to enter Traci's house, having a conversation with Clint's hard-eyed mother at her place, his brother's slovenly—the word popped into his head—wife at hers, Lee deduced they'd already figured out something was up.

In Jed Draper's place, three kids—two in diapers that needed changing—and a third with a nasty look in his eye and scabby knees—fought, wailed, whined until Lee's head throbbed.

But Sally Draper never deviated from her story, one that matched her mother-in-law's almost word for word.

She didn't know where the men had gone—certainly not hunting! Fishing more like, camping out for a day or two. And if that ungrateful Traci said her brother laid a single hand on her, she was a liar on top of being a lazy slut.

Bea Draper, the matriarch, had run the same line, and added a few flourishes. How Traci had a terrible temper, threw things at her hardworking boy. Was clumsy as a two-legged mule, always tripping over things—mostly as she didn't put shit-all away.

Lee took note of the field glasses in both houses, set on the sill of the window facing Traci's backyard.

He considered it all as he made his way back to the house where Traci had lived, and what he'd found—or hadn't found—inside.

She'd run off at dawn with only the clothes on her back and Zane's card in her pocket. Yet inside he'd found only two handmade dresses, both cotton and as shapeless as what she'd had on. No jewelry, no makeup—not even a tube of lipstick—two cotton nightgowns his grandmother wouldn't have worn, and not a single pair of shoes.

He'd grown up with a mother, a sister, had a wife, had lived with a girl he considered his own from her teenage years, so he knew something about what he thought of as female debris.

Nothing, just nothing normal inside that house.

And he hated, hated he'd had no power or authority to do anything about it. Until now.

He walked to the McConnells', found them both outside working their garden.

With a hand pressed to his back, Sam straightened, nodded. "Chief."

"Got some fine-looking tomatoes going there, Sam."

"We do that, and plenty of them. We can give you some to take home."

Lee scratched his chin. "Believe it or not, we got talked into planting some of our own this year. Just a couple bushes, but they're doing okay. Sure would appreciate having a few words with y'all."

"Figured you'd be by." Mary Lou adjusted her glasses. "I made some lemonade fresh this morning. You come on, sit down in the shade."

"That'd be right nice."

"Kids are coming later on for a cookout before we all head to the lake to see the show," Sam said as they walked.

"Should be a good one."

While Mary Lou went in to get the lemonade, Lee sat with Sam on the porch, let out a sigh as he got off his feet.

"I want to ask if you heard or saw anything from over Clint Draper's place last night."

"Can't say we did. We had the AC on, windows closed." Sam let out a sigh of his own. "He hurt that little girl again, didn't he?"

"I can tell you she lit out early this morning, pretty beaten up. Don't suppose you saw her go, or saw where Clint went?"

"Wish I had. Never seen her drive, so I'm guessing she took off on foot. We'd have helped her if we'd seen her."

"I know you would." As Mary Lou came out with a tray of glasses, Lee smiled. "That sure looks good, Mary Lou."

"She got away, honey," Sam told her. "She left him this morning."

Mary Lou set the tray down with a rattle. "Thank the lord. We worried when we saw you and the officers that he'd killed her this time. But she's all right?"

"She will be. My information is Clint went off with his daddy, his brother early this morning. Hunting's what I heard, fishing's what Mrs. Draper the elder claims."

"Hunting's more like, and we heard some shooting when we came outside." After handing out the glasses, Mary Lou took a seat. "The Drapers don't trouble themselves with hunting seasons, No Trespassing signs, or anything else. They do what they want and when they want."

"You wouldn't happen to know where they favor going?"

Now Sam shook his head. "I know they put up deer stands right on the property line, a few of them. And I'll tell you the God's truth, Chief, I wouldn't go looking for them up in the woods, not when they've got guns and cover. You were to step foot on their land, they'd unload on you and call it just."

"Bea Draper would've told them you've been around. They got walkies," Mary Lou added. "It was around nine, I guess—and after we heard the shooting—I saw her walk over next door, go right on in like she owned it. She didn't walk out happy. I guess she saw Traci wasn't there."

"She'd've been right on the horn letting the men know that," Sam continued. "And then y'all showed up. She'd have let them know to keep low, at least until you'd cleared out."

"Well." Lee drank some lemonade. "They're not going to stay up there in the woods. We'll do that clearing out, but we'll keep an eye on the place. I'd appreciate it if you'd do the same, give me a call if you see any of them come back."

"Happy to." Mary Lou patted her husband's hand. "But we'd be grateful if you kept our names out of it. They're vengeful people, Chief."

"There's no problem with that. You just call me direct, you hear?"

"You watch yourself," Sam added. "They won't take kindly if you lock up one of their blood."

"That's just what I aim to do."

Lee assigned a rotation of officers—in pairs—to watch the Draper land. He'd take his own rotation next shift, but decided he needed to get back, let his family know the status.

He found tables already covered with their colorful cloths, lights being strung, his sons hauling out more. And the little girl who called him Pap playing with the world's ugliest dog.

Audra wobbled to her feet, toddled over to him on those sweet, chubby legs, babbling and grinning with her arms already held out to him.

He scooped her up, gave her a toss to make her squeal. Ugly dog raced off to leap on Molly, start a mock fight, while their own Rufus just snoozed in the shade.

He smelled more lemonade and growing things, heard his wife's delicious laugh bounding through the open kitchen doors.

Normal, he thought. It was good, even for a little while, to come back to normal.

Audra wiggled down, toddled over to Darby, who—more squeals—hauled the baby onto her shoulders before she continued with the lights.

He went in, saw Emily checking potatoes on the boil for salad, and Zane struggling his way through peeling dozens of hard-boiled eggs.

"They ought to make a tool that does this," he complained.

"They do. It's called your hands."

Emily turned, and Lee saw the flicker of relief in her eyes as they met his. "And here's two more hands," she said brightly. "Where are Silas's?"

"I've got him and Ginny keeping an eye out for now. I'll switch with them in a bit."

"All right, you have a seat there with Zane. Want an iced coffee?"

"Babe, I'd've married you for your iced coffee alone. Anybody hear from Britt?"

"She's at the shelter with Traci and her mama," Zane told him. "She'll head back here soon. I take it the Drapers weren't home."

"That's right, but they'll come around. The women have walkies, so they'll know we're waiting for them."

He went to the sink—he'd been schooled more than once—washed his hands before he sat and picked up an egg. "The women were ready for us, had their stories together. Mary Lou McConnell said Bea Draper went over to Clint's place about nine this morning. She'd have seen Traci wasn't there, so they were ready for us with a couple loads of bullshit."

He peeled an egg—he'd been schooled there, too—reached for another. "I tell you something right now, that girl's lived a hard life over there. Both those women keep binoculars at the window that looks out at Traci's backyard. She wasn't lying when she said they watched her. And those kids—Jed Draper's kids? Filthy house, and two of them wearing nothing but dirty diapers with the older one looking like he'd smother them in their sleep if he could get away with it."

"Oh, Lee."

"There's a look, Em. He's young for it, but there's a look in the eyes, and he has it. And I come back here," he went on while he peeled a third egg, "I see our boys working together. And that sweet little girl comes running to me, smelling like fresh-cut grass and shampoo, wearing that pretty little—whatever it is."

"Romper," Emily added, setting down his coffee, standing behind him to rub his knotted shoulders.

"Well, she's romping in it, and now she's bouncing on Darby's shoulders out there, happy as ten puppies in a pile. It made me think those kids—no fault of theirs—but those kids, whoever's doing my job in fifteen, twenty years? They're going to lock those kids up. That's the odds they got."

"Some beat the odds," Zane said.

"Yeah, that's true. Best to remember some do."

Leaning over, Emily kissed his cheek. "You go on out there, play with your granddaughter. Zane and I can finish these."

"No, I'm fine here. Peeling eggs, it's mindless. I could use some of that." He reached back to pat Emily's hand, looked over at Zane.

"You're a good man, Zane. I want to say that to you in case I haven't recently. You suck at peeling eggs, no question about it, but you're a good man. Now, if I were you, I'd leave these to me, and I'd go out there to that long-legged woman, help her string lights, and give another shot at smooth-talking her into moving in here with you."

"Don't have to. She'll be moving in tomorrow."

Emily squealed, not unlike Audra, then wrapped her hands around Zane's throat as if to choke him. "I've been here more than an hour, and you're just telling me?"

"I've been concentrating pretty fiercely on peeling these eggs."

"You." Now she lightly swatted the side of his head. "Get out. Get those lights up, then you make sure your cousins have the rest of the tables set where they're supposed to be."

"Yes, ma'am."

He escaped.

"Damn it, my potatoes," she remembered, and dashed to take the pot off the stove.

"It's been a hard morning," Lee began.

Steady, Emily poured the boiled potatoes and water into the colander in the sink. "I know it."

"But that? It sure pushed away a lot of the hard."

She looked through the steam, through the window over the sink, out to where Zane plucked Audra off Darby's shoulders and settled her on his own.

"Our boy's happy, Lee. I worried about him more than Britt—he shouldered so much. But he's happy. And that girl? They fit. Seeing they do, it settles something in me. I see Gabe out there throwing a ball for the dogs and Brody shaking his head and laughing. It all settles something in me."

"We did good work, Em."

She glanced over with a smile. "Don't feel I'm done yet, but yeah, so far, some pretty damn good work."

A few hours later, Zane figured he'd rather have a good, solid nap instead of hosting a party. He'd hauled tables, chairs, climbed up and down ladders, carted out huge coolers of lemonade, iced tea, galvanized tubs to fill with ice and beer and wine.

Every time he thought he could have a beer break, grab a shower, someone—usually female—gave him another chore.

Before he knew it, the band Emily insisted on arrived, started setting up equipment on the platform Lee and his boys had built.

"Zane, you need to set out those new trash cans." Busy filling colorful tubs with silly little prizes, Britt called out to him before he could sneak away. "With the liners! Brody, have you finished the signs?"

"Almost!" Brody, the only one of them possessing any semblance of artistic talent, sat working on a sign to indicate cans and bottles, others for the age-grouping of the prizes.

Zane set out the new trash cans, stowed extra bags in the bottom as Emily had taught him, opened two to line the cans.

Determined to get that beer and shower before somebody found something else for him to do, he headed for the kitchen doors.

Darby walked out.

She wore one of those sundresses that made men grateful for hot, sunny days. He wasn't sure he'd known she owned a dress, much less a bold yellow one with skinny straps that showed off strong shoulders, a swirly skirt that floated around long, bare legs.

She wore the pendant he'd given her, little dangles in her ears.

And she'd fussed with her face—especially her eyes so they looked long and sexy and read violet.

"Well, look at you."

"You'd better, as I spent some time getting on my summer picnic."

"We should have one every week."

Then she capped it by handing him a cold beer. "You're dismissed to get yourself ready."

"Praise Jesus." But he cupped the back of her neck first, drew her in for a kiss. "However long it took, so worth it. I need to take you to a fancy dinner in Asheville."

"How about we take each other out?"

"Works for me."

Since he had to get by Emily and Britt—both putting food together and talking cheerfully about just that—he moved fast and quiet.

It didn't take him long, a quick shower, a fresh shirt and jeans, a pair of black Chucks. When he opened his terrace doors, he heard a guitar, heard his family, so stepped out for a minute.

His younger cousin played—courtesy of one of the band. And Brody looked wildly happy as others took up instruments, picked up the tune.

All three dogs, worn out from the afternoon, slept in the shade. Audra in her red-and-white-striped romper and blue hair ribbon clapped at the music.

Despite all his misgivings at the size and scope, he realized it all looked just fine. Just absolutely fine, with the red, white, and blue covered tables, the white awnings casting shade, the stacks of matching plates and napkins and cups.

Too early for the lights, he thought, but that was going to look just fine, too.

Darby's clever beanbag boards stood colorfully on the lawn, as did a bigger one for softball pitching designed for older kids.

Music rang out, the sun shined, and his lady wore a yellow dress.

Yeah, he decided, it all looked just fine.

It felt fine, smelled fine, sounded fine when he manned the smoking grill and dozens of people swarmed his yard and house.

Dogs, revived, wandered the crowd hoping for a handout. Beanbags slapped against painted plywood. He got hugs, backslaps, cheek kisses as he flipped burgers and dogs onto platters. He smelled fried chicken and hoped he wouldn't be too late to get himself some.

"Good party." Silas strolled over to him. "Dave's gonna take over for you for a minute."

He caught the look in his brother-in-law's eyes, turned. "I hereby pass the ceremonial flipper and tongs."

"Got it covered," Dave told him, handed him a beer.

"How 'bout we take a little walk." With a glass of cold sweet tea, as he considered himself still on duty, Silas led the way around the far side of the house.

"What's up?"

"Just heard from Lee. The Drapers got back—without Clint. They're claiming he went off with some friends on a fishing trip yesterday. The usual bullshit about how Traci's a liar, probably banged herself up to make Clint look bad."

"What friends?"

"That's the next thing. How the hell are they supposed to know? He's a grown man, can come and go as he pleases. We're figuring he got wind, tapped one of his drinking buddies to meet him, and he's hiding out."

Silas glanced back, making sure they were out of earshot. "Lee said they had long guns, no fishing gear. Claim they stowed the gear back by the stream, which is bullshit, and had the shotguns for protection.

"They gave Lee plenty of grief, plenty of sass, but you know the chief, he handles it. We'll rotate out again, keep a lookout, but Clint's likely to stay low for a day or two."

"He can't hide forever, and Traci's safe." That, Zane thought, had to be good enough for now. "I'll draft up divorce papers tomorrow, go in to see her, let her look them over, explain what she needs to do now that she's had some time."

"Hope to hell she doesn't back off again. Well. You oughta get yourself some food, son. Enjoy your own party."

"I'll do that. You keep me updated. The sooner Draper's locked up, the better."

She'd be afraid, Zane thought as they rounded the house again. Traci would stay afraid until he was. And fear, he knew, either made you fight back or give up.

Still, he had to put it away for now. He had more than a hundred people eating, talking, playing. He managed to snag a drumstick before he grazed the food tables, piling his plate.

"Try that tortellini salad." Ashley sidled up beside him. "Nathan made it, and you won't be sorry."

"Didn't know you were here." He leaned down to kiss her cheek.

"Haven't been here long. And the minute we showed up, my parents confiscated my kids. This is an amazing house, Zane, and the grounds—wow! I need to make friends with Darby."

"She makes them pretty easy, which is why I haven't seen her for a while."

"Over there, helping run the kids' games."

He glanced around as he scooped up some of the tortellini, watched Darby cheer on a little girl at the softball throw.

Ashley tipped her head toward his shoulder. "Not a woman in the world who doesn't want someone to look at her like you're looking at Darby. Does she know you're in love with her?"

"Yeah. Shows, huh?"

"Big-time. I'm so happy for you, Zane. And now I'm going to find Nate and see if I can make him look at me just like that."

He squeezed himself into a place at a table beside Micah and Cassie, let the music and party noise wash over him while he ate.

"You actually know all these people?" Micah asked him.

As Zane looked around, he shrugged, shoveled in more tortellini—Ashley hadn't steered him wrong. "It's more like Emily knows all these people. They keep coming, don't they?"

"Music's tight, food's good. Who wouldn't?" Cassie wagged her fork at him. "If you do this again, you're going to have more. Word spreads, you know? People'll suck up to you just to get the invite."

Then she leaned over, dropped her voice. "I don't want to bring things down, but do you know if Traci's okay? Her mom and my mom are friends, longtime."

"She's with her mother, and in a safe place."

"Good enough. I'm just going to let my mom know." She wiggled out, then patted Zane's shoulder before she walked off. "Good deed."

"Guess I didn't tell you I had a little . . . altercation with Clint Draper a couple weeks back."

Zane paused, took a look at Micah. "Define 'altercation.'"

"Just a little contretemps. See, I'm walking down the street, gonna meet Cass at Grandy's for some eats. As I pass Clipper's Bar, Draper comes out, gives me a full-on shoulder bump, right? So I just say, like, Hey, share the road, man, keep going, but he comes after me, gets all up my grill, dig? What he is? Shit-faced."

Since he hadn't tried it on his first round at the food, Micah paused to stab a fork into Zane's tortellini. "Not even seven in the p.m., and he's shit-faced, which is why he's coming out of Clipper's, and why he's looking for a fight. They kicked his ass out."

"And there you are, real handy."

"Oh yeah. I just want to get some eats with my girl. Really don't want to fight a mean drunk, so I'm all, Hey, man, chill, but he doesn't want to chill. He gives me a couple shoves. I figure I can outrun him, but, shit, I just can't grow the feathers for that. I reckon I'm going to have to fight this drunk asshole, probably get my own ass kicked. But Cyrus came along. You remember Cyrus, right? Nice guy, was married to Emily for about five minutes back in the day."

"Yeah, I know him."

In fact, Zane picked him out of the crowd now simply by the red hair—some white streaked through it.

"He comes up, and *he* gets in Draper's grill, tells him to take off, and says if he gets in his truck to drive off, he's gonna call the law, cause he's skunk drunk. Draper walks off, shoots us the bird like that hurts our feelings. I wanna buy Cy a drink, but he rain checks it 'cause he's heading home. I figure that's that."

"But it wasn't?"

"The next morning when I leave for a job, my tires are slashed, all freaking four."

"Son of a bitch," Zane muttered. "Did you tell Lee?"

"Yeah, but what's the point? Can't prove it was Draper. And better the tires get slashed than me, bro. I'm saying he'll for sure try something with you, because like Cass said, good deed."

"Let him try."

"When he does, I've got your back. Keep me on speed dial, man. Seriously. Now, it goes in the box, lid on, 'cause we've got partying to do. Like Cass said, the music's tight. I'm going to find her and show these people how to dance."

How not to was more like it, Zane thought. Micah had never picked up anything approaching rhythm, but he sure as hell had a good time stomping around on the dance floor.

Zane hoped he'd have a chance to do the same with Darby, but knowing his obligations, walked back to relieve Dave at the grill. And found Lee already had.

"Hey, get yourself a beer and a plate," Zane told him. "I've got this."

"No, I need a little wind-down time first, and a little grilling for the masses does the job. We'll talk about the rest tomorrow."

Understanding, Zane backed off. "When you're ready, send up a flare."

"Count on it. Go find your girl."

"I believe I will." He walked through the crowd, stopping to talk here and there until he could get to Darby.

She still manned the softball pitch. He spotted Roy, a bunch of teenagers, including Gabe.

He heard the tail end of a challenge as Darby eyed Gabe and lightly tossed one of the balls in the air.

"If I do three in a row, you take over here."

"Over-sixteen distance," Gabe added. "Straight pitch, no underhand crap."

"Of course."

"Deal. You miss, you buy my lunch next Sub Saturday."

"Done. Give me room here," she said, and in her pretty sundress, stepped back to the flag planted to indicate the over-sixteen line.

She rolled her shoulders, tipped her head, took her stance.

She wound up, sent the ball straight through the hole in the plywood and into the net behind.

Zane's brows lifted as she said, "That's one." He already knew she had an arm, now could add she had damn good form.

She sent the next through with a nice little whiz, then picked up a third. She batted her eyes at Gabe as he rolled his.

And hit the sweet spot with the third.

As she polished her nails on her arm, she smiled at Gabe. "You're my relief. Oh, look, we've got another contender."

Even as Zane shook his head, she grabbed his hand, pulled him up to the line.

"I'm rusty," he claimed.

"What, you can't pitch three through the hole?"

"I'm looking for a dance, not a prize."

"A dance with me? That's your prize, slugger. Step right up."

She tossed him a softball. He preferred the size, the toughness of a baseball, but still it hit a chord with him, took him back.

What the hell, he thought, just a kids' game at a cookout.

He zipped the first one through, felt that quick snap in the blood. He took another, let it fly so it thwacked against the net.

Felt damn good.

He put some speed on the third, winced as the force of it had the net toppling over. "Sorry."

"You ain't lost a hair, Zane," Roy said as Gabe trotted over to fix the net. "Not a single hair. Takes me back."

"Yeah, me, too."

Darby ran a hand up his arm. "If you don't play for the Lakeview team next season, it's a crime against humanity."

"Crime against humanity's a little extreme."

"Baseball is humanity." Then she took his hand. "Let's dance, Walker."

CHAPTER TWENTY-FOUR

While Zane watched fireworks bang and bloom in the sky, Clint Draper decided to borrow his good pal Stu's pickup. Of course, with Stu passed out cold on the couch of his deaf bitch of a grandmother's basement, Clint couldn't exactly ask permission for the loan.

He owed Stu, not only for giving him a place to stay, but for digging into his supply of oxy and home brew to help take the edge off.

And still, he was royally pissed.

He'd teach Traci a lesson, a good, hard lesson when she came crawling back, but meanwhile he had others needing good, solid payback.

His pappy had taught him—and those lessons had often come hard—that when somebody fucked with you, you fuck them back. And worse.

He had the whole story now, knew who he needed to fuck back. And no point in waiting to start.

In a couple days, he'd come out of hiding, and good old Stu would swear on his grandmother's Bible that Clint had been with him up in the hills, fishing and camping all the time.

Nobody'd prove any different.

He raided Stu's paint supply. When Stu worked, he put time in painting houses, and always took what was left, claiming he'd used every drop.

He had a closet piled with paint cans, old brushes and rollers, dented pans. Plenty for Clint's purpose.

After carting a few cans to the pickup, tossing in a couple of brushes, Clint drove into town.

He liked being drunk, believed when he'd downed a few he thought clearer, saw clearer, got stronger, even smarter. He didn't care if he swerved onto the shoulder a few times.

It just woke him up.

When he veered toward Zane's office, the front left tire hit the curb, then bumped over it. At that time of night, Lakeview slept sound, so no one heard him whistling softly through his teeth as he got to work on the job at hand.

Maybe some paint splashed on him when he opened a can at random, and some dribbled on the sidewalk as he walked across. He sloshed a brush around in what was billed as Moulin Rouge and slapped on his message. Because he wanted nice big letters, he had to open a second can. Blooming Orchid merged with Moulin Rouge.

He'd quit school at sixteen, had a spotty attendance beforehand. Spelling hadn't been one of his strengths, but the meaning and the hate came across in the sloppy lettering and drips of clashing paint.

SUK MY DIK MUTHR FUKER

Stepping back, he studied his work with some pride and watched drips of paint slide down the pristine white of the building.

Pleased, he used more of the orchid to scrawl **FAGGIT** across the main door before heaving more paint on the window, dumping the rest on the porch.

Too drunk and stupid to think of fingerprints, DNA, or basic common sense, he left the empty cans on the porch before unzipping and releasing his bladder on the doorstep.

Besides, he considered good old Stu an ironclad alibi.

He got back in the truck, smearing paint from his hands onto the steering wheel. He swerved and weaved his way out of town, navigated the road up to Darby's house.

Bitch stuck her nose in his personal business? Bitch had to pay.

He considered burning the place down, but he hadn't thought to get a can of gas.

Next time, he vowed, and settled for defacing the house with a rainbow of Cerulean Blue, Daffodil Yellow, Mountain Mist, slopping ugly words over the wood.

CUNT HORE LESBO BICH

He attempted to depict a gang rape with stick figures, and to his bleary eyes considered it fine art.

Using his art as a visual aid, he masturbated, howling with satisfaction as he spattered cum over her welcome mat.

Far from finished, he stumbled back to the truck.

Now came the big guns. Literally.

Hunched over the wheel, he drove toward Zane's, and was far too drunk, much too focused on getting where he needed to go to notice the headlights keeping a steady quarter mile back in his rearview mirror.

Even shit-faced he remembered Zane's security. Everybody knew about it, especially since Bigelow got his ass kicked by that lesbo bitch. Which proved, in Clint's reasoning, Bigelow was a pussy, and too much of a pussy to have knocked his wife and kids around back in the day.

Buncha bullshit.

One thing Clint Draper wasn't, for fuck's sake, was some pussy.

He cut the headlights as he drove up the steep lane, pulled up a little better than halfway. Security, my ass, he thought. He'd slip right through it, do what he came to do, and slip right out again.

He got his rifle off the bench seat beside him—paint time was over—and hiked into the woods.

He had a nice, bright moon to guide him.

If Clint knew one thing and knew it well, it was how to hunt and shoot and make the ammo count.

He thrashed his way through underbrush—not worried about scaring off game, as what he wanted slept all nice and tidy inside the big house.

He didn't figure on killing them—yet—but he'd sure as shit scare the piss right out of them.

"Time to wake up, fuckers. You'll be eating floorboards and shitting your pants."

And maybe, just maybe, one of them would peek out a door, a window. If that happened, he'd put a bullet in them.

Didn't matter a good goddamn which one.

"Think you can take my wife from me, turn that stupid bitch against me? Gonna fuck you up, fuck you up real good."

He stumbled a time or two, scratched the hell out of his arms on brambles—and left plenty of fibers and bits of skin behind.

He wished to Christ he'd thought to grab a beer from Stu's stash so he could slake his thirst.

The warm, close night and all the work he'd done had him soaked in sweat. Even drunk he could smell his own stink.

No worries. He'd clean up at Stu's, grab that beer, maybe pop one of the old lady's Ambien.

Sleep like a baby after he finished his good night's work.

The moon cut through the trees, flooded over the house. Clint thought he couldn't ask for better.

He saw himself slipping in and out of the shadows, silent as a ghost even as he stumbled, thrashed, cracked twigs under his boots.

But the shadow behind him moved quiet and bided its time.

Clint took a stand, such as it was, at the edge of the trees, keeping back as he studied the house.

Word was they had a big, fancy bedroom in the front with the big glass doors so that pussy Walker could stand out there on the deck lording it over the town.

He shouldered the rifle, brought the doors into the crosshairs of his scope. He thought he might even get lucky, at least wing one of them.

Either way, he thought, either way, they wouldn't sleep easy after tonight.

He fired twice, hit the glass, watched it shatter, then added a spray that flashed through the opening, hit the jambs, the house.

Grinning, heart thumping, he kept his aim, picturing the shot if that fucking Walker had the balls to come to the doors.

The shadow moved in behind him. Clint knew an instant of

shocking pain when the rock smashed his skull. His rifle hit the ground seconds before he did.

Now the shadow smiled and thought: Interesting.

When an opportunity fell into your lap, only a fool ignored it. Coolheaded, he took the rifle, hauled Clint up and over his shoulder.

He'd just take his opportunity off to a more private location.

The shots ripped Zane out of sleep. Instinctively, he rolled over Darby, wrapped around her, kept rolling until they hit the floor.

"Stay down," he snapped as the dog sent up a howl.

"What—"

"Stay down. Somebody's shooting at the house."

"No. Maybe more fireworks."

"Fireworks didn't do that." He gestured at the broken glass, lifted his voice over the alarm as it began to shrill.

Zod nuzzled in, lapped his tongue over faces, shoulders, hands while Zane slithered over her, pawed his hand onto the nightstand for his phone, already signaling.

"Yeah, I've got a problem. Somebody's outside shooting at my house. Call the damn cops, now. Stay down," he ordered Darby again. "I want you to stay low and get into one of the spare rooms and hide. If you hear him break in, get out a window. And keep going."

She lay on the floor, clutching the dog, every muscle trembling. "Is that what you're going to do?"

"Just do it."

He stayed low, worked his way to the closet and inside. He came out with the Louisville Slugger Emily had given him for his twelfth birthday.

And saw that rather than getting to a hiding place, Darby had unplugged a bedside lamp, now held it much as he did the bat.

"Two weapons are better than one," she began.

"Quiet!" He shoved out a hand. "That's an engine starting up."

Moving fast, he darted to the broken doors before she could object—and caught just the quick flash of taillights.

"Son of a bitch. I'm going after him."

"He has a gun. Do you?"

Ignoring her, he grabbed pants, swore as he cut his foot on broken glass. "Stay here."

She only had a second to think: Like hell.

When he ran from the room, she was right behind him. "Wait. Think. I know you're mad. Me, too. But there could be more than one of them, with guns, for God's sake, Zane. They could be trying to lure you out, just like this."

Though it galled her, she pulled out another weapon—the only one she believed would work on a furious male.

"Please don't leave me here alone."

That stopped him. "Damn it, Darby, he can't outrun the Porsche. Hide in the pantry until the cops come."

It galled, more than a little. But deciding her pride wasn't worth his life, she wrapped around him, clung. "Don't leave me alone."

"All right. Okay." So he stood with her in the upstairs hall, holding her. "It's all right, darlin', I'm right here. It's okay."

As relief spilled through her, she tightened her grip. "It had to be Clint Draper, had to be. He won't get away, Zane."

"No, he won't. Look—I'm not going anywhere. I want you to take the dog into the spare room there—stay away from the windows. I'm just going down to wait for Lee."

"We'll all go down. Jesus, you're bleeding."

"Just stepped on some glass."

"Bathroom," she ordered. "We'll clean it up, then Lee or Silas or somebody will be here."

It gave her direction, something to focus on, so her hands stayed steady as she examined and cleaned the wound—nastier than she liked, not as bad as she'd feared.

"He didn't try to break in."

"He'd know about the security system. Everybody does. Probably too stupid to realize shooting the glass would spring the alarm."

Seconds before Zane heard the sirens, Zod began to howl again.

"Here they come. Darlin'? You're naked."

"Right. I'll take care of that and be right down."

He stood, favoring his injured foot. "You weren't afraid of being alone."

"I was afraid," she said simply, and went to put some clothes on.

The dog raced downstairs, barking ferociously, and Zane followed.

Still naked, Darby sat on the side of the bed, let the trembling come again. The broken glass, the bloody footprints, the tangle of sheets. And, she saw now, the holes bullets had torn into the wall just a few feet from where they'd slept.

What if he'd waited? Waited until morning, until Zane stepped outside as he did every day? Until they'd sat together on the back patio over cereal and coffee?

They'd have been defenseless.

Or if he'd come sooner, using the booming fireworks as cover, shot while there were children running around the lawn, while everyone looked up at the sky?

She wrapped her arms around her belly, rocked.

"Pull it together," she told herself. "Just pull yourself together. Ifs don't matter. It didn't happen. And they'll find him. They'll find him."

She walked back to the bathroom, splashed cold water on her face, and waited for the sudden wave of nausea to pass.

By the time she'd pulled on clothes, Zane had started back up the steps.

"Wanted to see if you were dressed. Lee needs to come up."

"Sure."

He walked to her, laid a hand on her cheek. "You're really pale."

"I'll be better after coffee. I'll go make some." She looked down to the base of the steps where Lee waited. "It's really good to see you, Chief." She continued down. "I didn't even hear the shots, the glass breaking. I woke up when Zane rolled me off the bed and we hit the floor."

"Don't you worry now, honey. We're going to take care of this. That I can promise."

She nodded, walked to the kitchen to make coffee.

She continued to sit, sipping slowly, when Lee and Zane came back down.

Darby considered herself pretty adept at reading a room, and this one struck her as even more grim than it had been.

"Oh God, he didn't shoot someone, did he?"

With a shake of his head, Lee sat beside her. "Silas called in. Zane's office was vandalized again. Obscenities painted all over the front of the building. Paint's still wet. I've got a couple of officers going up to your place to check it out."

"Okay. It might have been Draper who broke in before, before Micah added security."

"Could be. We're going to wait until daybreak to check and see if we can find where he was when he shot the doors. And we'll be checking on his place, and his family before that."

"All right."

Lee patted her hand. "You're a steady one, Darby."

"Not altogether, but I believe in the system. It stood up for me when I needed it. I know you'll find him. Where's he going to go? And you'll put him away. Except . . ."

"Except."

Her gaze flicked to Zane. "It'd be a wild coincidence if it wasn't Clint Draper, with the timing. But, Zane, you were a prosecutor. It's not impossible somebody you put away is out, and wants some payback. And I can see by your face you've considered that."

"Have to," he agreed. "But it's Draper. Hitting my office, that's bullshit stuff. It fits him like a glove. And I'm betting anybody I prosecuted who had the brains to track me here probably knows how to spell 'motherfucker.'"

Lee rose to answer his phone, wandered off, wandered back when the call was complete.

"Your place, too, I'm sorry to say, Darby. Paint, crude words. And . . . he left some DNA. We'll send that off. We've got Clint's on file already. Still, it takes time. Not as much for prints, and we're going to find them, too."

"I should go see—"

"No, you're not going to go see," Lee said before Zane could. "It's a crime scene now, and you're going to steer clear of it. You need anything from there, we'll get it for you."

She looked Lee dead in the eyes. "What kind of DNA?"

"You leave that to us." He patted her hand. "I'd appreciate it if you'd both stay here for now. We're going to go have a conversation with the Drapers. And leave the bedroom as is. One of my men'll be around to take pictures."

He bent down, brushed his lips over Darby's hair. "Nobody does this to my family. You can take that to the bank."

"I'll walk you out."

Darby stayed where she was, waited until Zane came back.

"What kind of DNA? He told you just now. I have a right to know."

"My office, he pissed on the porch. Your place? He jacked off on your doormat."

She blew out a breath. "Well. Glad I didn't pay much for it."

"I'd beat him bloody for that alone, and I say that as somebody who'd rather use words than fists. But for that, I'd beat him bloody. Darby, I'm—"

Her shoulders went iron hard. "Don't you dare say you're sorry. I picked her up on the side of the road. I brought her to you for help. We're in this together." Though her eyes stung with tears, her voice came fierce. "Don't you dare say you're sorry to me for any part of this."

She swiped the heels of her hands over the tears that escaped. "Zod needs to go out."

Since the dog all but danced at the door, Zane had to agree.

"I'll take him—on a leash. Any possibility you could try to scramble up some eggs?"

"I can do that, but I can't guarantee how they'll turn out."

"Can't be worse than mine."

He got the leash, clipped it on the delighted dog. "If you'd been alone at your place—"

"I just went through a bunch of ifs upstairs before I reminded myself ifs don't matter. You'd better work up a serious appetite if you're going to swallow down my eggs."

In the wash of his security lights, Zane walked the dog, and used the task as an excuse to aim toward where he figured the shooter had stood. He'd examined plenty of crime scenes in his past life, pored over countless police reports.

And since he had, he kept Zod on a short leash. Wisely, he decided when the dog sniffed the air and strained against it to move ahead.

"Easy. We mess anything up, Lee won't have to kick my ass. I'll kick my own."

Moving carefully, he didn't have to follow Zod's nose for long. He could follow his own. Only more cautious now, he picked the dog up, tolerated the wiggles, the lapping tongue as he studied ground already disturbed.

And the blood, still fresh.

"Now, what do you make of that?" he mumbled. "You just hold on." Crouching, he got a firm grip on Zod's collar, dug his phone out of his pocket. He took a couple of shots, then frog-walked back until he had enough distance to trust the leash again.

He had to tug the dog away, then lead him off to where Zod could do what he had to do without compromising the scene.

While the dog busied himself, Zane called Lee.

"I found something—and before you jump, I didn't compromise the scene. I'm going to send you a couple pictures. You're going to want to get somebody over here. There had to be two of them, Lee, and one of them's bleeding."

He sent the pictures, thought it through while he walked Zod back for a very early breakfast.

Darby stood by the stove, scowling at the skillet. "First they were runny, and then in like seconds, they're overdone. But I didn't burn them, so that's—"

She turned as she spoke, saw his face. "What? What happened?"

"They're gone. Don't worry."

"They?"

He nodded, bent to unclip the leash. "Zod sniffed out where they'd been. That's a good dog." He gave the dog a rub, then poured his food in his bowl. Zod pounced on it like a lion pounces on a gazelle.

"There's blood."

"Blood? But—"

"I'm not an investigator, but I've worked with them. Simplest to my eye? Two of them, and one bashed the other with a rock. You've got a bloody rock," he continued as he got out plates. "You've got blood on the ground, crushed brush, short drag marks."

He shrugged. "They'll find more once the sun's up, but simplest is two, and one hauled the other out after he coshed him with a rock."

She stood watching him while he got out forks. "You're pretty damn cool about it."

"Well, now it's a mystery, so that's interesting. And we're about to have eggs and coffee." He gave her arms a quick rub, much as he had the dog—with easy affection. "I'm still pissed, but now we've got something to figure out on top of it. Clint Draper's easy, almost certain to be him and we'd know why. But, darlin', why did Clint hit somebody with a rock when he had a rifle? Or why did somebody hit him with one?"

"To protect us? And that doesn't make any sense," she admitted as she scooped clumps of overdone eggs onto the plates. "Why would they be in the woods in the middle of the night? Why would they haul the other away and not say anything?"

"See." He shot a finger at her, sat to eat. "Got you thinking. Could be one of his pals, whoever he's using to hide out. They had a dis-agreement out there, one smacks the other."

"Hmm." She sampled eggs. Maybe more salt. "Then it's oh shit, we better get out of here. But that's just stupid."

He tried more pepper. "We're talking—most likely—Clint Draper, darlin'. They don't come much more stupid."

"Most likely," she echoed. "It is most likely, but you'll still check on people you helped put away that might want to hurt you."

"I've got files. I'll be looking, but odds are better Lee rounds Clint up pretty quick, and that DNA, the prints slam that shut." Because they weren't any worse than what he'd have scrambled up, he ate more eggs. "He's pissed. Lee."

"I could see that for myself."

"He'd do the job regardless, but being pissed? He'll round Clint Draper up pretty quick. Even so, what I'm going to tell you is—"

"There are other Drapers," she finished. "And—how's this for talking southern—they won't take kindly to having their kin locked up."

"Not bad for a Yankee, and no, they won't take kindly to it. So you're going to be careful. We're going to be careful," he corrected before she could. "Plus, we've got ourselves this fierce guard dog."

Darby glanced over at Zod. He'd finished his breakfast and now lay on his back, stubby legs in the air, wide tongue lolling out of the side of his mouth.

Smiling, she lifted the charm she wore around her neck. "That makes two of us."

"And we'll look out for each other." He closed his hand over hers. "All three of us."

As if jabbed with a needle, Zod leaped up and, barking madly, raced toward the front of the house.

"Cops coming back," Zane said. "One thing's for certain, nobody's going to be able to sneak in here with the General on duty."

He rose, took his plate and hers to the sink. "I'll get the dishes," he told her. "You call off our little and fierce."

She got up, breathed out. "I love you, Walker." When he turned, smiled, she lifted her shoulders. "It seemed like one of those just-right times to say so."

"Anytime's the right time. I love you right back."

Knowing it for pure truth, she went to call off the wildly barking dog, and let in the police.

CHAPTER TWENTY-FIVE

It took her back, having cops everywhere, the way they moved, the way they spoke. It pulled Darby back to the Bigelow attack, but oddly that violent encounter blurred in her mind. Everything about it so fast, so hard.

But the cop speak, the routine of the work, yanked her back to the morning she'd lost her mother. And with crystal clarity, the impossible shock and disbelief when the police came to the door with grim faces, terrible words rolled over and through her. Now, just like then, she had nothing to do, no action to take.

Just waiting, waiting, waiting.

She'd already given her statement, had nothing to add. For now at least, Lee remained firm. She needed to stay put.

She'd watched and read enough police procedurals to have a layman's idea of what was going on around her.

They'd take official photos of the place Zane found at the edge of the woods, take samples of the blood, take the rock. Others would take photos of the bedroom, dig bullets out of the wall.

Bullets, she thought again as she wandered from kitchen to great room. Waiting, waiting, waiting.

It all seemed unreal.

She felt a twinge of embarrassment—ridiculous—when Emily came in. Then Emily walked straight to her, wrapped around her, and just held her.

That twinge turned into a flood of relief.

"They don't want me to go outside," she began. "The dog can't, so I'm supposed to stay in with him. Zane's out there, but it's his house, so—"

"That's not altogether why." With a final squeeze, Emily stepped back. "He was a prosecutor. He knows these ropes. Come on, sweetie. I'll fix you some tea."

Now she sighed. Enough with the self-pity, because wallowing in it was worse than doing nothing. "A Coke'll do it. Do you want anything?"

"Not right now, thanks."

"I want to go to my place, see the damage."

"You will," Emily assured her. "And when Lee clears it, we'll help you put it all to rights. Are you sure you couldn't get a little more sleep? The sun's barely up."

"I'm totally awake. I had to call Roy, tell him what happened, because I'm not going to be able to work this morning. He'll get everything going."

"Working for you's steadied that boy. What are y'all working on now?"

"You're trying to distract me."

"If you see it that easy, it's not working."

Darby walked to the kitchen doors—closed tight—looked out at the grounds she'd designed, the waterfall she'd built. "I love it here. This house, what I see when I look outside. I love Zane, even though that part still gives me some nerves."

"And now twice in this house you've had to deal with violence."

"Yeah. Do you think some people are just fated—I know, I know, I *know* it sounds stupid. But are some just fated to have violence in their lives? Again and again."

"I don't believe that for a single New York minute."

"I don't want to believe it, but I've been pacing around here, waiting, and I started thinking how my life did a one-eighty when I met my ex. Up until then, even considering my father took off, I had a good, solid childhood, a calm sort of life. My mother and I, school, the neighborhood, friends, the work, boys. Pretty much smooth."

On a long expelled breath, she sat.

"Then Trent. I married him too young, too fast, but screw it, Emily, others do. It either works or it doesn't. But it not only didn't work, it put me in the hospital."

Emily caught Darby's face in her hands, tipped it side to side. "He put you there. *It* didn't."

"He'd have put me in again if he could've managed it. I'd never had anyone want to hurt me before that. Not that way. Then my mom, losing her the way I did. Coming here, fresh start, right? Then Bigelow, then finding Traci, now this. It just keeps rolling."

As if sensing the need, Zod laid his head in Darby's lap, looked at her with adoring eyes. And Emily sat beside them.

"You're a smart, sensible woman, Darby. And most times you've got a positive way about you. I can't blame you for having a hard time finding that positive this morning. But all that you're saying is just foolishness.

"I don't know Trent," Emily continued, "but I know who he is because I dealt with Graham and my sister for years. They're mean, violent, ugly people who wear a mask so well, so easily. I grew up with Eliza, I interacted with Graham all that time, but I didn't see through the masks, not all the way. That wasn't fate. It was their horrible skill."

"It is, isn't it?" Darby agreed. "It is a horrible skill."

"What happened to your mother happened because someone was selfish, careless, callous. And I hope to Christ they suffer terrible guilt every day for the rest of their life."

She put an arm around Darby's shoulders, tucked her close. "In a terrible way, you were able to fight off Graham because of what happened with Trent. I find that so admirable—which is why I'm going to nag you, at another time—about giving that self-defense course. As for Traci, it's your compassion and caring that helped save her, so you don't think otherwise, not for a second. And this?"

She sighed. "This morning is a stupid, violent, ugly man's attempt to show he has big balls, when in fact, he's a small, dickless asshole. My Lee will see he's behind bars before sundown. You can count on it."

"Thanks. I mean it. I needed that."

"I think what you need is to get out of here and go to work. To take this sweet dog and go do something productive. So. I'm going to go talk to Lee about letting you go on and do that. Where would you be working today?"

"I had a little something to finish on Highpoint Road—that's how I came across Traci—but I'll do that later. I sent the crew to the Marsh place, by the lake."

"All right then." She gave Darby's knee a pat, then rose. But before Emily could head outside, they heard feet running down the front steps. And the sound of the door slamming shut.

"That's just it." Darby jumped up, got the leash. "I'm not going to sit here another minute."

With the dog thrilled with new activity, and Emily beside her, Darby marched outside in time to see two of the police cars speed off.

"They must have found him." Darby aimed toward Zane as he strode toward them. "Or he's done something else. But . . . Did they find him?" she called out.

Zane kept coming. "Yeah, they found him. Clint Draper."

Something's wrong, Darby thought, and by the way Emily took her hand, she knew Emily saw it, too. "What is it? What happened?"

"They found him . . . floating in the lake. He's dead. Christ." He scrubbed his hands over his face. "Gabe called it in."

"Gabe. Oh my God. I need to—"

"No." Zane shifted to stop Emily's forward leap. "You need to stay right here. Lee's got this. He's already talked to Gabe. They were working. Your crew, Darby. And from what I got, Hallie spotted the body. Roy jumped in to try to help. Too late for that, and he shouted out for somebody to call nine-one-one. Gabe called his dad."

He took Zod's leash. "Let's go sit down. We need to keep Zod clear of the crime scene. They're finished, or were, but we should keep him clear for now."

"I need to talk to my boy," Emily insisted.

"You go on and call him. Darby, how about if we put our heads together and make some sweet tea."

"I'll do it." Emily waved them back. "I'll get it started, call Gabe. I need to call Brody, too, make sure he stays away from that part of the lake for now."

With a nod, Zane nudged Darby to a chair on the patio, put the loop of the leash around his wrist when Zod plopped under the table to snooze.

"Someone killed him," Darby began.

"Or he fell in, or he committed suicide. That's for the cops and the ME to determine."

"The blood over there, the rock, the drag marks. You put it all together, Zane, and somebody killed him and dumped him in the lake. The questions are who and why."

"They'll be talking to one of his friends. They found a truck shortly before Gabe called. It's got spilled paint, more cans of it, and blood. What it looks like is Stu Hubble came along with Clint on his spree, then they got into something, Stu smacked him with the rock. Probably didn't mean to kill him, but did, panicked, dumped him. But things aren't always what they look like, and that doesn't explain why Stu would leave his truck sitting on the side of the lake road.

"We wait for the facts."

"I need to talk to my crew."

"I know." He put a hand over hers. "Soon."

The shadow had become a man, and the man stood outside with an excellent view of the activity on the lake. He'd watched the yahoo jump in, swim to the floater.

It had given him a chuckle along with his morning coffee.

He'd stood right there when the bumfuck cops had come across the truck he'd left where a blind moron could find it. He suspected one Stuart Hubble—according to the registration—was in for a bad day.

But the floater, the too-late lifeguard, the whole scene of chaos really topped it off.

Then the cops came screaming up—man, what a show! This was the most fun he'd had in weeks. At least since he'd beaten that two-bit whore he'd picked up somewhere in Dickwad, Virginia.

Best thing he'd done, he thought as he watched the show, had been following his gut—and following the asshole with the paint cans.

Like fucking divine intervention, that's what it had been.

He hoped killing the stupid bastard brought some trouble down on Walker. Maybe it would, just maybe. Asshole vandalizes the shit-head's office, then vandalized the whore bitch he's fucking—

He had to stop, take a breath there, unclench his fists.

Then what does he do, but sneak his drunk way right up to Walker's place, pop a bunch of bullets through the glass.

Dead idiot could think of it this way. If he hadn't done him the favor of bashing his brains in, he'd be spending a nice stretch in prison.

Better off dead.

"You're welcome!" Snickering, he slipped back inside for another coffee, a croissant, some local jelly.

He brought it out on the porch, sat in the nice sturdy chair. And enjoyed his continental breakfast and show.

When Emily brought out the tea, she rubbed Zane's shoulders. "I'm going to make a big pasta salad, get it chilling."

"You don't have to do that," Darby began.

"Lee's letting the crew go, and every one of them wants to come here, see the both of you. So I'm going to put together some food from what I can find in your poorly stocked pantry. I'll be raiding your kitchen garden while I'm at it."

Zane reached back to squeeze her hand. "Best pasta salad going. Is Gabe okay?"

"He seems to be. I want to see him for myself. I'm having Ralph go by and pick Brody up. I want both my boys where I can see them. Then you'll have the lot of them to help you take down the rest of these canopies, and haul in the rest of the extra tables and chairs."

She looked around. "Hard to believe it was just yesterday all of us were out here celebrating." She lowered her head to kiss the top of Zane's. "Lee'll be a while yet. He's got a lot to deal with."

"Zane." Darby reached for him when Emily went back inside. "Somebody has to tell Traci."

"I want to do that, and in person. And as soon as I can," he added. "Will you be okay if I go into Asheville?"

"Of course I will. Do you want me to go with you?"

"You stay here, help settle your crew. I'm going to check with Lee, get his go-ahead. He has the tougher one. He'll have to notify the rest of the Drapers."

Which he would, but Stu Hubble had to come first. Lee found him snoring on the couch in his hovel surrounded by empty beer bottles, a scatter of pills not yet consumed, ashtrays full of butts—tobacco and weed, and what looked like the remains of a meat-lovers pizza along with a couple empty bags of Doritos.

The good hard shove Lee gave him loosened an enormous fart, followed by a belch that smelled nearly as foul.

"Fukov," Stu muttered, and attempted to roll over.

This time Lee used his foot, and helped Stu land on the floor.

"Sumbitch! What the—" He broke off when his bloodshot eyes focused on Lee. "Who the hell let you in? This here's my place. You got no right—"

"This here's your grandmother's place. Get your sorry, stinking ass up. You're under arrest."

"Am not. Didn't do nothing."

Considering, Lee narrowed his eyes. "Where's Clint Draper?"

"How the hell am I . . ." Stu blinked, got slowly to his feet.

He was a big guy with a big gut of hard fat. He had little eyes and bad teeth.

"Around, maybe in the can. We've been hanging out. Was gonna go camping, but it got too hot, so we come back yesterday, hung out. Ain't illegal."

"Defacing property is. And you were stupid enough to use your truck when you painted obscenities on Zane Walker's office, on Darby McCray's house."

"Did no such thing. Been right here. You ask my gramma."

"Paint's still in your truck, smeared all over the steering wheel."

But none, Lee noticed, on Stu, who obviously hadn't changed or showered in several days.

"Your paintbrushes, Stu. Your paint cans, your truck."

"Nuh-uh. Less'n somebody must've stole it. You ask Gramma, you ask Clint."

"I asked your grandmother, who's deaf as a post and hasn't been down those steps for six months or more. I can't ask Clint Draper."

"Why the hell not?"

"Because we fished him out of the lake this morning, not a quarter mile from where we found your truck. He's dead."

"Is not." Stu pushed around to see if any of the empty bottles had anything left. "Back in the can's where he is. We've been hanging out right here 'cause it's too hot for camping."

Lee pulled out his phone, brought up the crime scene photo of Clint Draper, eyes wide, face gray. And shoved it under Stu's nose.

He yanked back the phone, and himself, when Stu bent over and puked on his own shoes.

The stench, Lee thought, would wake a decomposed corpse.

"Did you have a falling-out, Stu, up at Zane's place when you were shooting at the house?"

"It ain't Clint, no way. You're tricking me."

"We fished him out of the lake this morning. He's got a fist-sized hole in the back of his skull. I expect he was dead before you dumped him in the lake."

"I never did that." Stu's tree-trunk legs wobbled until he thudded back on the couch. "I never done killed nobody in my life. Clint's a friend of mine. I never done killed nobody."

"Get your sorry ass up or I'll haul you up. You're coming to the station, and you'd better start telling the truth or I'll see you do some real time behind bars. You're up shit creek, Stu, and every lie takes you farther from shore."

"I never done killed nobody! I swear on my life." Tears began to leak. "Clint just came by yesterday—we never went camping, he just asked me to say so. He came by after he heard Traci took off and you was looking for him. I was just helping out a bud, that's all it was, and anybody'd do the same."

"You reckon anybody'd hide and lie for a man who beat his wife black-and-blue?"

"I don't know nothing about that. Clint, he was here, that's what I know. We had some beer and such, and I passed out, I guess. I don't know nothing about the paint or nothing. Jesus, he's dead? For real?"

A moron, Lee thought, a lazy, bullying bastard, but an unlikely killer.

"Get up. You're coming in, telling it all. If you don't want me to cuff you, get up. You got another pair of shoes?"

"Uh, yeah."

"Well, change them. I'm not having your puke in my house. Get a shirt and pants, too. I'm taking what you're wearing into evidence. They find any paint, any of Clint's blood on you, you're fucked good."

"I was just covering for a bud, like anybody would. I didn't do nothing. I never killed nobody."

Lee believed him, right down the line. But that didn't mean he wouldn't squeeze him first. If Stu knew anything, anything at all, he'd damn well squeeze it out drop by drop.

By the time the crew arrived with Brody in tow, Emily had the pasta salad in the fridge and a second pitcher of tea steeping. Darby went straight to Roy.

"I'm still wet," he began, but she hugged him close. After a second's hesitation, he clamped hard around her.

"Holy God, Miss Darby. Holy God. I've never seen—never gonna stop seeing. When I—when I got to him, grabbed on, he turned over. And his face . . ."

"Come on, sit down."

"I—I got some dry clothes in the truck. Any place I can change outta these?"

"Sure."

She waited while he got them, then led him in and to the lower level, past Zane's home gym, the home theater and into a full bath.

"Take a hot shower, take your time," Darby told him, then gripped his hand. "Roy, you're a hero."

"I didn't do nothing."

"You went in the lake, trying, hoping to save someone. And when you saw he was past saving, you still brought him in. You're a hero."

As his eyes went damp, he shook his head. "I never liked the son of a bitch, that's God's truth. Liked him less since it got out he was hitting on Traci. But . . ."

"That only makes you more of a hero. Take your time."

She went up to find her crew huddled together at a table, united in shock. And Brody sitting so close to Gabe they made a twin pack.

"Is he all right?" Hallie twisted her hands together, released them, twisted. "He's hardly said a word since . . . since he pulled Clint Draper out of the lake."

"He just needs some time."

"Can you tell us what's going on?" Ralph demanded. "I'd sure as hell like to know what's going on."

"Me, too, but I'll tell you what I know."

She didn't sit, couldn't. "Somebody—we have to assume Clint Draper—shot out the terrace doors to the bedroom upstairs."

"Son of a bitch." Ralph pounded a fist on the table, made Hallie jump, and sent his own glasses skipping down his nose. "That son of a bitch. Not supposed to speak ill of the dead, but hell with that."

"Where's Zane?" Brody demanded. "Is he hurt?"

"No, no. He went to get Traci's sister. They're going into Asheville to tell her. Before Clint came here, he painted a bunch of crap on Zane's office building, on my place."

"The Drapers are no good," Hallie muttered. "Never have been, never will be. We're going to help you fix it up, Darby, don't you worry about that."

"I'm in on that," Brody said. "We'll make it right. But . . . how'd he get in the lake?"

Darby let out a breath. "They found—well, Zane and Zod found where he shot from, and . . . You can see over there where the police tape is. There's blood, too. He had to be with somebody, and who-ever he was with must've hit him with a rock, then dragged him off, dumped him in the lake."

"Don't make a lick of sense," Ralph added.

"No, it really doesn't."

"It kinda does," Brody put in. "Could be two things that kinda do."

Intrigued, Darby pulled up a chair, looked into Brody's Walker-green eyes. "What two things?"

"He was probably drunk—they'll do a tox screening and find out. But everybody knows he gets meaner and more stupid when he's drinking. Dad's had to lock him up a couple times for drunk and disorderly."

Emily poured more tea. "And how would you know?"

"I've got ears, Mom," he said, adding a teenage eye roll. "Anyway, whoever was mean and stupid enough to be with him when he shoots at the house was likely drunk, too, right? Could be he wanted a turn with the gun, and they tussled over it, and bam. Probably didn't mean to kill him, but did, then what're you gonna do, right? Dump the body. Should've just left it lay and took off, but drunk, stupid, and mean."

"Put it that way," Gabe considered, "it makes some sense. What's the other way, Sherlock?"

Brody grinned, then shrugged. "Okay, so he's going around tag-ging Zane's office, then Darby's house. Somebody sees him. Maybe somebody as mean as Clint Draper was, and they follow him right on up to here."

"Why kill him?" Darby asked.

"Sometimes mean doesn't need a reason, just opportunity. I heard Dad say that once. Either way, Dad, Silas, and the rest of them will figure it out. It's what they do."

"That's right." Standing behind her son, Emily squeezed his shoul-ders. "It's what they do."

"If it's the second . . ." Gabe hesitated, drew a finger down the con-densation on his glass of tea. "They're even meaner than the Drapers. I don't know anybody like that. Except . . . is Dad sure Zane's—I mean, Graham Bigelow is still locked up?"

"He checked first thing." Now Emily shifted a hand to Gabe's shoulder. "He's locked up good and tight, don't you worry."

But wasn't the real worry, Darby thought, the possibility that someone in Lakeview was meaner than the Drapers?

And a killer.

After he took Stu's clothes into evidence, Lee left him with an officer and gave him orders to shower, change, and wait in lockup. He'd be damned if he'd interview the idiot while said idiot was still stinking of sweat and stale beer and puke.

In any case, he had to notify the deceased's family, and wouldn't that be a goddamn picnic?

Knowing the Drapers, he took both Silas and Ginny as backup.

Horace Draper answered his knock, stood sneering with his thin gray hair buzzed to his scalp, a home-rolled cigarette tucked tight in the corner of his mouth.

The air inside, barely stirred by a couple of standing fans, still smelled of breakfast grease.

"Y'all come out here looking for my boy, I'm gonna tell you again, he's off camping. You ain't stepping in without a warrant."

"We found Clint, Mr. Draper."

Something shifted in the old man's eyes. "All right, then you know he wasn't nowhere around when that lying bitch he married says he smacked her. Never smacked that lazy woman in his life. Might be she coulda used it."

He jabbed a nicotine-stained finger at Lee. "You got my boy locked up, I'm gonna have your badge for it this time."

Lee ignored the finger, ignored the threat. "Mr. Draper, I regret to inform you, your son Clint is dead. I'm sorry for your loss."

"That's a stinkin' lie!"

"His body was recovered earlier this morning from Reflection Lake."

From behind Horace, Bea Draper began to wail, "Not my boy! Not my boy! Not my boy!"

"You hush up, woman. They's lying!"

Lee took out his phone, brought up the crime scene photo. "Is this your son Clint, Mr. Draper?"

He saw it then, the moment when reality and the grief that came with it overtook belligerence. Draper stumbled out the door, dropped into one of the chairs on the rickety porch.

"My boy's gone?"

"Yes. I'm sorry."

Grief snapped into a wild rage that shoved Draper to his feet. "You done it!"

Before he could lunge at Lee, Silas had his arms yanked behind his back. The old man had plenty of ropy muscle with that rage fueling them. Ginny had to step in, help hold him back.

"We don't want to put you on the ground, Mr. Draper," she said. "We don't want to cuff you."

"We didn't find him alive." Lee spoke calmly. "The Lakeview Police Department didn't cause his death."

"Then who done it! My boy can swim like a shark. He didn't fall into the cursed lake and drown. Who done it!"

"We're investigating."

"Investigating, my ass! Cops is nothing but corrupt all the way up to the FBI. You don't give one good shit about me or my blood. Never have."

"I'll do my job. It's best you sit down, get yourself under control. It won't do your family any good if I have to take you in for assaulting an officer."

"I'll tell you who done it. That pissant Bigelow boy goes by Walker. The one who stole my boy's woman, got her to say lies about him. You best put him in a cell right quick, ya hear? Before me and mine find him."

"Be careful who you threaten. Now sit down before I put you down." Lee jerked his head to Ginny, signaling her to go inside where Bea Draper continued to wail and sob.

"Zane never hurt your boy."

"You'd say that."

"I know that. When your boy was killed, Zane was busy protecting

Darby McCray and himself from the bullets Clint shot through the exterior doors of his bedroom, and calling the police."

"Bullshit. My boy did no such thing. That Bigelow scum, he'd lie and you'd swear to it."

"We found Clint's rifle, recently fired, in the truck he took from Stu Hubble, and we dug bullets out of Zane's bedroom walls. They're going to match. We found Clint's prints on the steering wheel, smeared with the paint he used to deface Zane's office building, Darby's house shortly before he fired the rifle. The paint was still wet. Seeing as Zane had a half dozen cops in his house about the time Clint was dumped in the lake, he's got a damn good alibi."

"You'd lie, they'd swear to it. Every one of those useless police."

"You know that's bullshit. Even you know. We have the time logged on the nine-one-one. I've got Stu Hubble in lockup now, and from the looks of his place when I picked him up, he and Clint got good and drunk, smoked some weed, popped some pills before Stu passed out, before Clint took it into his head to grab some paint cans, his gun, and go on his vendetta."

He crouched down now, looked into Draper's eyes. "You think about this. If you and yours hadn't lied to me yesterday, your boy would be alive right now. He'd've had his day in court. He might've done some time, but he'd be alive."

"Fuck you."

"Yeah." Lee straightened. "That's what I thought."

He saw the fist coming, had a half second to calculate. He let it land, took the bare knuckles on the cheekbone.

"That'll do it. You're under arrest, assaulting an officer." With Silas's help, he wrestled Draper to the ground, cuffed him, while Ginny had to shift from comforting a grieving mother to restraining a wild woman.

CHAPTER TWENTY-SIX

After a difficult hour with Traci, Zane drove back to Lakeview. A quick text with Darby told him she'd been cleared to go to her place—with her whole crew, he was relieved to hear.

Satisfied, he drove into town to assess his own damage.

He pulled up, got out, stood on the sidewalk studying the ugliness behind the police tape.

Worse, he thought, worse than the broken window—and it would take a lot more time and effort to repair. Several people stopped, offering sympathy or supportive anger.

He glanced over at the sound of his name, waited as Britt hurried to him. She simply opened her arms and took him in.

"I talked to Emily, and to Silas. I know everything. I'm so sorry." She drew back, but kept her arms around him. "First I'm thanking God you and Darby weren't hurt. Then I'm sick and mad about everything else."

"We've been through worse. It's just paint."

She lifted her eyebrows. "Tell me how you really feel."

"I'm sorry he's dead. Part of the sorry is because I didn't get a chance to beat the crap out of him. If he'd aimed three feet lower, I don't know. But I know Darby sleeps closest to the doors."

"Where is she? Should I go see her? I can juggle appointments."

"She's up at her place—the crew's with her, and Brody, too. He wanted to help."

"He's a good kid. We'll all help, Zane. Make sure she knows that."

"Will do. Look, we're going to draw a crowd here, and I can appreciate the support and still just not want to hear it all right now."

"Got it." She gave him a last hug, stepped back for another look at the building. "He sure couldn't spell worth shit."

At least it gave him a laugh before he left to go buy a whole lot of paint.

With that task handled, he swung by the police station. He found Lee in his office, writing up a report.

Angling his head, Zane studied the bruise on Lee's cheek. "Bet you didn't run into a door."

"Old man Draper's cooling his temper in a cell. Sit. Want coffee?"

"I couldn't stomach any more, but thanks. I'll start." He took a chair. "Traci's pretty shaken up, but she's got her mom and her sister with her. She's going to stay where she is for a couple more days. Longer if you think she should."

"Day at a time." The chair creaked, a homey sound, as Lee leaned back in it. "We've got Clint's prints on the rifle, on Stu's truck, on the paint cans, the brushes, even scattered on your office building, Darby's house. He always was an idiot."

"Can't argue."

"It'll take longer for the DNA left at your office and Darby's place. It shouldn't take as long for the blood match, or the tox screen, the COD. And I've got a reasonably clear timeline from Stu Hubble."

"He's not a suspect, I take it."

"Can't see it. Was passed out cold in his clothes when I picked him up. We'll have the clothes analyzed, but no paint, no blood to the naked eye. No prints on the rock, but plenty of blood. He's as big an idiot as Clint, and wouldn't have thought to wipe the murder weapon—plus, it shows no sign of that.

"Clint got to his house about noon yesterday," Lee continued. "On foot. Stu's grandmother confirms that. Stu says they never left the basement, ate, drank, smoked, watched TV, played some games, watched some porn. He thinks it had to be after two when he passed out."

"So Clint helped himself to the paint and so on, helped himself to Stu's truck."

"How it looks."

"They didn't have another friend drop by, get drunk with them?"

"Not according to Stu, and he was too scared to lie by the time we got here."

"Maybe he ran into somebody," Zane speculated. "Or somebody with a grudge against him—and there'd be plenty—decided to see what he was up to. Killing him seems . . ."

"Extreme," Lee finished. "Lots of possibilities. He turns the gun on somebody, gets bashed. He's with somebody, trips and falls on the rock, they panic and dump him. Or somebody decides it's payback time, takes the opportunity.

"I'm going to sort it out, Zane."

Zane remembered the way Lee had sat with him on the cot in the pod in Buncombe after the worst night of his life. "Counting on it."

"I want you to be careful, you hear? Draper's got it in his head you must've killed Clint."

"How the hell did I manage that when I'm upstairs trying to keep us from catching a bullet—and calling it in? And about five minutes later letting cops in the house."

"Facts, evidence, logic—they don't matter to him. To any of them. He's going to make bail, so you watch yourself."

"Let me talk to him."

"Zane."

"Has he lawyered up?"

Lee let out a half laugh. "Doesn't believe in such things—until he does. At the moment, it's hang the lawyers, which would include you."

"Let me talk to him. You can observe. If he really believes I did this, Lee, Darby could get caught in the cross fire. She nearly did already."

"All right. All right, I'll take you back."

Lee led him back, unlocked the steel door to the trio of cells. Stu, his back to the doors, snored like a freight train on the cot in the far right cell.

Draper sat on the cot in the far left, and leaped up the instant he saw Zane.

"You sumbitch." He shot an arm through the bars, trying to grab Zane. "I'll kill you first chance."

"Making a credible threat in front of a police officer's only going to keep you from making bail."

"Fuck you, fuck your bail. I got other sons."

"Yeah, you do," Zane agreed, eyes steady. "Maybe you'd like to keep the rest of your family out of a cell. Here's how it is. I had people, dozens at my house last night, some of them up to about midnight. I'm with Darby McCray—"

"That whore help you kill my boy?"

His years in the DA's office had that sliding off his back. "I'd say we settled in to sleep about one this morning. About four—eight after, actually, as I looked at the clock when I rolled Darby to the floor—I was wakened by the sound of gunfire and breaking glass. The exterior doors to my bedroom shattered."

"Did that yourself, that's what I say. Trying to fuck with my boy."

Calmly laying out the facts, Zane continued, "I told Darby to stay down, got over to my closet, got my ball bat in case whoever was shooting broke in. We called nine-one-one. What time did the call log in, Chief?"

"Four-eleven."

"Sounds right. I stepped on some glass. I expect there are police photos of my bloody footprints. I was pissed, going to go out with the damn bat, but Darby talked me out of it. She cleaned up my foot, and the cops came. Arrival time, Chief?"

"Four-sixteen."

"You stop and think. How the hell did I get to Clint, get his rifle? Why the hell would I take him to my place, into the woods, bash him with a rock if I *had* his rifle and meant him harm? And how the hell did I manage to get him into the lake when I had a houseful of cops?"

"You wanted him dead!"

"No, I wanted him to face charges, to face a jury of his peers. And somebody robbed me of the chance to see to that. I want to know who."

"You was probably screwing that useless whore he married."

"Oh, for Christ's sake, *when*? You and I know your family kept eyes on her pretty much around the clock. I've got my own woman. I'll make you a promise right now. If anything happens to her, I'll come for you."

"Zane."

He shook Lee off. "That's the language he understands. Traci's my client, nothing more, nothing less. I'll do my best by her. But when it comes to my woman, I'll do a hell of a lot more. Stay away from me and mine, Mr. Draper, and use your head. Whatever you think of me, you're smart enough to know I couldn't be in two places at the same time."

He walked out, waited while Lee locked the steel door.

"Probably didn't convince him."

Lee puffed out his cheeks. "He's thinking about it, which is more than he did before. It's a big stretch to try to twist you into it, and he's starting to see it. It might not matter to him. You're part of the why in his head. So be careful."

"You, too, Chief. Same reason."

"Comes with the job. Go on home." Lee gave him a slap on the back. "Get some food in you."

He did head home, thinking he needed to board up the bedroom doors, call his insurance company, see when he could get the doors replaced.

Boarding up meant getting some plywood, which meant borrowing a truck.

Maybe he should buy a truck. He wouldn't be driving the Porsche through the winter anyway.

Just one more thing to think about.

He detoured to Darby's, tried not to panic when he didn't see her, the crew, the trucks. All he saw were the obscenities scrawled on her house.

The cops, he assumed, had taken the befouled doormat. One small blessing.

He pulled out his phone, texted:

Where are you?

On the job. The Marsh house. Lee cleared us to work. Where r u?

At your place. Can I borrow your truck?
Sure. ?

I need to go buy some plywood to board up the doors. Custom doors, may take a while to replace.

We boarded the doors before we left. You need paint. I went by your office before here. He didn't spell anything right. Roy would paint for you, but I'm keeping him busy. I'll send you the name and number of the couple of guys he says would do it pretty quick if you don't have it. The same ones who painted for you before.

I've got it. What about your place?

Soon. I'm not on Main Street. Go home, eat some pasta salad, make the calls.

You okay?

Better. Should be home by six. Late start today.

I'll be there. I love you.

Aww, first time in a text. Weirdly, I love u 2. Later.

He pocketed his phone, looked around. Wished he could do something for her.

Then it came to him, and seemed so simple. So right. He went home, took care of it, made the calls, ate a little pasta.

When she got home, just after six, he had the outdoor table set—with flowers he hoped he was allowed to cut. And wine ready to pour.

"Well, look at this."

Darby surveyed the table while Zod raced over to Zane as if they'd been parted for years.

"I figured we both deserved it."

Her gaze shifted to his. "Don't we just."

"I made crudités."

"You did not."

He shot a finger at her. "Did. I figured it would start off our three-course meal."

"Okay, what are the other courses?"

"Pizza and Ring Dings. The crudités are a sop to adulthood."

"I think I'm in love."

He took a firm hold of her face, kissed her. "Better be."

She laid her head on his shoulder, sighed. "Let me go up, get a shower, change so I can be worthy of this amazing meal."

"I set things up in the guest room, the front-facing one with the window seat."

She tipped back her head to look at him, then as her eyes blurred, just lowered her brow to his shoulder.

"I figured we deserved that, too," he added.

Because she didn't trust her voice, she tried to nod, then just tightened her grip.

"Hang on a second," she managed.

He did, just hung on in the quiet evening with the odd little dog sniffing their shoes.

"You've got a way, Zane. Such a good way. I told myself to suck it up. The boarded doors, the bullet holes. It's not the room, it was the man. It's a good room."

"It'll be a good room again. But for now, we've got others."

Steadier, she drew back, smiled at him. "Now I've got you all sweaty, and probably transferred some stone dust. You oughta come join me in the shower."

"You have the best ideas. Just let me feed the dog."

"He ate on the job." Taking Zane's hand, she started inside. "Later he can have a you-know-what while I sample your crudité."

In the shower, Darby sloughed off the sweat and grime of the work. With the mating of wet, slippery bodies, she sloughed off the stress that had curled tight in her all day.

She felt it release, slide away like the water down the drain. Even knowing it would come back, perhaps because she knew, she could steep herself with him, with what they gave each other.

Under the pulse of water, skin slick with soap, hands greedy and gliding, they pushed away the ugliness, embraced the joy.

They kept the door closed on painful reality, sent Zod into spasms of delight with a Milk-Bone. And lighting candles, pouring wine, they talked of anything but what had shattered the peace in the dark hours.

With the light softening, the dog snoozing under the table, Zane poured more wine.

"Ready?"

Darby took another sip, nodded. "Yeah. You?"

"Yeah."

"Okay. Start by telling me how Traci handled it."

"I'm glad her mother was there, even gladder I took her sister. She needed both of them to help her through the 'It has to be my fault' stage."

"She's been beaten down, physically, emotionally, so that's knee-jerk. There were women in my support group who automatically assumed blame for everything. My kid failed his spelling test—must be my fault, terrible mother. It rained yesterday when it wasn't supposed to, so I must've done something wrong."

"I saw that plenty with abuse victims back in Raleigh."

"Which is why having you there helped her, too."

"Hope so. In any case, she's going to stay in Asheville for a while longer. She's scared of the Drapers, and she's not wrong."

"Do you think they'd try to retaliate, against her?"

No point, he thought, trying to soften it up.

"Payback's a religion to some people. Darby, you need to know at least right now, they're twisting this whole thing around so somehow I set it all up, killed Clint."

"That doesn't make sense on any planet."

"Doesn't have to. I think Horace Draper's beginning to see that, but it doesn't mean they won't try to strike back. And you're part of that. Not just because you were here, because you're with me, but because Clint targeted your place."

"I've already figured that out. Maybe he had some problem with me before. He might've been the one who broke into my place."

Frowning, Zane studied his wine. "It doesn't seem like his style. Not the break-in, but the fact nothing really valuable was taken, nothing was wrecked. Still . . . you could connect his whacking off on your doorstep with taking your underwear. He was already pissed at me," Zane considered, "because I wouldn't take him on as a client. So . . . maybe."

He reached over for her hand. "Either way, you need to be careful."

"We both do."

"We both do. Meanwhile, Lee's already matched his prints to your place, my office, the truck, the paint cans, and so on. The idiot Clint was staying with gave Lee a good timeline, up until said idiot passed out. His truck, his paint supplies. They'll have cause of death, ballistics, a tox screen pretty quickly. The DNA will take a little longer, but Clint's was already on file."

She'd thought of all that during the good, physical work of the day. "But none of that's going to point to who killed him."

"No, it's not."

Reading his face, she tapped a finger on his hand. "You have theories, Mr. Prosecutor."

"Maybe."

Now she circled her hand in the air. "Please proceed."

"All right then. Clint wasn't what you call a popular guy, not outside his family and a few idiots like Stu Hubble. He pissed off a lot of people. He'd get drunk, start fights, or get grabby with somebody's wife, girlfriend, sister. He hounded people like the McConnells, he poached on posted land. There's a guy who lives farther up in the hills who claimed last year that Clint and his brother Jed poisoned his hunting dogs."

"Well, God!" In response, Darby rubbed a foot over the snoozing Zod.

"Couldn't prove it, but—Lee let me read Clint's file—he was adamant. So a lot of people didn't think of Clint kindly, you could say."

"And your theory is one of them saw him sneaking up here, followed him, took the opportunity to pay him back."

"That's one of them."

"You have another that worries you more."

"Yeah. Graham Bigelow."

"He's locked up." Alarmed, Darby spoke quickly. "Lee checked. Emily said—"

"Graham's locked up," Zane confirmed, "but that doesn't mean he couldn't be a part of this. He's spent nearly two decades in prison. He knows how the culture works inside. There's a chance he could have made a deal with another con who was up for release, or knows somebody on the outside. Somebody who'd come here, watch the routine, look for an opening—maybe break into your place and know not to leave prints, not to disturb too much."

That idea, even as a theory, sent a shiver down her spine. "But . . . why kill Clint?"

"Stretch the theory. He's right there. Take him out, cause trouble, upheaval. It took smarts, if we go with straight bad guy, not to take the weapon, not to leave prints again, not to break in and go after us. Smart would know cops would come pretty quick. Smart bides its time, looks for the next opening. If something happened to either of us now, who would Lee have to look at first?"

"The Drapers."

"You got it. And while he is, whoever did it walks away. I put more into the first theory, but we can't discount the second."

"The second's closer to one of Brody's."

Surprised, Zane paused in pouring the last of the wine. "Brody has a theory?"

"A couple, and both slide close to both of yours. Mean doesn't always need a reason, just an opportunity."

"Ain't that the goddamn truth."

She looked toward the western hills, the lowering sun that showered them. "I love this place. I know I haven't lived here long, but I love it, the look, the feel, the people. I know there's mean under it, because there's some mean under anywhere. But the mean's why the Drapers are the next thing to outcasts here."

She looked back at Zane, lifted her glass. "We're going to be all right, Walker. We'll paint over the mean. We know it's under there, but we don't let it win. To prove it, I'm painting my place Tangerine Dream."

Zane opened his mouth, closed it, cleared his throat. "Wouldn't that be orange?"

"It would, and the door and trim? Tango in Teal. Bold, happy, up-yours-mean type colors. What're you painting, your office building?"

"I bought white. A lot of white."

"Come on!" She made a dismissive gesture, flicking white away. "You can do better."

"It's a law office, darlin'."

She leaned closer. "Is the law boring?"

"I'm not painting it Tangerine Dream."

"I was thinking more Nautical Navy, Mystic Gray for the trim and porch. I'll show you on my paint fan."

"I bought white."

"I bet they'll take it back, exchange it, because white. Take the opportunity mean gave you, Walker, make a statement. I'll show you," she said again. "After we take this wine and walk the dog."

"White's classy and classic," he insisted as they got up, and Zod jumped to his feet as if an alarm had sounded.

"Yawn."

"The painters are starting tomorrow."

"And I bet they'd agree with me, if they have any taste." She took his hand in hers.

He had a feeling she was leading him to more than dog walking.

Later, when she showed him her paint fan, as threatened, he saw himself exchanging the damn paint in the morning.

While they walked the dog, the man who'd come to Lakeview and done murder took himself for a walk as well. As he strolled by Zane's office building, he made a point to stop, to gape.

"Terrible thing, isn't it?"

As he'd hoped, one of the local yokels stopped to chat.

"Just awful!" He put shock in his voice.

"You visiting?"

"I am, yes."

"My family lives in Lakeview. I can tell you this isn't usual."

"I should hope not."

"Promise." She smiled at him, a pretty young thing. Maybe he'd make a point to have a taste or two of Pretty Young Thing. Maybe he'd kill her after.

So many possibilities.

"And actually, I work there. Law offices. I'm an intern. Gretchen Filbert," she told him, friendly as a puppy.

"Drake Bingley. Nice to meet you. But . . ." He looked back at the smears of paint, calculated how soon the sun would go all the way down, how long it might take to lure Pretty Young Thing. "Aren't you worried?"

"I guess I would be, but the man who did it . . ." He watched her censor herself. "He won't be back. It's a nice town, Mr. Bingley. I hope you have a wonderful visit."

"Oh, I already am. Say, I wonder if you can tell me the best place to have a good steak, a good glass of wine. I'm in the mood."

"Oh, sure." She beamed at him, into quiet blue eyes behind scholarly wire-framed glasses.

He knew he looked like a professor, one taking a few summer weeks to work on his novel. He'd spent considerable time cultivating that look—letting his hair grow, adding the professorial (to his mind) goatee.

He wore faded jeans, Birkenstocks, and an ancient Grateful Dead T-shirt he'd picked up at a flea market.

He even had the man purse, holding a well-worn paperback copy of *The Grapes of Wrath* (as if) along with his wallet and false ID, a bandanna, and the 9mm Glock he'd stolen from his brother-in-law's collection.

"You can't go wrong with Grandy's Grill—just down a couple blocks and across the street."

"Sounds good. Say," he began again, only to be cut off when another pretty young thing ran toward them.

"Gretch! Sorry, running late. Luca just texted. He and John are already at Ricardo's, grabbed a booth. Sorry." Like Gretchen, she gave him an easy smile. "Am I interrupting?"

"No, just letting Mr. Bingley know where Grandy's is."

"One day I've got to get Lucas to take me there for more than a beer and nachos. We gotta book."

"Enjoy your steak!" Pretty Young Thing One called back to him as she rushed off with PYT Two.

Opportunity missed, he thought. For now.

Maybe next time.

He continued his stroll, decided he'd go ahead and have that steak. Maybe he'd strike up another conversation, find another pretty young thing.

Even not too young would do.

CHAPTER TWENTY-SEVEN

Though he wasn't a hundred percent convinced, Zane exchanged the paint. He worked through the morning while the paint crew covered Clint's nasty art with primer.

He had to go through the story—an abbreviated version—with every client, accept their outrage on his behalf before getting to the business at hand.

He glanced up from his notes when Maureen came in.

"Your friendly reminder you have to leave for your appointment with Mildred Fissle."

"And her cats. I'm gearing up for it, and today's change in her will."

"Her granddaughter in Charlotte sent her flowers for her birthday. So she's back in. You've got two hours clear. Take a long lunch after."

"I might do that."

"Call Micah or Dave, see if they can meet up with you for lunch."

He angled his head. "Worried about me?"

"I love you, Zane, almost as much as I love my new shoes I got in the Independence Day sale. You know Horace Draper made bail."

"He's not going to come into the Sunshine Diner gunning for me, Maureen."

"Do it anyway."

"Fine. I tell you, women are running my life."

"We're so good at it. And speaking of that, you should think about getting Gretchen on board for next summer. She's just right, and when she passes the bar, she'd make you a nice associate."

"I thought of it myself, so don't go all smug thinking it was your idea."

She only smiled, smugly. "I took Cubby and Mike out a cold drink a bit ago. Cubby showed me what they're going to paint. I figured you'd stick with white."

"I should've, right?"

"Only if you wanted to be usual and boring, which you were going to because Milly at the hardware told me you bought white, then brought it back when they opened this morning for that nice strong blue and that pretty gray."

"Know-it-all," he said, and began to load his briefcase.

"Darby nudge you there?"

"Maybe."

"I'm giving you credit." She waited a beat. "For having the good sense to hook up with a woman of vision and taste."

"I'll take it. Now get back to work. I don't pay you to chat up the boss."

Amused, she stepped to him, kissed one cheek, then the other. "Call Micah or Dave—or both. You'll do that for me, won't you, honey?"

"Yeah, yeah." He left by the back to avoid the painters, and texted Micah—and what the hell, Dave—as he circled around for his car.

After he dealt with Mildred Fissle, her cats, her ever-evolving will, he wanted to drink his lunch. But refrained.

Since both Dave and Micah were available—he imagined Maureen had told them they'd better be—he decided on a manly lunch of meatloaf under the bright lights and within the orange walls—Tangerine Dream?—of the diner.

"Meatloaf, huh?" Micah considered the laminated menu as he gulped down some fizzy lemonade. "Cassie's making noises about going vegetarian. Ain't gonna happen. Make it two."

"To be young and able to eat the meatloaf special midday. Screw it. Make it three, Bonnie."

"Will do. Yours is on the house today, Zane. Show of support."

"You don't have to—"

"Done." She tapped a sharp finger on his shoulder and left to put the order in.

"Some bennies from a wad of crap," Micah said.

"And it saves me from paying for your lunch as my show."

"Hey." Micah waved a hand. "I'm still here. Just to finish up the wad of crap before we eat? Word is the other Draper boys are coming back for the, you know, funeral. The one's getting a day pass, under guard, then it's back in the slammer. The marine's got bereavement leave or whatever."

"Great."

"And Stu Hubble showed up at the clinic last night with a busted-up face and a broken arm. Said he fell down the steps, but that's bogus, man. You know Jed Draper gave him a beatdown."

Dave shook his head, looked unsurprised. "Blaming Stu Hubble's ignorant, illogical, and typical of the Drapers. We can hope Jed Draper got it out of his system."

"But you don't think so," Zane said to Dave.

"That kind always blames someone else. He's going to end up behind bars sooner or later. I can hope for sooner."

"They gotta know it wasn't you, bro."

"Yeah, they have to know."

But they had to know it hadn't been Stu Hubble either, Zane thought. Then again, Jed Draper would find it a lot harder to give him a beatdown than he had Stu Hubble.

He didn't like knowing a part of him looked forward to the attempt.

At the first patter of rain and grumble of thunder, Darby and her crew grabbed up tools and headed for their trucks.

Patsy Marsh popped out of her back door and gestured.

"Y'all come on up here, have a seat on the veranda. You're going to have a glass of tea and some of my pound cake."

"You don't have to trouble," Darby began, then switched gears. "Did you say 'pound cake'?"

"My mama's secret recipe. All y'all sit, take a load off. This rain isn't supposed to last."

"It's a fine place to watch a storm rolling," Ralph said. "Sure do appreciate it."

"Saves my Bill from eating more cake than he should."

"Can I give you a hand, Miz Marsh?" Hallie scraped off her shoes on the mat.

"You sure can. And how's your mama, your grandmama?" Patsy asked as they went inside.

Darby dropped down on the glider because Ralph had it right. It was a fine place to watch a storm. It whipped the trees, stirred up the water of the lake that went bright with the first slash of lightning.

And with it, the air blissfully cooled.

As Ralph took a padded chair, Darby patted the space beside her for Roy. "Doing okay?"

"Yeah." Still, he let out a long breath with his eyes on the lake. "Can't help but think about it. I sure wish they'd catch who did it."

"Tell you what I think." Ralph hunched forward in his chair. "I think Clint got one of his asshole friends, might be his own brother, to go on up and cause trouble at Zane's place. Drunk and stupid, argued about something. One asshole picks up a rock, smacks the other. Doesn't mean to kill him, but that deed's done, so he does the rest to cover. And what else? Whoever did it was likely stupid enough to think the cops'd figure Clint fell in and drowned."

Darby said nothing for a moment. She calculated Ralph had used more words in a single minute than he normally did in a full week.

"That's what Adele thinks," Roy put in, "like it was more accident than deliberate. Drunk and stupid."

Because although she didn't agree, the idea seemed to comfort Roy, Darby said nothing.

"So, you know, anyway . . ." Roy let out another long breath and the patter of rain turned into buckets, beating the roof of the veranda like war drums. "I'm engaged."

"You—" Darby punched his arm. "When?"

"Asked her last night."

"And you wait all damn day to tell us?"

"Still getting used to it myself." But it drew a quick head-duck grin out of him. "I didn't want to ask till I had a ring. What I see is women can be pretty particular about there being a ring, and I didn't have time to get one. Then yesterday, after . . . everything, I thought how life's pretty damn unpredictable, and I had to make a move. So I went out and bought a ring. She seems to like it just fine, so I guess I did okay. I asked her, and she said yes."

"What's this I hear?" Patsy, carrying a fat pitcher full of amber liquid, stepped out with Hallie right behind her with a tray. "Roy Dawson, am I hearing you finally had the good sense to ask that nice girl to marry you?"

"Yes, ma'am, I did."

"Isn't that fine news?" She set down the pitcher, began to pour tea into the glasses on Hallie's tray. "I bet your mama's just tickled."

"She sure is."

"You set a date?"

"Well, Adele wants spring, when it's warm enough to do it out-doors. She and my mama and her mama are already diving into it, so I'm just going along. I might miss a few days," he said to Darby, "with the wedding and a honeymoon."

"You don't worry about that one bit."

"First slice to the groom," Patsy declared, and passed Roy a dessert plate with a generous wedge of pound cake. "This is fine and happy news, just what we need."

A little teary-eyed, she passed out cake. "These young ones, Ralph, they don't know yet how fast it all goes, how you have to grab onto all the pieces, good and bad, to make the pictures you want to leave behind."

"Gotta take the storm with the sunshine, my own mama used to say."

"Isn't that the truth? I like a good storm," she said quietly. "It washes away the heat and the hard, at least for a little while."

And, Darby thought, wouldn't part of the hard be stepping out on her really pretty veranda, looking out at the lake she loved, and remembering the body pulled out of it?

As if she'd heard the thought, Patsy turned, smiled brilliantly. "What you're doing to what was an eyesore and a frustration to me down that slope is the best thing since my mama's pound cake."

"And it's real good cake, ma'am." Gabe shoveled in the last bite. "Real good."

"Storm's passing," Hallie said. "I'll take these dishes in for you before we go back to work."

"Don't you fuss with that, honey. I believe I'm going to sit out here, enjoy the cool a bit, and watch y'all work."

Darby thought about storms, and grabbing all the pieces, about the simple kindness of offering cake as she dug the next hole. The sun broke free, burned bright on the water, and turned the storm-damp air to steam.

Boats came back to glide, and kids leaped into the lake from a raft, filled the world with laughter and squeals.

Death didn't stop life, not for long.

It was life she thought of as she planted a trio of toothwort she'd chosen almost as much for its name—southern lady—as its foliage and flowers.

It would bloom early, she thought, start showing its stuff in the winter like a hellebore, then shoot up those sweet flowers at the first whisper of spring.

"Something on your mind, boss?" Hallie wondered.

"Just thinking it's late in the season now, but what a show this will make next year."

"It's pretty now, too."

"Yeah, it is, and we're going to be done here today. But next spring, and the summer that follows, and right into the fall. My oh my, what a job we'll have done."

She stepped back to check her positioning and, pleased, pulled out her phone to take a couple of shots. Walking down to the river rock Ralph and Roy had spread, she took some from a different angle before glancing out to imagine how it looked from the water.

She saw a little Sunfish sliding by, a lone man guiding it. Long, sunbaked hair spilled out of his fisherman's hat; the sun boomeranged off his mirrored sunglasses.

When he raised a hand in a kind of saluting wave, she felt a quick chill slice through the damp heat. But she lifted a hand in return before turning away.

"Well, gang." Odd, her throat felt tight. She unhooked her water bottle, soothed it. "We're about down to cleanup. Let's knock her out."

She caught herself glancing back, but the little Sunfish had sailed on.

Laughter had the man going as Bingley nearly capsized.

Looked right at him and waved! If he'd had his Glock, he could have shot her where she stood—and all the rest of them with her.

Maybe a couple of those idiot teenagers as well, screaming as they jumped off that stupid raft just to cap it off.

Maybe shooting her in the head wasn't his plan, but he just loved knowing he could have.

Time's coming, bitch, he thought, with the great good humor of the moment. Time's coming for you and the asshole lawyer.

And anybody who got in the way.

If he'd learned anything since going in, coming out of prison, it was he had a strong appetite for blood.

The spilling of it.

July moved on with its heat and quick, hard storms. Tourists flocked to Lakeview for their lakeside and hiking holidays. The summer people streamed in and out with murder barely making a ripple on their souvenir shopping.

Primer covered the ugly on Zane's building, so people streamed by it as well, and the bold new color began to make its statement.

While he waited for the other shoe to drop, knowing it would, Zane went on with his life.

It didn't surprise him to see Lee driving up on a lazy Saturday morning while he sat on his front veranda researching SUVs on his tablet.

He set the tablet aside as Lee got out of the car.

"Morning, Chief."

"Zane." His glance rose up to the boarded doors. "No doors yet?"

"Coming in next week, and my trusty painters are going to finish up at the office, fix the damn bullet holes in the bedroom here. Want something cold?"

Lee looked at Zane's tall glass. "Is that iced coffee?"

"It is. Come on in. I'll get you one."

"I won't say no. Darby around?"

"She had a couple consults this morning. She should be back before too long if you want to talk to her."

"Girl keeps busy," Lee commented as Zane led the way inside.

"She does. May be why she sleeps like the dead. So, are you on duty, Chief?"

"Summertime's usually all hands on deck. This one especially."

"Yeah." Zane got another tall glass, filled it with ice. "How's that going?"

"What we got is a victim nobody but his family and a few reprobates liked, drunk, pumped up with pills, out on a vendetta who ends up with his skull caved in on your property before he's dumped, already dead, into the lake."

After picking up the pitcher of room-temperature coffee he'd already brewed, Zane glanced over. "Do I need a lawyer?"

"It'd make my job easier if you did."

Zane poured coffee over ice, added milk from the fridge, handed it over. "If I'd gone out there, I might've seen something, someone."

"And gotten yourself shot."

"There is that aspect. How about we go porch sitting?"

"I won't say no to that either. You do make damn good coffee, Zane, hot or cold."

"The law thing doesn't work out, I could try a career as a barista."

They went back out, sat. Zane picked up the baseball he'd brought out with him, rubbed the seams. "I hear the Drapers are having Clint's funeral tomorrow."

"Dexter's Funeral Home. None of the Drapers are churchgoers, so that simplifies that. And they're burying him in their family plot."

"That's still legal, under some basic guidelines, in this state."

"It is, and in this case, simplifies things again. I've talked to everybody I know had a hard-on for Clint, or the Drapers in general."

"You get overtime for that?"

Lee let out a huffing laugh, drank some coffee. "I can tell you it took a hell of a lot longer than talking to those who ran with him. But in both cases, it's not falling in line. Turns out that Clint had some hard words with Richie Fields a couple weeks back, and Fields is the type who could bash a skull in. Thought maybe I had a line there, but at the time in question he was a guest of the county facilities after getting pulled over outside of Hickory for speeding, reckless driving, and DUI—which he added to by taking a couple swings at the county mounty."

"Well, you don't get a more solid alibi than that."

"You don't," Lee agreed, and drank more coffee, looked out at the hills. "With your work in Raleigh, you'd have gotten some threats."

"Goes with the job, Lee, just like it goes with yours."

"It does. I need you to start thinking if you got any credible, any that would've brought somebody here looking to cause you trouble."

"I have been thinking about it." Zane studied the ball, ran his thumb over the seams. "There might be a few."

"I'll want those names, son."

"Yeah." Zane turned the ball around and around in his hand. "I've been thinking about taking a trip to Raleigh, having a conversation with Graham."

"We're on the same page there, too. I've already had one with the warden. Graham's had a few cellmates in his time, connected with others. Some are back out in the world. We need to tug that line, too."

"The truth, Lee, while it doesn't feel like something he'd think of—he likes to be the one causing the pain—if it is his doing, I'm more worried about Darby. He'd never get over being put down by a woman."

"How about I make the arrangements, and we go talk to him together."

"I'm good with that. You let me know, and I'll work my schedule around it."

"I'll let you know. Meanwhile, are you really going to represent that idiot Cal Muldoon for popping Larry Easterday after he and Easterday got into that fender bender?"

"What can I say, Chief? Everybody's entitled to a defense."

"Lawyers." Lee let out a sigh. "This is damn good coffee."

"More where that came from."

Lee shook his head, set down his empty glass. "I gotta get on. You know," he added as he stood, "your building in town's looking pretty good. The mayor gave me some chatter about how maybe we should encourage other property owners along Main to think color."

"Always look for the upside."

Lee's eyebrows disappeared under the brim of his cap.

"Darby." Zane grinned, shrugged. "I'm trying to latch on."

"Good luck with that. I'll be in touch."

"Love to Emily."

"Always."

Zane sat, rubbed the baseball.

He'd send Lee the names from those credible threats, the data on them, but . . . Those weren't so worrying in his opinion. He had more concern about the ones he'd helped put away who hadn't made threats. Who'd been smart enough, careful enough not to make them while they bided their time inside imagining payback.

If Lee felt he'd eliminated anyone local, it was time to take a harder look back, time to dig through some case files.

He went inside, switched tablet for laptop. He had enough data on it to get started on what would be a long process.

He hoped Darby would be another hour or so, and not just because she'd promised (threatened) to give him a garden maintenance lesson on her return. He wanted to make some progress, eliminate or list possibles before she got back.

He didn't want to cloud their weekend with . . . undercurrents, he decided.

About twenty minutes in, he heard someone coming up the road, automatically saved his work, closed the file. And as cover brought back up one of the car dealerships he'd scanned before.

But it wasn't a truck, wasn't Darby.

Instinct had him taking a fielder's grip on the ball as the beige compact stopped beside his convertible.

He didn't recognize the man who got out, not at first, but saw tall, well-built, neatly dressed in khakis and a polo shirt, close-cropped brown hair, square jaw, probably late thirties.

Then the visitor removed aviator sunglasses, started forward.

Military, Zane thought, from the posture, the stride.

"Zane Bigelow—sorry," he corrected. "Walker."

"That's right." Putting it together, Zane got to his feet. "It's Bo Draper, isn't it? Sergeant Major Draper now."

"It is. I'm sorry to come to your home uninvited, but I hope to have a word with you."

"Come on up. Want some iced coffee?"

"I . . . That's very kind of you, but I'm fine. This is quite a place. New since I've been around Lakeview."

"About eight years old. You've been gone awhile."

"Just over twenty years now. I enlisted at eighteen. I haven't been back since, but . . ."

"It's hard to lose a brother."

"Even one you can't claim to know. I guess he was eight or nine when I left."

"Have a seat, Sergeant Major."

"I'm fine," he repeated. "I won't keep you long." He glanced at the baseball Zane still held. "I watched a few of your games well back in the day. Do you still play?"

"Not really." Zane set the ball down.

"That's a shame. Mr. Walker—"

"Zane."

"Zane, I've heard what my family has to say. I've heard what the police chief has to say. I'm not able to talk to Clint's widow, as she's . . . away. I'm leaving right after the funeral, but before I do, I'd like to hear what you have to say."

"Your brother's widow is a client. I can only tell you that she's in a safe place. It was necessary for her to seek a safe place as, by her account, which is credible, your brother physically assaulted her. Not just on the night of July third, but routinely. She came to me for help. I got her help."

"She'd be Allie Abbott's younger sister? I knew Allie a little when I lived here."

"That's right."

"My family claims Clint never laid a hand on her, then I hear them say he never laid a hand on her that she didn't deserve." Bo's jaw tightened. "I'm a married man, and I have two daughters. I wouldn't take kindly to anyone who laid a violent hand on them. I'm not my brothers. I'm not my parents."

"I'm not my parents either."

Bo nodded. "I heard some about that. My family's saying you and Clint's widow were having an affair."

"I met Traci twice since I got back to Lakeview. Once when Clint brought her with him to my office hoping to file a frivolous and, frankly, vindictive suit against his neighbors."

"The McConnells?"

"That's right. He wasn't pleased when I refused to take his case. I met her again when I went to their place because I saw the signs of abuse. She wouldn't talk to me, but I left my card. I'm involved with someone, seriously involved. Traci's my client, nothing more."

"The woman you're involved with—Darby McCray—she'd be the one who was here that night?"

"That's right."

"Clint defaced her property as well as your office. And the windows upstairs—doors," he corrected, "the ones that are boarded up. He shot them out."

"Evidence would indicate he did all of that. I don't know who killed your brother, Sergeant Major, whether it was friend or foe, a deliberate act or an accidental one. I do know it happened on my land, right over there, while the woman I love woke to have bullets from Clint's rifle hitting the wall three feet above her head."

"He was the runt of the litter, my pappy used to say. And he'd give the kid a smack just for the hell of it. That's not excusing what he did—and I believe he did all you're saying. But he was raised up mean."

"You were raised in the same house."

"I got out," Bo said simply. "The marines didn't just make me, Zane, they saved me. You were raised hard, and it seems to me you made different choices than my three brothers."

"My family saved me. My sister, my aunt, the man she married, my grandparents."

"I remember your grandparents," Bo continued. "They're good people. I can't say my family's good people, but I'm going to stand with them while we bury my baby brother. And I'm going to stand here now, look you in the eye, and apologize for what my brother did."

"Not necessary."

"It is for me. Maybe if I'd stayed longer I could've helped him see a different way of being. But I saved myself, and I can't regret it. I've got one brother in prison, another who's so like the old man you can barely tell them apart. Now I've got one going in the ground before he hits thirty."

"I'm sorry. I wasn't going to say it because I didn't feel it. But I can say it now. I'm sorry, Bo."

"I thank you for that. I'd like to pay for the damage my brother did to your home, your office, Ms. McCray's property."

"Absolutely not."

"If you won't take that, I want to ask you to let me pay for any of Traci's legal expenses."

"They're *pro bono*."

Bo sighed, squeezed the bridge of his nose. "You don't owe me or my family a single damn thing, but I'm asking all the same. There has to be some restitution. I want justice for Clint, I want to believe whoever killed him will be caught, tried, and punished. But there has to be restitution for what Clint did for me to settle myself on it all."

"If you give me your contact information, and a few days, I'll give you the name of a women's shelter. You could make a donation."

Bo closed his eyes briefly, nodded. "I can promise to do that." He took out his wallet and drew a card from it. "You can contact me when it's convenient. I'm going to do my duty to my family, then I'm leaving, going back to my wife, my daughters, my life. I won't be back again."

He held out a hand, and they shook.

"I appreciate you taking the time to talk to me."

"I'm going to say the same, and thank you for your service, Sergeant Major Draper."

Bo started back to his car, paused, looked back. "You couldn't have been more'n thirteen, fourteen when I lit out."

"That'd be about right."

"You sure could play baseball."

Zane watched him head down the road, then sat, picked up the ball again.

Maybe the marines had made Bo Draper, and saved him. But to Zane's mind, they couldn't have done either if he hadn't chosen to let them.

"Not just what you're born into, who raises you," he said aloud as he rubbed the ball. "It's what you do about it."

He set the ball down, picked up the laptop again, and got back to doing what he could do to protect what mattered to him.

CHAPTER TWENTY-EIGHT

Emily pulled up in front of the bungalow with her youngest in tow just after nine a.m. Together she and Brody hauled out the fresh sheets and towels, the soaps, shampoo, lotions, and the bags of groceries the guest had ordered.

Far from a morning person, Brody grumbled and scowled as they carted the supplies. "When I take over the business, I won't be cleaning cabins."

Emily just let out a snorting laugh. "Yeah? Let me know how that works out for you, pal."

Since she heard the television through the open windows, noted the Privacy sign absent from the front door, she shifted her load, knocked.

She had a smile ready when the door opened. "Good morning, Mr. Bingley. Is this a good time for housekeeping?"

He beamed a smile back. "It's always a good time if I'm not doing it. I was expecting Janey."

"Janey's mama tripped, broke her ankle this morning, so we're covering for her."

"I'm sorry to hear that. How's it going, big guy?"

Brody barely resisted the sneer, dragged out his polite voice. "Just fine, sir." He walked the groceries straight back to the kitchen. "Do you want to check, sir, make sure your order's correct?"

"I'm sure it's fine."

"Brody, you go on and put the groceries away, make sure to pin the receipt to the board there."

The polite tone dropped away like a stone in a well. "I *know*, Mom." Like he hadn't done it a zillion times before.

"Good, then you can start loading up the trash. I'll start in the bedroom, Mr. Bingley, if I won't be in your way."

"The handy thing about writing? You can do it anywhere. I'll just take my laptop out on the porch, and get out of *your* way. I'll see if the view inspires me to get my quota done this morning."

She wasn't bad-looking for an old broad, he thought as he unplugged his laptop from the charger. Definitely had a fine ass, but the tits probably sagged seeing as she had two kids.

Plus, she was married to the local cop, so best to keep hands off that one.

Her brat didn't look happy with his assignment. Couldn't blame him. Groceries, housekeeping—women's work.

"I bet you'd rather be off with your friends than cleaning houses, huh?"

Brody shrugged. "That's how it goes with a family business." He put the quart of milk, the bottle of mango juice in the fridge, glanced at the paperback on the kitchen table.

His mood perked up some, because book.

"I know that one won the Pulitzer and all, but I liked *Cannery Row* better."

"What?"

"That one's a total bummer if you ask me. Mom likes *East of Eden* best, and it's pretty good. But I still like *Cannery Row*."

He just gave the boy a blank stare. "Good for you."

Brody gave Bingley a long look. "My cousin got me into Virgil Flowers, and he's way cool. I'm going to do Sandford's whole series this summer."

"I don't watch much TV," Bingley said as he took his laptop out to the front porch, and ended any sort of conversation.

Thinking it over, Brody put away the rest of the groceries he figured Bingley was too lazy to go buy himself at the market.

Knowing his job—and his mother—he loaded the breakfast dishes Bingley had been too lazy to put in the dishwasher. Then, following routine, he dumped the kitchen trash into the big plastic bag before he noticed Bingley hadn't separated the recyclables into the second can.

With a strongly disapproving look aimed toward the front door, Brody did that job before carting the bag to the bedroom. His mother had already stripped the bed, loaded the sheets and bathroom towels into the laundry bag.

Brody started to speak, thought about open windows, and saved his comments.

He put the fresh sheets on the bed—something he'd rather do any day than clean somebody else's bathroom.

Just gross, man.

He knew he wasn't supposed to, but he eased the night table drawer open just a little. Condoms. Then the one on the other side of the bed. Nothing.

He did his job, emptying the other trash baskets, dusting off the furniture, putting the glass and plate beside the bed into the dishwasher.

He did both bedroom floors, though it didn't look like the guy had stepped foot in the second bedroom, left the second bath for his mother to wipe down, and did the dusting, polishing in the living area.

In a rhythm, he went out to sweep the back patio, check the water in the pots while his mom dealt with the kitchen.

In under an hour, they hauled out the dirty linens, trash, recyclables. And Brody noted instead of writing anything, Bingley had Candy Crush going before he toggled quickly to his screen saver.

"All done. Enjoy your day."

"You do the same," Bingley told Emily. "It sure is a peaceful spot. Oh, I meant to say the grounds are really beautiful. You must have a bright green thumb."

"I wish I did. You can credit Darby McCray and her crew from High Country Landscaping. We left you another marketing list, it's on the board with your receipt from today. You just let us know if you need anything."

"I'll do that. If I get my quota in, I may try some kayaking this evening."

"If you do, don't forget your coupon for the rental. It's in your welcome folder. Happy writing."

Brody waited until they were in the truck, until his mother started the engine. "Writing, my butt."

"Brody Michael Keller!"

"I'm serious, Mom. He was playing Candy Crush on his laptop."

"Well, God, Brody, so he was taking a break, or distracting himself while we were cleaning."

But Brody dug in. "If he's a writer, how come he thinks Virgil Flowers is a TV series?"

"I . . . not everybody reads popular fiction, even writers."

Brody just shook his head as Emily drove to the next bungalow on their list. "No way, Mom. Just no. He's supposed to be an English teacher, right? Like in college. But when I said something about *Cannery Row* and *East of Eden*—he had *The Grapes of Wrath* on the table—he didn't know what I was talking about."

"Of course he did."

"Uh-uh." When Emily pulled up at the next bungalow, Brody swiveled in his seat, his face set, even mutinous. "He didn't. And if he's an English teacher and a writer, how come he's only got one book in the whole cabin?"

"He probably uses a reader. He's probably got a Kindle."

"I didn't see one. And he—he looked at your butt when you walked away to start the bedroom."

"Oh my God! We'd better call your dad and have him arrested."

"I didn't like how he looked at it," Brody mumbled, unamused. "I didn't like him."

"Brody, we don't have to like every guest. We just have to give them good service. And that's what we're going to do for the Campbells right now. Four people, including two kids under ten, in this one. So expect more work."

He had more to say, but since his mother didn't get it, like at *all*, maybe his dad would.

He cleaned three bungalows with his mother—the Campbells' was definitely the worst—then rode his bike into town. He went by the station house, then hesitated.

His dad would listen, he knew that. And most likely his dad would tell his mom. Then he'd get a lecture.

Maybe not his dad then—at least not yet—but it ought to be family, and somebody who understood about bad guys and liars.

Family, an adult, a *lawyer*. And one who'd put bad guys away.

He turned his bike around, rode to Zane's office.

The building looked good, he thought. He hadn't seen the stuff Clint Draper had put on it in person, but one of his friends had taken a picture, and he'd seen that.

He figured Clint Draper was one of the bad guys his dad and Silas and Zane dealt with. But now he was dead so they didn't have to.

He left his bike out front, walked right in. Mrs. Carter looked up from her computer—he bet *she* wasn't playing lame old Candy Crush.

"Well, hey, Brody."

"Hey, Mrs. Carter."

"You got legal trouble?"

He smiled because she'd expect it. "I don't think so, but maybe I could talk to Zane about some stuff."

"You're in luck. He's got a half hour before his next appointment. You go right on back."

Gretchen, who he thought was really pretty—though he wouldn't look at her butt the way that Bingley lowlife had looked at his mom's—came in from the back with a thick file.

"Hi, Brody."

"Hi. I'm going back to see Zane."

"Great. How about you tell him I made those copies like he wanted?"

"Okay."

He kept going, pausing at the door to Zane's office, where Zane sat at his desk sort of frowning at his computer screen. Wouldn't be a game up there either, Brody thought.

He rapped his knuckles on the doorjamb. "Hey, Zane?"

"Hey, Brody."

No hesitation, Brody noted when Zane swiveled away from the screen. Some adults pretended to pay attention but they were still thinking about their other stuff.

His parents even did it sometimes unless you made them see it was important.

"I want to talk to you about something."

"Sure, have a seat. Something you need?"

"No. I don't know. Not exactly. Mom's not listening. So . . . Janey's mom broke her ankle."

"I heard. Or Maureen heard so I heard."

"I'm sorry and all, but I had to help Mom clean some of the bungalows so Janey could help her mom. I don't mind so much, but when I'm running things, I figure on having more standbys for housekeeping. Anyway, we cleaned the one that guy who's supposed to be a college English teacher who's writing a book's in."

"Supposed to be?"

Yeah, Zane listened. "Yeah, supposed to. If you had *The Grapes of Wrath* sitting on the table, and I said how I liked *Cannery Row* better, what would you say?"

"I'd have to say, even though *The Grapes of Wrath* is considered his masterpiece, I agree on that. Though I'm really fond of *Tortilla Flat*."

"I haven't read that—but see? You'd, you know, say something about the books. You wouldn't just go, like, blank. And if you were really an English teacher, you oughta have a bunch of shit to say."

"I'm going to agree with you again, but it could be he didn't want to talk. He may have been surprised a teenager could have opinions on Steinbeck. Not everybody's friendly."

"But he was trying to be, right? 'How's it going, big guy?'" Brody rolled his eyes. "I hate that. I'm not big so it's, like . . . patronizing."

"Okay." The kid liked puzzles, Zane thought. And since it intrigued him that Brody thought he'd found one, Zane leaned back, swiveled side to side. "Clearly, he hit you wrong big-time. What else?"

"Okay, first, before the book thing, he looked at Mom's butt."

"I gotta play devil's advocate here, pal. I've been known to look at a female butt in my time. I expect I'll do so again."

"Not like that. It was . . ." It made him uncomfortable still, had heat rising up the back of his neck. "It wasn't nice. It was like . . . it made me think I was glad I was there, that Mom wasn't alone with him."

The initial humor on Zane's face faded away. "All right. If you got a bad feeling from him on that, we'll make sure your mom doesn't go there alone."

The embarrassed heat washed away in relief. "You believe me."

"I believe you got a bad feeling, and that's enough."

"Okay, okay, good. A couple other things. So I got this wondering when he acted like he never heard of *Cannery Row* like that? I said how my cousin—you—got me going on Virgil Flowers, how I was going to finish Sandford's whole series this summer."

"That fuckin' Flowers. Great stuff."

"Yeah, it is. And he says to that? He doesn't watch much TV— even though the stupid TV's on right then anyway."

"Huh. Well, I pity his lack of taste in fiction, but—"

"He's got no books, Zane!" Rolling with it, Brody tossed his hands up. "No books except for that one paperback. I looked when we were cleaning. Not one book. And don't say e-reader, because he doesn't have one. I looked. You can't tell Mom or Dad—not any of this—but I looked in the drawers."

"I'll consider this attorney-client privilege, but you know better, Brody."

Because he did, and maybe he'd deserve the lecture—later—he rushed on. "He wasn't writing anything either. He was playing Candy Crush on his laptop. I think he's lying about being an English teacher, and lying about writing a book. How come he'd lie about that?"

"We can't say for certain he is, but people lie for all kinds of reasons. How long's he here?"

"I don't know. I couldn't check because Mom went back to the office. He's got a real expensive bottle of Scotch in the cupboard. The kind Pop gave Dad last Christmas. I saw that when I was putting his grocery order away. And his hiking boots hardly have any wear on them. He didn't recycle, and the bin's right there! How come some-body driving a Prius doesn't recycle?

"He's lying, Zane," Brody insisted. "People who're hiding out lie. Criminals lie. Criminals hiding out especially lie, right? Maybe he's the one killed Clint Draper and tossed him in the lake."

"Whoa, let's slow down. You're making some solid, salient points here. Don't overstate your case. What's his name?"

"Bingley. I don't know his first name, damn it. If Mom leaves the office, I can get into the office computer and find stuff out."

Jesus, Zane thought, the kid was a pistol already firing.

"Hold off on that, now. There's no point in you getting into trouble over this." Considering, Zane picked up his baseball, turned it in his hand. "You came to me, and I'm going to respect that. I'm going to respect you've got reasons for feeling what you feel. So I'll do a little poking around. If everything about him checks out, no harm, no foul. If it doesn't, I'll take it to your dad."

"Promise?"

Zane swiped a finger over his heart. "It might take me a couple days, but I'll look into it. You do me a favor back, and stay away from that cabin."

"Okay."

"Promise?"

The hesitation told Zane the "okay" had been cover, but the prom-ise would stick. Brody swiped a finger over his heart in turn.

To make it official, Zane took out a legal pad. "All right, let's get down what you know. Bingley, college professor—you know where?"

"Up north, but the Prius is a rental. He's maybe like your age, I guess. Not as tall as you. Maybe around six feet and like . . . one-fifty maybe. He's got blond hair, sort of long, one of those little beard-type things, blue eyes, and he wears glasses."

The kid paid attention, Zane thought as he noted it down. He tossed out a few basic questions, dug out what he could.

"I can work with this." Satisfied, Zane pushed up. "Let's grab a cold one before my next client comes in."

He walked to Brody, held out his hand knowing the shake would seal the deal on both sides.

Once he sent the boy off, Zane sat back down at his desk, made more careful notes from their conversation.

He knew Brody was a smart kid, and not just academically. And also a naturally friendly one. Something about Bingley had set him off. And while he hardly saw some guy renting a bungalow on Reflection Lake bashing in Clint Draper's skull, he'd follow through on his promise.

So he needed a full name, where he supposedly taught, maybe the address on record.

A simple matter—if he could ask Emily, or talk to Lee. But he'd made the promise, had to keep it.

He put the mission aside for his next client, and couldn't get back to it until the end of the workday.

But he had a plan.

He strolled out as Maureen and Gretchen shut down for the day.

"I should be in by eleven tomorrow," he said as if both of them wouldn't know. "I don't expect I'll be more than an hour in court."

"Regardless, your first appointment's at one-thirty." Maureen pulled her purse out of her bottom drawer. "You should grab lunch first."

"How about if I bring lunch back and we have ourselves a picnic on the back patio?"

"I'm in. Not pizza."

"You're a hard woman, Maureen. Say, I bet I know something you don't."

She gave him a smug, sidelong look. "Prepare to lose."

"We've got a budding Hemingway penning his literary classic in one of the Walker bungalows."

Maureen flicked her fingers in the air. "As if that's news to me. College professor from up north, spending a chunk of his summer here for the quiet and inspiration. About your age, I expect. Single since he's here alone and doesn't wear a ring."

"Oh, I met him." Gretchen shut down her computer, pulled out her own purse. "Mr. Bingley—or I guess it's Professor Bingley."

"John Bingley?"

"Ah." Gretchen paused, brow furrowed as she thought. "No, it was . . . Blake, Drake, Deke? Something like that. Not John. Why?"

"Not somebody I know then," Zane said easily. "How'd you meet him?"

"Oh, it was just in passing on the street a few days ago, really. He was looking at the building—like everybody before we had it painted again. I said something, he said something. He wanted to know where he could find a good steak and wine. I told him Grandy's."

"Good choice."

He locked up behind them, considered going down to Grandy's and poking there. But decided to start with the Blake, Drake, or Deke.

He texted Darby as he walked to his car.

Salt mines are closed. Heading home.

Me, too! I'm right now in line to order pulled pork sans, cole-slaw, sweet potato fries. We will feast.

I'll have a cold beer waiting for you.

Twenty minutes.

Good deal, he thought. Damn good deal.

He drove toward home, top down, looking forward to sharing Brody's story with Darby—as Brody hadn't included her in the no-tell. Plus, he wanted her take on it.

Because what was it with a guy driving a Prius who doesn't use a clearly marked recycle bin? Or an English prof who wouldn't enjoy talking Steinbeck with a teenage boy?

A puzzle, he thought, a mystery—and one he realized he wanted to get his teeth into. Takes me back, he realized, to working with investigators, to, yeah, puzzling out how to nail down the bad guys.

He turned up his road, wound around a curve. Hit the brakes hard.

The truck sat crosswise, blocking his way. Jed Draper already stood beside it.

And Zane sincerely hoped he wasn't about to be shot down a quarter of a damn mile from his own home.

He didn't see a gun as he got out—but it didn't mean Jed didn't have one handy.

Still, he had Jed by a couple of inches in height, and while Jed had that tough Draper look about him, Zane figured he could handle himself if Jed stuck with fists.

"You're blocking the road, Jed."

"My brother's in the ground."

"I know it. I didn't put him there."

Jed stepped closer, fists bunched, wiry body at the ready. "My ma thinks you did."

"I'm sorry your mother lost her son. I don't think there's anything harder than that. I didn't kill him."

"If you did, they'd cover for you. The whole fucking town would cover for you over a Draper." He spat in disgust. "So we're gonna settle it, right here."

"What's this going to change? You punch me, I punch you? Clint's still going to be dead, I still won't have killed him."

"He wouldn't be dead you hadn't took his wife from him. Whether you threw him in the lake or not, he'd be alive if not for you."

The hell with it, Zane thought. They weren't walking away from this without spilled blood and pain. "He'd be alive if he hadn't come on my land and shot out my doors."

"Got what you deserved there, less'n you deserved, for putting your nose in our family business. Think you're better'n him? Better'n me?"

Zane redistributed his weight, because it was coming. "Yeah. I know I am."

He blocked the first swing by pivoting into it, letting it bounce off his shoulder. Then, shifting his weight again, sent a roundhouse into Jed's solar plexus. It knocked Jed back, but didn't stop him. Zane felt the pain of bare knuckles glancing off his chin, used it to fuel his own blows. The fist he connected to Jed's face slit his lip.

Jed bared bloody teeth, charged like a bull.

Mistake, Zane thought, and simply danced away while his left pumped an uppercut on Jed's jaw.

"There's no point in this," Zane began, holding off as Jed shook his head clear.

And that was his mistake, not following through. As Jed steamed at him, he remembered Dave's words to a young boy who needed to learn to fight.

Outside the ring, there's no fair in fight.

Tasting his own blood, Zane waded in.

Singing along with Gaga—Zod wiggling as they took the road toward home—Darby decided she'd had a pretty perfect day, and looked forward to capping it off with a pretty perfect evening.

Then she hit the brakes, had one moment of sheer shock as Zod yipped in protest.

She leaped out of the truck, already grabbing her phone out of her pocket as she ran around Zane's car toward where a man with a bloody face swung a fist toward Zane's.

Zane snarled out, "No cops!" and the fingersnap of distraction had that fist landing.

She all but felt it in her own body. Her fingers tightened on the phone as the dog began to howl over the nasty sound of knuckles striking flesh and bone.

She made herself breathe—in and out—resisted punching nine-one-one only because she could see, for now at least, Zane had the advantage.

He had good form, she told herself, and Jesus, he could take a punch. But if he didn't end it soon, she would.

Winded, one eye already swelling, Jed circled, feinted. "When I finish you, I'm going to give your bitch a taste."

Zane heard his little sister screaming, saw his father dragging her by the hair. With that image in his head, he moved in with a cold fury. If he took more blows, he ignored them, just focused on that image, driving Jed back, driving him back.

Now Jed's swings went wild, went loopy as he staggered. And still, he stumbled forward, flailing out until his knees buckled.

When he went down, part of Zane wanted to leap on him, to pummel and pummel until he emptied himself out. But he wasn't his father.

He'd never be his father.

So he put a foot on Jed's chest to keep the man from getting up again.

"Stay down. Stay down, for Christ's sake, and use what brains you've got. I'm better at this than you, and I'm betting you know damn well I'm better at it than Clint was. I wouldn't have needed a rock to stop him." He crouched down, looked into those blackened, swollen eyes. "And if I was the type to use one, you'd be as dead as your brother. You know it wasn't me."

"Then who?"

"I don't know, but I'm not going to stop till I do. Whoever it was killed on my land, and I see that as a threat to the woman I love, the woman I want to spend my life with, build a family with. I won't stop until I know."

Straightening, he looked down at Jed with a mixture of revulsion and pity. "I didn't do this, I didn't cause this. You come at me again, it'll go worse for you than me. You so much as look at my woman, at any of my family, it'll go worse for you. You do anything to trouble Traci or her family, it'll go worse for you. You hearing me?"

"My brother's dead."

"That's a fact. You getting your ass kicked and having it end up behind bars—and I'll make sure both happen—won't change that. Now get up, get off my land. Don't come back here."

Saying nothing, Darby got back in her truck, pulled it to the side, and got out again to wait until Jed managed to get to his feet.

He didn't so much as glance toward her as he drove past.

Zane swiped the back of his hand over the blood on his face, tried a smile. "So. How was your day?"

CHAPTER TWENTY-NINE

Once inside, Darby ordered Zane to sit at the kitchen counter, got him an ice pack and a beer.

"Best girl ever," Zane decided, winced a little at the first sip of beer.

"I'll get what we need to clean you up. God, Walker, you're a mess."

"Hey, did you see the other guy?"

"I did. We'll talk. Sit." She got a beer for herself, and went to get the supplies.

Zane glanced down at the dog currently looking up at him with eyes all but dripping love and concern. "Not that bad, right?"

But when he shifted the ice pack to his left eye, he hissed.

"You forget how much it hurts. Shit, shit. I've got court in the morning. Oh, it's nothing, Your Honor. Just got in a fistfight with the brother of the guy killed on my property. No big deal."

He thought: Fuck, and took another sip of beer.

"I have court in the morning," he told Darby when she came back in.

She set down the first aid supplies, walked to the sink to run cold water over a cloth. "Truth or lie?" she wondered.

"I'm a lawyer, I can do both at the same time. It's not that bad, right?"

"You're going to have a black eye—left side. He didn't land any on the right. I can butterfly the cut over the bad eye. Your jaw's bruised and scraped up, same side—you need to work on the left guard. Cheekbone, left, that's cut up some. I can butterfly that, too, but you might need some X-rays."

"Nothing's broken. I know what it feels like."

Because she did, too, she nodded. "Any blurred vision, nausea?"

"No."

Face impassive, she turned back. "Strip off the shirt. Let's see the rest of you."

He started to, hissed again. "O . . . kay. He got some past me."

"More than some. You didn't mean it, at first."

He let her help peel him out of the shirt. "His brother's dead."

"And you holding back doesn't change that. He did a little number on your ribs."

Zane took her hand before she could test for breaks. "You pissed at me?"

"No, why would I be?"

He skimmed a finger down her cheek. "You look pissed."

"I *am* pissed, but not at you. I'm pissed you had to come home to that, that I did, that you had to fight off some idiot I've never even met. Hold the ice on the ribs while I feed the dog."

She poured food for Zod to pounce on, opened the kitchen doors so he could go out as he pleased. "You didn't want me to call Lee because you didn't want him—what was his name? Jed? You didn't want him to pay for it. You didn't end it sooner, and you could have, because you wanted to let him get a few in. You didn't stop holding back until he made that stupid crack about me."

"You're not wrong."

She turned to him, her face a study of fury and sorrow. "It wasn't our fault, Zane."

"Darlin', I know that. I don't even think he much liked Clint, but blood's blood. He didn't come here with a gun. I figure he wanted to beat a confession out of me, and instead, I have to figure he left knowing I didn't kill his brother."

"If it comes to anything like that again, don't you hold back."

"Probably won't." Gently, he wiggled his jaw. "Especially if I have court in the morning."

It annoyed the hell out of her that she admired how he handled it. She wrung out the wet cloth in a bowl.

"Let me deal with that face of yours."

She had a good touch, he thought, gentle but not hesitant. And she didn't get all pale and weird when she squeezed blood out of the cloth.

He watched her eyes as she cleaned him up, those deep, dark blue eyes. She smelled of the earth and growing things.

"I guess I forgot to use my filter," he began, "when I said that stuff about the rest of my life, and building a family and all."

"Mmm. Gonna sting," she warned when she picked up the antiseptic.

He let out a stream of curses as she applied it to various cuts and scrapes. "Why is the cure nearly as painful as the cause?"

"Maybe to remind us to stay out of fights. Is that a legal term?" Carefully she fixed the butterfly bandage to close the cut over his left eye. "The filter?"

"I planned—as far as I planned—to give you more time before bringing up lifetime commitments, marriage, kids. Blame it on the heat of the moment."

"Okay." When she picked up another bandage, he took her hand again.

"Do you want kids down the road, Darby? Marriage, building a life with me?"

She just rested her brow against his. "Marriage still catches in my throat, but I want kids, and I feel like we're starting to build a life."

"Marriage is just a contract."

She eased back, met his eyes. "No, it's not."

"No, it's not. I can put the filter back on till you're ready."

"We're good, right, even with all this?"

"We're more than good from where I'm sitting."

She bent forward, touched her lips to the cuts and bruises on his face.

"I wondered if you'd get around to that."

"I had to work through being mad first. Not at you. I mean that. Did you box in college?"

"Some. The elbow thing's a problem."

She went to dump the bloody water. "I might be able to show you some moves to help you compensate for that."

"Aren't you handy?"

"In all things. Zane, you have to tell Lee. I'm not saying to press charges, or have him confront this guy, but he needs to know."

"I know it." And was already working out just how to approach it. "I don't have to like it, but I know it."

"Anybody who sees your face is going to know you were in a fight anyway." She got him three ibuprofen, a glass of water. "So tell him, get it over with. Then we'll have some pulled pork barbecue and another beer."

"You know you don't give me a choice but to be crazy in love with you."

"I'm a hell of a catch. You call him, talk it through. I'll get dinner warmed back up."

Calling Lee—and he should've known—meant Lee insisted on coming over to see Zane for himself. Which meant Emily and the kids came, too.

Then because Emily insisted on telling Britt, that brought the rest of them. At least Silas and Britt picked up a bunch more pork and sides.

So a violent confrontation morphed into an impromptu family gathering. Darby watched Audra kiss Zane's "hurts" much as she had, and cuddle against him to comfort.

She supposed she'd missed out on big, impromptu family gatherings, being the only child of a single parent. She decided being a part of them now landed on the plus side of living with Zane.

Even when Britt used the excuse of a gardening question to lure her away from the others and around to the front of the house.

"I just want to ask how you're feeling, if you're all right."

"Zane's the one who got punched."

"I know your history, and I know you've been through three violent experiences in the last few months. If you need to talk—as friends, just friends—I'm here."

"Then I'll be honest with you. Part of me hit panic, hit shaky when I drove up on Zane and the latest Draper problem. I had to push that back because it doesn't help. But the rest of me? The rest of me was impressed, because Zane, despite how he looks right now, had it under control."

She looked down at the lake, going soft in the quieting light. "I know how to take care of myself, and that's important to me. Now I know Zane can take care of himself, and me if he needs to."

"Yes," Britt agreed. "We grew up in a terrible place, but I always knew he'd look out for me. So I know exactly what you mean. But if the shaky comes back, you call me."

"I'm really hoping this is the end of this cycle of crazy." She tapped the tattoo on the back of her neck. "It's really time for the calm and easy to balance it out."

While Darby talked to Britt around front, Zane signaled Brody, slipped off with him and the dog for cover into the woods.

"Real quick, I want your go-ahead to share what you told me with Darby."

"Oh, hey, I don't—"

"Hear me out. Say you're right, and we've got a bad guy. She lives here, too. And more, I really want her take on it. If I tell her in confidence, she'll keep that confidence."

"She has to swear."

"Absolutely."

"Okay. But nobody else."

"Nobody else. I've got a line on his full name—without telling anybody else."

"You do?"

The kid's instant admiration gave Zane a lift. "Yeah, and I'm going to check it out after everybody goes home. I can't promise anything, Brody, but I've got a place to start. Now think about this. If I find anything illegal, or really off, we need to tell your dad."

At that, Brody gave a decisive nod. "If you find proof, we talk to Dad."

"Good enough." They shared a fist bump.

"Can you show me where Clint Draper got killed?"

"No."

"Aw, man." Brody kicked the dirt. "How about you show me how you knocked his brother on his butt, and made him stay down."

Zane faked a punch, then caught Brody in a headlock. "We're going back."

He nearly put off filling in Darby, as his family didn't leave until after nine. But since he wanted to start his search, he thought it best to get that take of hers.

He ran a hand down her short cap of hair as they sat another moment in the glow of the garden lights.

"I have a client who's given me permission to share some information with you on the condition of treating said information as privileged and confidential."

"Why would one of your clients . . ." She trailed off as he gave her that "just go with me" look. "Fine. I can keep my mouth shut."

"The client requires you swear to same."

"Your client—whoever it may be—has my solemn word to keep my mouth shut on this matter. What's up?"

"I'll tell you, but let's walk around some. I'm going to stiffen up if I sit too long."

"You're going to stiffen up overnight, but good idea."

The moon, little more than a thumbnail, curved its thin crescent in clear, star-drenched skies. The dog trotted along with them, pausing occasionally to leap at the wink of fireflies.

The night-blooming jasmine Darby had spotlighted drenched the air with scent.

And with all that calm, that lazy summer easy, Zane brought the strange.

She interrupted a few times, for clarification, to question.

When he'd finished, they'd circled to the front of the house and took seats on the veranda, watched that sliver of moon swim on the lake.

"I'd say that's a boy with good instincts," Darby concluded. "Because there's a lot there that doesn't add up. A single book? No way given what he claims to do for a living, what he says he's come here to do. But maybe Brody just missed the e-reader."

"Possible," Zane agreed.

"Or he could read on his laptop, but it's hard to believe a college English professor has one lonely paperback for an extended stay."

"Agreed."

"It's also possible he's just a jerk about recycling and got a good deal on a rental Prius. You can always work things around to another angle, right?"

"You not only can," Zane said, "but some of us make our living doing just that."

"Still . . . You're an English professor, so you've spent a good chunk of your life studying and teaching literature. You couldn't possibly blank on John Steinbeck. Popular fiction? Maybe he's a book snob, but why not just ask, Who's Virgil Flowers?

"And when you put it all together," Darby concluded, "it feels off. What's your next move?"

"It turns out Gretchen ran into him on the street. In my clever, lawyerly way, I got a name. Or names. She thinks Blake, Drake, or Deke Bingley. So since I don't know where up north, or what university or college he claims to be a part of, I start with that."

"That'll take the rest of your life. Hold on."

She got out her phone, held up a finger before he could object. "Hey, Emily, sorry. I forgot with Zane going ten rounds I was going to send a couple of the crew to do a little maintenance on the bungalows. I thought we'd start with five, then spread out from there. Is anyone in five?"

Darby made uh-huh noises. "We'll make sure we start midmorning then. Unless he's checking out soon. No? Oh really. Another Yankee? Where's he from?"

She sent Zane a smug smile. "New York City. Well, we'll make sure we don't disturb him. Yeah, I'll make sure he ices down again before we go to bed. I can do that, sure. See you tomorrow then."

She clicked off. "She called him Mr. Bingley, and it would've seemed weird if I'd asked for a first name. But she said he was work-ing on a novel, and came from New York City."

"That's helpful. You're good at that."

"I'm going to have to send crew over there—and I'm going to have to go by reception and show her again what are actual weeds in the rock garden—but it's part of the service."

She got to her feet, held out a hand. "Come on, let's get you an-other round of ice and you can get started. And I can get to my really delayed shower before I take care of some paperwork."

He needed a shower, too, but unfortunately not a fun one.

By the time he'd finished, and Darby used another spare bedroom to deal with her paperwork, he was more than ready for the ice, more ibuprofen. And the option to work in bed on his laptop.

She glanced in an hour later—no doubt, he thought, checking on him.

"How's it going?"

"Slow." He raked a hand through his hair. "There are well over a hundred colleges and universities in New York."

"You had to figure."

"Even eliminating specialties—dance, medicine, fashion, law, like that—there's a lot. And also considering he may have inflated the 'professor,' it's best to check all the staff. So far, I haven't come up with Blake, Drake, or Deke Bingley listed. But I've got plenty more to check."

Because he could feel himself stiffening, he got up—and boy he felt that—tried to walk and stretch it out. "It'd go a hell of a lot faster if I had an investigator on this, even a law clerk."

"I don't qualify for either of those, but I can take some. I'm caught up. And I'm invested. I kind of want to prove the kid right. Which is weird."

"It is weird. Weirder because so do I. But you'll be getting up in . . . six and a half hours."

"I'm getting up then anyway. Half an hour. Same for you, Walker." She smoothed a hand over the hair he'd disordered. "You're more worn-out than you think."

"I think I'm pretty worn-out," he admitted. "Half an hour."

At the end of thirty, it was Darby who called it because he really did look beat. And Zane who volunteered to let the dog out one last time because he needed to move.

When he got back, and Zod took his latest sock to bed, she was already out for the count.

Zane got in beside her, breathed out against the aches and twinges. Then took her hand, pressed it to his cheek.

"Don't make me wait too long to take that filter off, darlin'."

While Zane fell into a fitful sleep, the man who went by Bingley sipped his single malt, paced the cabin.

He didn't like the way that brat had looked at him. It had nagged at him all day, enough that he'd driven past where he knew the little fucker lived, hoping to catch him outside.

Lure him over to the car, take care of him.

But he hadn't seen him—which, he admitted now, had been for the best.

Another body in the lake? Wouldn't be good. Even adding on a missing kid? Too much attention.

He'd already stayed longer than he should have, he saw that now. He'd let the pleasure of building up to that ultimate goal keep him in this hick town. Not even in the hick town, for God's sake.

He was living in the freaking woods.

Done with it, he thought. Checkout time.

Once he'd done what he'd come to do, he'd get in that ridiculous tree-hugger car and be hundreds of miles away before anybody knew the difference.

Dump the car in long-term parking at the airport, where he'd parked his *real* car. Wait until dark, slip on home, cut the hair, shave the beard.

Over and done.

But now, he had work to do. He wanted to wipe down every inch of the bungalow, just in case.

After that, he'd wear gloves.

Darby woke at six sharp, slid out of bed to, as per habit, dress in the bathroom so Zane could sleep.

"Don't worry about it," he mumbled. "I'm awake."

"Hurting?"

"It's always worse the next day." He felt her hand brush over his hair as he eased up—ouch—to turn on the light.

"Ice and Advil. I'll get it."

"It's all right. I need to move anyway."

"Go slow. I'll get you started with it."

She trotted out—he no longer felt surprise at her ease of walking around the house naked—and he lowered his feet to the floor.

"Had worse. Lots worse." Stood, breathed out. "But I was younger."

He sat again.

As he did, he considered asking for a continuance, weighed the pros and cons of going into court with a black eye. A distraction . . . maybe some sympathy from the judge.

Maybe, maybe not.

"Don't be a wuss. You can handle the drive into Asheville, an hour in court," he told himself.

Before he stood again, Darby came back with the ice and Advil, studied him. "Looks worse the second day, too."

"Thanks for that."

"You're going to see for yourself soon anyway." She laid the ice bag on the left side of his face, then offered the pills and water.

"I got a really hot nurse out of it."

"The hottest. Look, I can call Roy, have him get the crew started, give you some more TLC."

"Just need to get moving."

"Did you sleep?"

"Off and on. During one of the offs I did another chunk from the New York list, so at least something productive. Still no Bingley."

"Brody's going to be right. I feel it in my bones."

"Maybe. Meanwhile during my on and off, I had another thought. He drives a car, so he's got to have a driver's license. I've got a pal or two on the force in Raleigh. Since I can't ask Lee, I can ask one of them to run him."

"Is that legal?"

"Eh . . ." He wiggled a hand in the air. "First, I'll just pay the fee, look him up—all three names—on a criminal search, which is absolutely legal."

"I'm going to get dressed, help you downstairs, make us some coffee. What does he look like?" she asked as she pulled out cargo shorts.

"From Brody's description, sort of blondish hair, long, a little beard, glasses. Around my age—he thinks—not as tall, thinner."

She paused as she pulled on a sports bra. "You know, I saw somebody who looked sort of like that out on the lake on a Sunfish the other day. And for some reason, he gave me the creeps."

Zane's eyes narrowed. "Did he do anything?"

"No, no." She dragged on a T-shirt. "I didn't get a good look anyway. He was just sailing by while we were finishing up at the Marshes'. He sort of waved, that's all. But I got creeped. Maybe I should take the morning off, help you finish with this."

"I've got it. But I could use that coffee. I'm okay here, darlin'. I don't have to be in court until nine, so I'm just going to pull on some pants and I'll be down."

"All right. Let's go, Zod." The dog leaped, willing and able. She paused at the door. "This is a nice room, but I'm going to be glad when we're back in ours."

"Me, too. Couple days more."

She'd said "*ours*," he thought as he grabbed some sweatpants.

Maybe he wouldn't need that filter much longer.

By the time he got downstairs where she had coffee and Cheerios with fresh strawberries, he'd worked out the worst of the stiffness.

"It looks worse than it feels," he told her.

"Well, I'm glad to hear it. Stop and pick up some arnica gel somewhere. I didn't think of it before because I'm out. It can help with the bruising."

He put it on a mental list, went for the coffee. "Where are you working today?"

"Considering this Bingley may actually be a bad guy, I'm going to have Roy and Ralph go over there later this morning, do that maintenance. I'll go by to see Emily at some point, but I've got to start on the north side of the lake. Do you know George Parkison?"

"Sure. He owns some rentals over there, lives in Asheville, but keeps a second home here."

"That's the one," she said as they ate. "Apparently the company he had doing his property maintenance gets a D-minus, so he's hired us. We're mowing, mulching, weeding, pruning, and so on. He has four rentals, so that's a nice new client."

She smiled over a bite of cereal. "Especially if we charm him into adding in his own place."

"Bet you do."

"With the shape the rentals are in, and with sending Roy and Ralph off for a while due to subterfuge, it's going to take us two solid days. Then I'm hoping Cherylee Fogel, who's a book club pal of Patsy Marsh, bites on the proposal I gave her yesterday. Apparently, she recently divorced husband number two, is now sitting pretty on a fat settlement from same, and wants to—as she put it—'reimagine her lakeside cottage, inside and out, top to bottom.'"

"I believe you could give Maureen a run for her money on knowing who's who and what's what in Lakeview."

"People tell me things. Such as Cherylee's second ex-husband is a cosmetic surgeon—and I can attest, as Cherylee and I were up close and personal, he does excellent work. They lived in Greensboro during their four-year marriage, had the cottage, which is actually a lovely home with a soaring atrium and a summer kitchen overlooking the lake, as a weekend/vacation home. She took up permanent residence almost a year ago, during the separation, got the house and a hefty settlement due to the fact the ex had not one but two lovers on the side.

"One lover found out about the other," Darby explained as she ate. "They bonded, and together they went to Cherylee. Due to female solidarity, the philandering doctor is now out the lakeside home and all it contains, two BMWs, several pieces of art and antiques, a monetary settlement to the tune of three-point-three million. Not including a separate percentage of stocks and bonds."

Zane listened, fascinated. "Introduce me, because if she gets married and divorced again, I'd like to represent her."

Darby grinned. "She says she's done with marrying, and intends to stick with casual and adventurous sex, at least until she's ninety."

"You're not making a bit of that up, are you?"

"No need. She's fifty-eight, looks maybe forty—like I said, excellent work. She never had kids, but dotes on a selection of nieces and nephews, has formed a good circle of friends in Lakeview. And after seeing what I did at the Marsh place, looked up my website, saw your water feature."

Darby polished off her cereal. "She wants one of her own—and canna lilies. She remembers her grandmother's fondly. And she wants a lot of other things. She told me I was adorable, which is sweet, but even more that she feels strongly about supporting female-owned businesses. If she bites, and I think she will, High Country Landscaping's going to be rolling right into the fall."

She took her bowl and, since he'd finished as well, his to the sink. "And one more. She's thinking about starting a small charitable foundation—that would be funded with her half of the worth of their private plane, not included in that monetary settlement number. I said she might want a local lawyer to help her work that out, mentioned you—along with the disclaimer we lived together. So, you may get a call."

Delighted, impressed, Zane just stared at her. "I'm seriously crazy about you, in every possible way."

"Who wouldn't be?" She came to him, linked her arms around his neck. "I have to ask you for something that feels a little strange to me."

"Go ahead."

"I need you to text me when you get to the courthouse. Then again when you get back to your office."

He laid his hands on her hips. "You taking care of me, darlin'?"

"Apparently. It's a little out of my usual range of motion, but I need you to text me."

"Then I will."

He nudged her into a kiss. Before she drew back, she touched her lips to his black eye, the cut above it, the bruised jaw. "I gotta go. Come on, Zod."

Breaking free, she grabbed her water bottle, her phone, her cap. "Don't forget the arnica. Pick up two," she added, as she strode away with the dog racing ahead of her. "I could use some in my kit."

He wouldn't forget, he thought. And believed it was time to bring her flowers again.

She opened the truck door for the dog, lowered his window partway as he wiggled his butt into the seat.

"New job site today, Zod, but same rules apply. No digging, no pooping until you're taken to a suitable location. No cat and/or other dog chasing," she continued as she started down the road. "No crotch or butt sniffing."

He sent her his dreamy-in-love look. "This one's pretty much straight cleanup," she told him. "But it could lead to more. If we do a good job, we might get the client to go for some perking up next spring. Gotta think ahead," she reminded him, and made the turn at the end of the road, then slowed when she saw the car on the shoulder, the hood up.

She pulled up behind it. "Just be a minute," she told Zod, and stepped out.

"Having some trouble?" she called.

She heard, likely muffled by the hood, what sounded like "Battery dead" in a heavy Spanish accent.

"I can give you a jump," she began as she walked toward the front of the car, "or—"

She had an instant to see shoes, jeans, the back half of the figure hunched under the hood.

The fist swung up so fast, so unexpectedly, she never saw it coming.

CHAPTER THIRTY

Because he had to move fast, he caught her before she hit the ground. He had the zip ties ready, secured her wrists—just in case—once he'd shoved her into the backseat. Tossed a blanket over her, another just-in-case, though he didn't have far to go.

In a little over a minute since she pulled up behind his car, he sat behind the wheel again, pulled out. He nearly laughed himself sick as he drove with the radio blaring.

And with it blaring, he didn't hear the dog, abandoned in the truck, begin to howl.

He had everything ready at the cabin, and forced himself to stifle his humor until he'd parked and taken a cautious look around. Barely sunrise, he thought, pleased. Even the lake was empty.

He hauled her out, carried her inside, dumped her on the floor while he made certain the Privacy sign was out, the door locked, all the shades pulled.

"Just you and me, baby doll. Just you and me."

When she moaned a little, stirred a little, he hit her again.

"Not quite ready."

He cut the zip ties, dragged her into the chair he'd placed in the center of the room. A good sturdy one, with some weight to it. He zip-tied her wrists to the arms, her feet to the legs.

"You won't be trying any of that Bruce Lee shit today, bitch. Oh yeah, I read all about that. Even found an interview online. I like to jerk off while I watch it."

He searched her pockets, put her phone in one of his own, her multi-tool in another. And gave her breasts a couple of hard pinches just for fun.

He checked the time. Right on schedule! Though he figured he could take a solid two hours with her, he'd promised himself he'd keep it to one.

He'd wiped the place, top to bottom, and had packed his things. Time to get started.

He yanked her head back, tried slapping her awake. But her head just lolled. Must've hit her a little too hard the second time, he decided. With a shrug, he got a cold bottle of Gatorade out of the cooler he'd stocked for the road.

He sat, laid the Glock in his lap, drank, and watched her.

She came to slowly, her face alive with pain. Bad dream, bad dream, she thought, dazed. Terrible headache.

"Wake up, sleepyhead!"

Her blood froze; her stomach dropped, then clutched like a fist.

When her eyes flashed open, the pain was nothing against the fear.

"Miss me, baby doll?"

Only one person had ever called her that. She knew him. The beard, the hair—long and a duller color—didn't change his eyes. She knew him.

When he rose, holding a gun so casually, fear sweat sprang to her skin, soaked it.

She tried to spring to her feet, to defend herself, to fight, found herself pinned.

"Scream," he warned, "and I'll shoot you, not to death, but it'll hurt. Then I'll gag you. I'm looking for a little conversation, but we can go with your bleeding on the floor and a monologue. Your choice."

"What do you want, Trent?"

"Didn't I just say?" He slapped her—not too hard, just enough so she'd know who the hell was in *charge*. "What did I *say*? Repeat after me. Trent wants a little conversation."

She had to swallow the bile that wanted to rise into her throat.

"Trent wants a little conversation. You don't need the gun, Trent. I'm tied to the chair. I can't go anywhere."

"Are you telling me what to do?"

"No. I'm asking if you'd put the gun down while we talk."

Her mind emptied but for terror when he stuck the barrel under her chin. "Denied! How about I just pull the trigger? How about that?"

"I can't stop you, but then I wouldn't hear what you came all this way to say to me."

"You're shaking, Darb. You scared?"

"Yes. Yes, I'm scared."

"Good. You should be." But he removed the gun, stepped back. "Scared little baby doll, aren't you? You'll give me whatever I want, won't you?"

When he pinched her breast, she couldn't stop the flinch, the shudder, but she made herself say, "Yes."

She'd thought she'd hated him to her capacity to hate. But she found more.

"Do you think I want sex from you? I could take it if I wanted, but you're not getting off, oh no. No goodies for you, bitch. You want to know what I want? I'll tell you what the fuck I want."

The rage in his voice had her bracing for another blow, but he spun away, spun back, gesturing wildly with the gun. "I want my goddamn life back, the life you stole. I want every minute of the time I spent in prison back. I want my business back instead of having my own fucking family shove me behind closed doors, paying me to keep out of the damn way, and not *embarrass* them. I want my fucking partners dead, my so-called-friends dead for cutting me out, taking what was mine. I want to stop pretending I'm sorry for smacking around my own wife when she deserved it.

"How about that, Darb? Can you give me what I want?"

His face, red with fury, shoved close to hers. Submission, she thought, he wanted her submission, her humiliation.

Maybe if she gave it to him she'd live.

She let the tears come, let them flow. "I'm so sorry, Trent. I'm so sorry."

"Are you, Darby? Are you? Were you sorry when you sat in court, when you testified against me? You didn't look sorry, you lying cunt, when they found me guilty and you and that bitch of a mother of yours hugged like it was your goddamn birthday."

Give him what he wants. "I was afraid, I was afraid and I made a mistake."

"A *mistake*? Is that what you call it? The first week I was in prison, because of your mistake, I got jumped. Bastards beat me up just because they could. Mistake?"

Oh, the irony, she thought, but kept her head lowered, her eyes down. "You were so strong. I was afraid."

"You belonged at home, at the home I gave you, under the roof I put over your head, not out grubbing in the dirt like some damn dog."

The dog, the dog, the dog. Someone would find the dog, her truck. Someone—

"Are you listening to me?" He yanked her head back.

"I'm ashamed, so ashamed. I don't know how you can ever forgive me. If you could let me try to make it up to you—"

"Do you think I want you?" With a wild laugh, he gave her hair a vicious yank, then let go. "Do you think I came all the way down here, holed up in this hick backwater, because I want you back? You're going to pay, Darby, pay for all the things I want and can't have back."

He jabbed the gun into her stomach. "How's this for a start? How's your mommy doing, Darb? How's she doing, mommy's little baby girl? You know how easy that was?"

She heard her own ringtone—incoming text? Distracted, Trent drew the gun away, pulled her phone from his pocket. "From Roy. Are you fucking him, too?"

Trent dropped her phone on the floor, stomped on it.

"Sorry, Roy, Darby can't come to the phone right now."

The shaking came back so her knuckles rapped, rapped, rapped against the arm of the chair. "What are you talking about? About my mother?"

"What? Oh right."

He strolled back for his Gatorade, took a good gulp. "You went running home to her, didn't you? Went running home to her while your lawfully wedded husband rotted in prison. Even got a fresh new restraining order against me when I got out, and stayed all safe and warm with Mommy."

"You . . ." Nothing, even after all he'd done, had prepared her. Nothing ever could. "You killed my mother."

"*You* killed her! You signed her death warrant when you put me in prison. I just stole a car—you learn some useful things inside. That's what they call it, you know. *In*side. Stole a car, put my bike in it, poured some beer on the floor, blew some weed inside. Just had to wait for her to come jogging along, and bam!"

He did a kind of dance across the floor. "Man, she flew! Just keep driving, dump the car, ride the bike to where I stashed mine. Boom, and boom. And boo-hoo-hoo, Mommy's dead."

Grief, rage, shock slammed into her, so she tried to rock up in the chair despite the restraints. "She did nothing to you!"

"She took you in when you belonged to me! She looked at me, over your shoulder in that courtroom, she looked at me when they took me away, with satisfaction. She shouldn't have done that. I'm going to kill you when I'm finished, and sometime, maybe in a year, maybe two, I'm coming back to kill that asshole you're fucking. I'll do a better job of it than that drunk rube who thought shooting at a house mattered a damn."

Not just a batterer, she realized through the screams inside her head. Not just a vicious, violent, selfish man. A murderer.

The mask he'd worn, even in court, had fallen away. She saw not only the killer under it, but one who found pleasure in the killing.

And she would die here, by his hand.

Though he had plenty of time before court, Zane got dressed, save for the tie, dropped a baseball in his suit coat pocket. Maureen was right about it spoiling the line, but he liked being able to turn it in his hand in there when he listened to his opponent examine a witness.

He folded the tie into his other pocket, then pulled out his phone when it rang.

"Walker. Hey, Roy."

"Hey there, Zane. Is Darby around?"

"She left nearly an hour ago." Something crawled up his spine. "Are you at the rentals?"

"Yeah. Might be she made another stop, but she's not answering her phone. Tried texting and calling. But lotsa spots around here service drops out."

"Yeah. Look, I'm heading out . . ." He'd call his contact in Raleigh when he got to Asheville. "I'll swing by Emily's. She might have gone by there first, just got caught up. I'll let you know."

"Appreciate that. You know, I think we'll call Best Blooms, just in case she decided she needed something from there."

"Good idea."

But he heard the anxiety in Roy's voice that echoed the voice in his own head. Darby wouldn't get caught up or make another stop that would make her late for work—not without letting the crew know.

He considered calling Lee as he hurried downstairs. Just go by, he told himself. It's probably nothing. Better to go by.

He tried her phone as he left the house, got voice mail.

"Call me," he snapped, and jumped into his car.

When instinct says something's wrong, he thought, listen to it. He started to hit his hands-free to contact Lee after all, made the turn.

Saw Darby's truck.

He tried to tell himself she'd just had a breakdown, but he knew, already knew, even before he heard the dog howling. Before he saw the cap, the one she'd put on as she left, on the ground.

The dog leaped into his arms when Zane wrenched open the door. Fighting for calm, he called Lee.

"Somebody's got Darby. Her truck's on the side of the road fifty feet from our turnoff. The dog was in the truck. Her cap's on the ground. Somebody's got her."

"I'm on my way."

He thought of Jed Draper, and following his rage, got back in his car, put the dog on the floor of the passenger seat. "Stay down there."

He peeled out, floored it. What had made him think Draper would take losing a fight without retribution?

Because he'd seen it, Zane realized. Because he'd seen it in the man's eyes when he'd gotten up off the ground. But if he'd been wrong . . .

He took a turn too fast, fishtailed, kept going.

I saw somebody who looked sort of like that out on the lake, Darby had said. *He gave me the creeps.*

No books in the house, playing computer games, no Bingley at any of the hundred-plus colleges he'd checked so far.

Didn't make any sense, no damn sense, but . . .

He aimed the car toward Walker Lakeside Bungalows.

"She wouldn't have pulled over for Jed Draper. That makes less sense. Stay," he ordered the dog when he pulled up just out of sight of Bungalow Five. To keep the dog where he was, on the floor of the convertible, Zane tossed Zod his tie.

Then moved quick and quiet to the edge of the drive.

He saw the shades down. Who pulled all the shades with that view? Bedroom maybe, for sleeping, but the rest of the house?

He kept moving, kept to the soft ground, searching for a chink in a shade where he could see inside.

As he circled around, he heard a man's voice, raised in fury. "You look at me, bitch. You look at me when I talk to you. I'll shoot you in both knees, then in your gut if you don't give me some respect!"

Zane took out his phone, texted Lee:

Bungalow Five. He has a gun.

Then turned off his phone.

With no intention of waiting for Lee, he circled back to the front of the house. Get him outside—set off the car alarm—get him outside, rush him. Get him outside, away from Darby.

And before he reached the front, Zod began to howl.

"Good enough," Zane murmured. He kept moving, felt the weight in his pocket, and curled his hand around the baseball.

"What the hell is that?" Trent demanded.

He moved to the front window, eased back the shade to peer out. Behind him Darby flexed, rocked.

Zod, having jumped out of the car and now tangled with Zane's tie, lifted his head and began to howl again.

"Stupid fucking dog. I got a spare bullet for a fucking ugly dog."

He cracked open the door, then stepped out on the porch, grinned as he took aim.

Zane stepped out from beside the pawpaw Darby had planted, winged the ball just like the boy who'd dreamed of playing short at Camden Yards.

It hit Trent's face with a nasty thud, and as he stumbled, the gun spurted out of his hand. From behind, Darby rammed the chair into him and Zane rushed forward to finish him off. Trent was out cold.

She fell back, nearly tipping over, chair and all, as Zane rushed to her.

"T-t-triple play," she said through chattering teeth. "Zod to Walker to McCray."

Then she began to weep as if her heart, and every part of her, was broken.

"It's all right now. He can't hurt you now." He slid the gun over with his foot, kept his foot on it as he stroked her face. "I need to get something to cut you loose, okay? I'm going to get you loose, take you away from here."

"It's Trent. He killed my mother. He told me. He killed my mother."

He had no words, could only press his lips to her face. "You hold on. Just hold on. Let me get something to cut these off you."

"He took my multi-tool. It's in his pocket. Is he dead?"

"Here now, here's Zod." Zane lifted the dog, set him, trailing tie and all, in Darby's lap. "You just hold on another minute."

Not dead. Zane found a pulse, found the multi-tool.

Fresh rage beat inside him when he saw how deep those ties had cut into her flesh.

"I'm going to get you home, okay? Lee's coming, then I'm going to take you home. I'm going to take care of you, of everything."

"He killed my mother because she loved me, because she was there for me when I needed her. He killed Clint Draper, he told me. Maybe because he enjoyed it, maybe because he wanted to cause you more trouble. Because I was with you."

"He's never going to hurt you again. He's never getting out again. I need to tell Lee what's happened, and have him call for an ambulance. We want him to live, Darby, believe me, we do," he said when he took out his phone, turned it back on. "For a long time, in a cell. Lee, he's down. I've got Darby. We need an ambulance. Yes, I've got her."

He slid the phone back in his pocket. "He was coming in quiet, but they're only seconds away. You don't have to talk to him now. I'll take you home."

Those gorgeous eyes of hers were huge, a little glazed, but she kept them on his. "You hit him with a baseball. You hit him in the face with a baseball. I want the ball."

"Sure, we'll get that in a bit. It's gonna have to go with Lee for now. Look, there he is now, and pretty much the whole Lakeview police force."

Lee ran toward them, gave Trent a long look. "Ambulance is coming. I'll have another sent along."

"I don't need one." Darby cuddled the ecstatic dog. "That's Trent Willoughby, my ex-husband. I stopped because I saw the car, looking like it was broken down, at the shoulder of the road. I don't know a damn Prius from a damn Toyota," she said to Zane.

"Darlin', a Prius is a Toyota."

"See? He knocked me out, and I came to tied to the chair. He came to kill me, but he had a lot to say first. He told me he killed my mother, and how he did it. He told me he killed Clint Draper. I'd rather say all the rest later. I'm a little shaky."

"That's fine. How about Zane takes you on to our place? It's close, and Emily's there. I'll be along directly."

She started to get up, swayed. Zane plucked both her and the dog into his arms.

"Just a little shaky."

"I've got you," Zane said, then looked at Lee. "I've got her."

"I see that. You take her to Emily." He looked down at Trent as Zane carried Darby away. "I've got this."

It took hours. While Emily soothed and fussed, Zane took a walk to settle himself. It didn't work, but he had enough left to pretend it did, for Darby's sake.

She gave her long, detailed statement to Lee, let Dave treat professionally the lacerations on her wrists and ankles, which Emily had bandaged.

Because she asked, Dave gave Darby an update on Trent's condition.

Concussion, detached retina, broken nose, chipped cheekbone. "Nice play, slugger," he said to Zane.

"But he'll live?" Darby pressed.

"He's in serious condition. Not critical. Oh, and he lost a couple of teeth, some major contusions on the backs of his legs."

"She hit him with the chair he'd tied her to."

"Another nice play. It wouldn't hurt you to see your doctor."

"It's not my first punch in the face. I hope it's my last." Steadier, she rose. "Emily, I can't tell you what it means that you were here when I needed you."

"Honey, I promise you I always will be."

"He took my mother from me." Her eyes welled again. "She'd have been glad to know I found someone to stand in for her." Breaking, she pressed her face to Emily's shoulder when Emily pulled her in.

When Darby steadied, drew back, Emily draped an arm around Brody's shoulders.

"I'll never doubt your instincts again, about anyone. Ever."

"I'm real sorry about your mom, Darby. I'm real sorry."

"Me, too. You're my hero, Brody." Darby leaned over, kissed him lightly on the lips. "I have a lot of those today."

She found more when Zane finally got her home. Her entire crew waited on the porch along with vases of flowers, casseroles, pies. A pound cake.

"We just wanted to see you for ourselves," Roy began. "We know you gotta rest, but we just wanted to see you for ourselves first."

He lowered his head when his voice broke.

"We got two of the sites cleaned up good." Ralph cleared his throat. "We figured that's the way you'd want it. We'll take care of the rest tomorrow, 'cause we don't want to see you on the job tomorrow, and that's that."

"Who's the boss?" she demanded.

"Don't care about that. I ever see who put those bruises on your face out in the open, he's gonna wish I didn't. That's that, too."

"How about I take you inside, get you settled down." Hallie moved down the steps. "And these men here can take all this inside. There's likely to be more coming," she continued as she put an arm around Darby. "Zane, you left the door unlocked," she added, steering Darby inside. "We didn't feel like we should just go in. More'll be coming," she continued, "as word's out about what happened. People want to help out as they can. You matter here in Lakeview, Darby."

"Hallie, I need to go upstairs so I can have a good cry."

"I'm gonna take you right up there. Gabe, give me one of those vases to take up."

"This one's from Miss Cherylee. It's nice and showy." He gave Darby a light rub on the back. "How about I give Zod a you-know-what, Darby. Seems he earned it."

"Thanks, Gabe. Thanks, all of you."

Hallie held her while she cried, then sat with her until she slept.

When she woke, she looked out the tall window at the view of the lake, the boats sailing on it, the kids jumping off the raft.

She looked at the showy flowers sent by a woman she'd only just met. Thought of the tableau that had greeted her when Zane brought her home.

Rising, she studied her face in the mirror, the bruised cheekbone, the black eye—a fairly mild one, all things considered.

"You've never been stupid," she told her reflection. "Except the times you thought you were."

She walked downstairs, found Zane pacing the living room, his phone at his ear. "She's up," he said with his eyes fixed on her face. "I'll call you back. Everybody's checking in to see how you're doing. I just looked in on you a bit ago. You got some sleep."

"Yeah. I feel better for it. Zane—"

"Please," he said, then rushed to her, drew her in—so, so gently— held on. "I just need this. Just a minute of it."

"Take all the time you need."

"When I found your truck, life stopped for a minute. Everything stopped. I should've gone to Lee with what Brody told me."

"No. No, and no. That would've been a betrayal, and Lee couldn't have done more than you were doing. If you blame yourself for even the tiniest bit of this, it takes it away from where it belongs. Don't do that."

She drew back. "Don't do that when your brilliant cousin, our incredible dog, and your excellent baseball saved my life. Can we . . ."

"Anything."

"Careful or it might be a trip to Aruba. Can we sit out on the veranda, and drink some wine?"

"Absolutely."

When he got the wine, settled in beside her, she laid a hand over his. "I want to get this all over and out. How did you know where to find me?"

"At first I thought Drapers, but it just didn't fit. Then I remembered you'd said you'd seen a guy like Brody talked about, that he'd waved at you from the lake. That he gave you the creeps."

"Just that?"

"That and everything Brody told us. Not being able to find anybody by the name he was using at a college in New York. My gut said go there, so I did."

"I'm going to drink to your gut."

"I'm so sorry about your mother, Darby. I know it must be like losing her again."

Tears swirled and spilled again. "At first it just emptied me out, just drained me. He bragged about it, gloated. Then it gave me what I needed to try to hurt him. I couldn't have done it without you and Zod, but I was ready to go down fighting."

After swiping at tears, she sipped a little wine.

"Something snapped in him, Zane. I think it was always there, pulled tight if you know what I mean."

"Yes, I do."

"He covered it, kept it below the surface. Those undercurrents, right? He lost control with me before, but not like this. This was, well, calculated crazy, I want to say. He planned everything after he saw the articles about me fighting off Graham. He planned it out, like he planned killing my mother."

She let out a breath. "I don't think it would've worked. I think he'd have been caught. But he didn't. He thought he'd get away with it because he'd gotten away with it before. And he liked it. He killed two people because he liked it."

"I'm going to say more."

"More . . ." Shock slapped her again. "More people?"

"A long time between your mother and Clint. When they're finished with him, I'm going to say more. At least one or two more."

"He was always going to snap," she continued. "He was good at hiding it. I was young and not as experienced as I thought I was. He was so charming, said everything I wanted to hear. Oh my God, he was so sweet with my mother."

"He knew she mattered most to you."

"Yes, he knew. But once he had me, he started to slip. I wasn't stupid. I figured out it wasn't going to work, but I had to try. You don't just get married one day, and throw it away the next. It wasn't stupid to try."

"Of course not."

"Inside, I've told myself I was stupid. Bad judgment, letting myself get carried away by a good-looking man who seemed so right for me. I was stupid for convincing myself I was stupid."

"I'm glad you worked that out." He kissed her hand, then her bandaged wrist.

"Convinced I was stupid, I told myself you and me—we'd just cruise along for a while, see what happened. I mean, after all, what I wanted was some good sex with a man I liked, a hot man who understands the life-giving properties of baseball, appreciates the appeal of an ugly dog, finds it in him to embrace my creative visions, and so forth."

"I am all that."

"You are all that, and a box of cream-filled donuts. And I love you—that's not stupid. I want to build a life with you, also not stupid. I want to make a family with you, not at all stupid."

"Are you going to marry me, Darby?"

"Yes, I am."

He got up, picked her up, sat down with her in his lap. "When?"

"That's tricky. I want simple, right out here, with a party in the back. But I've got Roy getting married next spring. Busy season, and he wants a honeymoon. I can't have both of us off."

He kissed her cheek, her eye, her lips. Lingered on the lips. "Labor Day weekend."

"Labor Day?"

"Even you have to take Labor Day off. Especially to marry me."

"But—you mean *this* September. Walker, that's practically tomorrow."

"Why wait? Especially when you're not stupid. And I happen to know some women who can plan one big-ass party in about five minutes."

"But I'd have fall maintenance, tree planting. I'd have—"

"We'd wait, take a honeymoon in the winter. Slow season. We can go to Aruba."

She had to laugh. "That's pretty damn clever of you."

"I'm not stupid either. Life stopped, Darby," he told her, and traced a finger over the tattoo on the back of her neck. "Let's not waste a minute of it now that it started again."

"You saved my life with a baseball. I want that ball. I want to put it in a display box, keep it in the office I'm going to make out of one of the spare rooms. Once I decide which one suits me best."

She framed his face. "Look at us. Black eyes and bruises. We're a freaking set. Labor Day weekend." She touched her lips lightly to his. "Deal."

"You can seal a deal better than that."

"I'm not finished yet," she said, pressing a hand to his chest to hold him off. "If we're serious about making a family, about having kids, one of us has to learn to cook."

He eyed her. "We can flip for it. Say, heads I learn, tails you learn."

"Rock, paper, scissors."

"Two out of three."

"You're on."

After, when she laid her head on his shoulder, he told himself learning to cook couldn't be that hard.

"One night a week is pizza night," he decided. "Frozen or delivery."

"That goes without saying." She pressed a kiss to his cheek.

Together, the dog snoring at their feet, they sat in the quiet, watched the sun set over the western hills and light its fire over the water.

Turn the page for a sneak peek at
Nora Roberts's next novel

HIDEAWAY

Available May 2020

Turn the page for a sneak peek at
Nora Roberts's bestseller

LEGACY

Available May 2021

CHAPTER ONE

Big Sur · 2001

When Liam Sullivan died, at the age of ninety-two, in his sleep, in his own bed with his wife of sixty-five years beside him, the world mourned.

An icon had passed.

Born in a little cottage tucked in the green hills and fields near the village of Glendree in County Clare, he'd been the seventh and last child of Seamus and Ailish Sullivan. He'd known hunger in the lean times, had never forgotten the taste of his mother's bread and butter pudding—or the whip-swat of her hand when he'd earned it.

He'd lost an uncle and his oldest brother in the first Great War, had grieved for a sister who'd died before her eighteenth birthday delivering her second child.

He'd known from an early age the backbreaking work of plowing a field behind a horse named Moon. He'd learned how to shear a sheep and slaughter a lamb, to milk a cow and build a rock wall.

And he remembered, the whole of his long life, the nights his family sat around the fire—the smell of peat smoke, the angel-clear voice of his mother raised in song, his father smiling at her as he played the fiddle.

And the dancing.

As a boy he'd sometimes earn a few pennies singing in the pub while the locals drank their pints and talked of farming and politics.

His soaring tenor could bring a tear to the eye, and his agile body and fast, clever feet lift the spirit when he danced.

He dreamed of more than plowing the fields and milking the cow, much more than the pennies gathered at the little pub in Glendree.

Shortly before his sixteenth birthday, he left home, a few precious punts in his pocket. He endured the Atlantic crossing with others looking for more in the cramped confines belowdecks. When the ship rolled and rocked in a storm, and the air stank of vomit and fear, he blessed his iron constitution.

Dutifully, he wrote letters to home he dreamed of posting at the end of the voyage and kept spirits up by entertaining his fellow passengers with song and dance.

He shared a flirtation and a few eager kisses with a flaxen-haired girl named Mary from Cork who traveled to Brooklyn and a position as a maid in some fine house.

With Mary he stood in the cool, fresh air—fresh at last—and saw the great lady with her torch held high. And thought his life had truly begun.

So much color and noise and movement, so many people squashed into one place. Not just an ocean away from the farm where he'd been born and reared, he thought. A world away.

And his world now.

He was bound to apprentice with his mother's brother Michael Donahue as a butcher in the Meatpacking District. He was welcomed, embraced, given a bed in a room he shared with two of his cousins. While in only a matter of weeks he grew to hate the sounds, the smells of the work, he earned his keep.

Still, he dreamed of more.

He found the more the first time he turned over a bit of that hard-earned pay to sit in a movie theater with Mary of the flaxen hair. There he saw magic on the silver screen, worlds far beyond everything he knew, worlds holding everything a man could want.

There the sounds of bone saws, the *thwack* of cleavers didn't exist. Even pretty Mary faded away as he felt himself pulled into the screen and the world it offered.

The beautiful women, the heroic men, the drama, the joy. When he surfaced, he saw all around him the enraptured faces of the audience, the tears, the laughter, the applause.

This, he thought, was food for a hungry belly, a blanket in the cold, a light for the damaged soul.

Less than a year after he saw New York from the deck of a ship, he left it to head west.

He worked his way across the country, amazed at its size, at its changing sights and seasons. He slept in fields, in barns, in the backs of bars where he traded his voice for a cot.

Once he spent the night in jail after a bit of a dustup in a place called Wichita.

He learned to ride the rails, and evade the police—and as he would say in countless interviews over the course of his career—had the adventure of a lifetime.

When, after nearly two years of travel, he saw the big white sign spelling out HOLLYWOODLAND, he vowed that here he would find his fame and fortune.

He lived on his wits, his voice, his strong back. With the wit he talked his way into building sets on back lots, sang his way through the work. He acted out the scenes he watched, practiced the various accents he'd heard on the trip from east to west.

Talkies changed everything, so now soundstages needed building. Actors he'd admired in their silence on-screen had voices that screeched or rumbled, so their stars burned out and fell.

His break came when a director heard him singing while he worked—the very tune the once-silent star was supposed to romance his lady with in a musical scene.

Liam knew the man couldn't sing worth shite, and had his ear to the ground close enough to have heard there was talk about using another voice. It was, to his mind, simply being sure he was in the right place at the right time to be that voice.

His face might not have appeared on the screen, but his voice held the audience. It opened the door.

An extra, a walk-on, a bit part where he spoke his first line.

Building blocks, stepping-stones, forming a foundation fueled by the work, the talent, and the Sullivan tireless energy.

He, the farm boy from Clare, had an agent, a contract, and began in that Golden Age of Hollywood what would be a career that spanned decades and generations.

He met his Rosemary when he and the pert and popular Rosemary Ryan starred in a musical—the first of five films they'd make together in their lifetimes. The studio fed the gossip columns stories of their romance, but none of the hype was necessary.

They married less than a year after they clapped eyes on each other. They honeymooned in Ireland—visiting his family, as well as hers in Mayo.

They built a grand glamour of a home in Beverly Hills, had a son, then a daughter.

They bought the land in Big Sur because, as with their romance, it was love at first sight. The house they built facing the sea they named Sullivan's Rest. It became their getaway, then as years passed more their home.

Their son proved the Sullivan-Ryan talent spanned generations, as Hugh's star rose from child actor to leading man. As their daughter, Maureen, chose New York and Broadway.

Hugh would give them their first grandson before his wife, the love of his life, died in a plane crash returning from a location shoot in Montana.

That son would, in time, place another Sullivan star on the screen.

Liam and Rosemary's grandson Aidan, believing, as with Sullivan tradition, he'd found the love of his life in the silky blond beauty of Charlotte Dupont, married in glittery style (exclusive photos in *People* magazine), bought a mansion in Holmby Hills for his bride. And gave Liam a great-granddaughter.

They named the fourth-generation Sullivan Caitlyn. Caitlyn Ryan Sullivan became an instant Hollywood darling when she made her film debut at twenty-one months playing the mischievous, matchmaking toddler in *Will Daddy Make Three?*

The fact that most reviews found little Cate upstaged both adult leads (which included her mother as the female love interest) caused some consternation in certain quarters.

It might have been her last taste of preadolescent stardom, but her great-grandfather cast her, at age six, as the free-spirited Mary Kate in *Donovan's Dream*. She spent six weeks on location in Ireland, and shared the screen with her father, grandfather, great-grandfather, and great-grandmother.

She delivered her lines in a west county accent as if she'd been born there.

The film, a critical and commercial success, would be Liam Sullivan's last. In one of the rare interviews he gave toward the end of his life, sitting under a flowering plum tree with the Pacific rolling toward forever, he said, like Donovan, he'd seen his dream come true. He'd made a fine film with the woman he'd loved for six decades, with their boys Hugh and Aidan, and the bright light of his great-granddaughter, Cate.

Movies, he said, had given him the grandest of adventures, so this, he felt, was a perfect cap for the genie bottle of his life.

On a cool, bright February afternoon, three weeks after his death, his widow, his family, and many of the friends he'd made through the years gathered at his Big Sur estate to—as Rosemary insisted—celebrate a life well and fully lived.

They'd held a formal funeral in L.A., with luminaries and eulogies, but this would be to remember the joy he'd given.

There were speeches and anecdotes, there were tears. But there was music, laughter, children playing inside and out. There was food and whiskey and wine.

Rosemary, her hair as white now as the snow that laced the tops of the Santa Lucias, embraced the day as she settled—a bit weary, truth be told—in front of the soaring stone fireplace in what they called the gathering room. There she could watch the children—their young bones laughing at winter's bite—and the sea beyond.

She took her son's hand when Hugh sat beside her. "Will you think I'm a crazy old woman if I tell you I can still feel him, as if he's right beside me?"

As her husband's had, her voice carried the lilt of her home.

"How can I, when I feel it, too?"

She turned to him, her white hair cut short for style and ease, her eyes vivid green and full of humor. "Your sister would say we're both crazy. How did I ever produce such a practical-minded child as Maureen?"

She took the tea he offered her, winged up an eyebrow. "Is there whiskey in it?"

"I know my ma."

"That you do, my boy, but you don't know all."

She sipped her tea, sighed. Then studied her son's face. So like his father's, she thought. The damnably handsome Irish. Her boy, her baby, had silver liberally streaked through his hair, and eyes that still beamed the bluest of blues.

"I know how you grieved when you lost your Livvy. So sudden, so cruel. I see her in our Caitlyn, and in more than the looks. I see it in her light, the joy and fierceness of her. I'm sounding crazy again."

"No. I see the same. I hear her laugh, and hear Livvy laugh. She's a treasure to me."

"I know it, and to me as she was to your da. I'm glad, Hugh, you found Lily and, after those long years alone, found happiness. A good mother to her own children, and a loving grandmother to our Cate these past four years."

"She is."

"Knowing that, knowing our Maureen's happy, her children and theirs doing well, I've made a decision."

"About what?"

"The rest of my time. I love this house," she murmured. "The land here. I know it all in every light, in every season, in every mood. You know we didn't sell the house in L.A. mostly for sentiment, and the convenience of having it if either of us worked there for any stretch of time."

"Do you want to sell it now?"

"I think no. The memories there are dear as well. You know we have the place in New York and that I'm giving it to Maureen. I want to know if you'd want the house in L.A. or this one. I want to know because I'm going to Ireland."

"To visit?"

"To live. Wait," she said before he could speak. "I may have been reared in Boston from my tenth year, but I still have family there, and roots. And the family your father brought me is there as well."

He laid a hand over hers, lifted his chin to the big window, and the children, the family outside. "You have family here."

"I do. Here, New York, Boston, Clare, Mayo, and, bless us, London now as well. God, but we're far-flung, aren't we, my darling?"

"It seems we are."

"I hope all of them come to visit me. But Ireland's where I want to be now. In the quiet and the green."

She gave him a smile, with a twinkle in her eyes. "An old widow woman, baking brown bread and knitting shawls."

"You don't know how to bake bread or knit anything."

"Hah." Now she slapped his hand. "I can learn, can't I now, even at my advanced age. I know you have your home with Lily, but it's time for me to give back, we'll say. God knows how Liam and I ever made so much money doing what we did for the love of it."

"Talent." Then he tapped a finger gently to her head. "Smarts."

"Well, we had both. And now I want to shed some of what we reaped. I want that lovely cottage we bought in Mayo. So which is it for you, Hugh? Beverly Hills or Big Sur?"

"Here. This." When she smiled, he shook his head. "You knew before you asked."

"I know my boy even better than he knows his ma. That's settled then. It's yours. And I trust you to tend to it."

"You know I will, but—"

"None of that. My mind's made up. I damn well expect I'll have a place to lay my head when I come visit. And I will come. We had good years here, me and your da. I want what came from us to have good years here as well."

She patted his hand. "Look out there, Hugh." She laughed as she saw Cate do a handspring. "That's the future out there, and I'm so grateful I had a part in making it."

While Cate did handsprings to entertain two of her younger cousins, her parents argued in their guest suite.

Charlotte, her hair swept back in a chignon for the occasion, paced the hardwood, her Louboutins clicking like impatient fingersnaps.

The raw energy pumping from her had once enthralled Aidan. Now it just made him tired.

"I want to get out of here, Aidan, for God's sake."

"And we will, tomorrow afternoon, as planned."

She whirled on him, lips sulky, eyes sheened with angry tears. The soft winter light spilled through the wide glass doors at her back and haloed around her.

"I've had enough, can't you understand? Can't you see I'm on my last nerve? Why the hell do we have to have an idiotic family brunch tomorrow? We had the goddamn dinner last night, we had this whole endless deal today—not to mention the funeral. The endless funeral. How many more stories do I have to hear about the great Liam Sullivan?"

Once he'd thought she understood his thick, braided family ties, then he'd hoped she'd come to understand them. Now they both understood she just tolerated them.

Until she didn't.

Weary to the bone, Aidan sat, gave himself a minute to stretch out his long legs. He'd started to grow a beard for an upcoming role. It itched and annoyed him.

He hated that, at the moment, he felt exactly the same about his wife.

The rough spots in their marriage had smoothed out recently. Now it seemed they'd hit another bumpy patch. "It's important to my grandmother, Charlotte, to my father, to me, to the family."

"Your family's swallowing me whole, Aidan."

She did a heel turn, her hands flying out. So much drama, he thought, over a few more hours.

"It's just one more night, and there'll only be a handful of us left by dinner. We'll be home this time tomorrow. We still have guests, Charlotte. We should be downstairs right now."

"Then let your grandmother deal with them. Your father. You. Why can't I take the plane and go home?"

"Because it's my father's plane, and you, Caitlyn, and I will fly home with him and Lily tomorrow. For now, we're a united front."

"If we had our own plane, I wouldn't have to wait."

He could feel the headache growing behind his eyes. "Do we really need to go there? And now?"

She shrugged. "Nobody would miss me."

He tried another tack, smiled. He knew, from experience, his wife reacted better to the sweet than the stern. "I would."

And on a sigh, she smiled back.

She had a smile, he thought, that just stopped a man's heart.

"I'm being such a pain in the ass."

"Yeah, but you're my pain in the ass."

On a quick laugh, she walked over, cuddled on his lap. "I'm sorry, baby. Almost sorry. Sort of sorry. You know I've never liked it up here. It feels so isolated it makes me claustrophobic. And I know that doesn't make sense."

He knew better than to stroke that shining blond hair after she'd had it styled, so he lightly kissed her temple instead. "I get it, but we'll be home tomorrow. I need you to stick just one more night, for my grandmother, my dad. For me."

After letting out a hiss, she poked his shoulder, then offered him her signature pout. Full coral lips, sulky and soft crystal-blue eyes dramatically lashed. "I better get points. Big points."

"How about a long weekend in Cabo points?"

On a gasp, she grabbed his face with her hands. "You mean it?"

"I've got a couple weeks before I start production." So saying, he rubbed a hand over his scruff. "Let's say we hit the beach for a few days. Cate'll love it."

"She has school, Aidan."

"We'll take her tutor."

"How about this?" Now she circled her arms around him, pressed her body, still in mourning black, against his. "Cate has a long weekend with Hugh and Lily, which she'd love. And you and I have a few days in Cabo." She kissed him. "Just us. I'd love some just us, baby. Don't you think we need some just us?"

She was probably right—the smooth patches needed tending as much as the rough. While he hated leaving Cate, she was probably right. "I can make that work."

"Yes! I'm going to text Grant, see if he can do some extra sessions this week. I want a perfect bikini body."

"You already have one."

"That's my sweet husband talking. We'll see what my hard-assed personal trainer says. Oh!" She hopped up. "I need to shop."

"Right now we have to get back downstairs."

The flicker of annoyance marred her face before she smoothed it away. "Okay. You're right, but give me a couple minutes to fix my face."

"Your face is gorgeous, as always."

"Sweet husband." She pointed at him as she started toward her makeup counter. Then stopped. "Thanks, Aidan. These past few weeks, with all the tributes, the memorials, it's been hard on all of us. A few days away, well, that'll be good for us. I'll be right down."

While her parents made up, Cate organized a game of hide-and-seek as the final outdoor game of the day. Always a favorite when the family gathered, the game had its rules, restrictions, and bonus points.

In this case, the rules included outdoors only—as several of the adults had decreed no running inside. The It got a point for every hider found, with the first found designated as the next It. If that hider, now It, was five or under, he or she could choose a partner on the following hunt.

If a hider went three rounds without being found, that meant ten bonus points.

And since Cate had been planning this game all day, she knew how to win them.

She darted off when Boyd, age eleven, started the countdown as the first It. Since Boyd lived in New York like his grandmother, he only visited Big Sur a couple times a year at most. He didn't know the grounds like she did.

Plus, she had a fresh hiding place already picked out.

She rolled her eyes as she saw her five-year-old cousin Ava crawl under the white cloth of a food table. Boyd would find Ava in two minutes.

She nearly backtracked to show Ava a better spot, but it was every kid for herself!

Most of the guests had gone, and more were taking their leave. But a lot of adults still milled around the patios, the outdoor bars, or sat around one of the firepits. Remembering why, she felt a pang.

She'd loved her great-grandda. He'd always had a story to tell, and lemon drops in his pocket. She'd cried and cried when her daddy told her Grandda had gone to heaven. He'd cried, too, even when he told her Grandda had had a long, happy life. How he'd meant so much to so many, and would never be forgotten.

She thought of his line from the movie they'd made together, while he sat with her on a stone wall, looking over the land.

"A life's marked along the way, darlin', by the deeds we do, for good or ill. Those we leave behind judge those marks, and remember."

She remembered lemon drops and hugs as she scurried to the garage, and around the side. She could still hear voices, from the patios and terraces, the walled garden. Her goal? The big tree. If she climbed to the third branch, she could hide behind the thick trunk, in the green leaves that smelled so good, ten feet up.

Nobody would find her!

Her hair—Celtic black—flew behind her as she ran. Her nanny, Nina, had tucked it back at the sides with butterfly pins to keep it out of her face. Her eyes, bold and blue, danced as she flew out of sight of the multitiered house, far beyond the guest cottage with its steps leading down to the little beach, and the pool that overlooked the sea.

She'd had to wear a dress for the first part of the day, to be respectful, but Nina had laid out her play clothes for after. She still had to be careful of the sweater, but knew it was okay to get her jeans dirty.

"I'm going to win," she whispered as she reached up for the first branch of the California bay, put her purple (currently her favorite color) sneaker in the little knothole for purchase.

She heard a sound behind her and, though she knew it couldn't be Boyd, not yet, her heart jumped.

She caught a glimpse of the man in a server's uniform, with a blond beard and hair pulled back in a ponytail. He wore sunglasses that shot the light back at her.

She grinned, put a finger to her lips. "Hide-and-seek," she told him.

He smiled back. "Want a boost?" He nodded, then moved forward as if to give her one.

She felt the sharp needle stick on the side of her neck, started to swat at it as she might a bug.

Then her eyes rolled back, and she felt nothing at all.

He had the gag on, zip ties on her wrists and ankles in seconds. Just a precaution, as the dose should keep her out for a couple hours.

She didn't weigh much and, as a man in excellent shape, he could have carried her the few feet to the waiting cart had she been a full-grown woman.

After shoving her into the cabinet of the service cart, he rolled it toward the caterer's van—outfitted for just this purpose. He pushed it up the ramp, shut the cargo doors.

In under two minutes, he drove down the long drive, wound to the edge of the private peninsula. At the security gates, he entered the code with a gloved finger. When the gates opened, he drove through, made his turn, then hit Highway 1.

He resisted pulling off the wig and the fake beard.

Not yet, and he could handle the annoyance of them. He didn't have far to go, and expected he'd have the ten-million-dollar brat locked inside the high-class cabin (owners currently in Maui) before anyone even thought to look for her.

When he turned off the highway again, started up the steep drive to where some rich asshole decided to build a vacation paradise stuck in with a bunch of trees, rocks, and chaparral, he was whistling a tune.

Everything had gone smooth as silk.

He caught sight of his partner pacing on the second-story deck of the cabin and rolled his eyes. Talk about an asshole.

They had this knocked, for Christ's sake. They'd keep the kid sedated, but wear masks just in case. In a couple of days—maybe less—they'd be rich, the kid could go back to the fucking Sullivans, and he, with a new name, new passport, would be on his way to Mozambique to soak up some sun in style.

He pulled the van around the side of the cabin. You couldn't see the cabin from the road, not really, so he knew no one would see the van blocked by trees around the side.

By the time he hopped out, his partner had run down to meet him. "Have you got her?"

"Shit yeah. Nothing to it."

"Are you sure nobody saw you? Are you sure—"

"Jesus, Denby, chill."

"No names," Denby hissed, pushing up his sunglasses as he looked around as if somebody waited in the woods to attack. "We can't risk her hearing our names."

"She's out. Let's get her upstairs, locked in so I can get this crap off my face. I want a beer."

"Masks first. Look, you're not a fucking doctor. We can't be a hundred percent she's still out."

"Fine, fine, go get yours. I'll stick with this." He patted the beard.

As Denby went back inside, he opened the cargo doors, hopped in to open the cabinet doors. Out, he thought, as in o-u-t. He rolled her out onto the floor, dragged her back toward the door—not a peep from her—then hopped out again.

He glanced back when Denby appeared in his Pennywise the Dancing Clown mask and wig, and he laughed like a loon. "If she wakes up before we get her inside, she'll probably faint from fright."

"We want her scared, don't we, so she'll cooperate. The little spoiled rich bitch."

"That'd do the trick. You're no Tim Curry, but that'd do the trick."

He slung Cate over his shoulder. "Everything ready up there?"

"Yeah. The windows are locked down. Still got a hell of a view of the mountains," Denby added as he followed his partner inside the rustic plush of the entryway, the open living area. "Not that she'll enjoy that, since we're keeping her out or the next thing to it."

Denby jumped as "The Mexican Hat Dance" played from the phone clipped to his partner's belt.

"Goddamn it, Grant!"

Grant Sparks only laughed. "Used my name, nimrod." He carted Cate up the stairs to the second floor, open to the first with its cathedral ceiling. "That's a text from my sugar. You gotta chill, man."

He carried Cate into the bedroom they'd selected because it faced the back and had its own bathroom. He dumped her on the four-poster

Denby had stripped down to sheets—cheap sheets they'd bought, and would take away with them.

The en suite was to avoid dragging her out of the room, avoiding a potential mess neither of them wanted to clean up. If she made one, they'd wash the sheets. Once they'd finished they'd remake the bed, nice and tidy and with the original bedding, and remove the nails hammered into the window locks.

He looked around, satisfied that Denby had taken out anything the kid could use as a weapon—as if—or bust out a window with. She'd be too drugged up for that, but why take chances?

When they left, the house would be exactly as they'd found it. No one would know they'd ever been inside.

"You took out all the lightbulbs?"

"Every one."

"Good job. Keep her in the dark. Go ahead and clip those ties, take off the gag. If she wakes up, has to piss, I don't want her doing it in the bed. She can beat on the door, scream her head off. Won't make a diff."

"How long do you figure she'll be under?"

"A couple hours. We bring her some doctored soup when she does, and that'll keep her out for the night."

"When are you going out to call?"

"After dark. Hell, they're not even looking for her yet. She was playing fucking hide-and-seek, as advertised, and headed straight for the grab spot."

He gave Denby a slap on the back. "Smooth as silk. Finish up, make damn sure you lock the door. I'm getting this crap off my face." He pulled off the wig, the wig net under it, revealing a short, stylish mop of sun-streaked brown hair. "I'm going for a beer."

ABOUT THE AUTHOR

Bruce Wilder

Nora Roberts is the #1 *New York Times* bestselling author of more than two hundred novels, including *Shelter in Place, Year One, Come Sundown,* and many more. She is also the author of the bestselling In Death series written under the pen name J. D. Robb. There are more than five hundred million copies of her books in print.